TRAVELS WITH A WRITING BRUSH

MEREDITH MCKINNEY is a translator of Japanese literature, both contemporary and classical. She lived in Japan for twenty years and is currently Honorary Associate Professor at the Australian National University in Canberra. Her translations for Penguin Classics include *The Pillow Book* of Sei Shōnagon, *Essays in Idleness and Hōjōki* by Kenkō and Chōmei, and two novels by Natsume Sōseki.

Travels with a Writing Brush

Classical Japanese Travel Writing
from the Manyōshū to Bashō

Selected and Translated by
MEREDITH MCKINNEY

PENGUIN BOOKS

PENGUIN BOOKS

UK | USA | Canada | Ireland | Australia
India | New Zealand | South Africa

Penguin Books is part of the Penguin Random House group of companies
whose addresses can be found at global.penguinrandomhouse.com.

This translation first published in Penguin Classics 2019
003

Translation and editorial material copyright © Meredith McKinney, 2019

The moral right of the translator has been asseted

Set in 10.25/12.25pt Sabon Next LT Pro
Typeset by Jouve (UK), Milton Keynes
Printed and bound in Great Britain by Clays Ltd, Elcograf S.p.A.

A CIP catalogue record for this book is available from the British Library

ISBN: 978-0-241-31087-8

The scenes of the journey's many places linger on in the heart, and the painful sorrows of nights spent sleeping in mountains and on moors become in turn the seeds of later traveller's tales, and a means to consort with Nature's wind and cloud.

Matsuo Bashō

The great home of the soul is the open road.

D. H. Lawrence

Contents

List of Maps

List of Illustrations

Introduction

A man or a woman sets out on a journey, and writes an account of it. If it is well-written, we consider it literature. Such is probably our general understanding in the West of what constitutes travel literature. In Japan too men and women have long set out on journeys, and many have written about them; but literary travel writing in Japan was for many centuries a very different thing from our conception of it, and it is worth understanding a little about it before stepping off into the texts translated in this book. We may be surprised at the lack there of much that we are used to – tales of adventure, of far lands and the curiosities found there, of the day-to-day difficulties and unexpected delights of the journey. But once we have adjusted our expectations, what we will discover instead is a kind of travel writing undreamed of in the West – a richly literary tradition extending through a thousand years and more, whose individual works together weave a dense and beautiful brocade of repeated patterns and motifs, tones and textures, varying and building through time to create a composite and moving poetics of travel.

This is not to say that 'travel writing' as such was conceived of as a literary genre. Rather, the theme of travel permeated every type of literary writing to a greater or lesser degree. This book contains examples of travel writing from almost every kind of literary composition – from diaries and tales of various sorts, to drama, songs and above all poetry. Yet through this multiplicity of what we would today call genres,[1] travel writing emerges as an identifiable tradition with its own particular characteristics, a strong set of continuities through time that connects the seventeenth-century writing of the great *haikai*[2] poet Bashō back through the intervening centuries and their literature to the tenth-century *Ise Tales*, which in turn grew out of the poetry of the *Manyōshū* around a thousand years before Bashō wrote.

In this it is typical of classical Japanese literature, which honoured tradition and continuity through all its evolving forms and styles, even when it undercut this powerful tradition with humour and parody. A consecutive reading of the works included here will provide an insight into the trajectory of classical Japanese literature generally, from its earliest manifestations in the form of song and poetry (scarcely distinguished in that early time)[3] through the evolution of the prose tale and the diary form of the Heian period – still considered the pinnacle of classical Japanese literature – to the explosion of new forms of writing that occurred during the tumultuous and war-torn Kamakura and Muromachi periods (Japan's middle ages), and on to the great changes that swept through Japanese culture with the advent of peace in the Edo period, which produced the works of Bashō.[4] This book thus allows the reader to follow the evolution of the single theme of Travel through its many variations down the centuries, against the backdrop of the wider forces that shaped it, which are touched on in the introductory sections.

The selection ends with Bashō because he was in many ways the end of the long literary trajectory traced in this book. After Bashō, Japanese travel writing entered the factual and sometimes farcical world of everyday experience and largely turned its back on the elegance of the long literary tradition charted here,[5] in which the pragmatic and the personal generally played a very minor role. Despite the relative unimportance of mere facts in this earlier writing, however, we should turn briefly to the realities of travel during the period covered here, to understand something of the actual experiences that underlay the literature of travel.

Travellers and the Roads They Travelled

For all its importance in literature, travel itself was generally looked on askance and only reluctantly undertaken until the Edo period; our modern association of travel with enjoyment would have astonished travellers of the time, most of whom would have given much to be spared its hardship and loneliness.

This aversion to travel is understandable. Roads were often little more than tracks, particularly the minor roads, and frequently infested with robbers. Commonly, they passed through difficult mountain terrain and over deep, swift rivers where travellers had to rely on the fickle services of a local ferryman or make their way over teetering bridges, while coast roads had the added peril of difficult crossings between tides.[6] Inns only gradually began to spring up along the major routes. Even then, more than a day's journey on a less-travelled road still frequently required sleeping rough, or begging a night's shelter from a local, usually in a poverty-stricken and flea-ridden dwelling. It was not uncommon for earlier travellers to erect some kind of temporary shelter by the road for the night, particularly if they travelled with servants to do it for them. The early eleventh-century *Sarashina Diary* paints a lively picture of these experiences and more, as the young author travels with her parents and their extensive household down what became known as the Tōkaidō, then barely a road let alone the important highway it later became.

Sea travel, the other option, was if anything even more nerve-wracking in all but the calmest weather. Travel by boat was plagued by wind and wave as well as the fear of pirates and shipwreck on the rocky coastline, as the tenth-century *Tosa Diary* vividly depicts. Japanese boats were relatively small and tended to hug the coast for safety; perilous official forays across the China Sea to Korea and China were the full extent of overseas travel until the late nineteenth century. After the early sea poetry of the *Manyōshū* (largely limited to the local waters of the Inland Sea) and the long sea voyage described in *Tosa Diary*, boats largely cease to be a presence in literary travel writing except as shapes distantly seen across the water.[7]

An understandable distaste for travel was heavily reinforced by the firm conviction that the Capital (present-day Kyoto), as it was generally called, was really the only place for a civilized person to be. During the Heian period, when literacy (and hence literary production) was largely limited to the elite and to monks, there was some justification for this view – the Capital was the central site of culture, and the land beyond its borders quickly shaded off into the cultural equivalent of 'the wilds'. Travel was experienced as a kind of exile, which it occasionally was, and provoked an intense yearning for the distant Capital and all it represented. Even when the warfare and political dislocations of the middle ages had made this attitude far less realistic, it continued to deeply colour the literature of travel, whose fundamental terms of reference were largely established in the Heian period.

Who, then, were the travellers who created this literature? During the Heian period, much of the literary prose writing was produced by provincial governors and their families, who faced the unpleasant necessity of taking up new posts in near or distant provinces every few years. More locally, women diarists[8] of the upper classes sometimes recorded day excursions or longer pilgrimages undertaken to temples beyond the confines of the Capital – the excerpts from *The Pillow Book* and *Sarashina Diary* provide some examples. Courtiers accompanying emperors on imperial pilgrimages and excursions, and later military men of literary taste, also played their part in this literary tradition. But it was above all Buddhist monks[9] who took to the road, sporadically in the Heian period and in greater numbers later, and it is they who primarily carried travel literature forward through the centuries into the Edo period, when they make their final appearance in the figure of Bashō before dropping almost completely from view.

Brief mention must also be made here of the sub-literate class of travellers whose largely unseen presences were everywhere from the beginning, men and women whose fertile creativity is seldom directly glimpsed because it went largely unrecorded, but whose performative arts fed into the new forms of literature that emerged in the middle ages and later.[10] Their voices are briefly heard in some of the poems of the *Manyōshū*, and in the precious collection of their songs called *Dust Dancing on the Rafters* (Chapter 9). Perhaps the most intriguing of these often wandering performers were the women here termed *asobi*,[11] in many ways the ancestors of today's geisha, who are fleeting presences in numerous travel accounts. They serve to remind us that a thriving performative literature of the people coexisted with, and in unseen ways influenced, the mainstream literary works translated here.

What They Wrote

Literature was one of the few comforts of the educated traveller; a writing brush and a literary sensibility were essential items in most cultured people's equipment for the road.[12] That sensibility was essentially poetic. A glance through this book will reveal that poetry is everywhere present, either on its own or embedded in prose. This is because, put simply, poetry was crucially central to classical Japanese literature. Once China's writing system had been manipulated to write the Japanese language[13] the first work of literature to emerge was the vast poetry collection called the *Manyōshū*, whose poems reveal how widespread and important poetry composition already was. Then and down the centuries, poetry composition was the mark of a civilized man or woman, not simply the preserve of professional poets, although the best inevitably made a name for themselves. Literature was first and fundamentally poetry, and so it essentially remained. It is not surprising, then, that poems are the core from which literary travel writing evolved, and remained central to that writing through the centuries.

This book traces how travel prose evolved by expanding brief contextualizing prose prefaces to poems (*kotobagaki*), first seen in the *Manyōshū*, into longer poem-centred anecdotes that began to appear in personal poetry collections, and that might in turn be strung together to chronologically present the poetic highlights of a journey. The important point to note here is the continued centrality of the poems. We read a travel journal for the story, but for Japanese readers and writers for many centuries it was above all the poems that were the point. As with the early *Ise Tales* so with Bashō's travel journals[14] more than seven centuries later – be it fact or fiction, throughout the central development of travel literature the underlying role of the prose tends to be to set the scenes for the poems.

This has important consequences for the literature of travel that may make it at first somewhat disorienting for the Western reader. Where we might expect a more or less continuous narrative of the journey, what we often find is a series of short, disconnected scenes or episodes, sometimes quite briefly sketched, that culminate in a poem,[15] bridged perhaps by a vague linking expression such as 'On I went, and then . . .' that vertiginously elides what can be a substantial amount of intervening time and space. The effect is a little like a series of glowing points on an otherwise dark map, a kind of montage of intense poetic experiences rather than a realistic description of the journey.

The poetic effect is reinforced by the prose itself. Both in style and in content, the prose of most literary travel writing until the Edo period was governed by what could be called a poetic (*waka*) sensibility. This shaped it in numerous ways, from imagery to language to choices of focus and emphasis, and shaped also the image of the traveller himself.[16] Changing tastes in poetry are closely reflected in the changing tone of the prose writing down the centuries. For much of the Heian period wit and wordplay were key elements in Japanese poetry, and likewise we find in works such as *Tosa Diary* or *The Ise Tales* a humour, urbanity and lightness of tone very different from the darker tones of later travel writing. As poetry evolved to become more evocative and sombre, so too did its associated prose. This book tells in outline a complex story of fundamental shifts in literary style and taste down the centuries, and the role played in this by historical forces and by Buddhism's increasing influence on the literary sensibility.

For all the changes in poetic sensibility between the *Manyōshū* and Bashō, certain key elements remained remarkably constant. Wit and wordplay never entirely disappeared even from serious poetry, and humour re-emerged in the later linked verse (*renga*) tradition that led eventually to the *haikai* style of Edo period poetry. But perhaps the most striking continuity, apart from the remarkable continuity of poetic form and rhythm,[17] is the core sensibility of poignancy (*aware*). In classical Japanese literature, one definition of good poetry is poetry that touches the heart. Celebration and delight, emotions that we may look for in poetry, play a relatively minor role,[18] as does the purely imagistic description that we in the West associate with haiku. Longing and absence, rather than fulfilment and pleasure, are at the heart of Japan's classical love poetry (one of the great poetic categories), and it was only natural that these became the dominant themes also in travel literature, in which the landscape itself evokes the *aware* of the lonely traveller savouring his longing for home and absent loved ones.[19] The anonymous author of *A Gift for the Capital*, a quintessential medieval travel chronicle, sums up the experience of the literary traveller in the following description:

> There were times when I slept alone, blanketed in the wind off the high peaks; times when I woke to waves pounding the rocky shore, sleeves soaked from the wandering traveller's sorrowing sleep. Times also when I chanced to hear in the grass by my pillow the small cry of insects weakening in the cold, and knew that autumn was at its end; or looking up from yet another bed in some fisherman's rough hut, knew from the sky that the moon was rising now above a flood tide.[20]

A lonely bed far from one's lover, cold winds from the peaks that pierce the traveller's heart, waves whose salt spray is one with the tears that soak his sleeve, a pillow of grass where autumn insects sing their soft mournful song, moonlight filtering through the roof of some rough dwelling – these are the stuff of poetic imagery, in which feeling and the natural world are one, rather than straightforward realism. Reality may provide such experiences in abundance of course, but whatever the actual journey might entail, it was essentially in poetic terms that literary travellers generally portrayed it.[21]

Modern readers, for whom the distinction between fact and fiction is of fundamental importance, may be puzzled by the way one merges seamlessly with the other in this writing. One way to understand this is in terms of the role that imaginative projection played in poetic composition, and by extension in writing generally. Japanese lyric poetry (*waka*) assumes but seldom makes explicit[22] a feeling subject at its centre, which is usually best translated as 'I'. This 'I' is by no means always the voice of the poet, however, as it conventionally is in Western lyric poetry. In fact, particularly during the Heian period, it was common to compose poetry to certain set topics (*daiei-ka*) or to accompany or respond to a painted scene (*byōbu-uta*) by imaginatively inhabiting the given situation. A topic such as 'On hearing the cries of the wild geese', or a screen painting of a lone figure making his way along a mountain path, could elicit a poignant travel poem from a man who had himself never set foot beyond the Capital, and which might in turn be included in his personal poetry collection. A direct connection between lyric poetry and immediate personal experience was never as strong as we assume it to be – even if someone composed his poem as he walked a mountain path, as a later traveller might do, he was in a sense imagining himself as a figure in a scene.[23]

The greatest pleasure a literary traveller could experience was the pleasure of arriving in person at a place hallowed in poetry. The brief scene in the early *Ise Tales* in which the man (traditionally identified as the poet Ariwara no Narihira) sends a poem to his beloved from distant Mount Utsu echoes down the centuries in the journals of travellers along the Tōkaidō, who continued to search out the place identified with this scene.[24] In fact there is no evidence that Narihira, whose poem it is, ever travelled in the area. His poem uses the name of Mount Utsu purely for its overlap with the word *utsutsu* (reality), in a kind of word play common in poetry. Many other places visited by the travellers in these pages originally gained their poetic fame in similar ways; it was not the characteristics of the place itself so much as the presence of its name in literature (or sometimes in history) that lent it special power. The term for such place names, and by extension for the places that bore those names, was *utamakura* (poem-pillow), and their central role in travel literature was one of its defining features.

Place names per se play a remarkably prominent role in this literature, and their constant listing can take on an almost incantatory quality that still seems to carry in it something of the early religious potency associated with places and embodied in their names. *Utamakura* places were in a sense sites of literary worship in a manner similar to holy places on a pilgrimage route, places where the traveller would pause in awe, perhaps recite the poem or poems associated with the site, and compose a poem in turn, often incorporating some allusive reference to that earlier poetry, almost as a pilgrim will offer up a prayer.[25] The much-travelled Tōkaidō highway was particularly dense in *utamakura*, and few literary travellers failed to pause at these increasingly famous places and to record their visit and its poem, thus adding their offering to the place's literary accretions. Those who ventured further afield, as later travellers increasingly did, clung to the presence of the occasional *utamakura* sites in the landscape they travelled through as to a friend from a distant world, that of the cultured literature of the Capital, met with in the wilds of the literary unknown.[26]

In this and in other ways, literature and participation in the literary tradition lifted the traveller out of the merely personal and quotidian experiences of travel into the exalted company of 'those of old' (*kojin*), who had figuratively and sometimes literally travelled this way before him. Just as a poem was never simply the spontaneous response to its occasion but, importantly, always gained depth by speaking in some way to the larger *waka* tradition (usually by means of allusion), so increasingly as the centuries passed the literary traveller was always shadowed to some degree by a kind of composite figure of those who had gone before. In this book we can glimpse the evolution of this suprapersonal figure – which might be termed The Traveller – above all through the poetry composed by and about travellers, and follow the ways in which, particularly from the late twelfth-century figure of Saigyō onwards,[27] literary travellers increasingly wrote in its voice.

This is not to suggest, of course, that the travellers in these pages were not men and women with their own stories, writing in varying ways from their own lived experience. Rather, the *waka* sensibility and its great literary tradition gave expressive form and depth to the articulation of individual experience, and often also to that experience itself. A traveller who was moved by an *utamakura* site, or by seeing far overhead a flight of wild geese in an autumn evening, was moved the more deeply by partaking in an experience shared with so many others, and thereby drawn into the force field of a greater tradition that imbued his or her own insignificant and contingent experience with far richer meaning. In such ways, both the land itself and the experience of those who travelled through it were overlaid with a complex palimpsest of the literary that integrated the two in much the same way that landscape and feeling might merge in poetry.

The *waka* sensibility and tradition described above – which, it is important to remember, encompassed far more than the theme of travel that is the focus of this book – governs to varying degrees

most of the works translated here. We can hear its presence behind the individual voices of Heian works such as *Tosa Diary* or
Sarashina Diary, then witness how it emerges with particular force
in the literature of the middle ages, and finally watch the slow evolution within it of a new, more personal and grounded kind of
travel writing that evolved with the vogue for linked verse (*renga*)
in the fifteenth and sixteenth centuries. Although the immensely
sophisticated communal verse-making of *renga* identified itself
with that elegant *waka* literary tradition and shared its sensibility,
within it lay the seeds of a new and different kind of poetry that
leapt to prominence in the seventeenth century – the *haikai* or
light and playful poetry that Bashō in turn reconfigured towards
the end of that century for his own profoundly expressive uses.

The last two works included here, Bashō's first concerted piece
of travel writing and the early sections of his final great *Narrow
Road of Oku*, reveal his evolving and complex relationship with
the thousand-year-old *waka* tradition that he both esteemed and
worked against, and how he sought to both inhabit and recon-
figure the Traveller figure of the great medieval travel chronicles
in his own *haikai* terms, in both his poetry and his prose. The
essential continuities with the old travel journals and their sensibility place Bashō firmly within that earlier tradition, yet in both
style and substance his travel writing takes its inspiration from
the mundane everyday world that was the antithesis of the elegant old courtly world of *waka*-style writing.

Bashō found ways to take the largely frivolous new *haikai* sensibility that had by his day replaced the long literary inheritance of
earlier times and bring it back into a radically new and profound
relationship with the traditions of the past. In this way he produced late in life the final work in the long evolution of travel
writing that this book traces. That tradition essentially died with
him. Already, the Edo period's new *haikai* sensibility was beginning to produce very different travel works,[28] full of farcical
humour, information and practical advice for the new kinds of
travellers from all classes who were taking to the roads. Some of
the more educated travellers, schooled in the old *waka* tradition,
continued to write earnest travel journals in the old style, but few
have proven worth preserving.

Bashō, never a central figure in the world of *haikai* verse even in his own day, was largely eclipsed after his death by the more popular *haikai* styles and their writers, and those who drew on his legacy in later times were no longer inclined to try their hand at travel writing as he had done. He and his writing remain the culmination and in many ways the greatest statement of a tradition that had flowered through a thousand years and produced many fine and moving works, a sample of which are translated here.

A Note on the Translations

Many of the works excerpted or given here in full also exist in other translated versions, and the interested reader is encouraged to seek these out for different perspectives on the works (see Further Reading). My own translations attempt to honour the literary qualities of the writing, while simultaneously aiming as far as possible to remain faithful to the linguistic level of the text. Although Japanese underwent considerable changes over the course of the thousand years covered here, its literary written language remained essentially remarkably stable. It valued elegance and suggestiveness, and although English translation inevitably requires clarifying much that is left ambiguous or implicit in the Japanese, I have tried to suggest these qualities in my choice of language and style. Rhythm, balance, phrasing and flow are all important aspects of much of this writing which I have tried in various ways to reproduce.

Occasionally the prose in these works can intensify and take on many of the qualities of poetry,[1] with almost incantatory variations on a 5/7 syllabic rhythm. Since syllable count means little to the English ear, and goes quite unnoticed in prose, I have translated these passages with particular attention to cadence and indicated their phrasing with spaced prose. One of the characteristics of these heightened passages in particular is a sinuous flow that blurs syntactical connections and slides seamlessly between sentences, an effect that the translation also attempts to suggest within the limits of natural English.

The pervasive presence of allusion plays a vital role in classical Japanese literary prose as well as in poetry, adding depth and resonance to the textual surface and serving to bind the work into the wider tradition. It provides a kind of enriching harmonic accompaniment to the single melodic line of the textual meaning, which can seem flat without it. Allusion assumes a readership alert to the echoes of other works, so its full effect cannot be reproduced in translation. Its presence should not be ignored, however. Where allusion becomes overt quotation, I have explained it in a note. More generally, I use *italics* to point up some (but by no means all) of the passing allusive echoes embedded in the prose,[2] in the hope that readers will register the pleasure of its presence if not its full force.

Poems, of course, provide particular challenges for a translator. Classical Japanese poetry is notoriously resistant to translation – rhythm, a delight in punning word play, the crucial role of allusion, pivot words and the syntactic folding together of meaning, concision, ambiguity, linguistic nuance and more besides: all these are virtually impossible to reproduce. The translator must simply hope that something at least of the spirit of the poem is conveyed in the translation, and perhaps a little of its elegance. Although the structure of Japanese poetry depends on syllable count rather than line division,[3] I follow the general custom of using line division to shape and add tension, to slow the eye and to signal it as poetry.

A final word about orthography. The pronunciation of Japanese changed continuously throughout the thousand years covered by this book. Rather than attempt to convey the nuances of these complex shifts, the Japanese transcriptions of the poems follow the ahistorical but straightforward rules of modern Japanese romanization.

Primary Texts Used

Bones on the Wayside: *Bashō bunshū*, Shinchō Nihon Koten Shūsei vol. 17, Shinchōsha, 1978, ed. Toyama Susumu

The Death of Sōgi: *Chūsei nikki kikōshū*, Nihon Koten Bungaku Taikei vol. 51, Iwanami Shoten, ed. Fukuda Hideichi et al.

Diary of the Waning Moon: *Chūsei nikki kikōshū*, Nihon Koten Bungaku Zenshū vol. 48, Shōgakukan, 1994, ed. Nagasaki Ken et al.

Dust Dancing on the Rafters: *Ryōjin hishō*, Shinchō Nihon Koten Shūsei vol. 31, Shinchōsha, 1979, ed. Enoki Katsurō

A Gift for the Capital: *Chūsei nikki kikōshū*, Nihon Koten Bungaku Taikei vol. 51, Iwanami Shoten, ed. Fukuda Hideichi et al.

Ionushi's Pilgrimage to Kumano: *Ionushi seikō*, Kokken Shuppan, 2002, ed. Masubuchi Katsuichi

The Ise Tales: *Ise monogatari*, Shinchō Nihon Koten Shūsei vol. 2, Shinchōsha, 1978, ed. Watanabe Minoru

Journal of the Kyushu Road: *Chūsei nikki kikōshū*, Nihon Koten Bungaku Zenshū vol. 48, Shōgakukan, 1994, ed. Nagasaki Ken et al.

Journal of the Tsukushi Road: *Chūsei nikki kikōshū*, Nihon Koten Bungaku Taikei vol. 51, Iwanami Shoten, ed. Fukuda Hideichi et al.

Journey along the Sea Road: *Chūsei nikki kikōshū*, Nihon Koten Bungaku Zenshū vol. 48, Shōgakukan, 1994, ed. Nagasaki Ken et al.

Journey to Shirakawa: *Chūsei nikki kikō bungaku zenhyōshaku shūsei*, Bensei Shuppan, 2000–2004, ed. Kishida Yoriko

Journey to the East: *Chūsei nikki kikōshū*, Nihon Koten Bungaku Zenshū vol. 48, Shōgakukan, 1994, ed. Nagasaki Ken et al.

Manyōshū: Shinchō Nihon Koten Shūsei vols. 6, 21, 41, 55, 66, Shinchōsha, 1978–84, ed. Aoki Takako et al.

The Narrow Road of Oku: *Bashō bunshū*, Shinchō Nihon Koten Shūsei vol. 17, Shinchōsha, 1978, ed. Toyama Susumu

Nōin: *Nōinshū chūshaku*, Shikashū Shūkaku Sōkan vol. 3, Kichōbon Kankōkai, 1992, ed. Kawamura Teruo

Pilgrimage to Kumano: *Chūsei kinsei kayōshū*, Nihon Koten Bungaku Taikei vol. 44, Iwanami Shoten, 1959, ed. Shinma Shin'ichi et al.

The Pillow Book: *Makura no sōshi*, Shōgakukan, 1997, ed. Matsuo Satoshi et al.

Sarashina Diary: *Tosa nikki, Sarashina Nikki*, Shōgakukan, 2008, ed. Kikuchi Yasuhiko et al.

Senjūshō: *Senjūshō*, Ōfūsha, 1988, ed. Kojima Takayuki et al.

Sumida River: *Yōkyokushū (chū)*, Shinchō Nihon Koten Shūsei vol. 73, Shinchōsha, 1986, ed. Itō Masayoshi

The Tale of Saigyō: *Saigyō monogatari*, Kōdansha, 1981, ed. Kuwabara Hiroshi

The Tale of the Heike: *Heike monogatari*, Shin Nihon Koten Bungaku Taikei vols 44–45, Iwanami Shoten, 1993, ed. Kajiwara Masaaki et al.

A Tale Unasked: *Towazugatari*, Shinchō Nihon Koten Shūsei vol. 20, Shinchōsha, 1978, ed. Fukuda Hideichi

Tosa Diary: *Tosa nikki, Sarashina Nikki*, Shōgakukan, 2008, ed. Kikuchi Yasuhiko et al.

Wakan rōeishū: *Wakan rōeishū*, Shinchō Nihon Koten Shūsei, Shinchōsha, 1983, ed. Ōsone Shōsuke et al.

Further Reading

General

Carter, Steven D., *How to Read a Japanese Poem* (Columbia University Press, 2019)

Keene, Donald, *Travelers of a Hundred Ages* (Columbia University Press, 1999)

McCullough, Helen Craig (ed.), *Classical Japanese Prose: An Anthology* (Stanford University Press, 1990)

Plutschow, E., and Hideichi Fukuda, *Four Japanese Travel Diaries of the Middle Ages* (Cornell East Asia Series, Cornell University, 1981)

Shirane, Haruo, Tomi Suzuki and David Lurie (ed.), *The Cambridge History of Japanese Literature* (Cambridge University Press, 2015)

Manyōshū

Cranston, Edwin A. (trans.), *A Waka Anthology: Volume One: The Gem-Glistening Cup* (Stanford University Press, 1993)

Levy, Ian Hideo (trans.), *The Ten Thousand Leaves: A Translation of the Man'yoshu, Japan's Premier Anthology of Classical Poetry, Volume One* (Princeton University Press, 1987)

The Ise Tales

MacMillan, Peter (trans.), *Tales of Ise* (Penguin Classics, 2016)

Royall Tyler and Joshua S. Mostow (trans. with commentary), *The Ise Stories: Ise monogatari* (University of Hawai'i Press, 2010)

Tosa Diary

McCullough, Helen Craig (ed.), *Classical Japanese Prose, An Anthology* (Stanford University Press, 1990)
Shirane, Haruo (ed.), *Traditional Japanese Literature: An Anthology, Beginnings to 1600* (Columbia University Press, 2007)

The Pillow Book

McKinney, Meredith (trans.), *The Pillow Book* (Penguin Classics, 2006)
Morris, Ivan (trans.), *The Pillow Book of Sei Shōnagon* (Penguin Classics, 1971)

Wakan rōeishū

Rimer, Thomas J., *Japanese and Chinese Poems to Sing: The Wakan Rōei Shū* (Columbia University Press, 1997)

Nōin

Mostow, Joshua S. (trans.), *Pictures of the Heart: The Hyakunin Isshu in Word and Image* (Michigan Studies in Japanese Classics No. 26, 1996)

Sarashina Diary

Arntzen, Sonia (trans.), *The Sarashina Diary: A Woman's Life in Eleventh-Century Japan* (Columbia University Press, 2014)
Morris, Ivan (trans.), *As I Crossed a Bridge of Dreams: Recollections of a Woman in Eleventh-Century Japan* (Penguin Classics, 1989)

Dust Dancing On The Rafters

Kim, Yung-Hee, *Songs to Make the Dust Dance: The Ryōjin Hishō of Twelfth-century Japan* (University of California Press, 1994)

The Tale Of The Heike

Tyler, Royall (trans.), *The Tale of the Heike* (Penguin Classics, 2014)

Watson, Burton, *The Tales of the Heike* (Columbia University Press, 2008)

The Tale of Saigyō

McKinney, Meredith (trans.), *The Tale of Saigyō* (Michigan Papers in Japanese Studies, University of Michigan Press, 1998)

Watson, Burton (trans.), *Saigyō: Poems of a Mountain Home* (Columbia University Press, 1991)

Senjūshō

Dykstra, Yoshiko K. (trans.), *The Senjūshō: Buddhist Tales of Early Medieval Japan* (University of Hawai'i Press, 2013)

Journey along the Sea Road

Konishi, Hiroko (trans.), *The Kaidōki: A Partial Translation with Notes* (University of California Press, 1967)

Journey to the East

McCullough, Helen Craig (ed.), *Classical Japanese Prose: An Anthology* (Stanford University Press, 1990)

Diary of the Waning Moon

McCullough, Helen Craig (ed.), *Classical Japanese Prose: An Anthology* (Stanford University Press, 1990)

Pilgrimage to Kumano

Brazell, Karen, ' "Blossoms": A Medieval Song', *Journal of Japanese Studies* 6:2 (Society for Japanese Studies, 1980)

A Tale Unasked

Brazell, Karen (trans.), *The Confessions of Lady Nijō* (Arrow Books Ltd, 1973)

A Gift for the Capital

Strand, Kendra (trans.), '*Souvenirs for the Capital*: A Travel Journal by Sōkyū', *Asiatische Studien – Études Asiatiques* 71:2 (June 2017)

Plutschow, E. and Hideichi Fukuda, *Four Japanese Travel Diaries of the Middle Ages* (Cornell East Asia Series, Cornell University, 1981)

Sumida River

Tyler, Royall (trans.), *Japanese No Dramas* (Penguin Classics, 1993)

Waley, Arthur (trans.), *The Noh Plays of Japan* (Tuttle Publishing, 2009)

Journey to Shirakawa

Miner, Earl, *Japanese Linked Poetry: An Account with Translations of Renga and Haikai Sequences* (Princeton University Press, 1979)

Journal of the Tsukushi Road

Carter, Steven D., *The Road to Komatsubara* (Harvard University Press, 1987)

The Death of Sōgi

Horton, H. Mack, *Song in an Age of Discord: The Journal of Sōchō and Poetic Life in Late Medieval Japan* (Stanford University Press, 2002)

Bones on the Wayside

Barnhill, David Landis (trans.), *Bashō's Journey: The Literary Prose of Matsuo Bashō* (State University of New York Press, 2005)
Yuasa, Nobuyuki (trans.), *The Narrow Road to the Deep North and Other Travel Sketches* (Penguin Classics, 1967)

The Narrow Road of Oku

Barnhill, David Landis (trans.), *Bashō's Journey: The Literary Prose of Matsuo Bashō* (State University of New York Press, 2005)
Hamill, Sam (trans.), *Narrow Road to the Interior* (Shambhala Centaur Editions, 1991)
Sato, Hiroaki (trans.), *Bashō's Narrow Road: Spring and Autumn Passages* (Stone Bridge Press: The Rock Spring Collection of Japanese Literature, 1996)
Yuasa, Nobuyuki (trans.), *The Narrow Road to the Deep North and Other Travel Sketches* (Penguin Classics, 1967)

Further Reading on Haiku

Kern, Adam, *The Penguin Book of Haiku* (Penguin Classics, 2018)
Shirane, Haruo, *Traces of Dreams: Landscape, Cultural Memory, and the Poetry of Bashō* (Stanford University Press, 1998)

1: General Map of Japan

N

Japan Sea

Straits of Hayato

• Yamaguchi **Bingo**

Miyazu •

Tanb

Dazaifu •

Miyajima •

Hiyodori Pass

Capita

Naniw

Inland Sea

Sanuki

Sumiyoshi •

Awaji **Izumi**

SHIKOKU

Nara •

Tosa Ōminato

Yamato

KYUSHU

Ōtsu Nawa

Kumano Mts

(TSUKUSHI)

Murotsu

• Hongū

Ki

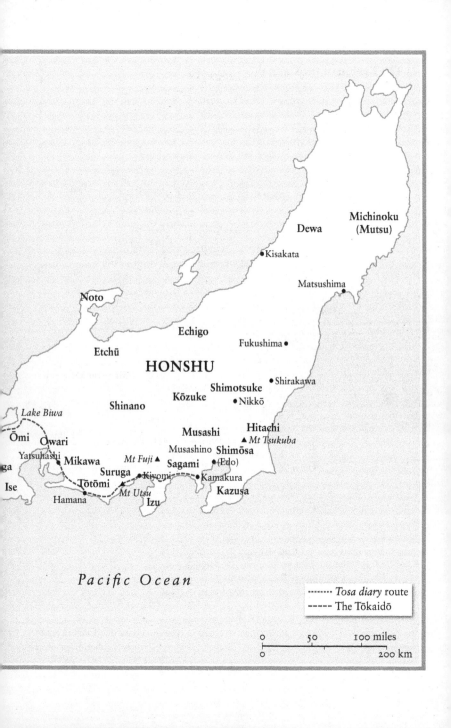

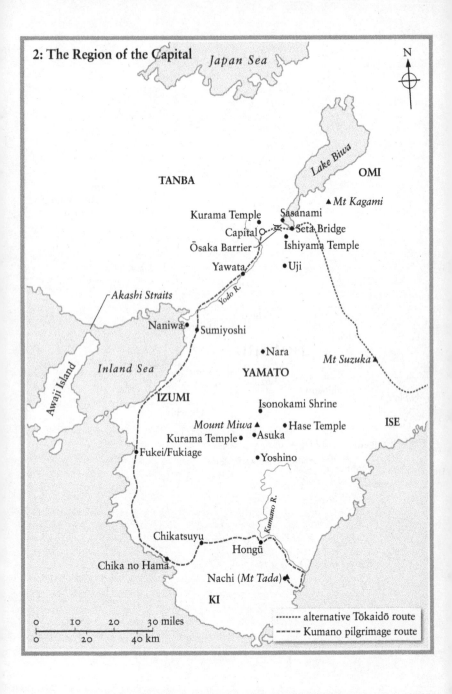

2: The Region of the Capital

Japan Sea

TANBA

Lake Biwa

OMI

▲ *Mt Kagami*

Kurama Temple • Sasanami

Capital ○ • Seta Bridge

Ōsaka Barrier • Ishiyama Temple

Yawata • • Uji

Akashi Straits

Yodo R.

Naniwa • • Sumiyoshi

• Nara

YAMATO

Mt Suzuka ▲

Inland Sea

IZUMI

Isonokami Shrine

Mount Miwa ▲ • Hase Temple

Kurama Temple • • Asuka

ISE

Awaji Island

• Fukei/Fukiage

• Yoshino

Kumano R.

Chikatsuyu •

Hongū •

Chika no Hama •

Nachi (*Mt Tada*) ▲

KI

| 0 | 10 | 20 | 30 miles |
| 0 | 20 | 40 km |

········· alternative Tōkaidō route

- - - - - Kumano pilgrimage route

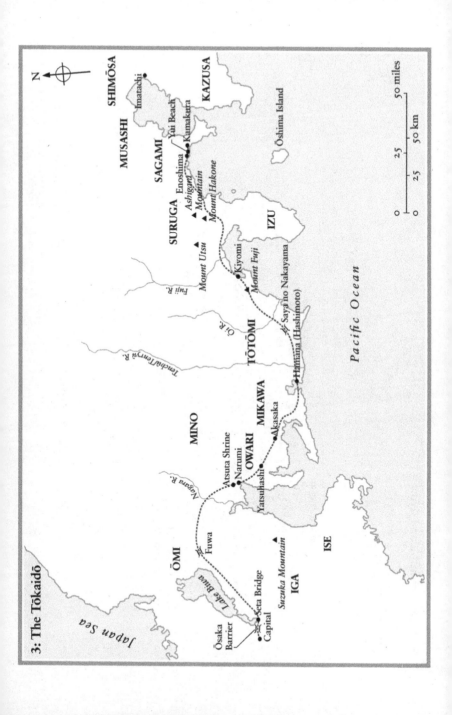

3: The Tōkaidō

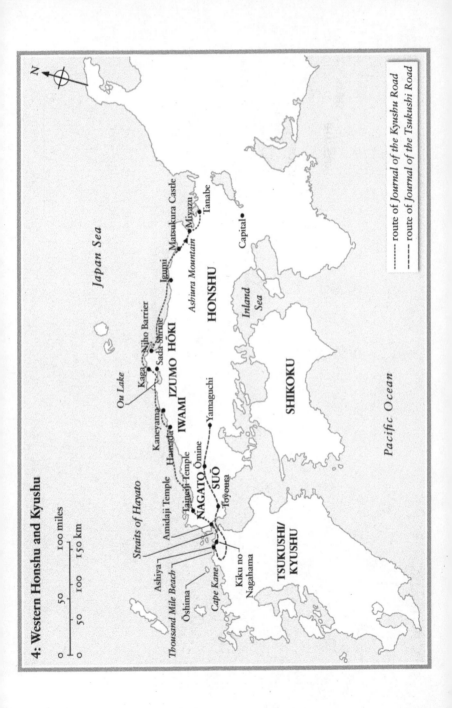

4: Western Honshu and Kyushu

Japan Sea

N

On Lake

Kaga
Niho Barrier
Sada Shrine
IZUMO HŌKI
IWAMI
Kaneyama
Hamada
Igumi
Matsukura Castle
Miyazu
Tanabe
Ashiura Mountain
HONSHU

Amidaji Temple
Taineiji Temple
Ōmine
Yamaguchi
NAGATO SUŌ
Tōyoura

Straits of Hayato

Ashiya
Thousand Mile Beach
Ōshima
Cape Kane
Kiku no Nagahama

TSUKUSHI/
KYUSHU

Capital

Inland Sea

SHIKOKU

Pacific Ocean

0   50   100 miles
0   50   100   150 km

----- route of *Journal of the Kyushu Road*
----- route of *Journal of the Tsukushi Road*

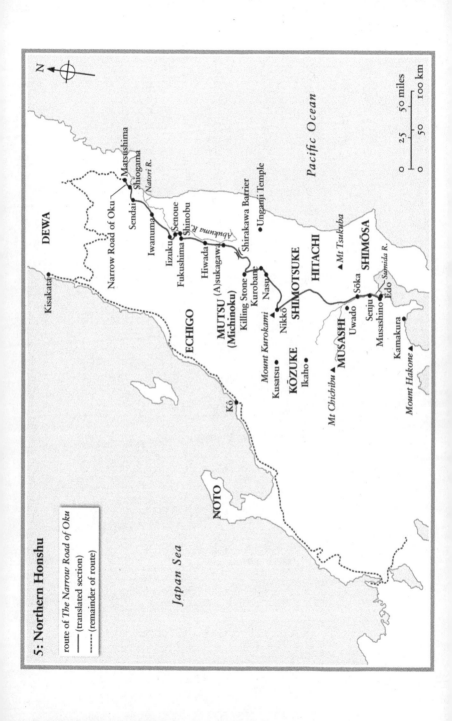

5: Northern Honshu

route of *The Narrow Road of Oku*
——— (translated section)
- - - - (remainder of route)

N

Pacific Ocean

Japan Sea

0   25   50 miles
0   50   100 km

DEWA

Kisakata

ECHIGO

NOTO

Kō

Matsushima
Shiogama
Sendai
Natori R.
Iwanuma
Senoue
Iizuku
Fukushima
Shinobu
Hiwada
(A)sukagawa
Abukuma R.
Killing Stone
Kurobane
Nasu
Mount Kurokami
Nikkō
Kusatsu
Ikaho
KŌZUKE

Narrow Road of Oku

MUTSU
(Michinoku)

SHIMOTSUKE

Shirakawa Barrier
Unganji Temple

HITACHI

▲ Mt Tsukuba

Mt Chichibu ▲
MUSASHI

Uwado
Musashino
Senju
Sōka
Edo *Sumida R.*
SHIMŌSA

Kamakura

Mount Hakone ▲

I

Manyōshū

The Manyōshū, *Japan's first extant work of literature,*[1] *is a huge and richly varied poetry collection containing more than 4,500 poems. Details of its compilation and date are unclear, but the last dated poem is from 759 and the compilation is thought to have been completed soon after this. One of the main poets represented, Ōtomo no Yakamochi (?718–85), was almost certainly among its multiple compilers, but the poems were probably gathered and arranged over many decades, and some originated much earlier. The result is a work that reveals the rapid evolution of early Japanese poetry into an accomplished literary form, establishing the lyric* waka *tradition that carried the* Manyōshū*'s legacy down the centuries.*

Poems of travel abound in the Manyōshū, *and give a telling picture of its world. The* Manyōshū *poems emerged from the seventh and eighth centuries which saw the establishment of the early Japanese state and the rapid development of its culture in the Yamato basin south of present-day Nara. By the time most of the poems were written, the Yamato state (centered on the emperor) had extended its reach eastward to somewhat beyond the present-day Tokyo area,*[2] *as well as north to the Japan Sea coast and as far west as northern Kyushu (Tsukushi), where at Dazaifu it maintained an important stronghold against possible aggression from the continent. There was thus much coming and going, not only of soldiers and officials but increasingly also of men from the provinces bearing tributes (taxes) to the capital. The custom of moving the site of the capital with the death of every emperor also caused considerable upheaval.*

The Yamato state was impressively quick to establish roads along the official routes, although in practice they were difficult to maintain and generally provided far from easy travelling. Travellers' overnight accommodation was almost non-existent, however, and travellers either sought shelter with local people or slept rough – the hardship and loneliness of sleeping on a journey are a pervasive theme in travel poems both in the Manyōshū *and later, and gave rise to many of its stock images.*[3] *More locally, the poems suggest considerable coming and going, often over mountains along rough tracks. The frequent mention of the corpses of dead travellers encountered on the road, and the fears and fervent prayers of those left behind, attest to the dangers inherent in travel in this period. This was particularly the case with sea travel, which plays an important role in these poems.*[4] *Although sea journeys were largely confined to the protected Inland Sea, boats were comparatively small and very vulnerable to bad weather and rough waves, and drownings were far from uncommon.*

One of the remarkable things about the Manyōshū *is its inclusiveness. It presents without distinction poems by emperors and commoners, by courtiers and lowly provincial soldiers, by both women and men in all walks of life. Almost half the poems are anonymous, and many would have been composed and transmitted orally and recorded only later.*[5] *Some of the poems are undoubtedly very old, although secure dating is impossible. The selection found here attempts a possible chronological order, beginning with a poem that was clearly orally transmitted and is probably early.*

*The compilers used a variety of ordering devices, among which chronology played only an occasional role. Most commonly, poems are categorized by type or theme, the three most important categories being the elegy or lament (*banka*), poems of relationship (*sōmonka*) – overwhelmingly love poems – and the general category of miscellaneous poem (*zōka*). The theme of travel is a pervasive presence in all three categories, and occasionally travel is accorded its own category (*kiryo no uta*).*

The very small selection given here attempts to give a sense not only of chronological developments but of the wide variety of composers, as well as the recurring identification of travel with longing, a theme that continued to resonate strongly down the following centuries. It also provides examples of the frequent borrowings and echoings of image and expression that signal the early evolution of what might be termed a communal poetic tradition.[6]

Finally, a brief word on the forms of poetry[7] *found in the* Manyōshū.

The chōka (*long poem*), *of varying length, and* tanka (*short poem*), *of thirty-one syllables, had both become established forms by the age of the* Manyōshū, *but the* chōka *form slowly gave way to the* tanka *during the eighth century and virtually disappeared from Japanese poetry thereafter. It is a syntactically loose flow of usually alternating 5- and 7-syllable phrases generally culminating in a final 7/7 couplet, and particularly in the hands of the great Hitomaro (? – c. 708) its rhythms and momentum made it a deeply expressive poetic form. Because the* chōka *form is essentially midway between heightened prose and poetry, my translations[8] follow the Japanese custom of writing it as a continuous line with spaces demarcating the phrases, and where possible attempt to give a sense of the syntactic flow of one 'sentence' into the next. The rhythmic propulsion onward from phrase to phrase allows no real pause, but for ease of understanding I retain a fluid sentence form.*

Chōka *are often followed by one or two envoys* (hanka) *in the form of 31-syllable* tanka *which act as a kind of coda, rephrasing and refining the* chōka's *central images and emotional statement. The history of the* tanka's *evolution remains unclear,[9] but its tendency to more personal lyric expression is evident in the relationship of* hanka *to* chōka, *and the dominance it achieved by the end of the* Manyōshū *period signals the direction Japanese literature would take.*

Some of the Manyōshū's *poems are accompanied by a brief headnote* (kotobagaki), *which might fill in the circumstances of composition or name the assigned topic.[10] These* kotobagaki, *which could occasionally extend to several lines, contain the seeds from which prose travel literature seems to have evolved.* (See Map 2)

FROM *MANYŌSHŪ*

388/89[11]

Anonymous. The note following this poem states, 'Wakamiya no Ayumaro recited this poem, but its author is unknown.' The poem, which has almost the air of a sailor's song, was probably primarily intended as a kind of invocation of and offering to the local gods for safe passage. It is an example of the oral transmission that would have been common, and of the related importance of recitation. It is specifically categorized as a travel poem.

watatsumi wa   kusushiki mono ka   awajishima   naka ni tate-okite   shiranami o   iyo ni megurashi   i-machi-zuki   akashi no to yu wa   yū sareba   shio o mitashime   ake-sareba   shio o hishimu   shiosai no   nami o kashikomi   awajishima   isogakuri-ite itsushika mo   kono yo no akemu to   samorau ni   i no nekateneba taki no ue no   asano no kigishi   akenu to shi   tachi-sawaku rashi iza kodomo   aete kogi-demu   niwa mo shizukeshi

A travel poem; with *tanka*.

The sea god must be   a god divinely powerful   to place in its centre   Awaji Island   and to circle Iyo   with white cresting waves   to swell the tide   through Akashi Straits   when evening comes   drawing it back   at daybreak.   Awed by the pounding waves   we seek our shelter   by Awaji's rocky shore keeping watch   wondering unsleeping   when the night will end   till above the waterfall   the pheasant in the scrubby brush declares the daybreak   with his clamorous cry.   Come my fellows   let us dare row out   for the level sea lies calm

Envoy

shima-tsutai	As we go rowing
minume no saki o	around the cape of Minume
kogi-mireba	hard by the island
yamato koishiku	longing for Yamato
tazu sawa ni naku	cranes flock and cry

3333/34

Anonymous. A poem that in many ways echoes the one above. It is apparently composed from the perspective of the waiting wife, whose husband has undertaken a sea voyage on imperial orders, probably to Tsukushi. The dangers of sea travel prompted fervent prayers and offerings to the gods by both the traveller and those left behind. The style suggests that it is an early poem.

ōkimi no   mikoto kashikomi   akizushima   yamato o sugite
ōtomo no   mitsu no hamabe yu   ōbune ni   makaji shiji-nuki
asanagi ni   kako no koe shitsutsu   yūnagi ni   kaji no oto shitsutsu
yukishi kimi   itsu kimasamu to   ura okite   iwai-wataru ni
tawakoto ka   hito no iitsuru   waga kokoro   tsukushi no yama no
momichiba no   chirite suginu to   kimi ga tadaka o

In duty to his lord   my love has gone   through Yamato and out
from the shores of Mitsu in Ōtomo   setting forth his great boats
with their strong-threaded oars   in the morning calm   the sailors
chanting   in the evening calm   the rowlocks creaking   oh he
is gone   and when will he come again   I begged to know   with
divination offerings to the gods   and ritual purifying   but
someone told me   mad though the words may be   that as the
autumn leaves   on Tsukushi's mountains   faithful as my heart
have drifted down and perished   so has the mortal being of my
love

Envoy

tawakoto ka   Mad they must surely be
hito no iitsuru   those words that someone
                              spoke
tama no o no   for he promised me
nagaku to kimi wa   that we would be together
iiteshi mono o   long as the endless jewelled
                              braid

1409

Anonymous, probably eighth century. This poem belongs to the important Elegy category, and is one of a run of poems relating to the dead.
The soul was long believed to enter death by travelling along a mountain path, an association of mountains with the realm of the dead that
reflected the custom of burying the dead in the mountains.

akiyama no   Drawn by the autumn leaves
momichi aware to   she has gone

uraburete	downcast into the mountain
irinishi imo wa	and though I wait
matedo kimasazu	she does not come again

85

Attributed to Iwanohime, consort of Emperor Nintoku (early 400s?), and as such among the earliest datable poems in the Manyōshū, *although in fact it almost certainly comes from a later time. The fusion of the twin themes of travel and yearning expresses a lyrical mode that remained dominant down the centuries.*

A poem composed by Empress Iwanohime in yearning for the Emperor.

kimi ga yuki	Long now are the days
kenagaku narinu	since you went, my lord.
yama tazune	Shall I go into the mountains
mukae ka yukamu	in search to meet you?
machi ni ka matamu	Or shall I watch and wait?

415

Attributed to Shōtoku Taishi (574–622), the revered early statesman who established the foundations of the modern Japanese state. This poem also belongs to the Elegy category. It is noteworthy that, despite his exalted status, the poet speaks directly in personal imaginative response to the misfortune of an unknown other, a traveller who has died by the roadside.

A poem composed in sorrow when Prince Shōtoku of the Upper Palace was making an excursion to Takahara Well, and saw a dead man lying on Mount Tatsuta.

ie naraba	Were he at home
imo ga te makamu	his love's arm would pillow him

kusamakura	poor traveller
tabi ni koyaseru	fallen on the journey
kono tabito aware	grass for pillow

1666

Anonymous. The headnote identifies it with the occasion when Empress Saimei (r. 655–61) made an excursion to mountainous Ki, possibly the imperial excursion of 658. Following the Chinese model, it was usual for members of the entourage to compose poems on imperial excursions. Needless to say, the image of the lone and beleaguered traveller is in this case a conceit.

Composed when the Empress who ruled from the Okamoto Palace made an excursion to the land of Ki.

asagiri ni	Drenched clothes
nurenishi koromo	undried
hosazu shite	from morning's mist
hitori ka kimi ga	do you cross alone
yamaji koyuramu	over the mountain path?

17–18

Princess Nukata, mid–late seventh century. Nukata, an impressive early poet, was beloved of Emperor Tenchi and later consort of his brother Emperor Tenmu, and adroitly survived the Jinshin coup of 672 in which she became entangled. Here, she is travelling from the capital in Asuka to what had been Tenchi's capital at Sasanami in Ōmi,[12] a journey of several days. This chōka is an example of the early mode of delighting in one's native landscape, depicted here like a lover at parting. Expressions such as 'of the sweet sake' and 'pale-earthed' are conventional epithets (makurakotoba).

umasake   miwa no yama   aoniyoshi   nara no yama no   yama
no ma ni   i-kakuru made   michi no kuma   i-tsumoru made ni
tsubara ni mo   mitsutsu yukamu o   shibashiba mo   mi-sakemu
yama o   kokoro naku   kumo no   kakusau-beshi ya

Princess Nukata composed this poem when she went down to
the land of Ōmi.

Mount Miwa of the sweet sake   till you hide at last   behind the
mountains   of pale-earthed Nara   till bend pile upon bend of
road   I would gaze my fill on you   I would glimpse you from
afar   over and over.   Is it right   these clouds so heartlessly
hide you from me?

Envoy

miwa yama o   Why do you hide from me
shikamo kakusu ka   lovely Mount Miwa?
kumo dani mo   Clouds, you at least
kokoro arana mo   should have a heart more
                              feeling
kakusau-beshi ya   than to keep it veiled

25

*Emperor Tenmu (d. 686). Already plotting the Jinshin coup that would
make him emperor, Tenmu (at the time Prince Ōama) renounced his
position as crown prince and travelled to Yoshino, ostensibly to become
a monk. He would have had much on his mind, as the poem describes.
(This is one of two variant texts.)*

miyoshino no   mimiga no mine ni   toki naku zo   yuki wa furikeru
ma naku zo   ame wa furikeru   sono yuki no   toki naki ga goto
sono ame no   ma naki ga goto o   kuma ga ochizu   omoitsutsu zo
koshi   sono yamamichi o

Composed by the Emperor.

In lovely Yoshino   on Mimiga Peak   snow fell without season
rain fell without cease   and like that timeless snow   like that
ceaseless rain   deep in circling thoughts I climbed   bend upon
bend   along that mountain path

135/6/7

*Kakimoto no Hitomaro (?–c. 708), one of Japan's finest poets, who
infused both the* chōka *and* tanka *forms with a new and compelling
lyric power. Here, Hitomaro leaves his wife behind as he travels to the
capital over the mountains from the remote Japan Sea coast where they
lived. The first mountain pass crossed on a journey, the last place from
which one's home was visible, was a key transition point, often marked
by a roadside shrine at which to pray for safety on the road. Travellers
were traditionally accompanied to this point and then farewelled.*

tsuno sawau   iwami no umi no   koto saeku   kara no saki naru
ikuri ni zo   fukamiru ōru   ariso ni zo   tamamo wa ouru
tamamo nasu   nabiki-neshi ko o   fukamiru no   fukamete omoedo
sa-neshi yo wa   ikuda mo arazu   hau tsuta no   wakareshi kureba
kimo mukau   kokoro o itami   omoitsutsu   kaeri-mi suredo
ōbune no   watari no yama no   momichiba no   chiri no magai ni
imo ga sode   saya ni mo miezu   tsuma-gomoru   yakami no yama
no   kumoma yori   watarau tsuki no   oshikedomo   kakurai-
kureba   amazutau   irihi sashinure   masurao to   omoeru ware
mo   shikitae no   koromo no sode wa   tōrite nurenu

At Kara Cape   in the Sea of Iwami   the deep sea *miru* weed
grows over sea rocks   the jewelled seaweed grows   over the
rocky shore   and like that jewelled weed   my girl leaned in to
me in sleep   she whom I love deep   as the deep *miru* weed   yet
the nights were few   when we slept thus together   and now I
am torn away   like clinging vine   and my heart aches   with
thoughts of her   turning to look behind   but the yellow leaves
upon Mount Watari   come fluttering down   and shroud from

view   the sleeve she waves to me   the sailing moon   glimpsed
among clouds   over Mount Yakami   then hid once more
from my longing sight   and across the heavens   the travelling
sun sinks shining.   Strong man   though I thought myself to be
the sleeves of my robe   are soaked with tears

Envoys

aokoma ga	So fast
agaki o hayami	my grey steed gallops
kumoi ni zo	that my love has gone
imo ga atari o	far among distant clouds
sugite kinikeru	as I come away
akiyama ni	Fluttering leaves
chirau momichiba	over the autumn mountains
shimashiku wa	halt a while
na chiri-magai so	your whirling fall
imo ga atari mimu	so I might see her still

194 /95

Kakimoto no Hitomaro. This chōka *is a lament for the death of Prince
Kawashima (d. 691), in the form of an intimate imagining of the
intense grief of his consort Princess Hatsusebe (Tenmu's daughter).
Prince Osakabe was Kawashima's brother. The imagined journey that
the mourning wife undertakes evokes the common conviction that the
dead still inhabit geographical space.*

*tobu tori   asuka no kawa no   kamitsuse ni   ouru tamamo wa
shitatsuse ni   nagare-furabau   tamamo nasu   ka yori kaku yori
nabikaishi   tsuma no mikoto no   tatanazuku   nikihada sura o
tsurugi tachi   mi ni soe neneba   nubatama no   yotoko mo aruramu   soko yue ni   nagusame-kanete   kedashiku mo   au ya to
omoite   tamadare no   ochi no ōno no   asatsuyu ni   tamamo
haizuchi   yūgiri ni   koromo wa nurete   kusamakura   tabine ka
mo suru   awanu kimi yue*

A poem presented by Kakimoto no Hitomaro to Princess Hatsusebe and Prince Osakabe.

In Asuka River   of the flying birds   the jewelled waterweed
of those upper reaches   twines down to stroke the lower   yet
he whom you love   twines no longer   this way and that about
you   sinuous as waterweed   that tender flesh no longer   lies
like a sword beside you   and through these black nights   your
bed lies chill and desolate   so that comfortless   perhaps you go
in hope of meeting him   dragging your jewelled train   through
mud and morning dew   on the great plains of Ochi   drenching
your robes   in the evening mists   sleeping upon your journey
grass for pillow   in search of him you will not meet again

Envoy

shikitae no	My love has gone
sode kaeshi kimi	he whose sleeve and mine
tamatare no	once lay together, gone
ochino sugi-yuku	beyond the plains of Ochi
mata mo awame ya mo	and will we ever meet again?

220/1/2

Kakimoto no Hitomaro. This famous poem begins with a typical pref-
acing passage of ritual praise of a place and its gods. It echoes the theme
of the ostensibly much earlier 415 above, but embeds the scene within
a rich narrative sweep.

tamamo yoshi   sanuki no kuni wa   kuni kara ka   miredomo
akanu   kamu kara ka   kokoda tōtoki   ametsuchi   hitsuki to
tomo ni   tari-yukamu   kami no miomo to   tsugi-kitaru   naka
no minato yu   fune ukete   waga kogi-kureba   tokitsukaze   kumoi
ni fuku ni   oki mireba   toinami tachi   he mireba   shiranami
sawaku   isana tori   umi o kashikomi   yuku fune no   kaji hiki-
orite   ochikochi no   shima wa ōkedo   naguwashi   samine no
shima no   arisomo ni   iorite mireba   nami no oto no   shigeki

hamae o   shikitae no   makura ni nashite   aratoko ni   korofusu
kimi ga   ie shiraba   yukite mo tsugemu   tsuma shiraba   ki mo
towamashi o   tamahoko no   michi dani shirazu   ōoshiku   machi
ka kouramu   hashiki tsumara wa

Poem composd by Kakimoto no Hitomaro on seeing a corpse
among the rocks on the island of Samine[13] in the land of Sanuki;
with *tanka*.

The land of Sanuki   of the jewelled seaweed   by its very nature
untiring to the eye   its gods by their very nature   mightily
sacred   known through the ages   as the face of a god   ever
more pleasing   in earth and heaven   with the passing days
there in Naka's bay   we set our ship   and came rowing   when
a sudden tide-wind   blew from the heavens.   We looked to
seaward   where the curved waves rose high   we looked to
shoreward   where the white waves clamoured   and bent our
hurrying oars   almost to breaking   from awe at the whale-rich
sea.   Of all the many   scattered islands   most finely named
Isle of Samine   there on its wild shore   we built our shelter
and I saw where you lay   tumbled on that rough bed   the wave-
loud clamorous shore   spread for pillow.   If I knew your home
I would go there and tell them   if your wife but knew   she
would come here seeking.   She will not know even   the lance-
straight way to take   but waits in trembling yearning   your
beloved wife

Envoys

tsuma mo araba	If your wife were here
tsumite tagemashi	she would have plucked and fed you
sami no yama	these wild asters
no no e no uwagi	now withered on the fields
suginikerazu ya	of Sami Mountain
okitsu nami	You who sleep here
ki-yosuru ariso o	taking for your own
shikitae no	spread pillow

makura to makite
naseru kimi ka mo

these wild rocks
where the waves come beating

66

Okisome no Azumahito (dates unknown) was a court poet and a contemporary of Hitomaro. Like poem 1666 above, this is an imperial excursion poem, composed when he accompanied Empress Jitō (r. 690–97) to the palace at Naniwa (here Ōtomo).

A poem at the time the retired Empress made an excursion to the Naniwa palace.

ōtomo no
takashi no hama no
matsu ga ne o
makurakinureba
ie shi shinowayu

I take for pillow
a pine tree's root
on the shore of Takashi
in the land of Ōtomo
but my heart yearns
    for home

67

Takayasu no Ōshima. We know nothing more than the name of this poet.

tabi ni shite
mono kōshiki ni
tazu ga ne mo
kikoezu ariseba
koite shinamashi

Far from home
and haunted by longing
did I not hear
the cries of the cranes
I might die of sorrow

79

Anonymous. The headnote identifies this poem as depicting the 710 relocation of the capital to Nara, which became its first permanent site.

The earlier palace was dismantled, floated downriver, and recon-
structed at the new site. (Envoy omitted.)

kimi no   mikoto kashikomi   nikibi ni shi   ie o oki   komoriku no
hatsuse no kawa ni   fune ukete   waga yuku kawa no   kawakuma
no   yasokuma ochizu   yorozu tabi   kaeri-mi shitsutsu   tamahoko
no   michi yuki-kurashi   aoniyoshi   nara no miyako no   sahogawa
ni   i-yuki-itarite   waga netaru   koromo no ue yu   asazukuyo
sayaka ni mireba   tae no ho ni   yoru no shimo furi   iwatoko to
kawa no hikogori   samuki yo o   yasumu koto naku   kayoitsutsu
tsukureru ie ni   chiyo made ni   imase ōkimi yo   ware mo
kayowamu

Another book states that this poem is of the time when the capital was moved from Fujiwara to Nara.

In awed obedience   to our lord's command   leaving behind
our loved familiar homes   we set our boats   upon the spirit-
dwelling   River Hase   and as we sailed   at every river bend
each of those eighty river bends   we turned back to gaze   travelling the lance-straight road   until we came at last   to Saho
River   in the capital   of pale-earthed Nara   and above the
robes   blanketing us by night   we saw the dawn's clear moon
while in its light   night's frost   lay white as whitest cloth   the
river frozen   like a sheet of stone   so cold the nights   and yet
unresting   coming and going we   have built that mansion.
Oh my lord   reign there a thousand ages   and we will come to
you as long

265

Naga no Okimaro (dates unknown). Roughly contemporary with Hito-
maro. This poem established Sano Crossing as an important utamakura
for later generations, although its location was in fact unclear.

kurushiku mo   A cruel rain
furi-kuru ame ka   beats down on me

miwa no saki   and at Sano Crossing
sano no watari ni   by Miwa Cape
ie mo aranaku ni   there is no house for
                                         shelter

273

Takechi no Kurohito (active late seventh to early eighth century), a court poet known particularly for the set of eight travel poems of which this is the first. This poem evokes the thronging birdlife once found in Lake Biwa (here called a sea). It is a relatively rare descriptive poem uncomplicated by any overt subjective element, although the image of abundance links it to the old land-praising tradition which by implication is praise of the ruler.

One of eight travel poems by Takechi no Kurohito.

iso no saki   As we go rowing
kogi-tami yukeba   around the rocky cape
ōmi no umi   in Ōmi's sea
yaso no minato ni   each of its eighty inlets
tazu sawa ni naku   is thronged with crying
                                         cranes

449

Ōtomo no Tabito (665–731). Tabito was head of the great Ōtomo clan, and spent his late career as governor of Dazaifu, where he encouraged poetry among subordinates and held influential poetry gatherings. Here he laments his wife's death in Dazaifu.

imo to koshi   With my love I came
mimune no saki o   to Mimune Cape
kaerusa ni   returning now alone
hitori shi mireba   again I see it
namida-gumashi mo   and my eyes fill with tears

351

Sami Mansei (active early eighth century). Mansei took the tonsure in 721, and is known by his Buddhist name. He was part of Ōtomo no Tabito's poetic circle. This poem is one of the most frequently quoted poems in classical poetry and plays a key role in later travel poetry, although it was better known in a later variant form. It is a rare example of a Manyōshū *poem that expresses a specifically Buddhist sensibility.*[14]

yo no naka o	To what shall I compare
nani ni tatoemu	this world?
asabiraki	It is like a boat at daybreak
kogi-inishi fune no	rowing away and gone
ato naki ga goto	leaving no trace

366/67

Kasa no Kanamura (active 715–33), a court poet in the early decades of the Nara period. The poem depicts a sea voyage off the distant Japan Sea coast, undertaken on official business. Replete with makurakotoba, *the poem weaves elegant variations on many themes found in the early poetry of sea travel.*[15] *The image of local 'fisher girls' burning salt in kilns on the beach long continued to be a common trope in classical travel poetry.*

koshi no umi no   tsunoga no hama yu   ōbune ni   makaji nuki-oroshi   isana tori   umiji ni idete   aekitsutsu   waga kogi-yukeba   masurao no   tayui ga ura ni   ama otome   shio yaku keburi   kusamakura   tabi ni shi areba   hitori shite   miru shirushi nami   watatsumi no   te ni makashitaru   tama tasuki   kakete shinoitsu   yamato shimane o

A poem by Kasa no Asomi Kanamura when he took ship at the port of Tsunoga; with *tanka*.

From Tsunoga   in Koshi's Sea   we set forth the great boat
thrusting down   threaded oars   into the whale-rich   ways of
the sea   gasping as we rowed   and in the Bay of Tayui   that
cord that brave men weave   smoke rose from the salt kilns   of
the fisher girls   but here on this journey   grass for pillow
there was no point   in gazing all alone   for like that jewelled
cord   the sea god twines   about his hands   a longing bound
me   a longing for home   in the land of Yamato

Envoy

koshi no umi no   In Koshi's Sea
tayui ga ura o   here on this journey
tabi ni shite   at Tayui Bay
mireba tomoshimi   gazing on all this beauty
yamato shinoitsu   I longed for Yamato

1747/8

*Takahashi no Mushimaro (active 720s – 730s). We know only that he
travelled extensively, probably in a military capacity, both to the East
and to Tsukushi. Naniwa was the site of an imperial palace constructed
in the 720s. Cherry blossoms, which play such a dominant role in later
Japanese poetry and culture, here make a rare early appearance.*

*shirakumo no   tatsuta no yama no   taki no ue no   ogura no mine
ni   saki-oiru   sakura no hana wa   yama takami   kaze shi
yamaneba   harusame no   tsugite shi fureba   hotsu eda wa   chiri-
suginikeri   shizue ni   nokoreru hana wa   shimashiku wa   chiri
na magai so   kusamakura   tabi yuku kimi ga   kaeri-kuru made*

[One of] two poems composed in spring in the third month,[16]
when the various nobles and high-ranking officials went down to
Naniwa; with [one of] two *tanka*.

On Tatsuta Mountain   white with cloud   above the falls   on
Ogura Peak   the cherry trees   bent low with blossom   blow

in incessant winds   from those high mountains   and the soft
spring rains   drift down unceasingly   so that the bough-tip
blossoms   have fallen now.   Oh blossoms on the under-boughs
stay a while   and do not scatter   until he comes again   home
from his far travels   grass for his pillow

Envoy

waga yuki wa   Surely our journey
nanuka wa sugiji   will not be more than seven days
tatsutahiko   oh god of Tatsuta
yume kono hana o   do not let the winds
kaze ni na chirashi   scatter these blossoms

1681

*Anonymous and undatable. The age-old role of the waiting woman
echoes the early poem attributed to Iwanohime (poem 85 above).*

okure-ite   Left behind
wa ga koi-oreba   I wait in longing
shirakumo no   while perhaps today
tanabiku yama o   you cross those mountains
kyō ka koyuramu   where white clouds trail

3132

*Book 12 contains a group of fifty-two poems described as expressing
'thoughts on a journey' (kiryo hasshi), 'thought' being largely synonymous with feelings of love and yearning. The following five anonymous
poems belong to this section.*

na iki so to   Going, I look back
kaeri mo ku ya to   hoping perhaps to see her
kaeri-mi ni   turning, begging Do not go
yukedo kaerazu   but she does not come again
michi no nagate o   down the long road I travel

3140

This poem appears to offer an early glimpse of the ubiquitous wandering female entertainers (asobi) *who haunt the margins of travel literature down the centuries and only disappeared from Japan's roads in the first half of the twentieth century. Sexual favours were an inevitable part of what many of them offered. Here, the woman is wistfully recalling her lover of the night before as she goes on her way.*

hashiki ya shi	Wretched now
shika aru koi ni mo	at last I understand
arishi ka mo	how much I loved you
kimi ni okurete	now that I travel on
koishiki omoeba	thinking of you behind me

3144

Explicit references to lovemaking such as that seen in the following poem were not uncommon in Manyōshū *poetry.*

tabi no yo no	So many nights
hisashiku nareba	spent on the journey
sani tsurau	how I yearn now
himo toki-sakeba	thinking how long since my hands
kouru kono koro	loosened her crimson undersash

3145

A lover's visit in a dream was believed to indicate that she was thinking of you. The following poem is a more sexually explicit variation on this usually elegant theme.

wagimoko shi	It seems my love
a o shinou rashi	must be yearning for me

kusamakura	for as I slept, grass for pillow,
tabi no marone ni	the knot of my undersash
shitabimo tokenu	somehow grew loose

3174

*This poem provides an example of the way a prefacing image (*jo*) could support and enhance the poem's statement. The first three lines are the* jo, *which folds syntactically into the final statement (translation is forced to make the metaphor explicit).*

izari suru	As steadily, as surely
ama no kaji-oto	as the steady sound of
	oars
yukuraku ni	in the rowing fishing boats
imo wa kokoro ni	so surely, steadily my love
norinikeru ka mo	rides in my heart

Book 15 of the Manyōshū *contains an unusual run of 144 poems composed by members of the ambassadorial expedition to Silla, the state that ruled the Korean peninsula at the time. They left the port of Naniwa in the summer of 736 and returned six months later after a difficult journey during which several had died. Typically, the poems do not depict the journey itself so much as the feelings of the travellers as they yearn for home. The following three anonymous poems represent the stages of the journey, the last being the return.*

3578

muko no ura no	Once nestled close
irie no sudori	as sea birds on the strand
hagukumoru	of Muko Inlet
kimi o hanarete	now you and I are parted
koi ni shinu beshi	and I die of yearning love

3669

tabi ni aredo
yoru wa hi tomoshi
oru ware o

yami ni ya imo ga
koitsutsu aruramu

Though travelling
by night I sit
warmed by the fire's
   light
while alone in darkness
my love will be pining

3716

amakumo no
tayutai-kureba
nagatsuki no
momichi no yama mo
utsuroinikeri

Wandering
like the shifting clouds
at last I come
to find the autumn leaves
have drifted yellow on the
   mountains

Relations with the Korean peninsula were often troubled, and fear of possible aggression from abroad necessitated that a garrison be maintained in Tsukushi, manned largely by men conscripted from the remote East. In 755, the great poet and compiler of the Manyōshū *Ōtomo no Yakamochi was stationed at Naniwa overseeing the processing of these frontier guards* (sakimori) *before they embarked for their three-year tour of duty. He gathered a large collection of their poems and selected the finest for inclusion in the* Manyōshū, *with names appended. Nothing is known of these men, though recurring reference to parents rather than lovers suggests the extreme youth of many. The poems would have been orally composed, and some are recorded verbatim in the rough Eastern dialect, distant forerunner of today's Tokyo speech. Yakamochi was so taken with these artlessly touching poems that he composed several himself 'in the manner of the frontier guardsman'. The poems are included in the final book of the* Manyōshū.

4337

mizutori no
tachi no isogi ni
chichi haha ni
mono hazu kenite
ima zo kuyashiki

As the water bird
takes sudden flight I came
away without a word
to my father and mother
and now I am sorry for it
                    Utobe no Ushimaro

4340

tochi haha e
iwaite matane
tsukushi naru
mizuku shiratama

torite ku made ni

Oh father, mother
wait and pray for me
till I take from the deep
its white brine-steeped
    pearls
and bring them home
    from Tsukushi
                Ōtomo no Yakamochi

4343

waro tabi wa
tabi to omoedo
ii ni shite
komechi yasuramu
waga mi kanashi mo

This journey of mine
I know must be my journey
yet how I love her
my wife who stays at home
haggard with child and
    waiting
        Tamatsukuribe no Hirome

4347

ie ni shite
koitsutsu arazu wa

Rather than stay
pining for you at home

na ga hakeru
tachi ni narite mo

iwaite shi kamo

I wish I could be
the long sword hanging at your
    waist
to keep you safe from harm
        The father of Sakabe no
        Omiminaka

4351

tabikoromo
yaeki kasanete
inoredomo
nao hada samushi
imo ni shi araneba

Though I sleep wrapped
deep in many layers
of traveller's cloak
how cold my skin
that cannot feel my love
        beside me
            Tamatsukuribe no Kunioshi

4352

michi no e no
umara no ure ni
hao mame no
karamaru kimi o
hakare ka yukamu

I must go
torn from your twining arms
like the winding bean
clinging to the thorny briar
that grows beside the path
                    Hasebe no Tori

4388

tabi to edo
matabi ni narinu

ie no mo ga
kiseshi koromo ni
aka tsukinikari

Journey they call it
but now how real that
    journey is
for the cloak that she
wrapped about me when I left
is soiled with the long road's dirt
                Urabe no Mushimaro

4400

ie omou to   Thinking of home
i o nezu oreba   I lie here wakeful
tazu ga naku   the reedy shore
ashie mo miezu   where cranes gather calling
haru no kasumi ni   unseen in spring mist
                                              Ōtomo no Yakamochi

2

The Ise Tales

Well over a century separates the Manyōshū *from the odd and intriguing* Ise Tales *(Ise* monogatari*). Much had changed during these years. A new era, the Heian period (794–1185), had arrived with the establishment of a permanent capital[1] where the city of Kyoto now stands. The resultant stability rapidly produced an impressive cultural flowering centred on the imperial court, which drew its wealth from the provinces. These were now officially administered by provincial governors drawn from among the middle-ranking courtiers, who vied for postings as close to the Capital as possible and dreaded their years away from its cultural and political world.*

While the Manyōshū *poems had been selected apparently indiscriminately from every class, literature was now essentially the domain of the elite and reflected its world and values. The literary image of travel that emerges from this period assumes that separation from the Capital constitutes something close to exile, a central theme that continues the* Manyōshū *travellers' longing for home. The famous travel sections of* The Ise Tales *exemplify this attitude, and in this and other ways foreshadow not only the tone but the style of travel writing to come.*

Another crucial development that had occurred during the intervening years since the Manyōshū *was the evolution of a script for writing the Japanese language. The* Manyōshū *was written with an immensely cumbersome system which used Chinese characters to represent sometimes the meanings assigned to them in Chinese and sometimes simply their Chinese pronunciation, which when strung together could be made to sound out Japanese words. Few could master it, and a hundred years later even fewer knew how to read it.[2]*

The Manyōshū *form of phonetic writing had by now evolved into a far simpler and more straightforward, though still complex, phonetic system* (kana) *which was in common use among the educated for writing the Japanese language. The prestigious Chinese language, however, was the official written language of the court and of the educated gentleman, who was schooled in the composing of Chinese poetry. The newly evolved phonetic* kana *writing system thus became primarily associated with women, who were denied the formal Chinese education of the public male sphere, and with the private realm of letters and love affairs and the* waka *poetry that was an inseparable aspect of both. These developments are crucial to* The Ise Tales, *and they help explain why so little Japanese literature of real worth had appeared in the years separating it from the* Manyōshū, *a time during which all the 'serious' literature was written, usually not very successfully, in a difficult foreign tongue.*

The Ise Tales *is a collection of* 125 *short, largely unconnected 'episodes'* (dan), *some a mere few lines long, each with a core of one or several poems. Neither its date nor its authorship can be established; it is thought to have reached its present form through a series of accretions by various hands from perhaps the late ninth to the mid-tenth centuries. Although the episodes almost never specify a name, the 'man' who is their protagonist has by long tradition been identified with the renowned poet Ariwara no Narihira* (825–80), *whose poems appear in a number of episodes and probably inspired the work's earliest form.*[3] *A courtier*[4] *who was by reputation a handsome playboy, Narihira became for subsequent generations the epitome of the debonair and witty lover who was the ideal of the courtly* miyabi *aesthetic.*

This image is largely due to The Ise Tales, *which depicts the anonymous 'man' in various dalliances and cleverly elegant poetry exchanges with women. As he is a courtier at play in the private world of love, his poetry naturally takes the form of the Japanese* waka, *and the stories created to support the poems are likewise written in Japanese. They are essentially elaborations of the form of the brief contextualizing headnotes or* kotobagaki *that often accompanied poems from the* Manyōshū *onwards, while their sensibility draws heavily on the* monogatari (*prose romances*) *that were a popular form of private entertainment at the time.*[5]

Although most episodes are implicitly set in the Capital, by definition the home of all that is elegantly miyabi, *among the most famous are the so-called* Azuma-kudari (*going down to the East*) *episodes that depict the travels of the 'man' and his companions into the wilds of the East and beyond to Michinoku, still the outermost reaches of the Japanese nation at the time. These episodes, above all 9, became a key reference text for later travellers along the route that came to be called the Tōkaidō, and played a crucial role in establishing important poetic* utamakura *sites along the road. They make no pretence at realistic description; their aim is to entertain with brief stories that fit the poems, the mood varying from the melancholies of the journey that were* de rigueur *for sophisticated travellers from the Capital, to humour at the expense both of the rustic locals and of the refined young courtiers reacting to the unaccustomed rigours of travel in uncouth lands.*

The selection of episodes given here provides a taste of the disconnected nature of The Ise Tales, *as well as of the tales' recurring fundamental structure, variety of tone and general style. Although each episode begins afresh, the* Azuma-kudari *section can be read as plotting a journey that takes the hero east to the area of present-day Tokyo (episodes 7–11), then on into Michinoku (episode 14), where he has a passing affair with an artless local girl with self-deluded aspirations to* miyabi *culture, who is humorously mocked in a way that may make us wince today. The final episode included here is a later one that depicts the young nobleman using the opportunity of a visit to his country estate to take his friends with him on the kind of elegant excursion[6] from the Capital that provided most of his class with their only taste of the wider world.* (See Map 3)

FROM *THE ISE TALES*

7

There was once a man. Finding life in the Capital difficult, he set off for the East, and as he was travelling along the coastline between the lands of Ise and Owari he saw the waves breaking wonderfully white, and composed this:

itodoshiku	Travelled distances
sugi-yuku kata no	reach back and back to home.

koishiki ni	Yearning for all I love
urayamashiku mo	I watch with envy
kaeru nami kana	the returning waves

9

There was once a man. Having taken it into his head that he was worthless, he decided to put the Capital behind him and instead set off for the East to search for a place to live. With him were one or two old friends. None of them knew the way, and they kept getting lost.

They arrived at a place called Yatsuhashi, Eight Bridges, in the land of Mikawa, so named from the eight bridges spanning the streams that flowed out in all directions like the legs of a spider.

They dismounted in the shade of a tree beside this marsh to eat their dried rice cakes. Irises were blooming beautifully in the marsh, and someone suggested they compose a poem on the theme of Travel, with the first syllable of each line to spell the word for iris, *ka.ki.tsu.ba.ta*. He composed this:

karakoromo	I have a wife
kitsutsu narenishi	intimate and dear to me
tsuma shi areba	as a long-worn robe
harubaru kinuru	swathing my thoughts with love
tabi o shi zo omou	through this far journey's distances

At this, they all shed tears onto their rice cakes till they grew quite soggy.

On and on they went, until they reached the land of Suruga. Having come to Mount Utsu,[7] they found the path ahead very dark and narrow, and overgrown with vines and maples.

Just as they were miserably contemplating their predicament, they happened upon a mountain monk. 'How do you come to be in such a place?' the monk asked. Our man recognized him, and wrote a letter to his beloved in the Capital, which he gave to the monk to take to her.

The meeting on Mount Utsu

suruga naru	Here on Mount Utsu's side
utsu no yamabe no	in the far land of Suruga
utsutsu ni mo	there is no meeting her –
yume ni mo hito no	neither in reality
awanu narikeri	nor yet in dreams

Looking up at Mount Fuji, he saw that it was white with snow, though it was by now late in the fifth month.

toki shiranu	Timeless Mount Fuji
yama wa fuji no ne	the falling snow
itsu tote ka	dapples your peak –
kanoko-madara ni	what season
yuki no fururamu	can you think it?

The size of this mountain is about twenty times as high as our Mount Hiei, and its shape is like a salt cone.[8]

On they travelled, until between Musashi and Shimōsa they came upon a very large river. Its name was Sumida River.[9]

They sat down in a group beside it, cast their minds back over the journey, and lamented together how very far away they now were; but the ferryman hurried them onto the boat, saying the sun would soon set. They boarded the ferry to cross, but every one of them was feeling wretched, since none was without a sweetheart back in the Capital. White birds about the size of a snipe, with red beak and legs, were floating about on the water and devouring fish. These birds were never seen in the Capital, so no one knew what they were. They asked the ferryman, and he told them they were known as 'Capital birds'. Someone composed this:

na ni shi owaba	Capital bird
iza koto towamu	if your name is true
miyako-dori	then tell me –
waga omou hito wa	she whom I love
ari ya nashi ya to	does she live or die?

And everyone on the boat burst into tears.

II

Once, as the man was on his way to the East, his friends received word from him:

| *wasuru na yo* | Do not forget me |
| *hodo wa kumoi ni* | though I am distant |

narinu to mo   as the drifting clouds.
sora yuku tsuki no   The travelling moon comes
                                          round
meguri-au made   and we will meet again

14

Once, the man went wandering off east all the way to Michinoku.[10]
A woman of those parts, no doubt impressed by the marvel of
someone from the Capital, fell deeply in love with him. She wrote:

nakanaka ni   Rather than die
koi ni shinazu wa   a futile death for love
kuwako ni zo   better to be a silkworm
naru-bekarikeru   bonded to its mate
tama no o bakari   through this brief life[11]

Even her poetry was rustic![12]
    He was clearly moved by her in some way, however, for he went
along and slept with her. When he left late that night, she composed this:[13]

yo mo akeba   When the dawn comes
kitsu ni hamenade   I've a mind to shove that rooster
kutakake no   into the water tub
madaki ni nakite   for he crowed too early
sena o yaritsuru   and sent my darling off

The man announced he was going back to the Capital, and composed this for her:

kurihara no   If only the famous pine of
                                          Kurihara
aneha no matsu no   were of human form
hito naraba   I would say Come with me
miyako no tsuto ni   back to the Capital
iza to iwamashi o   and be my traveller's gift

She was delighted by this,[14] and told everyone it was clear he loved her.

66

Once, the man took his brothers and friends to Naniwa with him, since he had property down in the land of Tsu. Noticing a number of boats along the shore, he composed this:

naniwazu o	I have seen this morning
kesa koso mitsu no	the many bays of Tsu
uragoto ni	afloat with boats –
kore ya kono yo o	frail grief-tossed vessels
umi wataru fune	plying the seas of life

Everyone was deeply moved, and home they went again.[15]

3

Tosa Diary by
Ki no Tsurayuki

While The Ise Tales *is plagued by questions of date, authorship and evolution, with* Tosa Diary *(Tosa nikki) we are suddenly on remarkably firm ground. We know with reasonable certainty that its author was the courtier and littérateur Ki no Tsurayuki (?870–?945), that it was written around 935, and that the version that has come down to us is a direct and apparently faithful copy of Tsurayuki's original manuscript[1] – a matter of astonishing luck, given that works from around this time and later generally exist today in several variant forms and include inadvertant errors and intentional changes made by a series of copyists.*

Tosa Diary *is also, on the face of it, a fairly straightforward diary of a real journey, and as such is the first in the long tradition of literary travel journals that culminates in Bashō's* The Narrow Road of Oku *750 years later. It describes in diary entry form the 55-day sea voyage undertaken by Ki no Tsurayuki and his entourage when he was returning to the Capital after his four years from 930 to 935 as provincial governor of Tosa, on the south coast of the island of Shikoku. Humorous, tender, personal, often poignant, and replete with convincing detail, it asks to be read as a realistic diary of day-to-day events. We experience with the writer the passing pleasures, the frustrations of endless delays en route, and the terror of bad weather, rough seas and pirates, as the boat makes its slow way[2] around the coast of Shikoku and on to the mainland, clinging close to shore and constantly putting in at tiny ports along the way for shelter.*

Yet Tosa Diary *is full of intriguing irony and artifice. The most striking example is introduced in the opening sentence, where we read that the writer is a woman. The fiction of this female persona, implicitly someone among the ladies in the governor's retinue, is maintained throughout the diary, although from time to time the guise slips and the voice is most easily read as that of Tsurayuki himself. The fiction and its ambiguities can be maintained with a light touch thanks to the lack of a need for explicit grammatical subject in Japanese sentences, so that Japanese readers are often only subliminally aware of precisely whose experience is being described.*[3]

There is a playfulness in this sometimes thinly maintained disguise, which allows Tsurayuki to present an ironic portrait of himself through the eyes of an observer, and frees him to imagine and inhabit the feelings and responses of someone apparently very different from himself. It also allows another pervasive pretence that the casual reader is less aware of – it seems that the poems that the ostensibly female writer and others compose during the voyage were in fact all composed by Tsurayuki himself. By this means, he could dramatize and add variety, texture and an extra layer of irony to what would otherwise have been a simpler and more monotonously straightforward personal account. Most importantly, the technique seems to have allowed him some emotional distance from what was clearly his own great grief for a recently deceased child, a recurring theme that adds a deep poignancy to the journey.

Although so different from The Ise Tales, here too poems and their circumstances of composition form the core of the work, which provides a vivid insight into some of the roles that poetry played in the lives of the educated elite. We see the members of Tsurayuki's party constantly resorting to poetry both in personal response to passing sights and experiences, and as a form of elegant group entertainment to set against the remote and sometimes daunting situation they found themselves in. This depiction is surely reasonably accurate, even if the scenes themselves may be fictionalized. The poetry, too, is typical of the era in its frequent reliance on wit, language play and the pose of what is known as elegant confusion,[4] a lightness of touch that offsets the weightier poems of sorrow and longing much as the gently humorous scenes of Tosa Diary offset the underlying grief, longing and hardship of the journey.

Ki no Tsurayuki was in fact the great arbiter of poetic taste of his age, and is best known as the chief compiler of the Kokinshū (c. 920), the seminal poetry collection compiled by imperial decree.[5] This hints at what may have been an underlying motive for his creation of Tosa Diary. Writing in the Japanese language, long eclipsed by Chinese at the court for both poetry and prose, had recently begun tentatively to reassert itself with the growing acceptance of Japanese waka verse as a legitimate poetic form among the men at court,[6] culminating in the compilation of the Kokinshū. Tsurayuki, a keen advocate of this emergent native kana poetry, may well have written Tosa Diary as a semi-playful experiment that extended the reach of native Japanese literature by creating a prose work in kana with the subjective waka sensibility, to set against the more objective and formal Chinese literary mode[7] that was then the accepted norm. Tosa Diary's famous opening sentence, which announces the transgressive nature of this diary as a woman's appropriation of a strictly male form – diaries (nikki, itself a Chinese word) were essentially simple aides mémoires kept by men in Chinese to record the day's activities – can also be read as covertly announcing a radical new literary form, in which the 'female sensibility' of Japanese-language kana prose lays claim to a new legitimacy.

Though written by a man, Tosa Diary opened the way for the subsequent flowering of women's diary writing at the Heian court that produced some of the greatest works of early Japanese literature. As the first extant travel diary, it might have been expected likewise to spur on the further evolution of this genre also. In fact, another three centuries would pass before a similar mode of travel writing emerged, and Tsurayuki's diary seems to have had little influence on the history of Japanese travel literature.[8] Radical as it was, this travel journal seems to have been in many ways unique in Heian literature, despite its importance in paving the way for the tradition of native prose literature that rapidly evolved after its time. (See Map 1)

FROM *TOSA DIARY*

I have heard that men write diaries, but a woman will try her hand at one here.

We set out on our journey, leaving our front gate at the Hour of the Dog[9] on the twenty-first day of the twelfth month of a certain year. I will just write a little about our travels.

[. . .]

Twenty-seventh day. Our boat set off from Ōtsu, bound for Urado.[10]
In the midst of all that had happened, the little girl born back in
the Capital had suddenly died in this far land, and there was one
among us who spoke not a word as he watched[11] the bustle of preparations for departure. Faced with this return, he was filled only
with sorrow and longing for his little daughter. Those with him
also found the loss hard to bear. A poem someone wrote and gave
him at this time:

miyako e to	Yearning for home
omou o mono no	and yet somehow this grief –
kanashiki wa	for there is one
kaeranu hito no	for whom there can be
areba narikeri	no return

And on another occasion:

aru mono to	Forgetting
wasuretsutsu nao	I think her here
naki hito o	the child now dead
izura to tou zo	and weep to find myself
kanashikarikeru	saying Where can she be?

In this vein, we arrived at a place called Kago Promontory, where
brothers of the governor and various others arrived, having followed us bringing sake and food. We alighted and sat on the shore
together, lamenting the sorrow of parting. People remarked to
each other that those retainers from the governor's establishment
who had come after us in this way showed a particularly delicate
sensibility, and indeed they seemed to. Speaking of parting's sorrow, all put their shoulders to the net together, so to speak, and
hauled in a fine catch of poems. One went:

oshi to omou	Hoping that perhaps
hito ya tomaru to	one loath to fly might stay
ashigamo no	we flocked here
uchimurete koso	like the wild ducks that flock
ware wa kinikere	among the shoreline reeds

The poem was roundly praised, and one among us composed this:

sao sasedo	Deep as the ocean's depth
sokoi mo shiranu	unfathomed though our oars
watatsumi no	probe its currents
fukaki kokoro o	so deep too the heart
kimi ni miru kana	that I perceive in you

But our oarsmen too had been tippling, quite without any deeper sense of poignancy, and now they cried that we must be quick and leave – 'The tide's at the full, and a wind's blowing up!' – so we prepared to board.

At this point, some among us recited certain Chinese poems that were apt for the occasion. Another sang a parting song from an Eastern province, for all that we were in the West. 'With a voice like that you'll make the very dust on the boat's rafters dance and the clouds pause to hear you on their way!' the men apparently exclaimed.[12]

This night, we stopped in Urado. Fujiwara no Tokizane, Tachibana no Suehira[13] and others followed us there.

Twenty-eighth day. We rowed out from Urado heading for Ōminato. Yamaguchi Nochimine, the son of the former governor, had brought along sake and fine food, which were loaded into the boat, and we ate and drank as we went along.

Twenty-ninth day. We have stopped in Ōminato. The doctor came all the way out to present us with New Year sake and medicinal spices for it[14] – a kind man, it would seem.

New Year's Day. We are still in the same port. Someone decided to prop the spices up by the boat room overnight, and the wind gradually dislodged them so that they slipped overboard, with the result that we had none to drink. Nor did we have any of the traditional New Year sweet potato stems and seaweed or tooth-hardening foods.[15] Such things are lacking in this part of the world, and we hadn't ordered any in beforehand. All we could do by way of celebratory feasting was to suck on salted sweetfish. What can those fish have thought of the mouths so eagerly clamped to theirs?[16]

We spent the day with our thoughts turned to the distant Capital, imagining together how the gates of the houses must be looking now, all hung with New Year decorative straw rope, mullet and false holly.

Second day. We are still in Ōminato. The head priest of the local temple sent food and sake.

Third day. Still here. Perhaps the wind and waves are reluctant to see us go. It does make us anxious.

Fourth day. The wind prevents us from leaving. Masatsura[17] has sent sake and fine food. We cannot simply do nothing in return for the gifts these people bring us, so we make small gestures of thanks. But we have nothing really to give. We may look prosperous, but we feel far less so than them.

Fifth day. The wind and high seas continue, so here we still are. There has been an endless flow of visitors.

Sixth day. Still as before.

It is the seventh day. The day of the White Horses ceremony[18] in the Capital. I couldn't help picturing it, although it was pointless to think of it here. The only white to be seen was the white foaming waves. Meanwhile, a long box filled with fresh water and ocean fish arrived on the shoulders of servants, a delivery from someone's home in a place called Ike. The name means 'pond', but although there were roach and other varieties, both freshwater and sea fish, there were none of the pond carp that the name suggested. The fresh herbs that were included reminded us that today is the Festival of Young Herbs.[19] There was a most amusing poem with the gift:

asajifu no   Here among moors
nobe ni shi areba   thick with *asaji* reeds

mizu mo naki	in this waterless Pond
ike ni sumitsuru	I have plucked for you
wakana narikeri	these young herbs

The poem is apparently that of a fine lady who has followed her husband into the provinces to live.

The food in this box was a gift for all of us, the young included; we gorged ourselves till we could eat no more and so did the boat's lads, who beat their drum-tight bellies loud enough to alarm the sea into fresh turmoil.

Thus our time has passed here with quite a variety of events.

Someone visited today with a retainer bearing boxed food[20] for us – now let me try to remember his name. In fact, he turned out to have come intent on composing poetry. After some general talk, he bewailed the rough seas that were holding us back, and composed this:

yuku saki ni	Loud cry the white-capped
	waves
tatsu shiranami no	that rise to bar your way
koe yori mo	but louder still my cries
okurete nakamu	that will rise here behind you
ware ya masaramu	to see you depart

Loud indeed, in that case! It was good food he brought, but what to make of his poem? We all made out that we were suitably moved, but no one composed one in return.[21] Even those among us who could have been most expected to respond simply devoted themselves to praising his poetry and devouring his food till the night grew late.

Finally the poet rose to his feet and left the room, though he announced that he wasn't going home yet. At this, somebody's young child murmured, 'Let me make a poem for him.'

Startled, we all declared this was an excellent idea. 'Can you really manage it?' we asked her. 'If you have a poem, be quick and recite it.'

'I'll wait to recite it until the man who left saying he wasn't leaving has come back,' she said, so a search went out for the fellow, but it seems the hour had grown so late that he had indeed gone home.

'So just what is it you've composed?' we asked dubiously. The child was, of course, too embarrassed to say, but after much questioning she finally came out with:

yuku hito mo	The sleeves of we who leave
tomaru mo sode no	and you who stay
namida-gawa	are awash with floods of tears
migiwa nomi koso	that rise until they overflow
nuremasarikere	the banks of Weeping River

Well fancy that. She was such a sweet little girl, this was quite unexpected. 'Of course it wouldn't do coming from a child,' our master said. 'One of us old ones should set our name to it. It doesn't matter whether it's bad or good, let's send it to him if we get the chance', and with that he apparently noted it down.

Eighth day. Things have prevented us from leaving, so we are still here. This evening, watching the moon sink into the sea, we thought of the poem of Narihira's that goes, 'would that the mountain's rim / would flee before it'.[22] If he were composing it by the sea, he would have made that 'would that the ocean waves / would rise to block its going'. Recalling the poem, one among us composed:

teru tsuki no	Watching the shining moon
nagaruru mireba	go floating down the sky I know
ama no gawa	the river of the Milky Way
izuru minato wa	must flow to the sea
umi ni zarikeru	as our own rivers do

Or at least I think it went like this.

Early on the ninth day, we set off from Minato toward the port of Nawa. A great many people decided they must accompany us until we crossed the province's border;[23] among them Fujiwara no Tokizane, Tachibana no Suehira and Hasebe no Yukimasa, who had faithfully followed us hither and yon ever since we had left the governor's headquarters. The devotion of these men was quite as deep as the ocean we travelled over. Now we would be leaving them behind, and so they had come along to bid us farewell.

On we rowed. Those left ashore grew more and more distant; we in the boat shrank to invisibility. Our friends on the shore were no doubt longing to speak to us still, while we too yearned back towards them – but to no avail. Full though my heart was, I could only murmur to myself this one poem:

omoiyaru	My thoughts reach back to you
kokoro wa umi o	across far seas
wataredomo	yet with no way
fumi shi nakereba	to send you word by letter
shirazu ya aruramu	how could you know them?

On we went, past Uta no Matsubara. Pines in untold numbers stood along the shore, untold ages old. Waves lapped at the feet of every one; restless cranes thronged around every branch. Unable simply to stand and gaze in wonder, one on board composed this:

miwataseba	Gazing upon these pines
matsu no uregoto ni	it seems the cranes
sumu tsuru wa	nesting on every branch
chiyo no dochi to zo	must take the trees for friends
omoubera naru	a thousand generations old

This poem doesn't do justice to the actual scene we saw.

On we went as we gazed on, while the mountains and sea slowly grew dark, and the night deepened. We could no longer make out east or west, and in our fear of the weather we could only have faith in our captain. Even the men among us were wretched at feeling so at sea with things, while we ladies bowed our heads to the deck and simply wailed aloud. And yet the sailors and captain sang sea shanties as they went along, quite unperturbed. The songs went:

haru no no nite zo	There you stand in the spring field
ne o ba naku	a-sobbing and a-wailing.
wakasusuki ni	Your Mummy and your Daddy will
te kiru kiru tsundaru na o	gobble up those nice fresh greens
oya ya maboruramu	you cut your little hands to pick.
shūtome ya kuuramu	Your mother-in-law she'll eat 'em –
kaera ya	*Come on, let's get on home.*

Another was:

yonbe no unai mo ga na	If I could lay hands on that kid from last night
zeni kowamu	I'd demand what he owes me.
soragoto o shite	He lied when he told me
oginori waza o shite	he'd be back with the cash.
zeni mo mote kozu	He's brought back nothing
onore dani kozu	not even himself.

And many more besides, too many to write. Hearing everyone laugh at these songs brought a little calm to my storm-tossed heart, for all that the sea was still so rough.

So we spent the night, until we arrived at the port. One old man and an old lady among our number were feeling particularly ill, and they sat huddled silently, unable to eat a thing.

Tenth day. We spent the day here in the port of Nawa.

Eleventh day. The ship set out at first light for Cape Murotsu. No one was up yet, and there was no way to judge the state of the waves. One could only tell east from west by looking at the moon. Dawn arrived as we went on, and while we washed our hands and gathered ourselves together morning turned to day.

Now we have arrived at a place called Hane. One of the young children asked, 'Is Hane the same as the *hane* (wing) of a bird?' He was only little, so everyone laughed, whereupon a young girl composed this:

makoto nite	If only Hane were
na ni kiku tokoro	in truth a bird's wing
hane naraba	as its name suggests –
tobu ga gotoku ni	oh that we could speed our way
miyako e mo ga na	and fly to the Capital

We all, both men and women, were longing for some way to reach the Capital as quickly as we could, so we all committed this poem to memory because it felt so true at the time, though it wasn't very good.

The child who asked that question brought to mind the little girl we had lost; indeed when was she ever forgotten? This was a day when the mother's grief was particularly intense;[24] we were returning home with our numbers diminished, and one of us, recalling the lines from the old poem that go 'one among them / will not be coming on the homeward journey',[25] composed:

yo no naka ni	Casting about
omoi-yaredomo	this sorrowing world of ours
ko o kouru	I find no sorrow stronger
omoi ni masaru	than the aching love we bear
omoi naki kana	for one who is our child

Such were our thoughts that day.

Twelfth day. No rain. The boats of Funtoki and Koremichi[26] arrived late to Murotsu from Narashi Port.

Thirteenth day. At dawn there was light rain, which fell for a while and then ceased. Some of the women disembarked and set off to bathe in a suitable place nearby. Looking at the sea, someone composed:

kumo mo mina	Even the clouds here
nami to zo miyuru	have the look of waves.
ama mo ga na	Oh for a fishergirl
izure ka umi to	so we might ask which is the sea
toite shirubeku	and know at last

The moon was now past its tenth night,[27] and shone enchantingly. Since the day we boarded we ladies have not worn any of our fine deep scarlet robes for fear of arousing the sea god. But here we were tucked away among a few reeds, so what could be wrong with hitching our skirts above our shins and more, to display those maidenly mussels of ours that go so deliciously with sea cucumbers? [28]

Fourteenth day. It rained from first light, so we stayed where we were. The governor observed a day of abstinence.[29] Owing to a lack of the proper vegetarian food on board, he broke fast early at noon with a sea bream that the captain had caught the day before, exchanging it for rice since he had no money on hand. There were other such occasions too, the captain several times bringing along a bream and receiving rice and sake for it. The captain was far from displeased with these exchanges.

Fifteenth day. No festival red bean stew[30] was cooked. This was bad enough, but the weather was also inclement. We sat about miserably all day, aware that more than twenty days have now passed since we set off. Idling the day away, everyone just sat around staring at the sea. A little girl recited this:

tateba tatsu	When they rise they rise together
ireba mata iru	when one calms the other calms –
fuku kaze to	what loving friends
nami to wa omou	the wind and the waves
dochi ni ya aruramu	must surely be

This was really very appropriate, though it came from a mere child

[. . .] Twenty-first day. Our boat set out around the Hour of the Hare.[31] The various accompanying boats also sailed out with us, and though it was spring[32] the sea looked as if it was scattered over with colourful autumn leaves. Our particularly fervent prayers seem to have had their effect, for there was no wind and the day had grown fine when we set off.

With us was a youngster who had asked to come into our service. He now sang a very moving boat song:

nao koso kuni no   And even so I find myself
kata wa miyararure   gazing back towards my home
waga chichihaha   thinking that there
ari to shi omoeba   wait my father and mother –
kaera ya   *Come on, let's go on home*

Off we sailed with this song in our ears, and there on the rocks stood a flock of those birds known as black birds.[33] At their feet, the waves broke white against the rocks. 'Look, white waves breaking beneath black birds', remarked the captain – a very ordinary remark, but it did sound clever somehow.[34] One noticed it because it was so unexpected from someone like him.

And so we went on. Our master composed a poem, prefacing it with the following: 'These seas are all the more frightening for those rumours we've been hearing ever since we left that pirates[35] might attack; it's turned my hair quite white. Here you have an old man of seventy or eighty, all at sea.

waga kami no   Guardian of these islands
yuki to isobe no   tell me true
shiranami to   which is the whiter
izure masareri   those white waves on the rocky
                                            shore
okitsu shimamori   or this snow upon my head?

You tell me, captain.'

Twenty-second day. We set out from the port of Yonbe, bound for a new one.

Mountains were visible far off. A boy of nine, who looked still younger, noticed that as we rowed the mountains seemed to move, and astonished us with this poem:

kogite yuku	Watching from this boat
fune nite mireba	that rows its way
ashihiki no	even the foot-heavy mountains
yama sae yuku o	move along with us –
matsu wa shirazu ya	can their pines not sense it?

A suitable poem for a young child to compose.

The waves were rough today – snow tossed against the rocky shore, or a white bloom of wave-flowers. Someone composed this:

nami to nomi	To the ear they sound
hitotsu ni kikedo	simply as waves
iro mireba	yet to the confused eye
yuki to hana to ni	seeing that white they seem
magaikeru kana	flying snow or blossom

[. . .]

And so we went on,[36] gazing out over the water and longing for one absent, when suddenly the wind blew up, and though we rowed and rowed we were pushed back and back, and came very close to capsizing.

The captain declared that since the god of Sumiyoshi was a fierce sea god,[37] he must be demanding to be given something. How very modern of him. The captain instructed us to present sacred *nusa* offerings, which we did, but the wind went right on blowing. Stronger and stronger it blew, and higher and higher rose the waves. Things were so dangerous that the captain then declared, 'If our offerings don't go down well with the god, we're the ones who'll go down. We must offer him something that will please him better.' Again we did as told, and since there was no help for it our master, announcing 'Two precious eyes, but only one of these',[38] tossed into the sea our single precious mirror – a great shame. No sooner had he done so than the sea surface grew mirror-calm. Someone composed this:

chihayaburu	This calm we see
kami no kokoro o	reflects the gentle heart
aruru umi ni	of the tempestuous sea god
kagami o irete	for when we tossed the mirror in
katsu mitsuru kana	the wild sea grew still

This god certainly isn't that deity of the pretty epithets conventionally associated with him in poetry, such as 'grasses of forgetting' or 'little pine upon the bank'. His heart was reflected there mirror-clear and plain for all to see – and the captain's heart was at one with it.

Sixth day. We set out through the navigation markers,[39] arrived at Naniwa and entered the river at Kawajiri. All of us, the old included, clasped our hands before our foreheads in unparalleled delight. The old lady from Awaji who was so seasick raised her head from the floor in joy at approaching the Capital, and composed this:

itsu shika to	Wretched we wondered
ibusekaritsuru	when that day might ever come
naniwagata	yet look – our boat is here
ashi kogi-sokete	pushing through the river reeds
mifune kinikeri	of Naniwa Inlet

People were amazed that such an unlikely person should compose such a poem. Our master, who was in poor shape himself, praised the poem highly. 'Who'd have guessed it, from the way you've been looking?' he said.

Seventh day. Today we set off rowing upstream from Kawajiri, plagued by how low the river is. Progress is extremely difficult in the shallow water.

As we went, our sick master – a rough-and-ready man who knows nothing really of poetry – was nevertheless so impressed by the old Awaji lady's poem, and no doubt also moved by his

own joy at approaching the Capital, that he somehow managed
to produce a poem himself.

ki to kite wa	Come we have at last
kawanoboriji no	but now our river passage
mizu o asami	is damned by shallow water
fune mo wagami mo	and neither boat nor I
nazumu kyō kana	make headway through our
	woes

He was no doubt referring to the fact that he was feeling ill. One
poem was not enough to satisfy him, and he composed another.

toku to omou	Swiftly though I urge
fune nayamasu wa	the boat to go
waga tame ni	I languish here
mizu no kokoro no	due to the shallow sympathy
asaki narikeri	this river bears me

This poem must have come from his overwhelming delight at
approaching the Capital.
   'But they're not a patch on the Awaji lady's poem. Damn, I
wish I hadn't recited them,' he added regretfully. And with that
we went to bed, for night had come on.

Eighth day. We continue to make poor progress up the river, and
stopped for the night in the area known as the Imperial Pastures
of Torikai. This evening our master's illness grew worse again,
and he was in great pain.
   Someone brought along some fresh fish, and we repaid him in
rice. 'An example of "fishing with fine rice to catch fingerlings",[40]
a few of the men remarked quietly. There had been similar
exchanges before, here and there along the way. In fact, however,
as today was a ritual day of abstention from flesh, the fish were
useless.

Ninth day. In our anxiety to arrive we set off before dawn, towed
by a rope from the riverbank, but there was so little water in the

river that we simply crawled along, scraping our knees as we went.

Along the way we came to a place called Wata no Tomari no Akare where people begged rice and fish, which we gave.

Towed along, we watched the place known as the Nagisa Villa[41] go by, a lovely place that recalled the past. Pines stood on the hill behind; a plum tree bloomed in the central garden. 'This place was famous once,' people remarked to each other. It is where the late Ariwara no Narihira composed this poem when he was here with the late Prince Koretaka:

yo no naka ni	If in this world
taete sakura no	the cherry never bloomed
sakazareba	think how serene
haru no kokoro wa	our springtime hearts
nodokekaramashi	would be

One who stood here today composed this on how the place now looks:

chiyo hetaru	A thousand generations
matsu ni wa aredo	these pines have stood
inishie no	yet the song they sing
koe no samusa wa	keens in the same chill voice
kawarazarikeri	unchanged through time

Another composed this:

kimi koite	Down the years
yo o furu yado no	recalling him with love
mume no hana	this ancient villa's plum tree
mukashi no ka ni zo	blooms still with the scent
nao nioikeru	it had of old

And in this vein we approached the Capital, full of joy.

None had had children when we left the Capital, but many among us had borne children while we were away. They all now gathered, and wherever the boat docked along the way they could be seen getting on and off, their little ones in their arms. Watching this, the mother of the little girl we left behind was overcome with sorrow. Weeping, she composed this:

nakarishi mo	Children return
aritsutsu kaeru	who once were not
hito no ko o	here on this earth
arishi mo nakute	while in sorrow I
kuru ga kanashisa	return without the child
	who was

What can the poor father have felt, too, on hearing this?

It is surely not for the pleasure of it that we feel and compose poetry like this. In China too, as here, poetry arises when feeling overflows, or so I believe.

Planning to arrive in the Capital after dark, we took our time.[42] The moon rose, and by its light we crossed the Katsura River. 'Unlike the Asuka River of poetry, this river's shallows and deeps have never changed,'[43] people remarked, and someone composed this:

hisakata no	High on the moon there rises
tsuki ni oitaru	an ancient *katsura* tree[44]
katsuragawa	while here the River Katsura
soko naru kage mo	holds within its deeps
kawarizarikeri	another changeless moon

Another composed this:

amakumo no	Katsura River
haruka naritsuru	long distant as the heavens
katsuragawa	today I have crossed you
sode o hitete mo	sleeves soaked
watarinuru kana	to arrive at last

And another composed:

katsuragawa	The River Katsura
waga kokoro ni mo	though it flows not
kayowanedo	through this heart of mine
onaji fukasa ni	yet flows as deep, it seems,
nagaruberanari	as my heart's feelings

Our joy at seeing the Capital was so excessive that it produced an excess of poetry.

The night drew on, and we could see nothing of what was around us. We entered the Capital filled with delight.

We came to the house, and as we passed in through the gate everything was revealed in the bright moonlight. The place had deteriorated beyond words, even more than we had been warned. It was not only the house that was derelict – those in whose care we had left it had equally clearly grown derelict in their duties. Despite the intervening fence, the place next door was virtually an extension of our own, so they themselves had offered to keep an eye on it from where they lived. And then there was the endless flow of gifts we had pressed on them whenever they sent news of the place. But we didn't voice our opinions openly this evening. Despite their evident negligence, we plan to thank them.

The garden has a water-filled depression that serves for a pond, with pines at its edge. The five or six years of our absence could have been a thousand years, for half of these have died, while young saplings have sprung up here and there among the others. In fact it is all in such a state of ruin that everyone exclaimed at the sorrow of it.

And how particularly sad, in the midst of the flood of nostalgic memories, to know that the little girl who had been born in this house had not returned with us. Amid the throng of noisy children surrounding the others who had come with us, one whose sadness was overwhelming quietly shared this poem with another who well understood:

mumareshi mo	She who was born here
kaeranu mono o	does not return –

waga yado ni   now in my garden
komatsu no aru o   I watch the young pines thrive
miru ga kanashisa   and sorrow fills me

This was not enough to satisfy him, it seems, for he composed
another:

mishi hito no   I might have seen that child
matsu no chitose ni   live long as the pine
mimashikaba   that stands a thousand years –
tōku kanashiki   why must I grieve instead
wakare semashi ya   torn so far from her?

So much haunts the memory and fills me with grief, too much to
express. One way and another, I plan to destroy this forthwith.[45]

4

Ionushi's Pilgrimage to Kumano by Zōki

About fifty years after Ki no Tsurayuki made his long boat journey back to the Capital, an elderly monk by the name of Zōki quietly set off from the Capital on a far more arduous journey to the wild and mountainous land of Ki, to visit the holy shrines of Kumano.

We know almost nothing about Zōki (his Buddhist name), though his life seems to have spanned from the mid-tenth into the beginning of the eleventh century. Buddhism, at first the preserve of temple-based priests and monks, had by now evolved in Japan to play an important role in the culture of the educated and aristocratic classes, where it became a custom to 'take the tonsure' and retire from active life to one of devotion and prayer in the face of old age, or a crisis in public or private life. Zōki's writing contains strong hints that it was the death of his patron that prompted him to take this path. He seems not to have been attached to a temple, but to have followed the increasingly common pattern of choosing an independent life of reclusion in a lowly hut (io or iori), from which he made numerous pilgrimages to shrines and temples[1] in the pursuit of his Buddhist practice.

Given that he was a Buddhist monk on pilgrimage, one might expect that his description of the journey would focus on its religious content, but this is not the case. Zōki was clearly a highly educated man, and as such he practised the art of waka poetry, by now established as an essential cultural practice in his world. It was common for a skilled poet late in life to gather his or her poetry into a collection (shikashū) for distribution to friends, and that is the fundamental form that Zōki's writing takes. But while shikashū were traditionally collections of discrete poems and their brief introductory kotobagaki, in the first section of his shikashū[2] Zōki experimented by expanding the form towards narrative.

Rather than write in the first person, he chose to make himself the third person protagonist in his own story,[3] giving himself the whimsical name Ionushi (literally 'master of the hut') and borrowing from the prose romance (monogatari) *tradition to give the story a sense of adventure and some degree of narrative coherence.*

This hybrid piece of writing is fascinating for a number of reasons, not least its innovative blending of genres. It echoes The Ise Tales *in expanding the poems'* kotobagaki *into little narrative episodes in their own right, but unlike* The Ise Tales *the episodes are loosely connected scenes that sequentially trace the clear stages of a real journey.[4] Zōki seems to have aimed at providing an episodic but coherent account of the journey in the face of the fragmentary nature of the* shikashū*'s inherent structure, and at times that structure seems stretched to breaking point. Several particularly lengthy episodes radically depart from tradition by having no core poem at all; in these, Zōki seems to have been experimenting with the possibilities of wittily allusive conversational exchange as a literary substitute for an episode's poetic core.[5] The tone veers rather haphazardly between conventional poetic melancholy laced with Buddhist renunciation of the world, and a lighter pleasure in wit and humour such as we also find in* Tosa Diary. *Above all, as the journey continues Zōki seems for a while increasingly concerned with recording his own observations in loose diary fashion.*

These sections provide a rare and precious glimpse of the enormously popular Kumano religious cult – a popularity that has found a new form today in the tourist hiking trails that follow the old paths of what is now the Kumano Kodō World Heritage pilgrimage site. The history of this sacred mountainous terrain goes back to earliest recorded myth, and by the mid-tenth century it had become a significant pilgrimage destination attracting great numbers of people.[6] Internal evidence suggests that Zōki made his pilgrimage as a fairly old man, around the end of the tenth century, and he depicts a chaotic throng of ascetics like himself living in cobbled-together huts clustered around the great central shrine of Hongū. Buddhism and the native 'Shinto' worship had by now largely accommodated each other, and the native deity of the great Hongū shrine was considered an avatar of the Bodhisattva Amida, an increasingly popular object of faith in Japanese Buddhism, making Hongū a powerfully attractive centre of devotion.[7] The ascetics we see gathered at Hongū would also have included in their practice strong elements of the syncretic shugendō *or mountain monk religious tradition whose practitioners still walk the Kumano mountains and conduct ceremonies at its shrines today.*

A man of his time, Zōki too made no distinction between worship at native shrines and the various Buddhist practices decribed above. His pilgrimage to the rugged Kumano area was an arduous journey that was in itself a form of ascetic practice, and his account notably lacks the usual laments over the sorrows of the journey, since its difficulties were an integral part of his purpose in going there. Instead, he gives us a brief but fascinating travel account of a monk who was at the same time a poet and who writes primarily as littérateur and acute observer of scenes and experiences met with along this famous pilgrimage route. (See Map 2)

FROM *IONUSHI'S PILGRIMAGE TO KUMANO*

Once there was a man who decided to turn from the world and live as his heart chose; he set off to visit all the delightful places he had heard tell of, as a way of comforting his sorrows, while at the same time praying at holy places to purge his sins.[8] His name was Ionushi. When he left on his pilgrimage to Kumano, around the tenth day of the tenth month, there were others who suggested coming with him, but since they were not people after his own heart he chose to set off secretly, accompanied by just one lad.

The day he left the Capital, he went to Yahata to pray,[9] and stayed the night there. That night the moon was beautiful, a cool breeze whispered in the pines, and the air carried the soft cries of autumn insects and the distant call of deer. Here in this unaccustomed place, he grew lonely for his hut as the night deepened. In such a place, he thought, one can feel the presence of the gods.

koko ni shi mo   Here is the gushing spring
wakite idekeru   of Iwashimizu's gods.
iwashimizu   Would that I could draw

kami no kokoro o	from the heart of that holy water
kumite shiraba ya	guidance for my way

On the evening of the second day, he arrived and worshipped at the shrine of Sumiyoshi.[10] There was a most delightful view out to the distant sea. To the south an inlet flowed into the bay, where a great variety of water birds floated happily about. There was also a little house with a reed fence, no doubt the home of fisher folk. The lingering feel of autumn in the air, the marvellous evening sky – all was deeply moving. Inside the shrine precincts the garden was quite invisible beneath a multicoloured carpet of fallen leaves, and the place seemed withdrawn into winter retreat.

Hearing the sound of voices chanting sutras, he thought quietly to himself:[11]

toki-kaketsu	Here I have hung
koromo no tama wa	among the hallowed pine leaves
suminoe no	of Suminoe Bay
kamusabinikeru	my offering – the jewel of truth
matsu no kozue ni	hidden from sight and mind[12]

Thus he went on from shrine to shrine, and in his heart he prayed: This world is as nothing, *more transient than foam on the water or dew upon the grass*.[13] I have turned from the world with the deep urge to extinguish my sins from past lives and secure my enlightenment for the life to come, and I pray that, though my eyes see the blossoms and the autumn colours of this world, my heart may remain unmoved by the lure of their worldly scents and colours; and though I observe the dew of dawn or the evening moon, I may understand the truth of this world's transient nature.

yo no naka o	Let me turn
itoi sutetemu	from this unhappy world
nochi wa tada	and henceforth place my trust
suminoe ni aru	in the patient pine
matsu to tanomamu	of Suminoe Bay

In the woods of Shinoda in Izumi, something prompted this poem:

waga omou	Measured against
koto no shigeki ni	these thronging thoughts
kurabureba	this tangle in my heart
shinoda no mori no	Shinoda's twisted branches
chie wa mono ka wa	are as nothing

A very beautiful moon hung above Fukei Beach in the land of Ki. There is a legend here that a heavenly maiden frequently appears on the beach.[14] Fascinating. The sight of this evening sky was most moving and melancholy. As the night deepened a lonely wind blew up, such a wind as lifts the frost from the goose's downy wing, and there was unspeakable poignancy in the distant cry of a crane calling for its mate. Other birds also gathered, calling in great flocks above the point, so that even he, unfeeling though he was,[15] grew deeply mournful.

otomeko ga	Here at Fukei's bay
ama no hagoromo	the heavenly maid
hiki-tsurete	seems to descend before me
mube mo fukei no	a swirl of feathered robes
ura ni oruramu	fluttering all about her

On seeing the waves come washing in continuously through the moonlit water:

tsuki ni nami	Waves and moonlight –
kakaru ori mata	I long to ask these fisherfolk
ariki ya to	if such a moment
fukei no ura no	has ever been before
ama ni towaba ya	on Fukei's bay

The waves stirred his heart.

nami ni mo are	Even these waves alone –
kakaru yo no mata	had such a night
araba koso	ever been before
mukashi o shireru	surely the fisherfolk
ama mo kotaeme	remembering would speak of it

Staying that evening at Fukei Bay, he set off again while the night was still dark. Seeing the waves rising high:

ama no to o	Along Fukei's beach
fukei no hama ni	the leaping waves
tatsu nami wa	beat so high
yoru sae miyuru	about the windblown fishers' huts
mono ni zo arikeru	even in the dark we see them

Sleeping the night on Shishinose-yama, Deerback Mountain, and hearing a deer calling:

ukarekemu	The crying deer
tsuma no yukari ni	seeks for his wandering wife
se no yama no	on Deerback Mountain
na o tazunete ya	perhaps in hope
shika mo nakuramu	the name will conjure her[16]

Sleeping the night on Iwashi Moor, something prompted him to compose this:

iwashi no	Could I but tell
mori tazunete to	the silent woods of Iwashi
iwaseba ya	to ask their ancient pines
ikuyo ka matsu wa	how many ages past
musubi-hajimeshi	branch first wove with branch

At the thought of picking up a pebble from Chika no Hama Beach:

utsu nami ni	I here relinquish
makasete o mimu	all to these washing waves
waga hirou	for we are so much less
hamama no kazu ni	even than the wave-tossed stones
hito mo masaraji	I reach for on the shore

At Nanbu Beach he happened upon a man he knew who was on his way home from the holy mountains of Kumano.

'All things being equal,' Ionushi said, 'why don't you turn back and come along with me on my pilgrimage?'

'I have a feeling you have something secret to pray about on your own,' the man teasingly replied.

'What do you mean?' Ionushi demanded. 'I hear tell that the

gods punish people who go casting aspersions, you know,' and he jokingly threw the little spiral shell that he had picked up and was fingering.

'Hey, this thing's spiralling out of control! Don't get so mad, hermit!' said his friend, and in return he flung a hermit crab shell.

Then, seeing some sea grass washing in on the waves, Ionushi remarked, 'Look at that. A rare glimpse of something "sunk from sight upon the flooded rocks".'[17]

His friend made a knowing face and responded, 'Well, you know, "a day spent longing" . . . '[18]

'But I must let my Kumano pilgrimage take its course,' Ionushi said.

'It's "the beach lilies of Kumano's bays",'[19] the friend came back with.

'No, "not a single night spent folded",'[20] Ionushi responded.

' "Why then you have no cause",'[21] declared the friend, and he recited this:

moshio-kusa	Though waves wash over
nami wa uzumu to	the sea grass in the tide
uzumedomo	to bury deep its secret
iya araware ni	yet with each washing wave
arawarenumeri	it shows more clearly

Ionushi replied with:

mikumano no	What comes washing in
ura ni ki-yosuru	on Kumano Bay's washing waves
nuregoromo no	is just a smear upon my name
naki na o susugu	and I would have you know
hodo to shiranamu	I'll wash it clean

'Well then,' said the friend, 'I'll see you back at the Capital.'

To this Ionushi responded, 'Sleeve pressed to eyes to staunch my tears!'

'Dangerous words!' the friend said. 'Well, see you on "Mount Later",'[22] and he went on his way.

That night he stayed at the port of Muro. He built himself a temporary shelter beneath a tree using autumnal branches of oak, and crawled in there to sleep. Late at night a passing shower fell.

itodoshiku	Already lamenting
nagekashiki yo o	the sufferings of this world
kaminazuki	now on my autumn journey
tabi no sora ni mo	out of this traveller's sky
furu shigure kana	a chill rain mingles with my
	tears

Approaching the holy mountain, he saw beneath every tree a little wayside shrine – so many of them. The night he slept at Mizunomi he composed:

yorozu yo no	So many gods
kami chū kami ni	from so many ages past
tamuke shitsu	I pray to as I go –
omoi to omou	surely every hope within me
koto wa narinamu	will be fulfilled

Three days later, he reached the holy mountain. Wandering about taking in the scene, he was intrigued to find there two or three hundred huts, each set up after the owner's particular fancy.

He visited a close friend there, finding him fast asleep with a charred log as pillow and only a straw rain coat wrapped about his loins.

'Hullo there!' he called.

'Come on in!' his friend cried, startled awake. 'Do have something to eat,' he went on, and produced a huge taro root about the size of a basket for storing *go* pieces, which he proceeded to cook.

'You could call it the mother of all taros,' he remarked.

'I can imagine it's as sweet as milk then,' said Ionushi.

'Yes, I'd do better feeding it to some child I suppose,' the friend responded as he dished it out. Then the bell rang, and they retired to the worship hall to pray.

There was a great gathering from hither and yon of untold numbers of ascetics, heads cloaked and straw coats draped about their shoulders, and when they left after the regular worship had ended some remained there before the deacon. Others stayed kneeling at the feet of the pillars, their straw coats drawn up, faces carefully hidden from view. Some bowed their foreheads to the floor, chanting *darani* mantras. There was such a hubbub of voices that each was hard to distinguish, but some loud voices he found too obtrusive.

[. . .]

He stayed on there until the twenty-first day of the eleventh month. As he wandered one day along the banks of Otonashi River, making plans to leave, another tried to dissuade him. 'Stay on a little longer,' he said. 'The gods wouldn't want you to leave either, you know.'

Just then, Ionushi happened to notice a white-headed crow.

yamagarasu	Even the mountain crow
kashira mo shiroku	now has a whitened head
narinikeri	so long has passed –
waga kaerubeki	surely my time to go
toki ya kinuramu	comes round at last

He called in on someone's dwelling, where the man was tending a fire of cypress wood which danced and crackled. When Ionushi picked up a piece of the wood to examine it his friend remarked, 'The charred wood on this mountain has special powers. They call it *hata-hata*.'

'That must be what it cries as it burns!' said he as he left.

He set off, and on his way down the river, at a place named Mifuneshima, or Sacred Boat Island,[23] he composed:

yama no o ni	Who poled the sacred boat
tare sao sashite	to meet the mountain
mifune-shima	and first decreed
kami no tomari ni	Mifuneshima to become
koto yosasekemu	the portal of the gods?

At the foot of the great waterfall on Tada Mountain:[24]

na ni takaku	In this high rope of water
hayaku yori kishi	twisting from times long gone
taki no ito ni	down the famous falls

yo yo no chigiri o   I have bound my vows
musubitsuru kana   for ages still to come

This mountain is a place of such moving holiness that no words could describe it to others.

About to set off on his homeward journey, he bent to pick up a shell on the beach and happened to wet his sleeve.

fujigoromo   I reach to take
nagisa ni yosuru   a frail shell from the waves
utsuse-gai   and find the sleeve
hirou tamoto wa   of my rough woven robe
katsu zo nurekeru   soaked as with tears

5

The Pillow Book by Sei Shōnagon

*At around the time that Zōki set off from the Capital on his pilgrimage
to the mountains of Kumano, a lady-in-waiting to the young Empress
Teishi (977–1000) in the imperial palace was writing the work known
today as* The Pillow Book *(Makura no sōshi). We know little about
Sei Shōnagon (?966–c. 1025) beyond the fact that her father was from
the provincial governor class, and that in about 993 she followed a
common custom among well-born girls of becoming a lady-in-waiting
at the palace. It was here that she began and wrote much of the miscel-
lany of observations, anecdotes, lists, opinions and occasional poems
that became one of the great works of classical Japanese literature.*

*Sei Shōnagon wrote her unusual and compelling work in the heyday
of court culture, a time later ages would look back to as the pinnacle of
Japanese civilization. Half a century after prose in the native Japanese*
kana *style began to claim a place as legitimate literature, women had
made this style their own. A* nikki *was no longer 'what men wrote' as
it had been when Ki no Tsurayuki dared to appropriate the form for
the* Tosa Diary*'s fictional female* kana *diarist. It had become a powerful means of personal and literary expression for educated women,*[1]
while men still continued to largely confine their kana *writing to letters and* waka *poetry, and to couch their serious literary compositions
in the Chinese language. The other important genre of the age, the*
kana *romance tale* (monogatari), *was also associated primarily with
women,*[2] *and while Sei Shōnagon was perhaps still adding to her* Pillow
Book, *at the court of a rival empress another lady-in-waiting, Murasaki
Shikibu, was already at work on her* Tale of Genji *(Genji monogatari), the greatest of Japan's classics and arguably the world's first novel.*

The Pillow Book *is not exactly a diary, though its intimate first-
person voice and eye for everyday detail owe much to that genre. It is*

essentially a chronicle of Sei Shōnagon's world, a world almost com-
pletely confined to the absorbing indoor life of the imperial palace. If she
knew more about the world beyond the Capital[3] *she clearly had little*
interest in revealing it. For ladies of the genteel classes, there was adven-
ture enough in the occasional legitimate opportunities to see the wider
world beyond the home in the guise of travel through the city streets on
visits, local excursions, and most importantly, pilgrimages. The excite-
ment and interest of such journeys for Sei is palpable in the descriptions
included here.

Sei's fascination with the world is acute, heightened no doubt by the
confinement in which she spent her life. Conventional poetic pathos was
not her mode.[4] *Her aim is to record what moves and delights, and pleas-*
ure (or occasionally the irritating lack of it) is the keynote of her writing.
Her delight in detail gives us far richer vignettes of the real world than a
more inward and self-consciously literary writer would think to provide.
Thanks to Sei we have a vivid picture of what it was like a thousand
years ago to travel inside a screened ox carriage as it brushed the passing
foliage or forded a stream; or to go on pilgrimage to a distant temple,
observing the lives of commoners along the way, and spend time there in
solitary retreat. Where personal experience failed her a lively imagin-
ation could provide equivalent detail, as we see in her thoughts on some
of the hazards of being in boats, which provide an early glimpse of the
women who until very recently still dived for pearl and abalone off the
shores of Japan.

Nothing quite like The Pillow Book *was ever written again.*[5] *We can*
only speculate about what kind of writing might have been produced if
future Japanese travel writing had borrowed more from Sei's acute and
engaging way of depicting the world around her.

FROM *THE PILLOW BOOK*

Things that make you feel cheerful – an ox carriage crammed with
ladies on their way back from some viewing expedition, sleeves
tumbling out in profusion,[6] with a great crowd of carriage boys running with it, skilfully guiding the ox as the carriage hurtles along.

[. . .]

Around the fifth month it's great fun to make an excursion to a mountain village.

In swampy ground, the grass and water together form a single wide swathe of green to the eye, with the surface a beguiling luxuriance of grasses, but if you take your time and travel its length it's delightful how the unexpected water beneath, though not deep, will burst forth under the weight of a human tread.

As you go on your way, the various hedges to left and right will thrust an occasional branch into the carriage, and you quickly try to snap one off as you pass, lamenting the way it's gone again before you can seize it. And then there's the lovely moment when some wormwood gets caught and crushed by the carriage wheel, whose turning then carries it around and up, right to where you're sitting.

[. . .]

Deeply irritating things – rain on the day when you're to go out for some special event or a temple pilgrimage.

[. . .]

Around the end of the fourth month, we went on a pilgrimage to the temple at Hase.[7] Our carriage was loaded on to a ferry at the famous Yodo Crossing[8] en route, and as we crossed the river we noticed what looked like quite short stems of sweet flag and reeds growing in the water nearby, but when we had them picked they turned out to be extremely long. It was fascinating to see boats loaded with reeds ferrying to and fro across the river. It looked precisely like the scene of that line from the song, 'Cut from Takase Pool'.

On our return on the third day we saw a most delightful scene, such as one finds painted on screens – a light rain was falling, and there were men wearing very small sedge rain-hats, their clothes tucked up high above their long shanks.

[. . .]

It's delightful to be on retreat at a temple over the New Year when it's terribly cold and there's a feeling of snow in the freezing air. On the other hand, it ruins the mood of the occasion if the skies are instead heavy with the threat of rain.

You've come on pilgrimage to the temple at Kiyomizu,[9] say, intending to seclude yourself in one of the private seclusion rooms; the carriage is drawn up to the foot of the long stairs leading up to the temple, and while the room is being prepared you observe the young monks, dressed only in little waist-robes and wearing those high clogs they wear, trotting perfectly nonchalantly up and down the steep stairway, murmuring scraps of sutras or chanting the four-word verses of the Kusha Sutra[10] as they go. It's a scene that goes perfectly with the place [. . .]

A priest comes over to you from the other side of the dividing lattice screen and engages you in conversation. He tells you that he has presented your petitions to Kannon most satisfactorily, and asks how many days you're staying, mentioning the names of some others who are also in retreat here. Then he disappears, and you are brought a brazier, snacks, a water scoop into which hand-washing water is poured, and a little handleless bucket to hold the water. Finally, monks appear and announce which rooms your attendants are to lodge in, and as they're called they rise in turn and go off.

It's a comforting feeling to think, as you hear the bell rung for the sutra recitation to begin, that it is also ringing on your own behalf. Next door you can hear a man, someone of quite high birth it seems, chanting and praying, and to judge from the way he sounds as he discreetly prostrates himself and rises, you have the impression that he's someone of considerable sensibility. He continues this throughout the night without pause for sleep, and you find it most moving to think of him there, so ardently engaged in his austerities. When he does break off from his prayers it's to chant sutras, at a decently moderate volume, and this too you find touching and inspiring. You rather long to be able to speak to him, and the way he tearfully blows his nose from time to time, though not at all loudly or unpleasantly, sets you to wondering just what it is that's weighing on his mind, and wishing you could somehow help his prayers be answered.

The priests keep up a great clamour of sutra chanting throughout the night, so that you get no sleep. After the pre-dawn service you manage to doze off, when suddenly you're jolted awake again by the sound of fierce and awe-inspiring chanting. The voice, which is reciting the special sutra of the temple, belongs to a man who seems to be a mountain monk,[11] and not a particularly impressive-looking one, who's spread his straw coat out to sit on as he chants. It's most moving to hear him.

[. . .]

Things one must be wary of [. . .] Boat crossings. It is marvellous weather, the water is splendidly smooth and calm, as if swathed in glossy pale-blue silk, and there's not the slightest hint of danger in the scene. The young lady is in *akome* gown and skirted trousers;[12] her youthful retainer is singing splendidly as he pulls at what I believe is called the 'oar',[13] and it's altogether the sort of charming picture that begs for an exalted audience to appreciate it. But as they ply their way, a fierce wind suddenly blows up, and the sea surface turns wild and choppy. Now as they hurry towards their destination, faint with terror, the waves flooding over the boat make it impossible to believe that only a moment earlier the sea could have been so calm and smooth.

Now that I come to think of it, there is no one so impressive and downright awe-inspiring as men who go about in boats. Even if the water's not particularly deep, how can they go rowing off so nonchalantly in such a frail and unreliable thing? Let alone when there are unfathomable depths of water below! Then there's the boat at the loading wharf – it is already stacked so high that the water is lapping a mere foot or less below the rim, yet the lads are fearlessly dashing about on it, though you'd imagine that the slightest wrong move would send it to the bottom, and it's down-right terrifying to watch them blithely tossing up to half a dozen great pine logs, each quite two or three feet thick, on to this over-loaded boat.

The boats are rowed from the roofed end. The person on the inside looks far more secure. It's the sight of the man who stands on the edge that makes you feel faint with terror for him. The loop of rope that holds the oar in place looks so precarious! What would happen if it snapped? He'd be certain to tumble straight into the water. Yet even such a vital bit of rope is far from thick.

The boats I have travelled in are beautifully made, and when you open up the double doors and raise the lattice shutters, you don't feel you are right down on the level of the water, so it's rather like being in a tiny house.

The thing that really fills you with unease is looking out at the little boats round about. The ones in the distance look exactly like bamboo leaves fashioned into tiny vessels and scattered here and there over the water. It's also charming to see the boats in the port at night, each with its individual light burning.

The sight of a tiny two-man craft moving over the water in the early morning is very moving. The 'white retreating waves' of the poem[14] really do disappear behind it in no time. One certainly feels that a boat is no way for people of quality to travel. Of course travelling on foot is also rather frightening, but at least it is far, far more reassuring to be on firm ground.

A stretch of water may seem terrifying, but your spirits sink still further at the thought of the fisher girls who dive for shells. If that thin rope tied to their waist snapped, whatever would they do? It would be all very well if it were men doing the diving, but it must feel miserable for women. The men are on board, singing away lustily, moving the boat along with the women's waist ropes dangling into the water. You imagine they would be feeling full of anxiety and trepidation. Apparently, when the woman wants to come up to the surface she tugs on the rope, and you can quite see why the men should scramble to pull her up as fast as possible. Even an onlooker must weep salt tears to witness the gasp of the woman as she breaks surface and lays her hand on the edge of the boat – really, I find it utterly astonishing to see those men sending the poor women overboard while they float lazily about on the surface!

6

Wakan rōeishū compiled by Fujiwara no Kintō

The Wakan rōeishū (c. 1013) (*'Chinese and Japanese Poems to Perform'*) *was another significant literary work produced at the Heian court at the height of its power and prestige, and it became an essential part of the library of later generations. It is a compilation of poems, most of which were already considered classics, specifically for use as a kind of* libretto *for performance purposes.*[1] *Its aristocratic compiler, Fujiwara no Kintō (966–1041), was not only a notable poet himself but one of the greatest literary and aesthetic arbiters of his time, and exercised his taste by producing several influential poetry anthologies. With the* Wakan rōeishū *he created a genre that was to have numerous later imitators, though none attained this work's fame and reach.*

The work brings together over 800 short poems and excerpts of longer poems, the great majority of which are in Chinese and the remainder (less than a third) Japanese waka. *This balance is an accurate reflection of the continued dominance of Chinese literature at the time. The intended audience would naturally have been male, since 'Chinese learning' still remained a purely male prerogative, although in fact women seem to have been familiar enough with the more famous Chinese poems to be able to identify them if not completely understand them. They would have commonly heard them chanted or sung, often by a group of men, either as straightforward entertainment or in elegant response to a situation that prompted the association – a fall of snow, say, might prompt the recital of a poem describing a snowy landscape, or a branch of bamboo provoke someone to sing impromptu a famous line from a Chinese poem on the subject.*[2]

The Wakan rōeishū *was essentially intended as a handbook of verses worthy of memorization for anyone aspiring to the kind of literary education that marked the sophisticated man, rather than as a work to refer to when performance was required. Precisely how these poems were performed remains unclear, although evidence suggests that recitation styles varied from a simple chant on one or several tones, through more melodic variations, often produced extempore and sometimes performed more formally with musical accompaniment. Later copies of the work sometimes include musical notation, indicating that performance was gradually formalized, but when the collection was first compiled it seems improvisation was common.*

The first part of the anthology is devoted to poems on the seasons, the most important of the poetic categories. The remainder consists of Chinese and Japanese poems arranged under a wide variety of topics, one of which is Travel.[3] *Many if not all of these poems would have been composed in specific response to the poetic topic of Travel, rather than spontaneously in response to direct personal experience, though they are no less evocative for that. Just as Sei Shōnagon could vividly imagine and describe a scene that she had probably never witnessed, such as the abalone divers, it was common literary practice to imaginatively inhabit and respond to scenes and situations (such as those depicted in paintings or tales) outside one's personal experience, and it may well be that the composers of these travel poems had seldom if ever left the Capital.*

It is noteworthy that only one of the Chinese poems translated here (the first) is the work of a Chinese poet. Not only did Japanese male poets commonly compose poems in Chinese, they had evolved a particular method of reading and reciting the Chinese that amounted to a kind of awkward translationese, in which a version of the Chinese pronunciation of the text's words was supported by the addition of Japanese syntactical constructions to make the whole more or less comprehensible as Japanese.[4] *The poems were sung both in the original Chinese and in this hybrid form (the transcriptions given here are in the latter form). The continuing pre-eminence of Chinese literature and language lent this stilted style of Sino-Japanese considerable prestige, and its vocabulary and constructions increasingly penetrated the native language, rather as Latinate words and syntax did with English.*

While helping to promote the prestige of the native Japanese waka, *the popularity of Kintō's* Wakan rōeishū *thus also inadvertently aided the spread of Sinified Japanese. Besides its importance as a collection of verses to be performed, it also became an essential handbook in the education of future generations as well as a key source of texts for calligraphic practice, and later literature made frequent reference to its poems through allusions that a reader could be relied upon to recognize.*

FROM *WAKAN RŌEISHŪ*

Travel

(Chinese)

kokan ni yadoru toki	Earth cloaked in wind and rain
kazeame o obitari	the night I stayed at the lonely inn.
enhan no kaeru tokoro ni	A single stretch of cloud and water
mizukumo ni tsuranaru	far out where a sail heads home.
	Hsü Hun (China, 791–?854)

(Chinese)

kōkō to shite kasanete kōkōtari	On, on you travel, farther still.
meigetsukō no akatsuki no iro tsukizu	Dawn's colours boundless over Bright Moon Gorge.
byōbyō to shite mata byōbyōtari	Carried far, far across the bay
chōfuho no yūbe no koe nao fukashi	the wind's cry deepens into evening.
	Minamoto no Shitagō (Japan, 911–83)

(Chinese)

akatsuki chōshō no hora ni ireba	Dawn, I enter the great pine-shaded grotto –
gansen musete reien ginzu	smothered trickle of spring from rock; monkeys keening on the peak.
yoru kyokuho no nami ni shukusureba	Night, I lodge by a far wave-washed bay;

seiran fuite kōgetsu susamaji   rough gales among summer's
                                                      leaves; a wilderness of bright
                                                      moonlight.
                                                  Yoshishige no Tamemasa (attrib.)
                                                      (Japan, dates unknown)

(Chinese)
tokō no yūsen wa   The idling ferry at the dock
kaze sadamate izu   puts out as the wind settles.
hatō no takusho wa   Over foamy waves the land of
                                                      exile
hi harete miyu   lies clear before me in the
                                                      brightening day.
                                                             Ono no Takamura
                                                             (Japan, 802–52)

(Chinese)
shūro no yoru no ame no   Night rain among the river
                                                      reeds
takyō no namida   brings tears of longing in a far
                                                      land.
ganryū no aki no kaze no   Autumn wind in the banks of
                                                      willows
ensai no kokoro   stirs sorrows in this distant
                                                      fort.
                                                  Tachibana no Naomoto (Japan,
                                                      dates unknown)

(Chinese)
sōha michi tōshi   Far is the sea road over green
                                                      waves
kumo senri   cloud for a thousand miles.
hakubu yama fukashi   Deep among white-misted
                                                      mountains
tori hitokoe   a bird's single call.
                                                  Tachibana no Naomoto

(Japanese)
honobono to
akashi no ura no

asakiri ni
shimagakure-yuku
fune o shi zo omou

My thoughts
follow a boat over Akashi's
    Bay
faint in first light
through morning mist
now slipped away among
    islands

                    Kakimoto no Hitomaro
                        (Japan, ?–708)

(Japanese)
wata no hara
yasoshima kakete
kogi-idenu to
hito ni wa tsugeyo
ama no tsuribune

Men in your fishing boats
tell them that I have gone
rowing my way
toward the scattered islands
over a wide sea

                    Tachibana no Naomoto

(Japanese)
tayori araba
miyako e ikade
tsuge-yaramu
kyō shirakawa no
seki wa koenu to

How might I find a way
to send word back
to the far Capital
that today I crossed
the Barrier at Shirakawa[5]

                    Fujiwara no Kanemori
                        (Japan, ?–990)

Landscape, attrib. Sesshū

7

Eight Poems by Nōin

The quintessential travel poet of the Heian period was Nōin (988–?1058), whose personal poetry collection Nōinshū *provides almost all the reliable information we have about his life. Nōin was his Buddhist name, and like Zōki before him he seems to have taken the tonsure in his mid-twenties – poems from this period dedicated to a woman and subsequent poems lamenting her death suggest that grief lay behind his decision to take this radical step. His poetry collection is structured roughly chronologically, and although he makes no attempt to link the poems into a continuous narrative as Zōki does, this structure and the brief contextualizing headnotes allow us to reconstruct a life that seems to have been impressively dedicated to travel.*

Despite the improvement of the major routes to and from the Capital, lengthy travel was still generally shunned among the literate classes and largely limited to provincial governors and their entourages,[1] as it had been in the days of Tosa Diary *a century or so earlier. Nōin's friendship with several such men provided an impetus for some of his journeys in later years, when he apparently spent time with his friends in their remote postings, but he is above all associated with two arduous earlier journeys to the wilds of the distant Michinoku (Oku) area, then still the farthest outpost of the Japanese nation. The first journey, made when he was thirty-eight, inspired him to return a few years later and spend around three years in reclusion there. Poems 109, 115 and 149 included here date from this trip.*

As with Zōki, it was Nōin's choice of the life of a non-monastic Buddhist monk that gave him both the freedom and the incentive to travel. Where Zōki apparently made pilgrimages from the beloved home base of his simple hut near the Capital, Nōin's writing shows little sign of attachment to any home and instead embraces a wandering existence as

the essential expression of his chosen life. The fundamental Buddhist prin-
ciple of non-attachment was embodied in the concept of life on the road
(michi, a term in itself synonymous with the Buddhist 'Way'), freed
from the bonds that tie one to the world, and the image of the lone wan-
dering monk 'making his way' as he drifts through the world would
shape the self-image of travel writers, tonsured or otherwise, down the
coming centuries. Poem 184 is a quintessential statement of this ideal,
which Nōin was among the first and most influential to articulate in
Japanese poetry. To what extent he actually followed the ideal of the
wandering beggar monk is less clear,[2] but there is little doubt that his
many journeys would have been rigorous and challenging enough to
constitute the kind of austerity appropriate to one who 'spurns the
world'.

Given this, it is ironic that Nōin was known to later generations pri-
marily for aesthetic rather than ascetic travel. In fact, he combined the
two in a form that was beginning to emerge as a 'way' or practice in
itself, the 'way' of the aesthete recluse (suki no tonseisha).[3] The custom
of members of the educated classes choosing, in response to some setback
or to advancing age, to 'leave the world' and become non-monastic
'recluse monks', had by now produced a sub-culture of cultivated and
literary men[4] with the freedom and inclination to practise the arts of
poetry, music and calligraphy as an integral part of their chosen reli-
gious practice. The result was a way of life which embraced artistic
reclusion as in itself a means to religious awakening.[5] Nōin, one of the
earliest of these suki no tonseisha, self-consciously travelled both as
poet and as wandering recluse monk, and took his poetry as seriously as
his religious practice.

In these poems, the wit and wordplay of an earlier era are no longer
the dominant style. Nōin's poems use sombre tones – autumn, evening,
drifting smoke – to evoke a resonance of feeling in which landscape
and mood merge, as in poem 109 where the sound of a snipe's wing-
beats stirs the receptive heart as they stir the unseen water of the bay.
This poem beautifully embodies the emerging poetic aesthetic of yojō,
the lingering resonance or stirred feelings and associations that emanate
from a poem's imagery. Nōin's poems strive for evocation and suggestion
rather than explicit description, and one of the key means of achieving
this in his travel poetry is the crucial presence of place names. He gave
added depth to his poems by the use of utamakura,[6] conventional place

name associations, by locating the poetic moment in a place whose famous name in itself evoked ripples of feeling and association for the reader.

Nōin's travel poems also create yojō *by their skilful use of the unseen and imagined. Poem 83, the only one of the poems translated here that responds appreciatively to witnessing a beautiful scene, gains depth of feeling by the poet's implied solitude and longing for an absent other. Other poems achieve a similar depth by balancing the experienced moment against an imagined elsewhere.[7] That elsewhere is often the Capital, object of yearning for literary travellers since the* Manyōshū *but in Nōin's poems the embodiment of the world he has spurned, with its mindless bustle and transient illusory pleasures. In poem 115 travel in far places is presented as the encapsulation of the life of spiritual reclusion and awakening to deeper truth. Yet the constant tug of that other world (see for instance poem 242) still constitutes a kind of covert longing that gives the poems their poignancy and complexity.*

Nōin's evocative self-image of the poet-monk – as lone traveller in far places, spurning the foolish delusions of the transient world and choosing instead the spiritual austerities of the journey, yet attuned to the natural world's beauties and moved by the poetic resonances of the places he visits – became a touchstone for later travellers, as did his poetry. Poems such as poem 101 became so much a part of the mental furniture of later travellers that more than six centuries later, when Bashō arrived at the old Shirakawa Barrier on his famous journey north into Oku, with spring all about him, it was nevertheless Nōin's autumn wind that haunted his ears.[8]

EIGHT POEMS

83

Sent to someone from the land of Tsu, where I was staying around New Year.

kokoro aran	If only I could show
hito ni miseba ya	to some feeling heart
tsu no kuni no	this springtime scene –

| *naniwa no ura no* | the Bay of Naniwa |
| *haru no keshiki o* | in the land of Tsu |

88

When Ōe no Kinyori became governor of Sagami.

furusato o	Perhaps you are
omoi-idetsutsu	crossing Kiyomi Barrier
akikaze ni	thoughts of home
kiyomi ga seki o	haunting your memory
koemu to suran	in the autumn wind

101

In spring of the second year (1025) when I set off to visit Michinoku, composed at the Shirakawa Barrier.

miyako o ba	Though with the rising mists
kasumi to tomo ni	of spring I rose
tachishikado	and left the Capital
akikaze zo fuku	the autumn wind blows chill
shirakawa no seki	at Shirakawa Barrier

109

Sent to a friend in the Capital when I was staying at the Bay of
Shiogama.

sayo fukete	Melancholy
mono zo kanashiki	in the deepening night
shiogama wa	Shiogama Bay
momohagaki suru	rippled by the wind
shigi no hakaze ni	of a snipe's quick wingbeat

115

On going to Yasoshima in the land of Dewa.

wabibito wa	Far lands are best
totsukuni zo yoki	for one who spurns the world –
sakite chiru	back in the flowery Capital
hana no miyako wa	the fleeting blossoms come and go
isogi nomi shite	busy in their passing

149

The Tama River in Noda.

yū sareba	Evening draws in
shiokaze koshite	and the salt breeze
michinoku no	carries the cry of plovers
noda no tamakawa	wafting in across Tama River
chidori naku nari	in Michinoku's Noda

184

On planning to set off for the Bridge of Hamana.

sasurauru	Wanderer that I am
mi wa izuku to mo	and aimless
nakarikeri	I make my way
hamana no hashi no	toward the distant crossing
watari e zo yuku	at Hamana Bridge

242

Arriving at Iyo and fondly recalling the blossoms of the Capital.

moshio yaku	Here on this far shore
umibe ni ite zo	watching the salt kilns'
omoiyaru	drifts of smoke
hana no miyako no	my heart recalls the blossoms
hana no sakari o	that fill the flowery Capital

8

Sarashina Diary by Sugawara no Takasue's Daughter

In the summer of 1020, a provincial governor named Sugawara no Takasue set off with his family, servants and retainers for the long and difficult journey back to the Capital from his remote posting in Kazusa.[1] *With him was his impressionable twelve-year-old daughter, whose vivid memory of this journey forms the first section of the memoir she wrote many years later, which was subsequently given the title* Sarashina Diary (Sarashina nikki).

Like many other women of her class, she is known to us only by reference to a male relative, in her case her father.[2] *Sugawara no Takasue's Daughter (as she is called) was born in 1008 and spent her earlier childhood years in the Capital, but the opening words of* Sarashina Diary *make clear that the three years she spent with her family in distant Kazusa felt like a lifetime to her. Where others yearned for the Capital as the centre of life and culture, this young girl's longing to return was focussed on the romantic tales* (monogatari) *that she would at last be able to read to her heart's content there, above all Murasaki Shikibu's recently completed* Tale of Genji, *whose fame was quickly growing. With her later diary, this girl herself was to join the ranks of the great woman writers of the Heian period such as Murasaki Shikibu and Sei Shōnagon, who did so much to create and carry forward the native literary tradition of* kana *prose writing.*

Although this work is known as a 'diary' (nikki), *the term's literary meaning had loosened considerably since its early use in the* Tosa Diary *over a hundred years before. In the hands of women writers, the* nikki *had become more like a chronicle or memoir of personal experience which barely gestured at the daily record structure that the term implies.* Sarashina Diary *takes the form a stage further, by chronicling not just a certain period of time but experiences and episodes that together cover most of the author's life, sometimes with vast gaps of time between them. Intensity of memory and experience seems to be a key to what she chooses to include. Much of the diary describes her life in the Capital, her close relationship with her father and her rather unsuccessful time in service as a lady-in-waiting in one of the great households (she was much too timorous to enjoy the experience). But travel plays a far more important role in her writing than in any previous work of Japanese literature except* Tosa Diary, *and the long opening description of her journey to the Capital as a young girl broke new ground in the native literary tradition and is her diary's greatest claim to fame.*

A central reason for its importance, and perhaps also for why she wrote it, was that the route she travelled was already rich with poetic association. The Tōkaidō, as it came to be called, had long been the main route connecting the Capital with the nation's eastern regions, although as Sarashina Diary *reveals it was still far from anything one could term a highway. Certain evocative places along the way had been woven into poetry³ both by travellers and by those who had never seen them but knew of them through the poetic associations of their names. These* utamakura *were by now standard references for any educated person, and a large part of the author's interest as she travelled was in seeing and responding to these places at first hand. Being just a girl, her responses only occasionally produced a poem successful enough to be recorded here, but others in the party would have tried their hand at poetry whenever an* utamakura *place was passed, as would countless other travellers down the coming centuries.*

Indeed Takasue's daughter's travel account epitomizes what had long since become a well-established characteristic of travel for the educated classes⁴ – the pleasure and solace to be had from experiencing the journey through a literary lens. Her account of the journey manages to be both personal and shaped by the waka *sensibility, including the pleasure in wit and wordplay that were still the dominant tone in poetry, seen for example in the subtle ironies enjoyed by the travellers at the name of the Plains of China. A literary sensibility also lies behind many seemingly casual remarks, such as the apparently odd comment on the 'incongruity' of the moonlight that bathed her suffering nurse, and it aso helps explain the lengthy digressions to recount stories heard along the way, which impress the young girl much as do her beloved tales. Place names provide the ground of many entries on the journey's progress, in much the same way as they resonate in so much Japanese poetry.[5] At almost every turn, indeed, and not least in the sinuous beauty of its prose, the journey section of the* Sarashina Diary *registers itself for the discerning reader as a literary work. At the same time, it presents a vivid and compelling account of a sensitive young girl's experience of the joys and hardships of eleventh-century travel, including such precious vignettes as the breathless description of her encounter with the travelling women entertainers* (asobi).

It seems likely that the account of this journey, written many decades later in old age,[6] drew on a journal of some sort that Takasue's daughter kept at the time, but the descriptions of later pilgrimages, a sample of which are also included here, are clearly recorded in hindsight. Sei Shōnagon's vivid descriptions of pilgrimages in her Pillow Book *(see Chapter 5) were probably known to the author, along with others by previous women diarists,[7] but the* Sarashina Diary *devotes far more space and descriptive energy to the cumulative accounts of her pilgrimages than any previous work. Certainly it was a growing religious urge that set the author on these sometimes arduous journeys late in life, but her evident pleasure in recalling and recounting them is of a piece with the long, lively account of her early journey to the Capital. While Sei Shōnagon details the experience of her retreat at the temple, Takasue's daughter glosses over this core aspect of her pilgrimages and devotes her energies instead to accounts of key moments along the way. She was deeply moved by landscapes, and her descriptions of them are vibrant and full of delight. Her tremulous tendency to take fright at the mere suggestion of danger gives us another side of her highly strung personality; dangers did indeed abound along the routes she travelled, but her servants seem to have enjoyed provoking her terrified reactions with idle talk.* (See Map 3)

FROM *SARASHINA DIARY*

Raised in a land *far beyond even the farthest reaches of the Eastern Road,*[8] what an uncouth girl I must have been! – yet somehow, having learned that what they call tales existed out there in the real world, I became obsessed with the need to find a way to lay eyes on some myself. Idling away our days and nights together, I would listen to my sister or stepmother recounting stories from this tale or that, or describing the glowing Hikaru Genji,[9] and the more I heard the more I longed for more. But it was impossible for them to reproduce the tales from memory well enough to please me, and it drove me mad. My longing was so great that I had someone make me a life-sized statue of the Healing Buddha,[10] and when no one was about I would wash my hands and purify myself, and then slip in to the altar, fling myself face down and beg that I might go up to the Capital as soon as possible and be able to read every one of those many tales that people spoke of.

Finally, the year I turned thirteen,[11] the time came for our return. On the third day of the ninth month we made the preliminary move[12] to a nearby place called Imatachi, and the home where I had lived and played all those years was now torn apart and left bare and empty.

The sun was setting through an alarmingly thick mist when we set off, with a great deal of fuss and commotion. As I was about to board the carriage I paused for a last look back; there stood the Healing Buddha to whom I used to bow low in private worship, abandoned now, and I wept in secret sorrow to be leaving it behind.

Our temporary lodging was quite unprotected by any fence, a mere reed-thatched shack without so much as outside shutters, just reed blinds and curtains. To the south it looked far out over the plain. The sea lay close by both east and west, creating a fine view. It was all so very beautiful in the evening mist that I had barely a wink of sleep but stayed up drinking in the scene in every direction, mournful at the thought that we would soon be leaving it.

On the fifteenth day of that month, a day dark with rain, we crossed the border, and that night we stayed at a place called Ikada in the land of Shimōsa. It was such a downpour that our hut was virtually set afloat that night,[13] and I couldn't sleep from terror. Out on the plain, three lone trees stood on a little rise. We stayed on through the following day, drying our sodden things and waiting for the rest of our party who had left after we did.

Early on the seventeenth day we set off again.

Long ago in the land of Shimōsa, we learned, there lived a wealthy man by the name of Mano, who oversaw the weaving and bleaching of many thousands of bolts of fabric – the remains of his house were still visible from the ferry that carried us across the deep river. Four large posts still stood in the water, the ruins of the old gate posts. Everyone composed poems on the theme, and hearing them I privately composed this:

kuchi mo senu	If it were not
kono kawabashira	for these unrotted river posts
nokorazu wa	left standing here
mukashi no ato o	how could we know
ikade shiramashi	the past is with us still?

That night we stayed at a place called Kuroto Beach. On one side was a wide plateau, and a white sandy beach stretched far into the distance, with a fine stand of pines behind it; the moon was wonderfully bright, and the wind moaned piteously. We all delighted in the scene, and everyone composed poems.

madoromaji	Let me not sleep
koyoi narade wa	tonight, for if not now
itsu ka mimu	when might I see again
kuroto no hama no	this autumn moon
aki no yo no tsuki	over Kuroto Beach?

We set off again the next morning, and that evening we stayed at the ferry port of Matsusato on the border of Shimōsa and Musashi where the boats cross the Futoi River at the upper shallows. It took all night to slowly ferry everything across.

Here our nurse, whose husband had recently died, gave birth, which meant we had to travel on separately.[14] I missed her terribly and longed to visit her, so my older brother gathered me up and took me over to where she was. We were all lodged in flimsy makeshift shelters, but at least ours had been draped against the draughts, while the hut she was in was terribly primitive, as she had no man to set it up properly for her. There was only a single layer of reeds by way of roof, so the moonlight filtered in everywhere, and she lay there under a scarlet robe in the midst of her suffering bathed in moonlight – a somehow most incongruous scene, given the circumstances.[15] She was very pale and beautiful, and was so touched by my visit that she stroked my hair and wept. I was deeply moved, and couldn't bear to leave her, but my brother was in a hurry to get back and I was wrenched miserably away. The image of my poor nurse continued to haunt me that night, and instead of sitting up to enjoy the moon with everyone I simply went to bed, feeling very low.

The following morning our carriages were carried across, while the others who had come to send us off stayed behind on the far shore and turned for home.[16] We travellers lingered there, loath to leave, and there were tears on both sides when it came time to part. My childish heart too was moved to sadness.

Now we were heading into the land of Musashi. There was nothing really interesting to be seen here. These sandy beaches weren't so much white as muddy, and where one expected the fields of purple *murasaki*[17] there was only a rampant growth of tall reeds and rushes, so high and thick that the tips of the bows that our mounted escorts carried were quite invisible. Making our way through this, we came at last to a temple by the name of Takeshiba. In the distance, at a place called Hahasō, were the stone foundations of a ruin.

We asked about the place, and this was the story. In the old days, we learned, there used to be an estate[18] here by the name of Take-shiba. It happened that one of the local men was sent off to the Capital as night sentry to the palace to man the fire huts,[19] and one day as he was sweeping the imperial courtyard, he was overheard muttering to himself as follows: 'Why should it be my fate to suf-fer here? Just think, back home I could be watching the gourd ladles drifting to and fro on all those sake jars that stand about – northward in a south wind, southward in a northerly, eastward in a west wind, westward in an easterly . . . And here I am instead!'

Now the emperor's dearly beloved daughter happened to have come out all alone just then to stand at the edge of a nearby room, leaning against a pillar behind the reed blind and gazing out. She was extremely moved to hear the man's soliloquy, and was pos-sessed with a longing to see just what these ladles might be and exactly how they drifted about. So she lifted the blind and said, 'Come over here, fellow'.

He tremulously approached the railing where she stood.

'Tell me again what it was you were just saying,' she ordered, and he did as told. 'Take me there and show me. I have good reason to say this,' she declared.

He was thoroughly overawed, but feeling that fate must have decreed it he took her on his back and set off to return to his country. Arriving at the Seta Bridge that night, and sure that by now they would be after him, he set her down by the bridge while he ripped up the planks between two of the bridge posts. Then he leapt the gap, and with her on his back he made his way on to Musashi, arriving after seven days and nights of travel.

When they discovered the loss of their daughter the emperor and his consort began a panicked search for her, whereupon someone came forward to report that they had seen the sentry guard from Musashi go rushing off 'with something very fragrant[20] draped around his neck'. When they searched for the man and found he had indeed disappeared, they realized that he must have headed for home. The emperor sent his people to pursue him, but of course when they arrived at the Seta Bridge they found it broken and couldn't cross. It was three months later that they finally reached Musashi and set about asking after the man.

The princess then summoned them. 'Clearly all this was ordained to happen,' she said. 'I longed to see this man's home so I ordered him to bring me here, and he did as asked. I love it here. What will become of me if you arrest this man? I was destined from a former life to live and die in this place. Hurry on back and inform His Majesty of all this.'

There was nothing for it. Even if they arrested the man, it was too late to think of returning the princess to the Capital now. The man from Takeshiba couldn't be given the province of Musashi as a gift for life, of course, or any official position, but a simple decree went out that the land now belonged to the princess, and the man's home was rebuilt as a palace for her to live in. When the princess died, it was made into a temple with the name of Takeshiba Temple, and her children were given the family name Musashi. And after that, it seems, only women were appointed as sentries in the palace fire huts.

On we went through the wilds, making our way over miles of nothing but reeds and rushes, until between Musashi and Sagami we came to the ferry crossing at Asuda River made famous by Narihira's poem, 'if your name is true / then tell me', though in his poetry collection it is called the Sumida.[21] Here we crossed by ferry into the land of Sagami.

The Nishitomi mountains looked just like a row of beautifully painted screens. In the other direction lay the sea, and the view of those beaches and the returning waves was absolutely lovely.

We spent several days travelling over the long stretch of Morokoshi Plains (the Plains of China), with its beautiful white sand. The locals told us that in summer the place was ablaze with native pinks in various shades of pale and dark, like a spread brocade, but that since it was the end of autumn there were none left. In fact, though, here and there we saw splashes of colour, a few last flowers still blooming most touchingly. People were delighted by the sight, and enjoyed the irony of our native Japanese pinks flowering in a place called the Plains of China.

We arrived at Ashigara Mountain having spent what seemed four or five days travelling through quite terrifying darkness. Even as we made our way in to the foot of the mountain the sky did not lift, and all about us the forest stretched frighteningly dense.

We stayed the night below the mountain, and a dark moonless night it was, a night to lose one's way in. Out of this darkness three *asobi*[22] suddenly appeared as if from nowhere. One was a woman of about fifty, and the other two around twenty and fourteen. A broad parasol was set up outside our lodgings, where they sat to perform, and the servants lit torches to light the scene. One *asobi* announced that she was the granddaughter of a famous performer called Kohata. Her hair was wonderfully long and hung very prettily on either side of her forehead, her skin was white and unblemished. 'She could easily take her place among the palace servants,' people remarked admiringly. Then she sang, and her voice was incomparable – it soared pure and beautiful to the sky. Everyone was so impressed that they called her over, fascinated. 'Even the famous entertainers back home couldn't rise to this!' someone declared, and at that she sang a wonderful song along the lines of 'Should you compare me to the ladies of Naniwa'. She looked so polished and presentable, and sang so gloriously, that everyone wept at the thought of her setting off again through such fearful mountains, and in my own childish way I was distressed even to think she must leave the safety of our lodgings.

We crossed Ashigara Mountain while it was still first light. It had been frightening enough below, but words cannot describe how terrifying it was up there. We were so high we trod the clouds. Deep in the mountains, just tucked in under the shade of a tree, we were moved to find three little *aoi*[23] plants growing. 'Fancy them growing here, so far from the real world!' people exclaimed. We also crossed three streams up on the mountain.

Finally we struggled down to the other side, and that night we stayed at the mountain barrier gate. We were now entering Suruga. Beside the Yokohashiri Barrier was a place called Iwatsubo, an extraordinarily huge square rock with a hole in the middle of it from which gushed water that was marvellously pure and cold.

Mount Fuji is in Suruga. Back where I used to live, it was the mountain we could see out to the west. There is nothing like it. This extraordinary mountain looks as if painted cobalt blue, and its snows never melt, so that it seems to wear a rich blue robe cloaked with a white *akome* gown. Smoke rises from its slightly flattened summit, and in the evenings you can sometimes see flames leaping from it.[24]

The Barrier Gate of Kiyomi[25] with its many guard buildings stands beside the sea, and its palisade fence extends right into the water. Kiyomi's waves leap high, *spindrift to meet Fuji's smoke* perhaps. It was a truly marvellous scene.

The waves were high too at Tago Bay, where we rounded the headland by boat.

There is a crossing at the Ōi River. The water was most unusual, flowing fast and white, almost as if great sacks of rice flour had been tipped into it.

The Fuji River flows out from Mount Fuji.[26] Here we met a local who told us the following story.

A few years back, on his way somewhere he had paused by this river to rest from the heat, and noticed something yellow floating downstream towards him. It snagged on a nearby object, and he saw it was a discarded sheet of paper with some sort of writing on it. He fished it out for a closer look. The words were beautifully written with thick brush strokes in vermillion ink on yellow paper. Intrigued, he read it, and found that it seemed to be some kind of official court appointments list, and on it were written the names of the provincial governorships that would fall free in the following year. This province was among them, and beside it was one man's name followed by another. How strange! he thought. How extraordinary! He dried the page and put it carefully away. Sure enough, the following year's appointments list was precisely as this document had predicted, including the man who became governor of this province, but within three months that man had died, and his replacement was the second man named there. Such things really do happen, he said. It brought home to him that each year the gods all gather on Mount Fuji and decide on the following year's appointments. Truly marvellous.

We passed through Numajiri without incident, but as we made our way on to Tōtōmi I became very ill. We must have crossed the pass at Saya no Nakayama, but I have no memory of it. I was feeling so bad that we stopped by Tenchū River and set up temporary shelters, where I spent some days slowly recovering. Deep winter was upon us now and a dreadfully fierce wind blew off the river, which I found quite unendurable.

Crossing the Tenchū, we next came to the bridge at Hamana. When we'd come East there had been a log bridge there – I mean across the inlet – but there was no trace of it now so we crossed by boat. Out to sea it was wild, and the waves were huge. The sandbanks in the inlet were quite uninteresting, but glimpsed through the great dark stands of beach pine *the surging waves* beyond flashed like jewels and seemed about to *overwhelm the very tree tips*, a truly impressive sight.

On we went. Having climbed up a horribly difficult slope at Inohana, we next came to Takashi Beach in the land of Mikawa.

The famous Yatsuhashi[27] was there only in name – there was no trace of any bridges, and the actual place was quite unimpressive.

The night we stopped in the mountains at Futamura, our shelter was set up under a large persimmon tree. All night long persimmons rained down on the roof, and our people gathered them up.

By the time we crossed Miyaji Mountain it was late in the tenth month,[28] yet the colourful autumn leaves were still at their height and unfallen.

arashi koso	No winter storms
fuki-kozarikere	have touched Miyaji Mountain –
miyajiyama	see how the autumn leaves
mada momijiha no	still hang in all their splendour
chirade nokoreru	undisturbed

Between Mikawa and Owari lies Shikasuga Crossing; it was entertaining to find that it was indeed a place that was *cause for hesitation*, as in the old poems.[29]

We passed Narumi Bay in Owari. The evening tide was near full, but this was not really a place to stop for the night so we decided to make a dash for it, fearing that the rising tide would prevent us from crossing, and managed to somehow make it through.

On the border of Mino we crossed the river at a place called Sunomata, and stayed that night at Nogami. Here some *asobi* entertained us deep into the night with songs, and I recalled with a pang those *asobi* back at Ashigara.

The snow was swirling wildly as we passed the Fuwa Barrier and crossed Atsumi Mountain, and nothing we saw could arouse our interest. Once in Ōmi, we stopped four or five nights at the house of a man by the name of Okinaga.

At the foot of Mitsusaka Mountain we met with cold winter rain mixed with fine hail that beat down day and night, dimming the daylight and making me thoroughly miserable.

From there, we went on without seeing anything worth noting through Inukami, Kanzaki, Yasu, Kurumoto and so on. The lake[30] stretched far and wide beside us, and it was wonderful to see the islands of Nadeshima and Chikubushima in the distance. The Seta Bridge was in a terrible state, making it far from easy to cross.

We spent the night in Awazu and at last, on the second day of the twelfth month, we reached the Capital. It being the custom to

arrive after dark, we set off at the Hour of the Monkey.[31] Close
by the Ōsaka Barrier Gate there was a makeshift wooden fence
set back against the mountain, and beyond it I could just make
out the face of a half-made Buddha figure about five metres high,
still only roughly carved, staring down at us.[32] 'Poor Buddha,' I
thought, gazing at it as we passed, 'sitting out here so far from
everyone in the middle of nowhere!' Of all the places we had
passed through, none rivalled the Kiyomi Barrier in Suruga and
the Ōsaka Gate.

That night in heavy darkness we reached our home to the west
of the Sanjō Palace.

[. . .]

*Takasue's daughter remained in the Capital. She eventually married
and bore three children. As she grew older she became increasingly religious and made a number of pilgrimages to temples, which gave her
fresh opportunities to travel. A selection of these pilgrimages from her
journal follows.*

At last I had come to understand and lament how foolish my
romantic fantasies of old had been, and I was vexed that I had never
gone with my parents on their pilgrimages. These days I lived in far
grander style, had brought up my children lovingly and well, and
had accumulated impressive wealth. Now I decided I must turn my
thoughts to the world to come, and so toward the end of the eleventh month, I set out on a pilgrimage to Ishiyama Temple.[33]

Snow was swirling down, and the road itself was full of delights.
Passing the Ōsaka Barrier Gate brought back to me that it had
also been winter back then when we came through on our way
home. Now too a fierce wind blew.

ōsaka no	Forbidding winds still blow
seki no seki-kaze	about the barrier gate
fuku koe wa	of Ōsaka
mukashi kikishi ni	crying with that same voice
kawarazarikeri	I heard so long ago

The imposing buildings of Sekidera Temple stirred memories of that rough-hewn Buddha face that had stared down at me, and I was moved to think how time had passed.

Uchiide Beach on the lake shore was also just as I remembered it. We arrived at the temple as dark was coming on, and disembarked to wash at the purification hall before climbing to the main worship hall. Not a voice was to be heard, and the wind off the mountain struck chill into my heart. Then during my prayers that night I drifted off, and heard a voice saying, 'We have received a gift of musk from the main temple. Please report this immediately.' Starting awake, I realized it was a dream. This must have an auspicious meaning, I decided, and it spurred me to continue my devotions till dawn.

The next day the wild snowstorm continued, and I comforted myself with talking to a dear friend from the Court who was there with me.

I spent three days in retreat there, then returned home.

The following year, there was a great flurry of excitement over the purification ceremony for the Great Thanksgiving Banquet that followed the enthronement.[34] I had already begun my own purifications for a pilgrimage to Hase[35] and this was the day set for my departure, but there were some in the family who believed this was madness.

'This is a rare spectacle, seen only once in a reign,' they declared angrily. 'Everyone near and far is coming to see it, and of all the times to choose, you plan to leave the Capital on the very day! You'll be the talk of the town!'

My children's father, however, took my part. 'Heavens, no!' he declared. 'You must follow your heart!' and he sent me on my way. I was very touched.

The people accompanying me were clearly longing to stay and watch the spectacle, and I did feel sorry for them. But I said to myself, 'What would be the point of seeing it, after all? I'm sure the Buddha will appreciate my urge to go off on pilgrimage at such a time and will answer my prayers.'

And so the following morning before dawn I set off. Crossing Nijō Avenue we made our way past crowds of people on horseback and in ox carriages coming the other way, all on their way to find early places in the viewing stands. They looked astonished at the sight of my procession, with its offertory torch bearers in the lead and attendants all wearing the white robes appropriate for pilgrimage. 'Good heavens, what's this?' they sneered derisively as we passed.

The front gate of the Chief Guard, Fujiwara no Yoshiyori, was standing wide open when we went by. He was clearly just about to set out for the viewing stands, and the men standing about in readiness chuckled when they saw us. 'Just look, there's someone on her way to a pilgrimage!' they jeered. 'On this of all days!' One man, however, did seem to have a finer sensibility. 'What point is there in delighting the senses with passing parades, after all?' he said earnestly. 'This lady must be impressively pious, and no doubt she'll be rewarded by the Buddha. All this is really quite senseless. We'd have done far better to spurn this spectacle and follow her example by going on pilgrimage.'

I had set out while it was still dark in order to avoid making a spectacle of myself en route, but we then paused at the front gate of Hōshōji Temple on the edge of the city to let those following behind catch us up, and also in hopes that the horribly thick fog would clear a little. An endless stream of people flowed by, coming in from the countryside to see the sight. There was simply no avoiding them, and as we forced our way through the throng everyone was leering at my carriage incredulously, vulgar, stupid-looking little brats included. The sight of them did make me wonder why on earth I had chosen to travel this road at such a time, but I concentrated all my thoughts on the Buddha, and finally we struggled through and arrived at the Uji River crossing.

Here too there was a vast crowd coming across, and the boatmen were looking very pleased with themselves at all the custom still awaiting them. They had rolled up their sleeves and pressed their faces to the oars, and we couldn't get anyone to bring a boat over to us for ages – they were quite blasé, humming and gazing about, pretending not to notice us. It seemed we would never get across. As I waited I gazed around, impressed to think that this was the place I had long wondered about, where the Uji maidens in Murasaki's tale[36] had been sent to spend their days. When at last we managed to cross, we called at the Uji mansion of the Chancellor,[37] and my first thought as I went in was that it must have been in just such a place that Ukifune lived.

We had set off late at night and everyone was tired, so we stopped at a place called Yairōchi to rest and eat. How it frightened me to hear someone in the party remark, 'Isn't this the notorious Mount Kurikoma?[38] And the sun looks close to setting. We'd all better make good and sure our things are secure!'

Having crossed the hills, we arrived at the banks of Nieno Pond just after the sun had sunk to the mountain rim. It was announced that we were to stop here for the night, and everyone scattered in search of lodgings for us. 'It's not much of a place,' they reported, 'but we did find a little peasant hovel, dreadfully run-down.' There was no help for it, so there we stayed.

Two scruffy-looking men came out and informed us that everyone else had gone off to the Capital. That night I didn't sleep a wink. The men kept walking in and out, till finally one of the maids asked why they were pacing about like this. 'Eh, here we are, putting up folk we know nothing of, and we can't sleep for worrying what we'd do if they made off with the cooking pot, that's why,' one of them replied, assuming we were asleep. It was both horrible and funny.

We left there next morning, and went on to worship at Tōdaiji Temple.

Isonokami Shrine[39] of course brought great age to mind, and it was indeed in a thoroughly decrepit condition.

We stopped that night at a temple in a place called Yamanobe. Hard though it was to summon the energy, I managed a little sutra chanting before dozing off and slipping into dream. I found myself entering the presence of a most exalted and beautiful lady. A fierce wind was blowing. Seeing me she smiled, and asked why I had come. 'How could I not?' I replied. 'You are to serve at the palace,' she said. 'You should consult the lady in charge of the Office of Staff.' I awoke thrilled, and with fresh conviction I threw myself still more fervently into my prayers.

Meanwhile, on I travelled, over Hase River and beyond, and that evening reached the holy temple itself. Having performed my purifications, I climbed the stairs to the main temple area.

Three days I spent there, and the night I was set to depart at dawn the following morning, I was startled from a light sleep. 'Look! A divine cedar from the Inari god!'[40] came a cry from the temple, and I sensed something being hurled. I woke and realized it was another dream.

We set off in the pre-dawn darkness. That day we didn't manage to find lodgings for the night until we reached a house this side of Narasaka.[41] It was another dreadful little place, and everyone agreed that they didn't like the feel of it at all. 'Be careful not to sleep,' they cautioned. 'Who knows what might happen. For heaven's sake don't scream or make a noise if anything happens, just lie there and hold your breath.' This filled me with fear and misery. It felt as if a thousand years had passed by the time the dawn came round. When first light finally arrived, I heard them declaring all over again what a den of thieves it was, and how suspiciously the woman in charge had behaved.

It was a terribly windy day when we crossed the Uji River, and the boat rowed quite close to the famous fishing weirs.[42]

oto ni nomi	I had no more than heard
kiki-watari-koshi	of the weirs on Uji River
ujigawa no	until I crossed today
ajiro no nami mo	and could count at last
kyō zo kazouru	the waves that lap them

Writing down in no particular order events that spanned two, three, five years makes it sound as if I have spent my time in constant prayer and pilgrimage, but this is not the case, for in fact considerable time passed between excursions.

One spring I went on retreat to Kurama Temple.[43] It was a soft, warm spring day, mist shrouding the mountain tops, and I was enchanted to see people coming down from the mountains carrying little bundles of yams and so forth that they had dug up there. The blossoms along the way had all scattered and there was no particular charm to the scene, but when I went again around the tenth month the mountain scenery as I travelled along was far more lovely. The mountain tops were covered in an autumn brocade, and the rushing stream sent up a crystal spray as it went tumbling along – a most wonderful sight. After worshipping I went to the monastery area, and oh the matchless sight of those autumn leaves glowing in the chilly shower that swept through!

okuyama no	How is it
momiji no nishiki	that the chill autumn showers
hoka yori mo	can dye so singularly deep
ika ni shigurete	this rich brocade of leaves
fukaku somekemu	here among far mountains?

I was deeply struck to see it all.

About two years later, I went on pilgrimage to Ishiyama Temple again for another retreat. All night long there I listened to the pouring rain, thinking gloomily what a dismal sound it was for travellers to hear, but when I opened the shutters and looked out at dawn the world was flooded in brilliant moonlight clear to the bottom of the valley, and what had sounded like rain was in fact a rushing stream tumbling among the tree roots.

tanikawa no	That mountain stream
nagare wa ame to	I heard as pouring rain
kikoyuredo	but there in the dawn
hoka yori ke naru	most beautiful
ariake no tsuki	spreads the moonlight

I went on another pilgrimage to Hase, a much more confident one than the first. Our progress was held up by the hospitality we received here and there along the way. The famous autumn leaves of Hahaso Wood in Yamashiro were at their loveliest. At the Hase River crossing:

hatsusegawa	Hase's swirling waters
tachi-kaeritsutsu	carry me round again.
tazunureba	Once more I come
sugi no shirushi mo	perhaps to gain at last
kono tabi ya mimu	the promise of that cedar[44]

The thought filled me with hope.

After three days' retreat I left, and sought lodgings in the same place this side of Narasaka. This time, however, there were too many of us to put up, so a temporary shelter was set up for us, while the attendants all spent the night sleeping outside. They spread riding overalls on the ground, put matting over them, and on this makeshift bed they saw in the dawn. Their heads were soaked with dew.

The dawn moon was astonishingly bright and clear, a truly lovely sight.

yukue naki	Beneath the far skies
tabi no sora ni mo	of this wandering journey
okurenu wa	the same dawn moon
miyako nite mishi	I knew back in the
	Capital
ariake no tsuki	keeps me company still

Circumstances took me down to Izumi[45] one autumn.

From Yodo onward we went by boat, and the scenery along the way was quite indescribably delightful and moving. On a dark night we docked at a place called Takahama, and very late we heard the sound of oars approaching. 'Who's there?' someone asked, and we learned it was a group of *asobi*. Everyone was very interested, and we had their boat draw alongside ours. It was extremely moving to see them, lit by distant firelight, long sleeves flowing gracefully and faces hidden by fans as they sang.

Next day, just as the sun was setting behind the mountains, we passed famous Sumiyoshi Bay. Sea and sky were one in the enfolding mist, and no painted picture could do justice to the wonderful sight of the pine branches, the sea surface, the waves breaking along the beach.

ika ni ii	How express it?
nani ni tatoete	How compare and tell
kataramashi	the beauty
aki no yūbe no	of the Bay of Sumiyoshi
sumiyoshi no ura	in the autumn evening?

So our boat glided on, while I could only turn and gaze behind, untiring of the scene.

I travelled back to the Capital that winter. We boarded our boat at the mouth of the Ōtsu River, and that night the wind and rain raged fierce enough to shift the very rocks, the thunder roared, and the sound of the furious waves and the winds that howled about us were so terrifying I was convinced my life was at an end. We drew the boat up a slope and there spent the night. Later the rain ceased, but the wind still blew and we couldn't put our boat out. Five or six days we spent there on that hill, going nowhere. When the wind at last died down a little I opened the blinds of our boat and looked out, and saw the sudden delightful sight of the evening tide in full flood, and the cranes calling full-throated down in the inlet.

A gathering of local officials had come to visit. 'If you had put out to sea that night,' they said, 'and gone on to Ishizu, you would have sunk without a trace.' Their words made me quite wretched at the thought.

aruru umi ni	What if we had set forth
kaze yori saki ni	before the wind blew
fune dashite	into that raging sea
ishizu no nami to	and now were gone
kienamashikaba	into Ishizu's waves?

Dust Dancing on the Rafters
compiled by Retired Emperor Goshirakawa

The Sarashina Diary *several times records a particular source of delight and wonderment for the author in her travels – chance encounters with the women entertainers who went by the general name of* asobi. *These women are haunting presences at the margins of many travellers' tales down the centuries,[1] but being themselves largely or completely illiterate they left no personal record of their lives.[2] Ironically, it is a retired emperor whom we have to thank for transcribing the fascinating songs that carry to us the voices of these and other illiterate performers, in an anthology that goes by the name of* Ryōjin hishō *(Dust Dancing on the Rafters).*

This name derives from a Chinese legend in which the very dust danced on the rafters at the marvellous voices of two women as they sang.[3] There is no doubt that many asobi *did indeed both sing and dance with real art, and prided themselves on being very much more than prostitutes, although prostitution inevitably played a more or less important role in their lives. Song and dance were ubiquitous forms of entertainment for both aristocracy and commoners, and although the more aristocratic forms of song were of the kind found in* Wakan rōeishū *(see Chapter 6), members of the court clearly found the earthier songs of commoners intriguing,[4] and were easily beguiled by the professional songs and dances of the* asobi *they encountered. In the twelfth century, versions of these songs became immensely popular at court under the name* imayō *('songs of the moment'), and their performance was cultivated as an art.*

A key impetus behind this passing aristocratic vogue[5] for popular imayō *was Retired Emperor Goshirakawa (1127–92), the compiler of* Dust Dancing on the Rafters. *Goshirakawa's immense energies encompassed a lifelong passion for* imayō *which he documents in the*

companion work to the collection, called Ryōjin hishō kudenshū.
There he describes an obsession with singing imayō *that drove him to
practise 'without break, day in day out, mindless of time', until he lost
his voice and his throat swelled so that he could barely swallow. His
urge to master the art prompted him to apprentice himself to famous
performers, and his court witnessed the startling sight of* asobi *coming
and going day and night from his chamber to pass on the secrets of their
art. Saddened at the thought that these songs were ephemera that
would be forgotten, he meticulously noted as many as he could gather,
adding detailed performance notes that have unfortunately been lost.*[6]
*Of their actual performance we know little more than that they were
usually accompanied by a drum and often also by dance. Their flexible
rhythm, often based on the traditional 5/7 beat with variations, is evident in their words, but we have no way of guessing melody or tempo.*

*It is impressive that Goshirakawa found the time and dedication to
both cultivate this art and record the songs so meticulously. He lived in
turbulent times, and was frequently at the centre of their tumultuous
events. By the time he was born, the stable world of the Heian court was
beginning to show cracks that would soon lead to its downfall. Factional
court politics was making increasing use of the military support of two
powerful warrior clans from the provinces, the Genji and the Heike,
whose rivalry complicated matters further. Goshirakawa found himself
briefly on the throne (1155–8) in the midst of a bitter succession dispute
which provoked the first of several bloody upheavals that would wrack
the Capital and result in the accession to power of first one and then the
other warrior clan, and the effective end of the Heian court's authority.
In his long and very active 'retirement' Goshirakawa himself proceeded
to manipulate events in ways that both furthered the chaos and inadver-
tantly aided the final supremacy of the warrior clans. By 1169, when he
was putting the finishing touches to* Dust Dancing on the Rafters, *the
great warlord Taira no Kiyomori had assumed the most powerful position in the land, and the world Goshirakawa had known had irrevocably
changed.*

*No one in the Capital remained untouched by the bloodshed and
turbulence of these decades. They shook the upper classes to their foundations, and starkly drove home the truth of the Buddhist teachings on
impermanence and suffering that so many of these songs also speak of.
Yet the melancholy tone that began to permeate Japanese literature and*

thought during this time is very different from the jaunty toughness in the face of adversity that we hear in the songs of the asobi *and other itinerant entertainers.*[7] *Their grand themes are, unsurprisingly, love (seduction) and relationships and, perhaps more surprisingly, religious faith. Travel is a constant presence in the songs, although relatively seldom an overt theme. While full of poignant lament, what these songs finally convey is the wry acceptance and humour of women and sometimes men inured to the hardships of a life lived at the difficult margins of society.*

This brief selection of songs provides only a glimpse of the great range that the work contains, but it gives a vivid picture of life on the road for this fascinating underclass. Pilgrimage, one of the main reasons for travel for both high and low, features in the first four songs, particularly the arduous and immensely popular Kumano pilgrimage.[8] *Suffering the difficulties of the route was an integral part of the austerities believed to earn one divine merit, and it is gently mocked in the first two songs. The third song, apparently sung by the* asobi *based at the river port of Yodo below the great pilgrimage shrine at Yawata, picks up the theme and turns it neatly into flirtatious suggestiveness. Songs 364 and 365, mothers' laments, sketch poignant portraits of men and women born to a life on the road, while 361 and 467 take up the voices of such travellers themselves and bewail the harsh treatment they often received. Song 429, which uses the list format seen most famously in Sei Shōnagon's* Pillow Book, *typically twists an initially melancholy tone to introduce a knowing wink at the end, as does song 457 for all its underlying heartfelt sadness.*

FROM *DUST DANCING ON THE RAFTERS*

257

kumano e mairu ni wa	Hey you pilgrims
nani ka kurushiki	what's so hard
shugyōja yo	about the road to Kumano?
yasumatsu himematsu	It's Easy Pine of Yasumatsu
goyōmatsu	Princess Pine and Five-Leafed Pine
chisato no hama	and the Beach of Chisato.[9]

258

kumano e mairamu	I'd like to go
to omoedomo	to Kumano
kachi yori maireba	but if I go on foot
michi tōshi	the way is far too long
sugurete yama kibishi	and the mountains far too steep
uma nite mairaba	and if I go by horse
kugyō narazu	there's no hardship in it
sora yori mairamu	so let me go by air then –
hane tabe nyakuōji	oh Nyaku-ōji,[10] give me wings!

261

yawata e mairan	I'd like to go to Yawata[11]
to omoedomo	but the Kamo River
kamogawa katsuragawa	flows so fast
ito hayashi	and oh so fast
ana hayashi na	flows the Katsura River!
yodo no watari ni	So set your boat out
fune ukete	at Yodo Crossing
mukaetamae	and come to meet me
daibosatsu	oh Bodhisattva![12]

300

warera ga shugyō ni	That time when I set out
ideshi toki	on my hard pilgrimage
suzu no misaki o	around I went past Suzu Cape
kai-mawari	oh far around I went
uchi-meguri	and when I left the cape behind
furi-sutete hitori	on I walked a-fortune telling
koshiji no tabi ni idete	along the Koshi Road[13]
ashiura seshi koso	and ah poor me
aware narishika	how my feet did hurt!

364

waga ko wa jūyo ni	My girl would now
narinuran	be in her teens
kōnagi shite koso	I hear she's on the road
ariku nare	here and there a-priestessing[14]
tago no ura ni	maybe she wanders
shio fumu to	the far salt paths
ika ni amabito	down by Tago Bay[15]
tsudouran	and how the fisher folks must flock
madashi tote	begging for their fortunes
toimi towazumi	taunting and teasing
nabururan	saying what a child she is
itōshi ya	my poor darling girl

365

waga ko wa hatachi ni	I guess my boy
narinuran	would now be twenty
bakuchi shite koso	gambling I hear
ariku nare	out along the roads
kuniguni no	in all the gambling dens
bakudō ni	but he's my own dear boy
sasuga ni ko nareba	so I forgive him.
nikū nashi	Oh gods of Sumiyoshi
makai-tamau na	and of Nishinomiya[16]
ōji no sumiyoshi nishinomiya	let him win!

361

kai no kuni yori	Down from the land of Kai I came
makari-idete	and crossed the pass of Shinano[17]

shinano no misaka o   hard climb it was
kurekure to harubaru to up that steep path
tori no ko ni shi mo   yes all that way I've come
                      and now

aranedomo   you tell me to go back
ubuge mo kawarade   a chick like me
kaere to ya   still barely feathered?

467

ame wa furu   The rain pours down
ine to wa notabu   and they tell me to get lost
kasa wa nashi   though I have no rain hat
mine tote mo   nor even a cape
motanu mi ni   to shelter under –
yuyushikarikeru   oh such mean
sato no hito kana   village folk they are
yado kasazu   to turn me away!

429

kokoro-sugoki mono   Things to make the heart
                      forlorn –

yomichi funamichi   night roads, boat trips
tabi no sora   skies of travel
tabi no yado   lodgings on a journey
koguraki   a voice chanting sutras
yamadera no   deep in dark forest
kyō no koe   in some mountain temple
omou ya nakarai no   and two lovers forced apart
akade noku   before love is spent

457

nami mo kike	Hear, waves!
koiso mo katare	Speak, rocky shores!
matsu mo miyo	Pines, bear witness!
ware o ware to iu	If a fair wind
kata no kaze	blew my way
fuitaraba	one that loved me as I am
izure no ura e mo	I'd drift with it
nabikinamu	to any shore it took me

10

The Tale of the Heike[1]

When the leader of the great Heike warrior clan, Taira no Kiyomori, seized effective power in 1167 he inherited a traumatized but still functioning court, and proceeded to embed himself and his family into its world with the aim of ensuring the continuing supremacy of the Heike clan after his death. But the turbulence that had swept him to power was not so easily laid to rest. It was not long before the ascendancy of the Heike was challenged and, after a long and bloody struggle, finally defeated by the great rival clan of the Genji. The battles between the Heike and the Genji convulsed not only the Capital but the country at large, and when the Genji came to power the imperial court found itself under the rule of a new seat of power, Kamakura, the home of the Genji clan in the distant East. Later historians have determined that this moment marks the end of the long and peaceful Heian period, which had lasted almost 400 years (794–1185), and the beginning of the middle ages with the Kamakura period (1185–1333) and the Genji's military rule.

The long military romance known as The Tale of the Heike *(Heike monogatari) was born of this immense upheaval and tells its story. It is like nothing that had come before it. While the literature of the Heian period had evolved within the court and remained the preserve of that little world,[2] with* The Tale of the Heike *Japanese literature as it were took to the road and went out into the wider world. Not only does its story range freely up and down the country from Kamakura in the east to the far western tip of the main island of Honshu as it follows the scenes of battle, but the* Tale *itself largely evolved from and was transmitted by minstrel reciters who were frequently itinerant themselves.*

Its origin is anecdotally traced to one Yukinaga, a former provincial governor who as a monk 'created The Tale of the Heike, *which he taught to the blind reciter Shōbutsu'.*[3] *This is rather too neat as an explanation for this epic work, which exists in a bewildering variety of texts and lines of transmission, but it at least points to several important facts about its creation. One is that, probably from the beginning, it was conceived as a work to be performed. The men who carried this work into the world, reciters such as the renowned Shōbutsu, were part of an ancient tradition of blind musicians and reciters that seems to have existed in different forms throughout the world, bearers of much of the oral literature of pre-literate societies.*[4] *Japan's professional reciters, known as* biwa hōshi, *were more or less itinerant monks who memorized and performed lengthy sections of* The Tale of the Heike *to the accompaniment of a stringed instrument called a* biwa[5] *for audiences ranging from courtiers to warriors and commoners. It is unclear what role the* biwa hōshi *played in the actual creation of the many variants of the* Tale, *but if a single individual such as Yukinaga did indeed first commit some form of the* Tale *to writing he probably did so by collecting and organizing material that was already in circulation within a few decades of the defeat of the Heike in* 1185.[6]

Another point to note in the anecdote of Yukinaga's role is that he was at the time a monk. This points to the pervasive presence of Buddhist teachings in the Tale, *specifically the teaching on Impermanence that underpins the* Tale's *relentless narrative of death and the reversal of fortunes. In many ways the* Tale *seems to have grown out of and been a tool of Buddhist preaching, whose influence is visible not only in the content but also in the structure and tone of many scenes as well as in the language itself. In* The Tale of the Heike *the traditional vernacular* kana *literary tradition gives way to a very different language and writing style that blends the old native Japanese of Heian literature with Chinese idioms and literary styles that had long existed side by side with it in the court and that were also the conventional language of Buddhist writings. The influence of the tough, colloquial warrior language and the Eastern dialect that the new rulers spoke is also strongly present in the language of the* Tale.

In content, style, language and concerns, The Tale of the Heike *is thus a masculine work, as befitted the times. But it is far from being simply a straightforward account of the battles and changing fortunes of the war and those who fought. The fact that the title[7] takes the perspective of the losing rather than the winning side is indicative of the*

Tale's approach to the stories it tells; above all, it aims to move the audience to pity and sympathy rather than simply to stir us with tales of derring-do. Fierce warriors commit heroic acts, but it is their deaths and defeats over which the Tale often lingers. We sense the Buddhist preacher behind the heart-wrenching scenes and descriptions that emotionally drive home the truth of the impermanence of all we cling to in this world.

The style and language of the Tale reflect this. While some versions of the work were apparently intended to be read, its nature as a performance piece is clear in the varying rhythms and rhetoric of its words. These sometimes abruptly shifting styles and cadences reflect the fact that certain passages were chanted and even sung, while others were more freely recited. At points of heightened emotional intensity the prose often tends to shift towards a loosely poetic rhythm of five and seven syllables, whose lyrical force sustains the emotion of the language. This urge towards lyricism and pathos connects the Tale with the old literary tradition that in so many other ways it steps beyond. Warriors are portrayed as men of sensibility, who can compose and appreciate poetry and are moved by the passing seasons. The Tale itself is a richly literary work, frequently beautiful in its language and evocations and compelling in the narration of its set pieces. Though the heyday of its reception was the immediate century or two following the Genpei Wars (as they were called), it continued to be read and performed down the ages, and has inspired countless other works into the present.

The two extracts translated here give a glimpse of the wide variety of content and styles found in the Tale. The first presents events leading up to the decisive battle at Ichinotani (in the area of modern-day Kobe), in which the Genji defeated the Heike forces with a pincer movement involving a daring descent down a perilous ravine. The narrative swings freely between the Heike and the Genji positions, but its emotional focus is the Genji feat of navigating their way to the top of Hiyodori Pass with the aid of an old horse, and then successfully descending the steep ravine under the guidance of a local hunter to take the Heike forces by surprise. The narration's lingering lyrical description of the route through the snowy landscape incorporates the poetic parallelism typical of the Chinese literary style.

The second extract, which takes the captured Heike warrior Taira no Shigehira (1157–85) along the road from Kyoto to Kamakura as he anticipates certain death, exemplifies how far from realistic the Tale *could be. Much of it consists of an extended passage depicting the journey in the lyrical elegiac style known as* michiyuki-bun *(literally 'going-along-the-road writing'), a style prefigured in the 5/7 syllable rhythms of* chōka *in the* Manyōshū *and very likely continued in some form in popular literature down the intervening centuries.[8] This dense weave of poetic images in 5/7 syllable style takes the sorrowing traveller along the Tōkaidō by means of* utamakura *place names, evoking the pathos of his fate. It is interrupted by a prose passage describing a famous poetic exchange with an* asobi *which later formed the basis of the great Nō play* Yuya, *just one example of the reverberations the* Tale *had in later literature.*

THE TALE OF THE HEIKE 9.9

Lord Munemori now sent Yoshiyuki as messenger to the Heike lords, saying, 'Word has come that Yoshitsune[9] has defeated our forces at Mikusa and has already thrust his way into the valley of Ichinotani. That mountain behind is a key place. Make your way there, every one of you.' The lords, however, all declined.

Next, he sent to Noritsune. 'I know I have asked this favour of you many times, but could you go?'

'Fighting goes well for me because for me fighting is all,' Lord Noritsune replied. 'A battle is not won by choosing to go only where there is promise of firm ground, as with hunting or fishing. I am prepared to set forth again and again, to meet the fiercest enemy. All will go my way, have no fear,' he added reassuringly.

Delighted, Lord Munemori sent ten thousand troops to Noritsune, with the former governor of Etchū Moritoshi at their head, and together with his brother, Lord Michimori, he secured the side up against the mountain – that is to say, the foot of Hiyodori Pass.

Michimori called his wife to Noritsune's temporary encampment, and there said his last reluctant farewells to her. Noritsune was enraged by this. 'I was sent here precisely because this was such a dangerous place, and indeed it is. If the Genji come hurtling down from the top of the pass, as they may at any moment, we will have no time to so much as seize our weapons. Even bow in hand, there would be no chance to fit an arrow. And even were arrow set to bow, there would be no drawing it to shoot. Yet look at you, idling and smooching like this! Utterly useless!' Michimori acknowledged that this was just, it seemed, for he hurried to don his armour and send his wife back.

On the evening of the fifth day, the Genji left Koyano and gradually pushed their way in to Ikuta Wood. The pine fields of Suzume, the woods of Mikage and off toward Koyano – wherever one looked one saw the Genji camps, scattered hither and yon, beacon fires burning. And with the deepening night their glow grew stronger, lighting the landscape like a risen moon above the mountains. 'Let us light fires too,' the Heike said, and there in Ikuta Wood they set a few ablaze. Gazing as the sky began to lighten, the Genji fires shone like a star-filled night. Now they felt the truth of that ancient poem that speaks of 'fireflies by a stream'.[10]

There camped the Genji, resting their horses; here they camped, feeding and grooming them, taking their time. As for the Heike, anxiety gripped them, fearing the Genji attack from moment to moment.

When dawn broke on the sixth day, Yoshitsune, who led the Genji troops, divided his ten-thousand strong army into two. Seven thousand or more horsemen he sent to the western side of Ichinotani under the command of Sanehira. He himself set forth with around three thousand via the Tanba Road, planning to attack from the rear down Hiyodori Ravine.

'That place is renowned for its dangerous steepness!' the warriors exclaimed to each other. 'I want to die against the enemy, not by tumbling down some ravine. If only there were someone who knew these mountains and could guide us.'

At this, Hirayama Sueshige from the land of Musashi stepped forth. 'I know how to take you,' he declared.

Yoshitsune responded, 'But you are a man of the Eastern provinces, seeing these Western mountains for the first time today. I cannot believe that you could know the way.'

Hirayama spoke again. 'How can you say this? A poet can intuitively know the blossoms of Yoshino and Hase, surely; just so, a brave warrior by instinct knows the way behind the enemy's defences.' To the others, this sounded arrogant bravado.

Next a young man of eighteen from Musashi by the name of Beppu no Kotarō stepped forth to speak. 'My father, the monk Yoshishige, taught me this – "Whether pursued by the enemy or hunting far over the passes, if you are lost deep among mountains you should sling the reins over the neck of an old horse and have him go ahead of you. He will be certain to lead you out."'

'Finely spoken, young man,' said Yoshitsune. 'There are indeed cases where an old horse has known the way, though the fields were buried in snow.' He chose an old grey horse, set a silver-trimmed saddle upon its back and a gleaming bit in its mouth, tied up the reins and threw them around its neck, and sent it on ahead of them into the unknown mountains.

It was early in the second month, and patchy snow still lying on the peaks might almost have been blossoming cherry trees. *Uguisu* sang in the valleys; spring mists sometimes hid their way. Climbing, they saw glittering white clouds that soared above; descending, the steep mountainsides were lush with leaf, and sheer cliffs fell away. *Even upon the pines the snow still lay*; the narrow path they followed was hidden deep in moss. At each rough gust of stormy wind, the flying snow might have been scattering plum blossom. East and west they whipped their horses, hurrying on till darkness fell over the mountain path, whereupon they alighted and made camp.

Musashibō Benkei led over an old man. 'And who is this?' Yoshitsune inquired.

'A hunter in these mountains,' Benkei replied.

'Well then, you must know the terrain. Speak frankly.'

'Indeed I do know it.'

'What do you think of the plan to send my forces down from here onto the Heike stronghold in Ichinotani?'

'It could never be done, sir. A ravine ninety metres deep, boulders close to fifty metres high – such places no man can go. Even more unthinkable to send a horse down. What's more, the Heike will have dug pitfalls inside the defences, and planted pronged stakes in readiness.'

'All right, can a deer do it?'

'A deer can do it. Once the world warms, your deer from Harima will cross through here to Tanba to lie in the deep grass, and when once the world grows cold again he will cross back

The Genji forces descend Hiyodori Ravine

from Tanba to Inamino in Harima to find food in the shallow snow.'

'Well then,' cried Yoshitsune, 'it's a walk in the park for a horse! Surely a horse can go where a deer can? Quick, lead us down.'

'I am old, sir, and could not do it.'

'Do you have a son?'

'I do,' he replied, and he brought before Yoshitsune a youth of eighteen named Kumaō.

A coming-of-age ceremony was swiftly performed for the youth, who was now given the name Washino-o no Saburō Yoshihisa, after the old man's name, which was Washino-o no Shōji Takehisa, and he was set at the head of the troops to lead them down.

Later, after the Heike were defeated and Yoshitsune had fallen foul of the Kamakura ruler, this Yoshihisa died alongside him when Yoshitsune was killed in the far north.[11]

THE TALE OF THE HEIKE 10.6

Taira no Shigehira (1157–85) was among the Heike warriors defeated at the battle of Ichinotani, where he was captured. Sent to the Genji headquarters in Kamakura, as described below, he was in fact spared by Yoritomo, the leader of the Genji, but later met his end at the hands of the Nara monks whose temples he had inadvertently destroyed in a fire.

In Kamakura Yoritomo was constantly demanding that Shigehira be brought to him, so it was agreed that it should be done. First Sanehira took him to Yoshitsune's quarters. Then on the tenth day of that same third month, Kajiwara Kagetoki led him off toward Kamakura.

Taken captive in the West, he lamented even returning to the Capital in this way. Alas, picture then his feelings as he found himself now setting out along the Eastern road.

Coming to Shinomiya by the stream his sorrowing thoughts turned back to Semimaru   fourth prince of emperor Daigo long ago   who at this border purified his heart   and plucked his *biwa* in the stormy gales   while by day in wind or calm and by night be it rain or fine   Hakuga no Sanmi[12] for three long years   trod

these paths and stood to listen   learning the secret repertoire
here *where that grass hut once stood*   ah sad to think of now.   On
over Ōsaka Mountain   the horses' hooves thundering   on Seta's
Chinese Bridge   through Noji village where the skylarks rise
spring riding on the waves of Shiga Bay   Mirror Mountain
blurred with mist   and northward the high peak of Hira   till
he drew near the heights of Ibuki.   And though it gave his heart
no pause   *the boarded eaves of Fuwa's barrier gate   in ruins* now
seemed so much more arresting.   Uncertain as the uncertain
tides that turn   at Narumi's tidal beach[13]   salt tears soaking his
sleeves   on he went into the land of Mikawa   to Yatsuhashi
where once Narihira sang   of one *dear to him as a long-worn robe*
his wretched heart as full of tangled thoughts   as those eight
tangled spider's legs[14]   and on past the Bridge of Hamana   the
wind chill in the pine tops   waves crashing at the inlet.   Oh any
journey is a mournful thing   and his heart grew darker still in
evening's deepening gloom   and so at last he came to the inn at
Ikeda.

They stayed that night with Jijū, the daughter of Yuya who
ran the inn. Seeing Shigehira, she exclaimed, 'Once I could
never have dreamt of even communicating with you, yet now
here you are, entering a place like this!'[15] and she composed this
poem for him:

tabi no sora	Here beneath traveller's skies
hanifu no oya no	lodged in this squalid hut
ibusesa ni	of rough earth walls
furusato ika ni	how you must pine
koishikaruramu	thinking of your old home

In reply, he composed this:

furusato mo	I do not pine
koishiku mo nashi	at thoughts of my old home
tabi no sora	beneath these traveller's skies
miyako mo tsui no	since even the Capital
sumika naraneba	offers no sure shelter till my end

'That poem is elegantly done,' Shigehira then declared. 'What
manner of person composed it?'

Kajiwara bowed. 'You have not heard of her yet, my lord? When Lord Munemori was governor of this province, he took her into his service and she became his favourite. She had left her old mother behind here, but although she constantly begged leave to come and care for her, he would not let her go. Then, early in the third month, she composed this:

ika ni semu	What's to be done?
miyako no haru mo	I would grieve to miss
oshikeredo	the spring flowers of the Capital
nareshi azuma no	but my beloved flower in the East
hana ya chiruran	may even now be falling

At this, he gave her leave to go. She is the finest poet along the Sea Road.'

He had now been many days on the road since leaving the Capital, the third month was half gone and spring was almost over. Blossoming trees on the far mountainsides seemed to the eye like patchy snow, while spring mists swathed the many bays and islands. His thoughts were filled with the road his life had travelled and what lay at its end. 'What miserable karmic fate has led me to this?'[16] he sighed, and his tears flowed without cease. Lady Nii, his mother, had bewailed his lack of children, and his wife Lady Dainagon-no-suke too had felt the lack and prayed to all the gods and buddhas for a child, but without result. 'It was a good thing,' he told himself now. 'How painful this would be if I had had a child.' It was some small consolation at least.

Coming to Saya no Nakayama Pass   he could not think that he would 'cross this way again'[17]   and fresh griefs added to his grief so that his sleeves were still more soaked with tears.   Forlorn, he walked Utsu's vine-tangled path.[18] Passing Tegoshi, he saw far to the north a mountain white with snow. 'What mountain is that?' he asked, and learned that it was Mount Shirane in the land of Kai. At this, Shigehira repressed his tears to recite:

oshikaranu	Though I do not lament
inochi naredomo	that life will end
kyō made zo	I have not fully lived

| *tsurenaki kai no* | until today, seeing at last |
| *shirane o mo mitsu* | white Shirane Mountain[19] |

He passed the barrier of Kiyomi, and now he was in the wide plains skirting Mount Fuji. Northward soared emerald mountains, the wind soughed lonely in the pines; to the south blue ocean stretched, waves thundered on the shore. On he went past Ashigara Mountain, whose god first sang the song that goes, 'If you loved me you'd be thin with pining / so I can tell you never really did'.[20] On then through Koyurugi Wood, over Mariko River, past the bays of Koiso and Ōiso, Yatsumato, Togami-ga-hara and Mikoshi Cape, and though they took their time along the way, slowly the days mounted up, and so he came at last to Kamakura.

11

The Tale of Saigyō

Once the Genpei Wars described in The Tale of the Heike *had shifted the seat of power from the imperial court in Kyoto to Kamakura in the East, the home of the new military government, there was much coming and going between the two distant centres. Suddenly the highway that linked them was a busy road thronged with military men, commoners and even the upper classes. Travel, until now a relatively rare experience for the literate classes, took on a fresh and vivid reality for many.*

Although civil power was firmly in the hands of the Kamakura government, back at the old Capital the emperor continued to play the role of figurehead, and the culture of his court remained the prestigious ideal. Waka poetry, the quintessential literary form, in fact reached what was arguably the highest point in its history in the early decades of the Kamakura period, with the great imperial poetry collection known as the Shinkokinshū. The greatest number of poems in this celebrated anthology (94 of a total of 1,978) were composed by a monk named Saigyō (1118–90). This alone was enough to ensure him a prominent place in Japanese literature, but it does little to explain why Saigyō became and has remained one of Japan's most loved poets and legendary figures.

The story of his life is surely part of that explanation. Saigyō was born into the minor aristocracy, and as a young man served the court in the relatively lowly position of palace guard, although legend assigned him rather more status at court as well as a doomed love affair with a high-ranking lady that ostensibly lay behind his decision at twenty-three to take the tonsure and 'leave the world'. Thereafter, like Nōin[1] before him, he became a wandering monk who spent considerable time on the road (legend largely ignores the lengthy periods he spent attached to various temples or coming and going from the Capital). Many of the poems he wrote seem to be born of this itinerant life, which he depicted at some-times unusual length in the introductory headnotes to the poems.[2] *His poetry was not only skilful but moving, with a striking directness and simplicity of diction, and with recurring key images, particularly the moon and cherry blossoms, that became his emblem for later generations. For all these reasons, the romantic figure of Saigyō, wandering monk and poet of moon and blossoms, took hold in the public imagination and influenced future literary travellers down the ages, not least Bashō.*

Perhaps another reason for Saigyō's popularity was that he seemed to embody and offer an emotionally satisfying answer to the times he lived in. He was thirty-eight (already approaching what was considered old age at the time) when Kyoto was first beset by the armed insurgencies that led on to the terrible Genpei Wars and brought the Heian period to an end, and he not only witnessed these traumatic decades but was closely concerned with the fate of some of those whose lives were ruined by them.[3] *The abrupt transition he had experienced, from an assured future in the ruling-class establishment of the old Heian court to a hard life on the road at the mercy of the uncertainties of fate, seemed to mir-ror the shocking and destabilizing transitions that the nation was experiencing. Yet as one of the pre-eminent poets of his day, Saigyō carried with him into this new world the reassuring continuities of the old high culture. Still more importantly, both his poems and his life attested to his embrace of the Buddhist Way, whose teachings offered a convincing answer to the bewildering experiences of the times. Given all this, it is hardly surprising that Saigyō became a figure of legend for this precarious age. What clinched his transition from mortal poet to some-thing approaching saint was a famous poem that uncannily foresaw the ideal death that he was widely believed to have achieved, 'in spring beneath the blossoms / under the second month's full moon'.*[4]

As with The Tale of the Heike, *it is likely that this and other stories about Saigyō were circulating in the early years after his death. It took the hand of an anonymous and talented writer, however, to transform all this at some unknown date into a work that would help to carry his legend down the ages, a work commonly known as* The Tale of Saigyō (Saigyō monogatari). *The structure of* The Tale of Saigyō *follows the same fundamental principle as that of* The Ise Tales[5] *three centuries earlier – the construction of narratives about a poet, built around a ser-ies of his contextualized poems.*[6] The Tale of Saigyō, *however, is a far more sophisticated and coherent work than its forebear. It describes and, where it suits the author's purposes, freely imagines episodes in Saigyō's life to create a sketchy and highly romanticized poetic biography – poetic in the sense that it not only depicts Saigyō above all as an idealized poet, but also depends for its structure on the poems which form the core of almost every episode, often reading more like an expanded form of the poetry collection style of* kotobagaki-*plus-poem than a work conceived as connected narrative.*

Indeed on every level, including that of the prose itself, The Tale of Saigyō *is essentially conceived of as belonging to the world of poetry. In this it bears a familial relationship with the heightened writing of the* michiyuki *journey description style seen in the roughly contemporary* Tale of the Heike.[7] *Lament and journey, always a natural pairing in Japanese literature, found a new expressive form in this age when both lamenting and journeying were touching the lives of so many.*

But Saigyō's journeying, which forms the core of The Tale of Saigyō, *also took on an extra meaning for the creators of his legend. As the popularity of Buddhism spread in this uncertain age, Saigyō was increasingly seen through a Buddhist lens, as a saintly wandering monk who had 'relinquished the world' and embraced the truth of the teaching of Impermanence. The complicated textual history of* The Tale of Saigyō[8] *strongly suggests that creative copyists increasingly reinterpreted the Saigyō figure in sternly Buddhist terms, as seen in the following extract in the extended description of his saintly victimhood at Tenchū Crossing, and in his encounter with the hermit of Musashino. Such scenes, which bear no known relation to the historical Saigyō, increasingly overlaid but never displaced the original poet figure that Saigyō's poems themselves had helped to create, and served to increase the potency of his legend down the centuries.*

The following extract takes Saigyō from one utamakura *site to another along what was by now the well-travelled Tōkaidō road, although the depiction is in purely poetic terms.[9] His journey continued into the remote north of Michinoku, still largely unvisited except by the more intrepid travellers, but this extract leaves him at the famous Shirakawa Barrier.[10]* (See Map 3)

FROM *THE TALE OF SAIGYŌ*

Saigyō had long felt an urge to visit the East. 'Who knows how short life may be,' he thought, so he made his preparations to depart, and a number of close friends gathered to send him on his way, beguiling themselves through the night with songs and music and together soaking their sleeves with the tears of parting.

It happened that on that night the moon was particularly splendid.

kimi mo toe	Grieve for me, and I
ware mo shinobamu	will think of you with love
saki-databa	whoever first departs this world
tsuki o katami ni	holding as keepsake in the mind
omoi-idetsutsu	this moon

He travelled eastward for many days, until he came to the place known as Tenchū Crossing in the land of Tōtōmi. Here he found a ferry filled with warriors that happened to be just departing, and he hurried aboard, but the large numbers already on board clearly made everyone worry for their safety, and they cried, 'Hey you, get off! Off with you, monk!' When Saigyō, taking this for nothing more than the banter that went with ferry crossings, paid no attention, they proceeded to take a whip to him and beat him mercilessly.

Blood pouring from his head, Saigyō was a pitiful sight indeed. Yet he showed not the least resentment of this treatment, simply clasping his hands in humble apology as he retreated from the boat. The monk who was his travelling companion wept with sorrow to witness this, but Saigyō gazed quietly at the weeping man, and then he spoke.

'This was what I meant when I said to you as we left the Capital that we would surely meet with pain and sorrow along the way. We must begrudge nothing, though our very limbs are severed, though we lose our very life. If we were to cling to our old attitudes, we should never have shaved our heads and dyed our robes black. The Buddha's heart holds compassion above all things, and saves poor sinful creatures such as us. If we exact revenge on our enemies, our anger and resentment will never cease. There is a teaching that says, "If you repay your enemy with kindness, your enemy will be extinguished," and in the sutras it is said, "A single evil thought will destroy countless *kalpas* of good deeds."[11] Then there is the Bodhisattva Fukyō, who ignored the pain of his beating but worshipped his attackers with the words, "Rather than despise and hate you, I have the deepest respect for you, for you are all on the path to becoming Bodhisattvas."[12] All these reveal the true nature of the Buddhist practice, which puts others before self. No doubt more events like this will continue to occur on our journey. This is painful for us both, so you had best leave me and return to the Capital.'

And so they parted and went their separate ways, east and west. Poor companion, he remembered well how Saigyō had been in former days, so it was only natural that he should grieve to see him treated like this.

As for Saigyō, though he had had the strength of heart to send his companion away, his heart was sore, for the man had been a good friend for many years.

All alone he travelled on, and came to Kotonomama Shrine at the hard mountain pass of Saya no Nakayama.[13] *Whatever the forms we see, whatever the sounds we hear, all can only lead astray. The Buddha cannot be apprehended with the senses,*[14] he intoned by way of prayer, and with that he crossed the pass, composing this:

toshi takete	Life has brought me back
mata koyu beshi to	to this dark pass of Saya.
omoiki ya	Little did I think
inochi narikeri	grown old
saya no nakayama	I would cross this way again

On he went[15]   alone and pierced by stormy winds   breasting the world's rough waves and floods of grief   great as the great Ōi River   tears and the dews of travel   together moistening his priestly sleeves   nor could he ever wring them dry   and so he arrived at a lodging place called Okabe in the land of Suruga, where he paused to rest at a dilapidated little temple building.

Happening to glance toward the back door, he saw an old cypress-bark rain hat hanging there. Intrigued, he looked more closely. On the hat were written the words: *I have no love of life or limb, I long only for the supreme Way.* Seeing this, he recalled that back in the Capital that past spring, when a companion in the Way had set off on a religious journey to the East, they had together made a vow that if one were to die first, he would return to this world and lead the other to paradise. Saddened at their parting, Saigyō had written these very words on his friend's hat as a keepsake.

The hat lay here before him, but his friend was nowhere to be seen. Sorrowing, Saigyō said to himself, 'Yes, it is the world's way that one or other should go before, "like dew on leaf-tip or the drop beneath".'[16]

Restraining his tears, he asked someone at his lodgings about the hat. 'A travelling monk came through here from the Capital this spring,' he was told, 'but he became ill and died in this building, and the dogs took him and gnawed him to pieces. You can no doubt find his remains somewhere hereabout.'

Saigyō searched, but could find nothing.

kasa wa ari	The hat remains
sono mi wa ika ni	but where now
narinuramu	is the body it once sheltered?
aware hakanaki	Ah sad and transient world
ame no shita kana	beneath the sky

And so, deep in thought, he travelled on, pierced by the chill winds of early autumn, moved at times by the sight of the wild moors, hearing the song of autumn insects in the grasses, and the cries of wild geese winging south from Koshi, though for him there could be no waiting for the message they might carry.[17]

Forlorn at heart, he composed:

aki tatsu to	No one announces
hito wa tsugenedo	that autumn has come
shirarekeri	but I know it

miyama no suso no	in the wind that brushes
kaze no keshiki ni	the landscape at Miyama's hem
obotsukana	Why is it –
aki wa ika naru	this vague
yue no areba	ungraspable
suzoro ni mono no	autumn sadness
kanashikaruramu	in things?
shiragumo o	Wings spread
tsubasa ni kakete	with the white clouds
tobu kari no	the far wild geese
kadode no omo no	yearn for their companion
tomo shitau kana	grounded in this household
	field

Passing along the mountain path of Utsu, where once Narihira lost his way among the vines and maples, and where he wrote of meeting 'neither in reality nor yet in dreams',[18] he thought with longing of the poets of old.

Arriving at the barrier gate of Kiyomi, the scene of the offshore waves that shattered on the rocks and the moonlight-flooded tide seemed to him still more wonderful than he had heard tell, and he composed:

kiyomigata	Kiyomigata
oki no iwa kosu	where the bright autumn moon
shiranami ni	tosses light
hikari o kawasu	with the white waves
aki no yo no tsuki	washing the offshore rocks

Approaching the land of Suruga, he felt the truth of Narihira's poem that asks if Mount Fuji knows the season,[19] yet gazing up at that distant peak of Mount Fuji he saw a somehow knowing smoke rising from its top. The mountain was half hidden in cloud, lakes brimmed at its feet, to the south stretched a broad plain and before it spread a rich expanse of sea with all its hoards for the fishermen.

Here he felt he could forget a while the trials of his long journey

from the Capital over the many mountains and rivers, bays and
seas.

kaze ni nabiku	Fuji's smoke
fuji no kemuri no	trails lingering in the wind
sora ni kiete	skyward and is gone
yukue mo shiranu	as my thoughts go drifting
waga omoi kana	out into nothing

itsu to naki	Floating thoughts
omoi wa fuji no	drift frail
kemuri nite	as Fuji's smoke
madoromu hodo ya	dozing
ukishima-ga-hara	over Floating Island Plain

Approaching Mount Ashigara, he recalled the long-ago words of
Sanekata, 'since Ashigara is that mountain's name', and the poet
who wrote, 'Deep among white-misted mountains / a bird's single
call'.[20] Just then, a gust of chill wintry wind pierced him through.

yamazato wa	Late autumn
aki no sue ni zo	in this mountain village –
omoishiru	now I learn
kanashikarikeri	the full force of sadness
kogarashi no kaze	from the wintry wind

As he passed through Togami Moor at a place called Ōba in the
land of Sagami, the mist over the moor parted a moment and a
stag's call carried to him on the wind.

e wa madou	Wife hidden
kuzu no shigemi ni	in the bewildering shelter
tsuma komete	of tangled vines
togami-ga-hara ni	the stag goes crying
ojika naku naru	over Togami Moor

At nightfall that evening, he heard the sudden sound of a snipe
rising from a nearby marsh.

Saigyō on his travels

kokoro naki	In autumn dusk a snipe
mi ni mo aware wa	lifts from the marsh
shirarekeri	and even this heart
shigi tatsu sawa no	that should no longer feel
aki no yūgure	feels the moment touch it[21]

Aimlessly lured on by moonlight, Saigyō made his way into the far land of Musashi. The moon within the glittering dew upon the plume grass tips scattered like jewels on the passing wind, and insects cried forlornly from deep in the bush clover. His mind was full of fond thoughts of the poets of old who asked the origin of Musashi's purple *murasaki* grasses, and as he went he murmured the old poem, 'This moon makes me forget the evening's lodgings / and journey on along tomorrow's path'.[22]

Five or six miles in from the path, he heard a distant voice chanting sutras. 'That's odd,' he thought, 'I heard that there was no human settlement for many miles beyond this point.' He set off to follow the voice, and found there a rough hut thatched with vine and reed, surrounded by a fence of bush clover, yellow valerian and many another autumn grass, with dry ferns spread against the eastern wall for

what seemed a sleeping place, while on the western wall was hung a picture of the Bodhisattva Fugen with before it the eight scrolls of the Lotus Sutra.[23] Everywhere in the garden, autum flowers bent low with dew, and the soft cries of autumn insects lent further pathos to the moving nature of the place. 'Who might ever call here?' he wondered, and indeed he found that the path petered out.

Peering in, he saw an old monk, surely over ninety, with snowy head and frosted brows, intoning the words, 'Reside in a quiet place, and pursue your Practice.'[24]

'Perhaps this is some kind of mountain sage,' Saigyō thought, bemused.

It was the night of the eighth month harvest moon, and the moonlight was indeed brilliant, so there was no mistaking this hermit's hut for some mere house tucked away from sight. He approached and stood before the old monk. They simply gazed at each other in mute astonishment, until eventually Saigyō asked, 'What manner of person are you, to live here like this?' But there was no reply.

Saigyō spoke again. 'I am from the Capital, and a yearning to see the East has brought me here. Finding the landscape of

Musashino far more moving even than I had heard tell of at
home, I made my way in here. I heard that no one lives for many
miles ahead. I long to hear the story of your past, and how you
manage to live here.'

Thereupon the old man said, 'I was once a retainer in the service of Empress Yūhōmon'in,[25] and when the Empress passed
away, I became a monk and travelled the land pursuing my practice. Arriving here, I felt that this was a place where I could retreat
from the world and follow the Buddhist Way, and I have now
been here more than sixty years, since the age of twenty-nine. I
have chanted the sutra more than seventy thousand times.'

Saigyō too was well acquainted with the circumstances of the
Empress,[26] and together they talked and wrung their tear-soaked
monkish sleeves. Loath as they were to part, at dawn Saigyō rose
to go.

ikade ware	How might I
kiyoku kumoranu	perfect the moonlight mirror
mi to narite	of my soul
kokoro no tsuki no	till it is burnished
kage o migakamu	to unclouded purity?
ikaga subeki	What's to be done?
yo ni araba koso	Were I still in the common world
yo o mo sutete	I would despair again
ana uki no yo ya to	and turn away
sara ni itowamu	lamenting its sorrows
aki wa tada	This evening alone
koyoi bakari no	should bear the name
na narikeri	of Autumn
onaji kumoi ni	though the moon rises pure
tsuki wa sumedomo	into the same skies of other
	nights

Going on into Michinoku, he stopped the night at a place called
the Shirakawa Barrier. Here he recalled Nōin's poem, 'Though
with the rising mists / of spring I rose / and left the Capital / the

autumn wind blows chill / at Shirakawa Barrier Gate',[27] and as the moon was particularly pure and beautiful that night, he wrote on a pillar of the old barrier house:

shirakawa no	In Shirakawa's barrier house
sekiya o tsuki no	the filtering moon beams
moru kara ni	now are its only guards
hito no kokoro o	but they halt
tomuru narikeri	the heart

12

Senjūshō

The anonymous collection of Buddhist tales called Senjūshō *('The Collection') seems to have been written around the middle of the thirteenth century. This probably makes it roughly contemporaneous with some versions of the* Tale of Saigyō, *but these stories present the same protagonist in a startlingly different guise. Where the* Tale of Saigyō *is primarily a literary work, and depicts Saigyō above all as the romantic figure of a wandering poet-monk,* Senjūshō *is written with austerely Buddhist intent and Saigyō is transfigured accordingly – in these tales 'Saigyō' is no more than a shadowy and occasional figure behind the first person voice of some of the stories, a wandering monk who writes with feeling of the saintly hermits he has encountered in his travels to far places. Yet despite his peripheral and nebulous role, the implied presence of Saigyō as author of the work was enough to earn it an important place in the evolving Saigyō legends that proliferated during the following centuries, and it was only in the early twentieth century that his presumed authorship was definitively dismissed.*

Senjūshō *belongs to the world of Buddhist tales or* setsuwa *that emerged in the late Heian period, when Japanese Buddhism began to extend its reach beyond the temples and monasteries and strive to make itself more accessible and relevant to the general populace. These tales often combined the entertainment of story with the serious intent of moral and spiritual teaching, and essentially grew out of an oral rather than a written tradition. In both content and style the tales in* Senjūshō *bear a close relationship to sermons: they first set out the story of a holy man, either as straightforward biography or as someone encountered by the narrating wandering monk, and this is followed by a stirring commentary intended to move the audience to tears of veneration at his sanctity.*

At the heart of these stories is the ideal of a particular form of extreme Buddhist asceticism popular at the time: the practice of the solitary hermit who rejects the social world (including that of the temple) and immerses himself in the purifying powers of nature, living alone and meditating in a cave or temporary shelter with only the bare essentials in clothing and food. These men were frequently wanderers who had relinquished all attachment to the illusion of stability and home, and sought out places that were particularly conducive to the act of 'purifying the heart' and thereby attaining enlightenment. Wild seashores and deep mountains were the ideal, although a hermit could if necessary practice reclusion surrounded by others, as does Shinpan in story 5:9, as long as he remained undiscovered. The key was to 'hide one's virtue' and appear a fool, and as much as possible to avoid all social interaction.

This urge to solitude and anonymity, however, was compromised by another Buddhist teaching, one that seems to have been a direct inspiration for Senjūshō. The concept of zuiki – to attain joy by witnessing and learning from the virtue of another – and more generally of the related kechien – to gain merit from contact with someone holy – encouraged one to seek out people of sanctity such as these holy men and either ask a teaching from them, as Saigyō does in 3:1, or establish contact in any way possible, as the villagers do in 5:9. These tales abound in stories of the desperate lengths the hermits went to in their efforts to escape attention and hide their virtue as the practice demanded, and to attain peace and solitude for their practice. Senjūshō is in fact written to provide a vicarious form of zuiki for its audience, by making vivid for them the experience of discovering and witnessing these holy men, and stirring the feelings of joyful reverence and gratitude that such contact would produce. Much as it sometimes exhorts readers and listeners to pursue such extreme practices themselves, its fundamental aim is to provoke the religious awe of the witness and thereby 'transfer merit' to a lay audience.

It is Senjūshō's particular genius to introduce to many of these tales the framing device of the narrator wandering monk, and to implicitly and occasionally explicitly identify him as Saigyō.[1] This allows an audience not only to hear the tale of a holy man but to hear it ostensibly from the lips of someone who himself is worthy of reverence and emulation. The wandering narrator monk is an intermediary figure, *an active seeker with the authority to approach and interact with holy men and bring the merit he thereby acquires back to the realm of the common people.*[2] *The typical Saigyō figure of legend is distinguished by being both approachable and 'other', both frail human and something close to saint, and thus is ideally suited to the role of narrator of these tales, which in turn helped to reinforce these characteristics of Saigyō's legendary figure.*[3]

Other aspects of the legendary Saigyō figure also fit well with Senjūshō. *His dual role of both poet and monk introduces a degree of movingly poetic sensibility to many of the stories he narrates, elevating them by association with his poetry and pointing up the responsiveness to landscape that also underlies the recluse ideal (as in the opening scene of 3:1). The poignancy of the forlorn and sensitive wandering poet-monk depicted in the* Tale of Saigyō *adds weight to the affecting sermon sections of the* Senjūshō *tales, with their frequent appeals to* aware, *a word that functions on the level of both poetic and religious sensibility.*[4] *The frequent reference to tears embodies this; the tears of* Senjūshō's *narrator are not simply the joyous tears of* zuiki, *but also echo the new medieval sensibility already seen in the more poetic sections of* The Tale of the Heike *and in* The Tale of Saigyō, *that is characterized by a sensitive embrace of sorrow and suffering. The tears that blur his eyes so that his brush falters (3:1) also blur the boundary between poetic and religious sensibilities.*

The two tales presented here give an idea of the varying styles of Senjūshō. *In the first (3:1), Saigyō the poet-narrator is clearly identified, travelling with a companion as he does in* The Tale of Saigyō *as well as in the* kotobagaki *to some of the poems in his own poetry collection. The hermit too is revealed as a man of poetic sensibility, their exchange of poems being typical of the poetic exchanges customary in establishing mutual credentials as cultivated people, and his poetic credentials are further hinted at by his association with the* utamakura Matsushima.[5] *Tale 5:9 follows the more usual form of the* setsuwa *tale in having no framing narrator. It offers a picture of the type of the hounded hermit who retreats into increasingly extreme isolation, although even here there is a hint of poetic sensibility in his choice of the* utamakura Utsu *for his retreat.*[6] (See Map 1)

FROM *SENJŪSHŌ*

3:1 The Holy Man Kenbutsu in his cave retreat

Once long ago, I set off with another recluse in the direction of the Koshi Road, and in the land of Noto,[7] in Inayatsu, I found a particularly enchanting place where mountain and sea mingled. It was far from any human habitation. The rocky cliffs were sheer, the shoreline wild. Deeply drawn by it all, I paused to rest a while and look around. Above me towered the crags, the trees and plants grew in delightful fashion, and there I glimpsed a most wonderful-looking cave.

Longing to know more I hurried over, and found there a monk of about forty sitting in meditation. This cave faced south, and the sea lay spread before it. The monk looked most pure of heart. He wore only a light unlined robe about his shoulders, and this seemed the sum of his possessions.

I was enthralled. 'Where might you be from?' I asked. 'You must find this a splendid place to live.'

Smiling a little, he spoke the following poem:

naniwagata	Who could think this
muradatsu matsu mo	a splendid place to live
mienu ura o	when this bay does not offer
koko sumiyoshi to	the crowding pines along the shore
tare ka omowan	of famous Naniwa[8]

Somehow this touched me, and I responded with:

matsu ga ne no	Seeing the waves that wash
kishi utsu nami ni	over these pine tree roots
arawarete	along the shore
koko sumiyoshi to	I cannot help but feel
omou bakari zo	this place is 'good to live'

The hermit in his turn was very taken with this.

I proceeded to question him. 'So what name might you go by?' I asked. 'And do you live here always?'

'Well,' he replied, 'people call me The Hermit of Tsuki-Matsushima. And no, this is not my permanent home. I come here regularly to live for ten days each month. During that time, I eat nothing.'

Awed and astonished, I realized that this must be the man known as Saint Kenbutsu. Nervously, I introduced myself. 'My name is Saigyō.'

'I have heard of such a man,' he said.

But we could not go on exchanging pleasantries in this way, and so reluctantly and tearfully I left him, after asking for a holy teaching to keep in my heart. On my way back from my travels I did not find him there, so I took the extra four days and went to Matsushima, where I spent two months in his temple.

All this rises again before me as I write of it now, and my tears pour faster to recall it till I can no longer see where to place my brush upon the page. What true integrity this man had, to turn his back on lovely Matsushima, such a holy and tranquil place where the heart might rest pure, and cross all the mountains and waters to distant Noto to deepen his meditations in the piney winds and wash his pure heart in the pounding waves. Could anything compare to such an exalted spirit – to come without companion, bringing no sustenance to preserve his life, and live like this for ten whole days? Perhaps somehow it could be done in spring and summer, but once the cold set in, if he were to die exhausted and frozen there ... oh it breaks the heart to think of that snowy cave of his beneath the winter skies of the Koshi Road.

How does it come about that people with the same urgings in their hearts should be as different from each other as if vast mountains separated them? For those whose urge to follow the Way is deep, it is the accepted thing to turn one's back on the world and live in some tranquil temple. But to leave behind you the utter calm and purity of the Matsushima temple, where the only voices are the soft twitter of birds and the wind that sometimes calls about the roof tiles and sweeps the garden clean; to live on a lonely beach in the teeth of the sea wind, the sleeves of your bare hemp robe tossed in those gales – *even this heart, that should no longer feel*[9] is moved to tears. His own disciples would not have known his whereabouts; there would be none to come calling on him. How deeply moving to think that though he was in lovely Matsushima he chose to disappear for the first ten days of every month, and that it was in that far cave in Noto that he chose to live. During this time the temple was in the charge of a disciple, and none would have been surprised at these absences since it seems they happened every month.

5:9 Concerning the priest Shinpan

In recent times there was a high priest named Shinpan, who lived for many years in Yamashina Temple.[10]

In his fifties, having arrived at old age, his urge to spurn the world grew deeper, and he left his temple and made his way to Shiga in the land of Ōmi, where he found a place good for secluded meditation, and there he built a scanty hut and lived in purity of heart. Though others were around him, before his hut lay open land, behind it rose a mountain path, a sparkling waterfall tumbled nearby, and the stream that flowed down past his dwelling was rare and beautiful to see.

Those who lived nearby drew their water from this waterfall. One day a group of little girls came along to fetch water, and as they passed his hut, singing vague snatches of song and chattering aimlessly together, one remarked, 'There's a holy hermit living in that hut, you know!' After this, a crowd gathered there to see and venerate him.

'I left my temple in order to purify my heart in peace and quiet and hide my virtues from the world,' Shinpan said to himself in dismay, 'but now they have come to light again here.' And so he set off wandering again with no direction in mind, walking aimlessly from place to place, striving above all to appear a worthless fool. Word has it that he made his way deep into the mountains of Utsu, where he purified his mind. He would come out to a village from time to time and spread his sleeve to beg for food, then retreat far into the mountains once more.

Intrigued to know where he went, one day some people hid to

watch him on his way and followed him to find that he pushed on and on, deeper and deeper into the mountains, to a ravine where a stream ran pure; here he sat facing south, as still as sleep, hands clasped in prayer before him.

Those who had gone to see proceeded to tell others. 'A true follower of the Way indeed!' they exclaimed. 'If this is how he lives, what will he do when the rainy season comes?' and they set about making him a hut for when the time came. Someone must go and enquire about his scant needs for food, they decided, and another messenger was sent into the mountains, but though he asked all manner of questions and did his very best to persuade him, the hermit replied not a word.

The messenger eventually arrived back at the village and explained what had happened. 'So you see, he really does seem to be a marvellous fellow,' he finished. 'Why don't we all go in together this time and talk to him?' and he set off back there with a great crowd – but the hermit was nowhere to be seen. How can this be? they wondered, and they went off in different directions and tramped all over the mountain in search of him, but there was not a trace.

A long time later, one of these villagers had business that took him on a journey through Kō in Echigo, and hidden there among the crowds in the town he spied the hermit. 'How do you come to be here?' he asked, but the hermit rang his little bell pretending to be mute, and said not a word. Having been discovered yet again, the story has it that he set off on his wanderings once more, this time towards the sea.

A moving tale indeed – that this man, once a high-ranking priest in Yamashina Temple revered by three thousand monks, now mingles with the dust of some far distant land, his virtues hidden from the world. Pointless to worship all the hundred million buddhas – if your own heart is not pure, all offerings are surely futile. The true enlightenment of the Bodhisattva lies only in this, to awaken your heart from the dream of illusion. Instead of making holy images or building fine worship halls, what you should do is purify your heart with the Buddhist Truth. If your urge to seek the Truth springs from wisdom, how can you fail to gain enlightenment? An awe-inspiring thought indeed! It is said that one gains joy from taking to heart the good deeds of another, and I can vouch that it is indeed so.

As to Shinpan, legend tells that he returned to Yamato, ragged and emaciated, and at the foot of sacred Mount Miwa he turned to face the east and died as if drifting into sleep, with on his lips a prayer to the Kasuga deity.[11]

13

Journey along the Sea Road

By the early thirteenth century, the Heian period's court-centred culture had given way to the new cultural forces set in motion by the rise of Kamakura's military regime. The road that linked the old Capital (Kyoto) with the new centre of government (Kamakura) was suddenly thronged with travellers,[1] among them a monk who in 1223 made the journey to Kamakura and back on foot and wrote a strikingly beautiful poetic account of his journey known as Journey along the Sea Road (Kaidōki).[2]

Journey along the Sea Road *is anonymous. Its author tells us only that he is a man of about fifty, living simply on the north-eastern outskirts of the old Capital with his aged mother. Having recently taken the tonsure and become a lay monk, he finally responds to the lure of all he has heard about distant Kamakura and sets off to see it for himself, apparently from sheer curiosity. His account is indeed full of the passing interests of the journey, and provides fascinating glimpses of life on the road. These are never more than glimpses, however.* Journey along the Sea Road *is written as a literary, not a factual account, and its details are carefully chosen to that end. Structurally, it follows the time-honoured tradition of moving from one poem-centred episode or place (often an* utamakura*) to the next along the route, and its sensibility is essentially poetic. With* Journey along the Sea Road *we enter the realm of the great medieval travel chronicles (*kikō*), self-consciously literary works that combine elements of the diary and poetic anthology traditions to create a lyrical and occasionally philosophical account of a personal journey.*

Journey along the Sea Road *is not only one of the earliest, but also among the longest and certainly the most strenuously 'literary' of the travel chronicles. For all his humility, its author was clearly a highly cultured man with a deep appreciation of the Chinese classics, as befitted an educated gentleman of the time. Writing at a time when the male tradition of* kanbun *Chinese writing was increasingly mingling with the native Japanese* kana *style that traditionally belonged to the world of women's writing and of Japanese* waka *poetry,* Journey along the Sea Road *represents a fascinating experiment in combining the two. Although it belongs to the* waka *rather than the Chinese poetry tradition, and is written in the native language, its prose bears the strong imprint of Chinese literary prose.[3] Parallel phrases balance each other in echoing or contrasting imagery and vocabulary that often derive directly from Chinese writing, so that the work sometimes reads almost like a translation from the Chinese. The result is a richly ornate style very different from the native lyrical prose style of a work such as* The Tale of Saigyō. *The elevated and rhythmically subtle prose of* Journey along the Sea Road *achieves an elegance and beauty that translation can do no more than gesture towards.*

Yet Journey along the Sea Road'*s stated aim is to record 'what has moved me' (*mono no aware*),[4] which places it firmly within the native* waka *lyric tradition. In fact, for all his stylistic experimentation, the author is carrying forward the literary inheritance of the earlier recluse poet-monks such as Saigyō, Nōin and Zōki[5] who combined the practice of* waka *with travel or wandering as essentially a form of religious austerity. The tone of* Journey along the Sea Road *makes clear that this journey is not undertaken for mere pleasure and interest, despite his self-effacing statement in the preface. Just as his account is far from being the simple record written in 'clumsy words' that he humbly claims it to be, the journey itself is in fact largely depicted in sombre colours, as a rigorous experience that befits the austerities of the wandering monk – 'for pillow the wayside grasses of life's fate, my monk's robes chill in the cloudy dawn, mat spread over mossy stones'. The traveller's musings turn again and again to Buddhist themes.[6] Although the author bears little similarity to the austere Buddhist ascetics depicted in* Senjūshō, Journey along the Sea Road *can be read as essentially a meditation on the Buddhist truth of Impermanence, as embodied in the experience of the road. Here, as in* The Tale of Saigyō *(which was probably first created at much the same time), poetic and religious sensibilities merge in the depiction of the journey.*

Despite its various forebears,[7] Journey along the Sea Road *is one of the key progenitors of the travel chronicle genre that flowered in the Kamakura period and throughout the middle ages and achieved its final great statement in Bashō's* The Narrow Road of Oku. *Its unknown author was perhaps the first to follow Zōki's early experiment in* Ionushi's Pilgrimage to Kumano[8] *by expanding the poetry anthology into a semi-continuous personal account of a journey, merging it fully with the diary form to produce an introspective and poetic prose travel account enriched by a religious sensibility. Others would quickly follow, but this work stands out both for its remarkable prose style (an impressive experiment which, however, had little direct influence on the travel chronicles that followed) and for its lasting importance to later travellers, who were still carrying precious copies of it on their journeys centuries later.*

By far the largest part of Journey along the Sea Road *is devoted to chronicling the journey from the old Capital to Kamakura, but it also includes a perfunctory description of his stay there and journey home, in which Buddhist themes increasingly predominate. The description of the journey proper is also prefaced by a section describing his circumstances, followed by a glowing description of the lure of Kamakura and the busy highway, and a quick poetic sketch of his own trip that serves as an introductory summary of what follows. The present extract includes part of this prefatory material, and follows the journey along the Tōkaidō as far as the great* utamakura *of Yatsuhashi.*

The prose of Journey along the Sea Road *is rich with literary allusion that creates a density of texture impossible to convey in translation. Only some of the more important allusions and passing quotations are highlighted. Where the allusions, particularly to Chinese literature, become too dense I have omitted them altogether.* Journey along the Sea Road *assumes a readership schooled in the Chinese and Japanese classics,[9] which makes it largely unapproachable in Japan today except by scholars in the field. Its evocative beauty deserves a wider audience.* (See Maps 2 and 3)

FROM *JOURNEY ALONG THE SEA ROAD*

[...] Inns are thronged with travellers coming and going, high and low, men and women, who crowd the road to Kamakura, weaving the work of court and government to and fro, through peace and through upheaval, along the length of the highway's clattering loom. Fool that I am, I had long heard of all this with indifference. And how many more days did I then spend merely talking of it? The boat of my heart had gone rowing out in fancy, while I had yet to dip a real oar into the waves of those many miles of sea road. My thoughts raced ahead down the highway like some unruly horse, though I had not yet plied my whip in fact over the border and into those cloudy distances. Now, however, chance came my way, and suddenly I was making plans for that far and solitary journey.

I set out one morning in the beginning of the fourth month of Jōō (1223), leaving the Capital in the early hours. Much though I had loathed my miserable hut until that day, now that I was leaving it *I felt a sudden fondness*, and I stayed loitering there until the temple bells sounded first light, when finally I tore myself away.

Winding south along Awataguchi's sunken road, I made my way towards the Ōsaka Barrier, while to my north the nine-tiered pagoda[10] slipped away and was lost to sight. Descending through the conifers of Matsuzaka Slope a pine torch lit my way, then in the dawn light I passed by pale Shinomiya Stream. Crossing the border at Koseki, I went on down towards Ōtsu Bay. I turned to see behind me to the left the gate of Sekidera Temple, my eyes startled by those fierce sculptures guarding either side;[11] crossing eastward over Seta Bridge, I was chilled by the foaming waves that raced below. The boats out on the lake set my heart yearning after them, but I hastened my horse on through the fields with whip in hand.

On, on I went, and the Capital withdrew into the distance. Ahead, a far blur of forest – *the merest tufts of young spring herbs* those trees seemed from a distance. Behind, the mountains fell away, now *buried deep in cloud*. Already the setting sun was slanting into evening, and a dark rain beat incessantly on my rain hat. Wringing my sleeves, I tasted for the first time the poignant sorrows of travel. I slept in a mountain lodging and left before the dew was gone; daybreak brought *a melancholy landscape*. Then a night beside water and away in the morning wind; a cheerless evening. Pines and yet more pines, mists high and low swathing a boulder-strewn path; then coming to water and still more water, *deep or shallow* the waves lapping the long embankment's shore.

Below the bridge at Hamana I pledged *what my heart held dear*; at Kiyomi's border gate I left my haunting longings and walked on. Seeking the smoke from Fuji's peak, I saw instead only December's snows still blowing there; in quest of the vines on Utsu's mountain path, I found that ancient tale gone like a dream, and only the wind's cry to startle me. Soft emerald banners swayed beneath every tree, soothing the sufferings of the passing traveller, while at each night's stopping place the woven *grasses of the traveller's pillow* lulled his sleep. *On, on I travelled, farther still*,[12] the delights of mountain, river, moor and bank growing yet deeper, *stronger and ever stronger*, while my life seemed to lengthen through the pleasures of seaside town and forest hamlet.

Perhaps it was the outstanding interest of this particular road among the four,[13] or perhaps that this journey of mine as solitary monk was my first, but where even seasoned travellers must pause to admire, I as a newcomer could not repress my delight. Yet that delight was *mixed with melancholy*, for I had left behind me an aged mother returned to infancy, with the uncertain promise that we would meet again. Oh what a wicked thing to do, to leave her and go drifting on my way, *a floating cloud* straying upon the skyroads, casting this dew-frail life to the wandering winds!

No one I met along the road knew me. Warmly though we spoke together, we went our separate ways. The long journey tired me out, and for ten days or more exhaustion overcame me. When I came at last to Yui Beach,[14] I paused and rested there three hours. As the sun sank into the west, yearning thoughts of home filled me and I longed for that reunion; then with the moon that rose in the eastern sky my thoughts turned to the eastern city ahead, and worries crowded in.

And so I have penned poems to speak my many thoughts, and written of the feelings of the journey. What I write here favours neither prose nor poetry; I simply aim to record how I have been drawn to these far places and what has moved me there, and I beg you to forgive my clumsy words.

I left the Capital at dawn on the fourth day of the fourth month. Meeting with rain that morning, I paused a while before crossing Seta Bridge, and went on again in a sorry state. As I went, my thoughts were of my aged mother left alone, her perilous days numbered.

omoi-oku	If fate decrees
hito ni ōmi no	that I will see again
chigiri araba	she whom I leave with love
ima kaeri-kon	this is the way I will return
seta no nakamichi	across the Bridge of Seta

The rain grew heavier once I crossed the bridge, and the grassy path over the moors was drenched. Miles on through the fields, I edged past other travellers coming along the track; passing a little hamlet, a strange dog barked madly after me. There I was, new to my journey, and furthermore soaked in the pouring rain. In no time my spirits had sunk into gloom to match the weather.

tabi-goromo	The sodden sleeves
madaki mo narenu	of this travelling cloak as yet
sode no ue ni	so new upon me
nuru-beki mono to	drenched by the rain
ame wa furikinu	in lieu of travellers' tears

On through fields and past farmhouses, further and yet further, till I came upon a row of farmers digging a fallow field, their rhythmic work song as they hoed sounding like the cries of migrating geese. Peasant women were gathered in a household field plucking *egu* herbs just as in the old poem, and I in turn found my *sleeves wet with tears*.[15] Behind the house, the willow by the stream shifted in the breeze, and with it a nearby *egret's trailing crest feathers*; deutzia blossom foamed on the bamboo fence, and a *hototogisu* chanted softly.

Thus, eyes fixed on Mikami Peak beyond, I crossed the Yasu River.

ika ni shite	How might I too
sumu yasukawa no	flow clear as Yasu's waters
mizu naramu	though I pass my life
yo wataru bakari	sullied by suffering
kurushiki ya aru	in this mortal world?

I went through Wakasugi and on past Yokota Mountain. It is said that by starlight this mountain is rife with robbers, and I hurried on to avoid such an encounter.

haya sugiyo	Traveller, hasten on!
hito no kokoro mo	Here hearts have gone awry
yokotayama	as in the mountain's name,[16]
midori no hayashi	and lurking in the green wood's shade
kage ni kakurete	robbers lie hidden

The shadows of night found me at Ōoka, where I took lodgings. Having long since learned the untrustworthy nature of this world and taken monk's robes, it moved me still more to now lay my head on a traveller's pillow. I thought of the *rain that night in the thatched hut* on Mount Lu, so affecting in Bai Juyi's famous poem,[17] and shame filled me at how little my own rough poem could express the deep emotion of this night's rain on the thatch of my lodging here at Ōoka.

sumizome no	Lying here alone
koromo katashiki	upon my ink-black monk's robes
tabine shitsu	to sleep a traveller's sleep
itsushika ie o	brings home to me
izuru shirushi ni	the home that I have left

On the fifth day I left Ōoka and journeyed on, on through Uchi no Shirakawa and Soto no Shirakawa, until I came to Suzuka Mountain. From this mountain onwards the road enters the land of Ise. Clouds seethed from *the layered peaks*, while beyond rose wall upon wall of cliffs thousands of metres deep; a piney wind sang about the summits, and before my eyes danced the figure of old Ji Kang.[18] In the woods a few rare blossoms hid among spring leaves, or lay scattered in *a fine brocade*. And there was more. *The mountain goddess* dyed her summer robes in the leaves' emerald green; the valleys echoed back the singing birds.

The path twisted steeply down, and *my stumbling horse* grew weary with the stones. Indeed it could be truly said of this one mountain that it contains many – thousand-foot cliffs tower to block the vision, and a single stream flows in a hundred rapids, soaking the feet of many a traveller. *Mountain upon mountain, stream after stream*, so that even though I travelled the high road, half my journey and more was yet to come.

suzuka-gawa	Suzuka River
furusato tōku	I will cross your waves
yuku mizu ni	feet soaked in the foaming rapids
nurete iku se no	that flow on and away
nami o wataran	away from my far home

At dusk, I stopped at Suzuka's barrier gate. A half-moon hung above the peaks, *a drawn bow* left upon the path of the wild geese returning. Downstream the water shot to the valley floor, an arrow to pierce a tiger rock like that swift arrow of old.[19]

And so my nights mounted up along travellers' roads, for pillow the wayside grasses of life's fate, my monk's robes chill in the cloudy dawn, mat spread over mossy stones. The *wise pine reached out* like the heavens over me, but it was *my friend the bamboo* that sheltered me where I lay at night.

suzuka-yama	On Suzuka Mountain
sashite furusato	drifting to sleep I thought
omoine no	of the far home behind me
yumeji no sue ni	and travelled back down dream roads
miyako o zo tou	to the Capital again

On the sixth day, once the cock had crowed in the valley as in the ancient tales, I rose and left with the dawn. More than halfway now over the mountain, on I went downhill. Carved *walls of cliff* towered about me, *a home to soothe the virtuous heart*; streams poured through deep-cut channels, flowing rich and fast to *delight the wise*.

And so I came out among village and field, and walking among

the paddy fields I saw to left and right a vista of newly planted
rice. Some fields were tilled, some fallow, with flooded fields
of seedlings dotted among them. The water channels were also
broken here and there, and the water *drawn at will into each field*;
the seedlings along the rows of paddy paths were lifted by each
farmer for his planting. Rich smoke from farmhouse kitchens told
of the benevolence of our rulers, whose virtues in turn spring
from that earth they plough. The dragon god tends the rice with
his summer rains, while thunder and lightning have long brought
the rice to head, anticipating autumn. The farmers labouring
through the spring produce those taxes paid in full come autumn.
Thus does the whip lie idle in times of order, and the reeds that
would once have made it are left to grow fireflies instead.

nawashiro no	There in the mirrored surface
mizu ni utsurite	of new-planted flooded fields
miyuru kana	I see the cloudy face
inaba no kumo no	of coming autumn
aki no omokage	with its low-bent grain

The days passed and I yearned for home. Turning to look back
along my way, mountain and stream were indistinguishable – all
was cloud. I could tell east from west by the light of the sun's rise
and set, but the continual pause each evening only to set off once
more with the morning's light made it hard to dwell on the transient brevity of our nights and days. My feet lifted themselves
along, step after endless step, swallowing the sense of distance so
that I found myself thinking in hope that I would indeed return
from this far journey. But what brought me sorrow was my painful thoughts of what was past and to come, here on this road that
links the far Capital behind with the remote land ahead.

furusato o	Where among those mountains
yama no izuku ni	did I cross to come
hedate-kinu	from my far home?
miyako no sora o	White clouds have buried
uzumu shirakumo	the skies of the Capital

Night's shadow drew in, and I stayed in a place called Ichigae. Before me and below, the sea had carved an inlet thronged with the sea-dwelling fish protected by their god, while high behind me towered peaks, *the locks of the mountain goddess* combed with wind. The night waves beating on the rocks flashed with a thousand fiery lights, and in the dawn the flying squirrel's cry broke through *my lonely pillow's dreams*. Staying there, I found my solitary heart purified, but in the morning I set off in company, invited by a travelling friend.

matsu ga ne no	Pillowed on the rocky shore
iwa shiku iso no	among the pine roots
nami-makura	used though I am to travellers' beds
fushinarete mo ya	why do these waves of sorrow
sode ni kakaran	soak my sleeve?

On the seventh day I left Ichigae, and went down by ferry from a place called Tsushima Crossing. Fresh spring reeds spread green about me, a scene to hold captive Shun'e's *untethered horse*.[20] Waves rocked *the floating water chestnut leaves*, but not a sound rose from the heedless frogs. A passing oar flung drops onto my sleeve, so I composed:

sashite mono o	No melancholy thoughts
omou to nashi ni	have made me tearful,
minare-zao	yet the oar that knows this water well
minarenu nami ni	has soaked my sleeve
sode wa nurashitsu	as I watch these unknown waves

Once we had crossed, we were in the land of Owari. At Kataoka the morning sun's rays shone strong, a skylark rose singing from the burnt fields, my horse went galloping free over the plain of Ozasa, and all felt suddenly very different from the struggling journey that had gone before.

In a garden plot I noticed a mulberry tree with a house beneath it. A wild-haired woman was bent over a silkworm box tending the silkworms, while in the garden plot an ancient fellow *wielded his hoe*. In these parts, little children have no thought of book learning but only of working muddied in the fields, and it touched me to see such young folk helping their parents. The father would surely not have gone out of his way to train them in Confucian piety, yet it seems they must come upon it naturally.

yamada utsu	In the tender spring
uzuki ni nareba	when the fields are tilled for
	planting
natsubiki no	the little children too
itokenaki ko mo	stand seedling-deep there
ashi hijinikeri	legs caked in mud

A hazy moon cast its soft light and people were already settled in their inns when I found myself a traveller's pillow and stopped the night at Kayatsu.

On the eighth day I left Kayatsu, and came to the sea at Narumi Bay.

Passing before the Shrine of Atsuta, I knelt to the god within, a Buddhist avatar,[21] and bowed my head in fervent prayer. I spent some time before the great shrine gate in meditation on the sacred syllable,[22] and it seemed to me that with the merging of these deities, the shrine itself had subtly transformed into a Buddhist paradise. Age has frosted the buildings, and the piney winds whistled high about their roof tiles, yet the god's powers *are ever new*, and the people's faith springs fresh as spring flowers in their hearts [. . .]

Far on past this bay, the morning tide was at the full, so deep that nothing but a fish could swim there. By noon the water had withdrawn, and I hurried my horse across before it turned.[23] To the west, wide sky merged *to dark sea*, cloud and water the same blue. Out in the offing, *the leaf-shape of a single boat* seemed to float gently upward into pale sky. Why did those young boys of legend grow old and withered in that boat?[24] Even though they never found the fabled island of Penglai, or laid hands on the draught of immortality, surely *simply to float upon the waves is a lifetime's delight*, and thus the means of prolonging healthful life.

oi seji to	One whose heart
kokoro o tsune ni	is fixed on holding age at bay
yaru hito zo	will thereby gain the draught
na o kiku shima no	of immortality
kusuri o mo toru	they say that island holds

As I went along this beach, I noted how the little crabs left their holes and came rustling out to scamper on the sand. Startled by the feet of man and horse, they leapt sideways or crouched and scuttled back to their holes in haste, and I watched as those about to be trampled ran to save themselves in some other hole, while others who could have stayed safe where they were instead dashed to a hole beneath our feet and were crushed. Poor things! *Suffering dogs us all*, and the little crabs too know deep attachment. Are we who see this and lament the fact of transience wise, or not? Is not the heart that is attached to this world of life and death still more transient and futile than that of these little crabs?

tare mo ika ni	Lost, I have wandered here
mirume aware ni	to this bay where the waves
yoru nami no	drift with seaweed
tadayou ura ni	moved as any man
mayoi-kinikeri	must be to see it

Mountain upon mountain, and more mountains yet; river after river, and yet more rivers crossed. Alone I had parted from my home, to travel down this new and distant road. Who knew the day I would return? Though there were many who travelled with me, stepping along together side by side, few shared my inner feelings; the differences between us were as lonely as a friend's rejection. And yet, although I am one who *has no heart to feel*,[25] the moment's experience still touches me . . .

Climbing Shiomi-saka, though nothing like that steep Mount Wu, my breath grew short on the hard ascent. My feet carried me on down that long road, through mountainous Miyaji and

Futamura. All mountains are mountains, but these are the finest of them; all pines are pines, but this forest ranks above others. Rain seemed to sound in *the greenleaf wind*, but from the cries of the cranes swirling among the clouds I knew of the clear skies above. *Oh pine, pine*, it is your thousand years of constant virtue that keeps you here unchanged; oh journey upon journey, my life is a brief moment, and I cannot hope that we will meet again.

kyō suginu	Today has passed.
kaeraba mata yo	If I return, you mountains,
futamura no	may I find again this path
yamanu nagori no	beneath the pines of Futamura
matsu no shitamichi	that haunt my longing heart

Deep in the mountains flows Sakai River. I crossed alone upon a floating boat, while beside me sunk in water deep below travelled my accompanying shadow.

Thus I came to the land of Mikawa. Passing the waystation of Chirifu and pressing on over the plain for some miles, I came to the little group of bridges that bears the name of Yatsuhashi.[26] Being summer, *the mandarin ducks that sleep here on the sand* had gone, but in the water the irises were at their peak. The flowers were those flowers of old, the colours remained unchanged, and here were those same bridges, but how many times down the years must they have been remade? . . .

14

Journey to the East

Less than twenty years after the anonymous author of Journey Along the Sea Road *went to Kamakura, another man followed his example by travelling the same route (in 1242) and writing his own travel chronicle, known as* Journey to the East *(Tōkan kikō).*

The now busy highway between the old Capital and the new political centre of Kamakura bore less and less resemblance to the arduous and lonely roads trodden by poetic travellers down the ages. Journey to the East *mentions in passing several places where the increasing traffic of passersby had led to new post towns and roads, and there would have been no shortage of reasonable accommodation for travellers such as him. The lonesome 'sorrows of the journey', that requisite emotion for every traveller of sensibility, would have been somewhat undermined by the bustle of other travellers on the road and the relative ease of travel generally. Yet in the face of these outward changes, it was in precisely these decades that the medieval travel chronicle or* kikō, *with its evocative depictions of the solitary traveller moving through a poetically charged landscape and responding to its poignant resonances, came into its own.*

Journey along the Sea Road, *which had largely paved the way, was written by a monk, and its depiction of the journey was infused with the melancholy of a Buddhist sensitivity to transience. The anonymous author of* Journey to the East *was clearly from much the same background, a well-read man of religious sensibility approaching old age, but unlike* Journey along the Sea Road'*s author he was neither as energetically committed to the religious path nor as richly steeped in the Chinese classics. The result is a travel chronicle in the style of* Journey along the Sea Road *but without its more extreme characteristics – transiency is a constant theme, but it is expressed in a more genteelly literary mode;*

Chinese language and literature infuse the writing, but they serve to enrich rather than dominate the Japanese waka *style and literary sensibility; the long descriptive and introspective asides of* Journey along the Sea Road *are absent, and the focus is on the poetics of the journey itself.* Journey to the East, *with its flowing and melodious prose style and its elegant balancing of Chinese and Japanese stylistic and linguistic elements, is an impressive achievement. In it the medieval travel chronicle can be said to have achieved its ultimate form, and it was read, admired and emulated by the long line of poetic travellers who came after it.*

The travel chronicle or kikō *as it evolved from* Journey along the Sea Road *through* Journey to the East *and onward is above all a literary form, and it is a mistake to attempt to read it as a straightforward or factual account of the personal experience of a journey. Rather, in this mode of writing the personal and immediate find their meaning through identification with the rich literary and cultural heritage of travel that had evolved through the centuries.*[1] *This is not to say that the author's repeated reference to his emotional responses is simply a matter of following convention by recording the required emotion. To pause at a place that recalls for you a poem or a famous moment in literature or history stirs a genuine emotion, and we can imagine that in this period, when travel was suddenly much more easily experienced and one could find oneself standing in the presence of famous and evocative places long known only from books, the thrill of emotion was real. The author of* Journey to the East *and other writers of literary travel chronicles sought to record those moments of the journey when their immediate experience touched something larger and imbued the merely personal with a deeper meaning. The poems that form the core of most of these episodes are an embodiment of that powerful connection and its resultant emotion.*

It was a happy coincidence that the road that drew these travellers along it had played such an important role in literature for centuries. The travel sections of the tenth-century Ise Tales *(Chapter 2) were the ultimate touchstone for poetic travellers along the Tōkaidō, and places such as Yatsuhashi or Mount Utsu that figured there were high points of the journey that required the traveller to pause, appreciate and if possible write a poem in turn.*[2] *At places such as these, past and present sometimes proved hard to reconcile; Yatsuhashi provided* Journey along the Sea Road*'s author with the fulfilling sight of irises and little bridges, as* poetic tradition required,[3] although he acknowledges that the bridges would have been rebuilt many times in the intervening centuries, but the author of Journey to the East was unlucky enough to arrive in autumn and find a very different scene (he makes no reference to the bridges, which would probably still have been there).[4] He has better luck at Mount Utsu, which is satisfyingly overgrown as in the old description, and here he has the added delight of being provided with another quintessential traveller's experience in the form of a hermit to interview. This is not only poetically fitting – The Ise Tales famously describes a meeting with a mountain monk here – but also draws on the more recent tradition of saintly hermits who deign to tell their tale to reverent travellers, as seen in Senjūshō.[5] A handy sign points to the man's hut, and it is tempting to think that this hermit had placed himself there with a keen eye to the passing trade of travellers eager for just such an experience. His disarming honesty in confessing his lack of religious impulse and understanding serves to identify him as a 'holy fool', innately saintly.

Like Journey along the Sea Road, Journey to the East devotes most of its description to the roughly two-week journey from the Capital to Kamakura, where the author stayed about two months before returning. He too probably wrote his travel chronicle not long after the journey, carefully selecting episodes for poetic effect and polishing his prose.

The previous extract from Journey along the Sea Road leaves the reader at Yatushashi, and this extract from Journey to the East joins him at this point and ends at Mount Utsu. The extract from Diary of the Waning Moon that follows this will trace the journey on along the road from Mount Utsu to its end in Kamakura.

FROM JOURNEY TO THE EAST

Close to the midpoint of a hundred years of life, my temples ever chiller beneath the white frost of age, and yet my time spent idly and with no fixed abode to see out my days, I sighed to see myself in those words of Bo Juyi, *like some floating cloud, head white as frost.*

I had never craved the worldly fortunes of such as Jin and Zhang,[6] and wished only for the humble house of one like Tao Qian.[7] But still I hesitated at the thought of actually retiring to some thatched hut deep among mountains, and so I lived a nebulous life at the edge of the Capital, trudging with all the others along the path of everyday existence. My body, as the saying goes, was *in the market-place, while my heart was in retreat from the world*.

And then, quite unexpectedly, in the autumn of the third year of Ninji (1242), in the middle of the eighth month, I had reason to leave the Capital and set off for the East. Far though the journey stretched before me, beneath *still unknown traveller's skies*, past mountain and bay, fold upon fold, pushing through hindering clouds and mists, I made my way ever on along that endless road. At last, more than ten days later, I came to Kamakura, having passed my nights *in mountain inns or rough lodgings among moors*, and come upon fine lonely scenes of river bank and seashore, writing as I went of the sights that struck me and the moving moments that stayed with me, in hopes that these words may perhaps remain for others who might thereby remember me.

I left my home in the foothills of the eastern mountains and crossed the Barrier of Ōsaka around the time of the eighth month's full moon, that time when the tribute horses are brought in;[8] the autumn mists hung thick, moonlight drenched the deep night, and the breeze was soft. The faint crow of a cock reached me, bringing to mind the image of that traveller who *travels still beneath the late moon's light*.[9]

[. . .] On, on I went, until I came to Yatsuhashi in the land of Mikawa. Thinking as I gazed around me of Ariwara no Narihira and that poem he wrote on the irises,[10] which made his fellow travellers weep onto their rice cakes, I searched about but could see nothing at all like irises, and only field upon field of rice.

hana yue ni	In memory perhaps
ochishi namida no	of those shed tears
katami to ya	that the flowers provoked
inaba no tsuyu o	dew is left clinging still
nokoshi-okuramu	upon the rice leaves

I was particularly moved to remember the poem that Minamoto no Yoshitane[11] sent to the lady he left behind when he came to this land as governor: 'when I cross alone / Mikawa's Yatsuhashi / my thoughts will be / only of pining love / for you who are not with me'.

Leaving the place called Yahagi, I crossed Miyaji Mountain and stopped the night at Akasaka. It was touching to think that Ōe no Sadamoto[12] had taken monk's robes and left the world for the sake of a woman who lived here. Different roads may lead people to take this step, but he set out on the path of Truth having turned his heart from its blind wanderings in the relentless sorrow of love's parting, a wonderful thing indeed.

wakareji ni	How did he turn
shigeri mo hatede	from his dark tangled course
kuzu no ha no	along that road of parting
ikade ka aranu	as the twining *kuzu* vine
kata ni kaerishi	will turn to new ways?

I made my way out to the plain of Honno, to a scene stretched hazy all about me, unbroken by mountain or hill. It felt as it would to gaze out over the *thousand and more miles of the Qin domain*, grass and earth together a vast green expanse. Fond thoughts of that landscape drew me to wonder how this might look in moonlight. It was easy to lose one's way among the jumble of paths trodden among the plain's thick bamboo grass, and I was moved by this to think of the willows that the former Musashi governor[13] had instructed those living nearby to plant as road markers. Though they were still too small to provide welcome shade, they could serve in their way as signposts.

Legend tells us that the Duke of Shao[14] was the brother of King Wu, and ruled over the land of Yan as one of the three ministers under King Cheng. When he was ruler of the western area, he would set up his court beneath a sweet pear tree. Under his rule, both officials and citizens maintained their livelihood; he judged all complaints fairly, and pardoned even the graver crimes. His rule filled all with such affection that after he was gone they carefully preserved the tree from the axe, and wrote poetry about it. It was no doubt in the spirit of this story that when he was still prince the later Emperor Gosanjō composed this Chinese poem for his tutor Sanemasa when he was appointed governor: 'Though the folk whom you will rule / write sweet pear poems for love of you / never forget the many years / of cultured pleasures that we led together'.

The former Musashi governor was moved by the same sympathy and care as these men of old to plant his willows by the road as shade for passersby, and it seems to me that those who see them now will, like those of old, follow his impulse and tend these trees with grateful love to become at last the travellers' shade trees.

ue-okishi	Here still the plain of willows
nushi naki ato no	though he who planted them is gone
yanagihara	their welcoming shade
nao sono kage o	recalling to the traveller
hito ya tanoman	the shelter of his generous heart

When I passed through the waystation of Toyokawa, someone told me that back in the old days there had been no alternative route here, but recently a great many travellers had suddenly taken to going by the new Watōtsu road instead, and now even the local people were moving away. It has ever been the way for people to *abandon the old in favour of the new*, but I do wonder why. It is such a shame to think of this place left to *crumble to ruins* like long-ago Fushimi village,[15] as those who have long lived here drift away.

obotsukana	Who can tell
isa toyokawa no	what man first changed the route
kawaru se o	to cross a different way
ika naru hito no	the shifting rapids
watari-someken	of fickle Toyokawa River?

At the border between Mikawa and Tōtōmi stands the famous Mount Takashi (High Mountain). As you cross it, you come upon a tumbling mountain stream where the water pours thunderously among rocks. Its name is Sakai River (Border River).

iwa tsutai	Here at High Mountain
koma uchi-watasu	I set my horse
tanikawa no	to cross from rock to rock
oto mo takashi no	where the river flows loud
yama ni kinikeri	as the mountain's fame is high

On to Hashimoto, whose scenery is as astonishingly lovely as reputed. To the south lies the ocean, where fishing boats bob among the waves; to the north, a lake with houses strung along its bank. A long point lies between the two, thick with pine trees. Wild winds moan constantly among the pines; the ear can barely distinguish between the sob of wind and wave. All who pass are affected by it, and those who spend the night sleep fitfully. The bridge that spans the lake bears the name of Hamana, a celebrated site from of old. The clouds that linger in the morning sky touch the heart more forlornly than in any other place.

yuki-tomaru	Another passing night
tabine wa itsu mo	of traveller's sleep
kawaranedo	yet forlorner here
wakite hamana no	to pass and leave behind
hashi zo sugiuki	the Bridge of Hamana

I did indeed spend the night at an inn here. It was a thatched house with tattered old eaves, and through the many gaps a dappling of unclouded moonlight filtered in. A large crowd of *asobi* had gathered, and I was most impressed when one who seemed a little older sang softly 'all night long beneath my bed / I see the clear heavens'.[16]

koto no ha no	The sensitive heart
fukaki nasake wa	that lay behind those words
nokiba moru	shone clear to me
tsuki no katsura no	in the pure moonlight
iro ni mieniki	filtering through the eaves

Loath though I was to leave, off I set again, and came to a place called the Plain of Maizawa. The land spread wide to north and south; westward, the shore lay close. No flowery brocade was threaded there, only white sand in heaps like snowdrifts. Among them an occasional pine tree grew, boughs visited by the moan of the salt wind. Rough thatched huts too stood here and there, no doubt the homes of fishermen and suchlike.

As I went on, gazing out over that vast expanse of land, a traveller joined me and told me the following: from time immemorial there had been on this plain a wooden image of the Bodhisattva Kannon. The little hall that once housed it must have rotted away, and now it passed the years in a flimsy hut of thatch that kept out neither rain nor dew. One year, a man from Tsukushi passed by on his way to Kamakura on legal business. Pausing to worship there, he made a silent vow that if his prayers were answered he would build for the image a proper hall on his way back. In Kamakura he did indeed win his case, and so he built the hall as promised, and since then many worshippers have come.

As soon as I heard this I took myself off there to worship too. The scent of incense drifted constantly on the breeze; fresh flowers at the altar still held the morning dew. What looked like written prayers were tied to the cords of the altar curtains, bringing to mind those sure words of the sutra,[17] 'The Buddha's vow of salvation is ocean-deep.'

tanomoshi na	What faith we feel
irie ni tatsuru	to know that deep fulfilling power
mi o tsukushi	that stands before us
fukaki shirushi no	firm as a marker to the passing ship
ari to kiku ni mo	in treacherous waters

There is a river crossing by the name of Tenryū, where the river is deep and the flow looks terrifyingly strong. It brimmed with the autumn rains, and boats were quickly swept away downstream, making it hard for travellers to cross. When the river is in flood boats can easily capsize, and apparently there are many corpses of the drowned lying below. It put me in mind of those swift waters of Wu Canyon,[18] and filled me with trepidation. Still, as the poet says, such torrents are nothing to *the shifting perils of the human heart*. The long hard road that is our human life surpasses all comparison.

kono kawa no	This river's swift
hayaki nagare mo	torrential surge
yo no naka no	bears no comparison
hito no kokoro no	with the fickle turbulence
tagui to zo miru	of the human heart

I arrived at Ima Bay in the land of Tōtōmi, where I found lodgings for a few days, and here I took a little fishing boat out to see the bay. A long point of land juts out into the sea; to the south waves soak the traveller's sleeve *upon far beaches*, while northward the winds in the towering pines pierce his heart with sorrow. It was very like that moving scene back in Hashimoto that I was so loath to leave. It seemed to me that if that scene had not so struck me, I might have been more moved by the one before me now.

nami no oto mo	Now in the Bay of Ima
matsu no arashi mo	the sound of waves
ima no ura ni	and wild winds in the pines
kinō no sato no	speaks to me of my longing
nagori o zo kiku	for that scene of yesterday

There is hereabouts a shrine by the name of Kotonomama,[19] and passing it a thought rose up my mind:

yū-dasuki	May the prayer
kakete zo tanomu	arising in my mind now
ima omou	find its fulfilment
koto no mama naru	through the power
kami no shirushi o	of this shrine's fulfilling name

I knew that the mountain pass of Saya no Nakayama was a place of poetic fame, forlornly described as *lying stretched to bar my view*[20] in a poem of the *Kokinshū*, and my heart grew all the more forlorn when I saw it. Deep mountains rose to the north, covered in wind-tossed pines and cedars, while southward stretched hills and plains where autumn flowers lay drenched in dew. As I climbed up out of the valley toward the peak I seemed to penetrate the very clouds; the cry of the deer brought tears to the eyes, the soft plaint of insects deepened my sorrow.

fumi-mayou	Treading the frail path
mine no kakehashi	bridging the peak
todae shite	my feet lose their way
kumo ni ato tou	and I must ask the clouds
	for help
saya no nakayama	on Saya no Nakayama

Over the mountain and on, you come to a place called Kikukawa (Chrysanthemum River). I had heard that here, back in 1221, a certain Middle Counsellor Muneyuki[21] was arrested for a crime and brought to the East, and stayed the night at an inn here, where he wrote on the paper of the door this Chinese poem:

> At Chrysanthemum River in the land of southern Nanyang,
> they drew the downstream waters for long life;
> here at the eastern sea road's Chrysanthemum Stream
> I meet life's end upon the western shore.

Moved, I asked about the house, but it had burned down, I learned, and there remained no trace of his words. How ephemeral this world, I thought with sorrow, moved that even something left as a final remembrance before death should now have disappeared.

kaki-tsukuru	Even those words he wrote
katami mo ima wa	as keepsake for the future
nakarikeri	are now no more. Who said
ato wa chitose to	that written words 'remain
dare ka iiken	a thousand years'?

Crossing Kikukawa River, I very soon came to a village, whose name is Kohama. Climbing a little hill at its eastern edge I looked beyond, down onto the Ōi River, which flows in numerous shallow channels over the broad river plain in an untidy tangle that reminded me of the sinuous *sunagashi* effect in decorative paper.[22] It is far more interesting viewed from afar than when crossing, I decided, and though it was hardly the famous poem's distant view of *Tatsuta's tangled swirls of autumn leaves*,[23] still I paused long before I turned away.

hikazu furu	The journey's poignancy
tabi no aware wa	greater with each passing day
ōikawa	deepens like the hues
wataranu mizu mo	of this yet uncrossed
fukaki iro kana	Ōi River

Leaving my lodging at Maeshima, I went on past the new post town of Okabe. While I paused in the shade of a pine to eat my rice cakes, a fierce wind keened in the branches, and I was cold in my summer traveller's robe with its thin sleeves.

kore zo kono	Be tender
tanomu ki no moto	stormy wind
okabe naru	that rages so
matsu no arashi yo	around this pine in Okabe
kokoro shite fuke	where I come seeking
	shelter

When I crossed Mount Utsu the path was indeed still *overgrown with vines and maples*, just as of old.[24] Searching as I went for the place where Narihira might have given his message to the mountain monk, I came upon a sign on the side of the road announcing that a recluse who had cast off all ties with the world lived here. It wasn't far from the road, so I ventured in to see, and there sat a solitary monk in a tiny grass hut. A painting of the Bodhisattva Amida hung in the altar, with some words from the Pure Land Sutra. Otherwise, the place was bare of objects.

I asked him how he came to dedicate himself to the Buddhist path, and he told me that he was a man from these parts. He had had no particular religious urge, he said, and since he was without

learning he was too ignorant to understand much, and too lazy
to bother praying, and thus both unable to study the Buddhist
teachings, and without any inclination to meditate. But someone
had told him that it was a finer thing to sleep among mountains
than to be a monk down in the village, so he had built his hut
here and lived here many years.

Long ago, they say, Shu Qi went off to dwell among the clouds
of Mount Daoyang and pluck spring fern shoots for his food; Xu
You[25] too lived with the moonlit waters of Ying River, and hung
his single drinking gourd in a tree. There was no real sign of any-
where to cook around this hut, and this monk seemed to have
abandoned all thought even of the comfort of *breaking wood to
build a fire*. It touched me deeply to find him dwelling here, deep
among the gales on a lonely mountain, his heart in the pure realm
among far clouds, his saintliness unexpressed yet plain to see.

yo o itou	This heart that seeks
kokoro no oku ya	to turn from the sad world
nigoramashi	would surely have been
	sullied
kakaru yamabe no	did he not live
sumika narade wa	here in this mountain home

Not far from this hut I came to the summit, where I found a large
and ancient-looking stupa on which were written a great number
of poems. One was as follows:

azumaji wa	This I name the high
	point
koko o se ni sen	of all the Eastern Road
utsu no yama	this narrow vine-wreathed
	path
aware mo fukashi	deep in the mournful
	mountains
tsuta no hosomichi	of Mount Utsu

Moved by this, I wrote beside it:

ware mo mata	I too would call this
koko o se ni sen	the high point of the Eastern Road
utsu no yama	where the dew lies
wakite iro aru	among the richly coloured leaves
tsuta no shita-tsuyu	of vine-wreathed Mount Utsu

15

Diary of the Waning Moon
by Abutsu

Among the increased flow of traffic along the Tōkaidō were a number
of women, one of whom wrote the travel chronicle Diary of the Waning Moon *(Izayoi nikki), some time between the date of her journey*
(1279) and her death four years later. Her name was Abutsu, a Bud-
dhist name indicating that she had taken the tonsure. Unlike the other
important travel chronicles of the age, however, there is no hint of any
religious concerns in what she wrote, nor in the reason why she took to
the road. Her journey was the culmination of what seems to have been
a passionate and somewhat combative life, and her travel chronicle
provides a window into her unusual story, as well as into the highly
charged politics of waka *poetry at this time.*

Abutsu in fact twice took the tonsure, but in between she managed
to raise five children to two men, become one of the most important
poets of her day, and lay claim to the contested inheritance of the
Mikohidari lineage of waka, *one of two important rival schools of*
poetry at the time. Her first retreat into religious life came while she
was still in her teens, as a reaction to a failed love affair. She seems to
have subsequently married, however, and then at thirty-one destiny
led the great poet Fujiwara no Tameie, head of the Mikohidari House,
to commission her to make a copy of The Tale of Genji *for his daughter.*
The two became lovers – she became in effect his second wife (polygamy
was accepted at the time) – and their long-standing relationship pro-
duced three children. This in itself was not unusual according to the
customs of the time, but Abutsu, clever and ambitious, also became the
recipient of important documents and archives of the Mikohidari House
which were by right of inheritance the intended property of Tameie's old-
est son by his first wife. In the last two years before his death in 1275,
Tameie officially retracted his will and left the inheritance of both

substantial property and poetic lineage to his and Abutsu's son Tameuji. The subsequent quarrel with his earlier family restored these rights to the oldest son, but Abutsu refused to accept defeat. In her mid-fifties, already an old woman by the reckoning of that time and a tonsured nun after the death of her husband as custom dictated, she set off on the two-week journey to carry her case to the law court in Kamakura and win back the rights for her beloved son.

Her travel chronicle reflects all this in a number of ways. It opens, not with the customary introductory poetic passage humbly sketching in the writer's background, tendency to reclusion and urge to take to the road, but with an impassioned presentation of her credentials and sense of grievance, and the righteous cause which led her to 'forget all hesitations, abandon all thoughts of myself', and set off to appeal to the authorities in Kamakura for a return of her son's inheritance. With her went one of her older sons, a high-ranking priest.[1] There is thus no pretence of the usual solitary wanderer of poetic tradition. Abutsu's pragmatism also colours her prose, which is generally quite plain and perfunctory rather than reaching for elegance. This does not mean, however, that her chronicle is not 'poetic' in the accepted ways; indeed the role of poetry is absolutely central to it. It seems likely, in fact, that this chronicle was specifically intended to display her poetic credentials and further her case to the authorities, by reinforcing her claim to be the able upholder of her husband's poetic legacy as her introduction asserts.

For this reason it is almost a textbook record of a skilled poet's journey. Her chief aim en route is to visit the utamakura *and respond in appropriate fashion, demonstrating her mastery of the poetic tradition in her poems.[2] The prose frequently acts essentially as headnotes to the poems, and the work in this sense bears a closer relationship to the traditional personal poetry collection (shikashū) than to the more expanded travel chronicles that some others were now writing. But it is nevertheless a personal record of her journey, its details carefully selected and presented for poetic purposes, and it provides us with numerous glimpses of life on the road.*

The chronicle does not end with her arrival in Kamakura but goes on to document her long stay there, focussing on poems written and exchanged and culminating, surprisingly, in a long chōka[3] *which reads as an impassioned poetic plea to the authorities for justice. After*

*several years she finally returned home, where she died not long after,
her case still unresolved.*[4]

The extract given here takes the journey along the Tōkaidō from the
utamakura *of Mount Utsu (where we left the author of* Journey to
the East*) to arrival in Kamakura.* Journal of the Waning Moon *is
far shorter than the previous two travel chronicles, and this extract
is correspondingly short, although the distance covered does not differ
substantially from that of the previous two. It inadvertently provides
an important record of the fact that Mount Fuji had become dormant
in recent years – a disappointment to visiting poets, who now found it
more difficult to refer to the traditional drifting smoke in their poems.*
(See Map 3)

FROM *DIARY OF THE WANING MOON*

As we were passing over the mountains of Utsu, we happened to
cross paths with a mountain monk of my son's acquaintance. It
was astonishing, almost as though the scene had been set up pur-
posely to echo Narihira's 'neither in reality / nor yet in dreams'
encounter[5] – a mixture of delightful, moving and poetically perfect. He told me he was in haste so I had no time to write many
letters for him to carry to the Capital for me, and only sent one to
a particularly exalted person.[6]

waga kokoro	My heart here on Mount Utsu
utsutsu to mo nashi	lost to reality
utsu no yama	while far away
yumeji mo tōki	down that path of dreams
miyako kou tote	the Capital it longs for
tsuta kaede	Even when wintry showers
shigurenu hima mo	do not dye the vines and maples
utsu no yama	to a blood-red tint
namida ni sode no	my sleeves here on Mount Utsu
iro zo kogaruru	are dyed deep with tears

This night we stayed at a place called Tegoshi, where people had flocked on account of a certain high-ranking cleric who was on his way to the Capital. All the inns seemed full, but we did manage to find one place where there was room.

Twenty-sixth day. We crossed a river called, I think, Warashina-gawa, and came to Okitsu Beach, which immediately recalled to me the poem 'Oh moon, seek after me'.[7]

At the place we called in on next day I noticed a rough box-wood pillow, and since I was feeling very bad I lay down for a while. Having an inkstone[8] to hand, I wrote the following on the nearby paper door as I lay there.

naozari ni	A passing sleep, a dream
miru yume bakari	upon this transient pillow
kari-makura	but pillow, do not dream
musubi-okitsu to	of telling others that I lay
hito ni kataru na	this borrowed hour with you in Okitsu

Just on dark, we passed the Kiyomi Barrier. It was charming to see the waves tossing white foamy robes over the rocks.

kiyomi-gata	Let me ask you
toshi furu iwa ni	ancient rocks of Kiyomi
koto towan	how many layers
nami no nureginu	of those sodden robes
iku-kasane kitsu	have been flung at you?[9]

It quickly grew dark, and we stayed in a seaside village nearby. Smoke from the place next door filled the room, no doubt something to do with the fishermen's work, and it smelled dreadful, reminding me of the poet who spoke of 'the stench of the inn at night'.[10] A wild wind howled all night long, and the waves raged loud at my very pillow.

narawazu yo	Never have I lain
yoso ni kiki-koshi	as wakeful to the wild shore's waves

kiyomigata   as here at Kiyomi
araiso nami no   till now a place
kakaru nezame wa   only of distant rumour

When we saw Mount Fuji, no smoke rose from it. Long ago when I came this way with my father, that trip when I composed the poem 'What will become of me / oh Bay of Narumi?',[11] I remember clearly seeing Fuji's smoke rising morning and night, but though I now asked when it had ceased no one could give me a clear answer.

ta ga kata ni   Who drew that smoke
nabiki-hatete ka   from Fuji's peak
fuji no ne no   to drift away
kemuri no sue no   yearning, lingering, then gone
miezu naruramu   toward its unknown end?[12]

Recalling the words of the Preface to the *Kokinshū*:[13]

itsu no yo no   How many aeons
fumoto no chiri ka   have those grains of earth
fuji no ne no   at Fuji's feet been building
yuki sae takaki   to make at last this mountain
yama to nashikemu   high with building snows?

kuchi-hateshi   If the smoke of Fuji
nagara no hashi o   no longer rises, would that I
tsukuraba ya   might build anew
fuji no kemuri mo   that ancient Bridge of Nagara
tatazu narinaba   that rotted long ago

This night we stayed in an inn worthy of the description 'upon the waves'[14] – on all sides the wild waves sounded and I could not sleep.

Twenty-seventh day. After sunrise we crossed Fuji River. The morning river was chill, and I counted a total of fifteen river branches forded.

View of Mount Fuji from Suruga Bay

sae-wabinu	Painful with cold
yuki yori orosu	my sleeves this wintry day
fujigawa no	frozen in the river's wind
kawa-kaze kōru	blown from the snows
fuyu no koromode	of Fuji's peak

It was a beautiful sunlit day when we arrived at Tago Inlet. Fisherfolk were out fishing. I wanted to say to them:

kokoro kara	It was by choice
ori-tatsu tago no	you came down to Tago Bay.
amagoromo	Never lament to others
hosanu urami mo	the unwrung sorrows
hito ni kakotsu na	of your fisher's robes

We stayed the night in a place called Kō in Izu. While the evening sun still lingered, I took myself off to worship at Mishima Shrine, where I presented these poems to the gods.

aware to ya	Perhaps the god
mishima no kami no	of Mishima may see
miyabashira	with pity in his heart
tada koko ni shi mo	how I have come thus longing
meguri-kinikeri	to pray at the pillars of his shrine

onozukara	Surely the gods
tsutaeshi ato mo	will recognize the ancient lineage
are mono o	of the poetic Way
kami wa shiruramu	that flows down through me
shikishima no michi	from ancient times[15]

tazune-kite	I have come
waga koe-kakaru	seeking the help of gods
hakoneji ni	for an assurance that the path I take
yama no kai aru	over the hard Hakone mountains
shirube o zo tou	will bear fruit at last

Twenty-eighth day. We left Kō and set out on the Hakone Road. The night was still dark when we departed.

tamakushige	Though I hasten
hakone no yama o	over Hakone Mountain

isogedomo	dawn does not lift
nao akegataki	the sky where trailing clouds
yokogumo no sora	still hang in darkness

We had taken the Hakone route having heard that the road over Ashigara Pass[16] was a roundabout one.

yukashisa yo	I long to see you
sonata no kumo o	Ashigara Mountain
sobadatete	but you sent up
yoso ni nashitsuru	such a forbidding wall of cloud
ashigara no yama	we must remain estranged

We descended a precipitous mountainside, so steep that it was hard to brake the feet. Its name was Yusaka Slope. Having finally managed the mountain crossing, we came to a river by the name of Hayakawa (Fast River) at its base, and it was indeed very fast. Seeing numerous logs go floating by, I asked about it and was told that they were sending the logs down to the bay for the fisherfolk to use in boiling the seaweed for salt.

azumaji no	Over Yusaka Slope
yusaka o koete	along the Eastern Road
miwataseba	before my eyes now
shioki nagaruru	the swift waters of Hayakawa
hayakawa no mizu	bearing salt logs down

From Yusaka we emerged at the bay. The sun was setting, but we were still far from our night's lodging. The sea stretched away to Ōshima Island in the distance, and no one could tell me the name of the place when I asked. The only dwellings round about were fisher folks'.

ama no sumu	Could I but find
sono sato no na mo	some inn to stay at
shiranami no	here in this wave-worn village
yosuru nagisa ni	its name erased
yado ya karamashi	even for those who live here

We made our way in the pitch darkness over a river called Mariko-gawa, and this night we stayed in a place named Sakawa. The following day we would reach Kamakura.

Twenty-ninth day. Leaving Sakawa, on we went along the shore. Above the dawn sea hung a slender moon.

uraji yuku	Dawn's wan moon
kokorobososa o	thin above the waves
namima yori	shows me my own heart
idete shirasuru	faint and forlorn
ariake no tsuki	upon this seaside road

Mist shrouded the waves that came and went along the beach, and nothing could be seen of the many fishing boats that were there earlier.

ama obune	Mists of morning
kogi-yuku kata o	rise with the waves
miseji to ya	perhaps to hide
nami ni tachi-sou	the distant place
ura no asagiri	to which those boats
	go rowing

Distant too seemed the far Capital, like a dream.

tachi-wakare	Needless this journey
yo mo uki nami wa	tear-soaked with the floating waves
kake mo seji	and far from those I love
mukashi no hito no	if only he of old
onaji yo naraba	were still of this world

16

Pilgrimage to Kumano
by Myōkū

*For all the upheavals of the Kamakura period, literary culture remained
as important as ever, and its touchstone was still* waka *poetry. Eager to
prove their cultural credentials, the new warrior elite busied themselves
with studying the approved classics and practising the revered art of
poetry. But where poetry remained strictly beholden to tradition, new
literary forms and fashions were also emerging, among them a new
kind of song known as* sōga *(or* sōka*) that became a fashion in the late
thirteenth century.*

*Sōga were later termed 'banquet songs' (*enkyoku*) because that is
where they were largely sung, as part of the entertainment performed
either professionally or by the guests themselves. We know almost nothing of how they were sung and performed, although their influence
on the development of Nō drama may hint at similarities in singing
and possibly dancing style.[1] The name* sōga *means 'fast song', and their
remarkable length[2] also suggests that they were sung quite fast. Like
Imayō and other song forms, they are structured on an alternating
rhythm of seven- and five-syllable phrases, with considerable variation,
indicated in the translation by the two-part structure of each line. There
is a breathless flow to the language and the swinging rhythm that suggests
performance could have been somewhat mesmeric, broken by occasional interjections ('kono!' and 'ano!' in the extract below perform
this function).*

*Sōga come down to us from anthologies that appeared in 1296–1319.
Most of the songs are attributed to one of two creators[3] (Pilgrimage
to Kumano is listed as by Myōkū) whose names indicate a Buddhist
affiliation, and who are believed to have had close connections to the
court in Kamakura. Whoever they may have been, they were clearly well-
educated. Where the simple* imayō *songs of earlier courtly popularity*

originated among the class of lowly entertainers, sōga *were elaborate literary creations that made extravagant use of time-honoured poetic techniques such as parallelisms, pivot words, literary allusion and quotation. Their virtuoso linguistic and literary cleverness can so dominate the words that meaning becomes of only secondary importance and sometimes disappears altogether beneath the weight of the dazzling textual surface. It seems fitting that such overt and dramatic displays of literary skills should emerge from a warrior culture impressed by hard-won acquisition of the literary arts.*

Pilgrimage to Kumano (Kumano sankei) *is one of the longest and most elaborate of the* sōga, *and well illustrates this impressive literary style. It depicts the pilgrim's journey from the old Capital (Kyoto) to the great pilgrimage shrines of the mountainous Kumano region in present-day Wakayama prefecture.*[4] *This ancient and arduous pilgrimage, popular from the Heian Period onward, took pilgrims by various routes deep into the mountains to the shrines at Hongū and on to the holy waterfall at Nachi, traversing a sacred geography that was studded en route with minor shrines known as* ōji. Pilgrimage to Kumano *traces the pilgrims' journey around the coast, then turns inland at present-day Tanabe and follows the mountain path via Chikatsuyu to Hongū and on down the Kumano River to end at Nachi. Its language enacts the route in a continuous litany of the names of some of the* ōji *shrines*[5] *in geographically correct order of encounter, which forms the core of its structure. The tone is far closer to ritual evocation than to realism: the names (indicated in the translation with initial capitals) are usually seamlessly woven into the descriptive substance of the song like figures in a densely woven fabric, through forms of word play also found in* waka. *A description such as 'where the waves Beat over Rocks' embeds the* ōji *name Rock Beating (iwauchi), while the name Itoka, which includes the character for 'thread' ('ito'), is incorporated in the description 'green trailing willow threads' and in turn leads into the associated image of the pilgrims 'threading swift-footed through the days'. Other names can be split across several lines or buried unobtrusively in seemingly straightforward descriptions. The result of all this, when read literally, creates an endless flow of discontinuous and often startling imagery whose single structuring principle is the progress of the pilgrim from one sacred site or* ōji *to the next along the route.*

The breathless forward motion of this long poetic depiction of the journey, the structural centrality of place names, the richly lyrical language and juxtapositions of disconnected imagery, all identify Pilgrimage to Kumano *as a sustained* michiyuki *such as that found in* The Tale of the Heike *10.6 (see p. 114f), an emotionally heightened evocative form of rhythmic prose-poetry.* Michiyuki *generally depict intensely poignant journeys, and* Pilgrimage to Kumano *is unusual in evoking not sorrow but mounting joy as the pilgrims approach the shrine. The poignancy lies in the arduous nature of the journey, a suffering willingly undertaken as a form of spiritual practice that purifies the pilgrim and prepares him or her to approach the gods.*[6] *Although* sōga *such as* Pilgrimage to Kumano *were typically sung as a form of entertainment, it may well have simultaneously performed the more serious function of ritually singing performer and audience through the surrogate experience of the pilgrimage itself*[7] *and thereby bestowing its benefits.*

Pilgrimage to Kumano *consists of five lengthy sections punctuated by the repeated invocation 'All praise to the nation's greatest holiness / the miraculous pilgrimage to Kumano'. The following extract, roughly a third of the full song, is a translation of parts of the third and fifth sections, the first taking the pilgrim along the coast and the second following the route from the coast through mountainous country to arrive in the final lines at Hongū Shrine on the Kumano River.*[8]

The translation attempts to evoke something of the feel of the complex play of imagery that supports the invocations of the numinous names of the ōji shrines along the route. Other translations and interpretations are frequently equally possible, while much of the complexities of hidden allusion and poetic word play is impossible to convey. (See Map 2)

FROM *PILGRIMAGE TO KUMANO*

Sheer the mountains   piercing clouds.
Vast the ocean   wave-soaked deeps.
We pass the foothills   clamber up
cross Misaka Hill   and rest
Tamuke Ōji   sacred twists of rope
twined afresh with prayers   and on

shore upon endless shore   to Waka Bay
tidal flats where over lines of reed beds   pass the crying cranes.
Empty shells broken   on the beach
in the waves   a sunken sweet-oak log
god of sweet Tamatsushima   tossed
among lovely sea-tangled reeds   and blown
down Fukiage Beach   the salt sea wind
chiller yet   and song cool.
Summer mountains   by the flourishing eaves
sweet-scented orange   brushed perhaps
by sleeves of some past owner[9]   in long-gone evening breeze
Irisa Mountain   Kabura Slope
hold many branching   mountain paths
yet steady flows   the changeless Arita.
Far on from the river   the Beach of Nagusa
far and farther   runs the sea road
screening from view perhaps   Honomi Point
green trailing willow threads   of Itoga Mountain
as we thread swift-footed   through the days
finding the way   more surely as we go.
Yuasa Ōji   Kōno Rapids
Yura Harbour   now close by
round Far Mountains   winds the Ki Road
Mount Kōnose   called 'Deer-backed'
with reason   where deer graze Bush Clover Fields
Tomiyasu Ōji   a thousand ancient years
Komatsubara   beautiful to gaze on
Aitokuzan Ōji   we see afar
banks of Hidaka River   where the waves
Beat over Rocks   about the inlet road
where gods of the Salt-fire Kilns   bestow compassion
Inami and the Ōjis   of Ikaruga, Kirime
blessings many   as the palm leaves of Yashinoki
sacred dances offered   Ōji after Ōji
precious the voices   raised in reverent prayer
ALL PRAISE TO THE NATION'S GREATEST HOLINESS
THE MIRACULOUS PILGRIMAGE TO KUMANO

[. . .] [*The pilgrims turn inland at Tanabe*]
Look up to the mountains   tree branch tangle
pine and oak   green deep with shadow
steep winds the path   doubling around vast boulders
climb up and up   pausing at rocky Sekigan
on and ever on   dimmer yet and darker
kono!
peaks cloud-smothered   High Heaven's Plain far indeed
ice-covered deep-rooted rocks.   On past the shrine of Ōsaka
and now ahead yes surely   already close Chikatsuyu
beneath the trees   lush Hisohara
bare branches cold   snow tumbling
might be the cherry blossoms   of Tsugizakura
and far on to Iwagami   Yunokawa
over Mount Mikoshi   and along its side
deep in the valleys   scarce any sign of men
a bird's single call[10]   *ice at water's edge   snow on the peaks*
each thing has its own   sorrowful colour.
Oh what joy and what delight   gazing upward
here we have come   to Hosshin-mon!
Through its gate passing   pure and unsullied
Heart's Water drunk   at Mizunomi
limpid indeed   clear to the bottom
every sin swept away   at Haraido
and silently before it flows   Otonashi River
no ripple breaking   its quiet surface.
Now roof by roof standing   at last the holy shrines.
ano!
Oh three-fold diety   Waka-ōji
the Five Embodiments   the Four Jewelled Doors!

17

A Tale Unasked
by Lady Nijō

Most classical texts have come down to us in multiple copies that differ from each other in large and small ways, but there is only one precious copy of the remarkable memoir known as A Tale Unasked (Towazu-gatari). *It lay forgotten for centuries in an obscure corner of the archives of the Imperial Household until a scholar came across it in 1940, transcribed and published it. It proved an important discovery. Not only is this lengthy memoir impressive literature, but the story it told makes riveting reading with its first-hand revelations of the intimate affairs of emperors and other important figures in the imperial court of the late thirteenth century. It is perhaps not surprising that it was apparently only covertly read after it was written, was seldom mentioned, and later disappeared from sight altogether.*

A Tale Unasked was written by a woman known by convention as Lady Nijō from her title at court. She was born in 1258 into a high-ranking aristocratic family with connections that promised her a glowing future, and after her mother's death when she was four she was brought up in the imperial palace under the fond eye of Retired Emperor Gofu-kakusa. When she was fourteen she became his consort and bore him a son. Blessed with beauty, intelligence, impressive literary and artistic talent, and what was clearly a compelling personality, she was Gofukakusa's darling among his consorts, but her adventurous nature complicated her life. A Tale Unasked relates in considerable detail, though naming no names, the love affairs she had with several other highly placed men at court, among them apparently Emperor Kameyama, Gofukakusa's arch-rival.[1] Her father's death had by now undermined her position at court, the jealousy of Gofukakusa's principal consort was mounting, her little son had died and she had borne several children to other men, while Gofukakusa's affection for her was becoming increasingly fickle. Rumours of her affair with Kameyama may have proved the last straw, and in 1283 she was driven from the court.

Book IV of A Tale Unasked, the first section of which is given here, picks up her story again six years later without detailing the intervening years, but we can imagine that they were years of considerable hardship and sorrow. Somewhere during this time she became a nun. A more conventional woman would now have settled to a quiet life of reclusion and contemplation, but Nijō was never one to follow convention. In the spring of 1289, at the age of thirty-one, she took to the road, going first to Kamakura along what was by now the well-travelled route along the Tōkaidō. Subsequent sections depict a life that continued to be dominated by travel, as Nijō made pilgrimage after pilgrimage to places near and far – a small sample describing her pilgrimage to the important shrine on the island of Miyajima (off present-day Hiroshima) is included here. Travel clearly enlivened her as well as stimulating her literary talents, and the travel sections of her memoir are among the best travel writing in Japan's literature.

A Tale Unasked may have been written over many years but it took its final form some time after 1306, when its story ends.[2] The title carries a hint of defiance – she would tell her tale whether or not the world wanted to hear it. The remarkable trajectory of her life certainly made her story worth telling, and adds considerable poignancy to her travel writing. Although it was the convention to emphasize the sorrows of the journey, Nijō's sorrows were very real. Despite her other affairs she seems to have never ceased to love Gofukakusa, and she carried her heartbreak with her through life;[3] indeed it seems that she undertook the first journey below in the vain hope of somehow dealing with her grief. It provoked in her a fine empathy with the feelings and sufferings of others, particularly women she met along the way; the scene of her exchange of poetry with the asobi early in the journey is particularly touching, as is her time spent with the asobi community en route to Miyajima.

Early in A Tale Unasked Nijō relates that when she was a little girl she was deeply impressed by the idealized figure of the wandering poet Saigyō that she came upon in The Tale of Saigyō.[4] 'I had envied him ever since,' she wrote, 'and though of course I could never undergo such rigorous ascetic hardships, I longed to be like him and renounce the world, wandering wherever my feet led me, delighting in the blossoms and the dew, telling of my bitterness at the tumbling leaves of autumn,

and writing just such a chronicle of my own ascetic travels to leave in
memory of me when I died.'

This indeed she did, though not in quite the romantic fashion she
had envisaged. Her travel, undertaken essentially as a form of penance,
came closer to Saigyō's 'rigorous ascetic hardships' than her childhood
imagination could have guessed. Her literary skills produced a work of
at times impressive beauty, and if her poetry does not rise to Saigyō's
heights her prose more than compensates for it. Its masterful use of com-
pression, elision and allusion carries the reader smoothly forward from
one evocative description to the next. Like all literary travellers, she seeks
out the utamakura en route, and her lament at finding the famous
Yatsuhashi so changed provides a glimpse of the emotional significance
of such places. Like Saigyō and many after him, Nijō's combination of
poetic and religious sensibilities lends her writing depth. Yet in the end,
it is her rich humanity that leaves the most lasting impression as we
read her story. (See Maps 1 and 3)

FROM *A TALE UNASKED*

Near the end of the second month, I left the Capital with the
departing moon. Though I had severed my life from my old
home without a backward glance, thoughts of the uncertainties
of this world where no return can be relied upon drew belated
tears to my sleeves, and *even the moon reflected in those drops seemed
a tearful face*, so that it was with tremulous heart that I arrived at
the Barrier of Ōsaka.

Here I could not discover even the lingering traces of Semimaru's[5] famous hut of old, where he once lived and wrote the
words 'whether in palace or in lowly hut / all is boundless', and
the form I saw reflected when I bent to the Barrier's pure spring
waters moved me with the unfamiliar traveller's guise of my
departure's *first steps on the far journey*, halting my feet.

A single cherry tree stood there at the height of its blossoming,
and even this my eyes were loath to leave. There in the blossoms'
shade also rested four or five others on horseback, apparently
country folk though neatly dressed. Perhaps they saw those flowers
with the same feelings as myself.

yuku hito no	These cherry blossoms
kokoro o tomuru	halt the heart
sakura kana	of the passerby –
hana ya sekimori	barrier guards of sorts
ōsaka no yama	on Ōsaka Mountain

And with such thoughts I went on my way, to arrive at the way-station called Kagami, or Mirror.

It was just on dusk, and the sight of *asobi* wandering about in search of a night of love filled me with a deep melancholy at the cruel ways of this world. I was touched to sadness too by the dawn's temple bell that sent me on my way again.

tachi-yorite	Though I come to gaze
miru to mo shiraji	at mirroring Mount Kagami
kagami yama	it cannot know
kokoro no uchi ni	the image of that lingering face
nokoru omokage	that still haunts my heart[6]

Days went by, and I came to the waystation of Akasaka in the land of Mino. Unused to travel as I was, the passing days had been hard on me, so in my weariness I paused to stay here. The inn-keeper had two *asobi* with him, sisters who played elegantly on the *koto* and *biwa*, which brought back old times for me,[7] so I ordered up sake for them and asked them to perform. The one who seemed the older of the two was evidently deeply troubled by something, for though she was distracting herself by plucking the *biwa* tears filled her eyes, and I watched her full of sympathy to imagine that she was surely suffering much as I was. These tears of mine at memories of lost love, so unbecoming to a nun's black sleeves, must have troubled her, for she wrote this poem on the tray that held the sake cups, and handed it to me:

omoi-tatsu	What was in your heart
kokoro wa nan no	that prompted you to rise
iro zo to mo	and leave the world behind you

| *fuji no keburi no* | haunting as Fuji's smoke that drifts |
| *sue zo yukashiki* | on to some unknown end? |

Taken completely by surprise at this unexpectedly elegant gesture, I responded with:

fuji no ne wa	Mount Fuji's peak
koi o suruga no	lies in the land of Suruga
yama nareba	linking it with love[8]
omoi ari to zo	so the smoke that rises there
keburi tatsuran	must issue from love's fierce fires

Prone as my heart was to linger over all I loved, even this passing encounter was hard to leave behind me, yet there was nothing for it, and I went on my way again.

Arriving at Yatsuhashi, I found no flowing streams there.[9] Not even the famous bridges were to be seen, and I felt as if deprived of a friend.

ware wa nao	My heart still enmeshed
kumode ni mono o	with thoughts as tangled
omoedomo	as those spidery streams
sono yatsuhashi wa	but at Yatsuhashi now
ato dani mo nashi	all sign of any bridge is gone

I paused on my way to worship at Atsuta Shrine in the land of Owari. Praying at the sacred fence, memories suddenly flooded me. This shrine had been part of my late father's domain, and by way of a personal prayer offering in the fifth month he would always send a sacred horse[10] for the shrine festival; the year of his final illness he added a raw silk robe, but then the horse suddenly died en route at the waystation of Kayatsu. Dismayed, they found a substitute to offer from the stable of a resident governing official, we learned, but I remember that it troubled my mind, for it seemed to me that the gods had refused to accept his offering. All this came back to me now, and I spent the night there deep in sorrow and pining over the past.

It was past the twentieth day of the second month that I left the Capital, but being so little accustomed to the road, though my heart urged me forward I was travelling slowly, and it was by now the beginning of the third month. Seeing the evening moon rise resplendent in the sky recalled to me that same sight above the Capital, and I seemed to see before my eyes again the dear face of His Majesty. The flowering cherries in the shrine precinct looked so proud of their splendid blossoms. Just who was this beauty for? I wondered sadly.

haru no iro mo	Now the lovely flowers
yayoi no sora ni	come to spring's skies
narumigata	as I to Narumi
ima ikuhodo ka	yet how soon now will they pass
hana mo sugimura	leaving behind a cedar grove of green[11]

This I wrote on an offering card which I hung on a cedar tree before the shrine.

Having prayers I wished to make, I stayed in retreat here seven days, then set off once more. As I made my way ever onward over the tidal sands of Narumi, I paused to look back at Atsuta Shrine and glimpsed the red of its sacred fence, now hazed with mist, majestic in the distance, prompting unstoppable tears at my father's memory.

kami wa nao	Look on me, oh gods,
aware o kakeyo	with pity still
mi-shimenawa	though the rope of my life
hiki-tagaetaru	twines a different way now
ukimi nari to mo	and I wander here forlorn

I crossed the Barrier of Kiyomi by the moon, my heart full of sad ponderings on all that was past and to come. With thoughts more numerous than the white-spread sands of the beach that stretched before me, on I went around the skirts of Mount Fuji through Ukishima-ga-hara. Snow still lay piled deep on Fuji's peak, and as I gazed it seemed quite plausible that Narihira should have found *the dappled snow* still lying even in the fifth month. How pointless, I thought, to pile thought upon thought like these snows, when I must come to nothing in the end. Fuji's smoke too was now no more, it seemed – what was any longer left to *trail lingering in the wind*?[12]

Then I crossed Mount Utsu, but seeing no sign of Narihira's *vines and maples* thronging the path I was quite unaware of where I was and failed to take it in, only learning when I asked later that I had already passed it.

koto no ha mo	Where were those vines
shigeshi to kikishi	that have so thronged
tsuta wa izura	this road with words?
yume ni dani mizu	I knew of them, but even in my dreams
utsu no yama-goe	saw nothing as I crossed Mount Utsu[13]

Pausing to pray at Mishima Shrine in the land of Izu, I found that the offering ceremony was just like that of the Kumano pilgrimage, with a most awe-inspiring dragon image. A distinguished lady in traveller's garb was performing the Ten Thousand Venerations on the shore, a practice begun by the late Shogun Yoritomo,[14] and seeing her wretched figure pacing endlessly to and fro made me wonder if she was indeed as unhappy as I.

The long-awaited moon rose well into the night. *Brief nights are cause for sorrow*, but here it was beguiling to watch the shrine maidens making their strange gestures as they danced the sacred *kagura*. The overgown that they wear for shrine duties is somewhat like a child's robe. They danced something called the Eight Maidens Dance, and the sight of groups of three or four weaving around each other was so engrossing that I stayed up all night to watch, only leaving the shrine when the cocks' crows signalled the dawn.

It was after the twentieth day when I arrived in Enoshima, a place so lovely that words in fact fail me. I spent the night in one of the many rock retreats on the island, which lies far out over the boundless sea, a place called Senju Cave where an aged mountain ascetic was performing the Merit Accumulation austerities. Crude though his dwelling was, hedged only with the mist and with bamboos for screen, yet the place had true elegance. He was most hospitable, serving up shellfish and other local delicacies. When I presented him with a fan and other gifts from the Capital produced from my companion's satchel, he declared that living where he did, he heard no news from the Capital. 'The *visiting winds* certainly never bring me such gifts as these,' he went on. 'I have met with old friends this evening!' I could see just what he meant. Nothing more was said, and we all settled down for the night.

The night grew late, but lying there on the renunciate's mossy mat in *the long-worn robe* of my far journey, thoughts piling one on another, I did not doze enough to even dream. Sleeves soaked in the muffled tears I hid from others, I rose and went to stand outside the cave, where *billowing cloud mingled as one with billowing smoke*. Then *night's clouds lifted and disappeared, while the moon* seemed held there motionless, high and bright in the sky, and I felt that I had indeed wandered the poet's *two thousand miles from home*. From the mountains somewhere behind came the sudden shriek of a monkey – *it rent my heart*, and I felt all the sadness in me rise up as fresh as ever. I had left the Capital, I thought miserably, hoping perhaps to find a way to dry the tears of my lonely thoughts and griefs, but the sorrows of this world had covertly come along with me:

sugi no io	A simple cedar hut
matsu no hashira ni	rough pine for pillars
shino sudare	hung with coarse-leaved blinds –
ukiyo no naka o	could I but leave
kake-hanareba ya	the sad world far behind me

[. . .] The following morning I entered Kamakura.

After returning to the Capital, Nijō continued a life of active pilgrimage. The following journey dates from the late autumn of 1302, when she was forty-five. She is travelling by boat to visit Itsukushima Shrine on the island of Miyajima.

It was by this time early in the ninth month, and from the frost-withered grasses rose the soft intermittent cries of autumn insects that now sang their last. The boat drew in to shore and we spent the night at anchor there, and the *thousand, nay ten thousand beats* of a fulling block came to me bearing thoughts of wintry villages on dark nights, a sorrowful sound to hear from my listening pillow on the waves. Then it was moving to see the boats on Akashi Bay, *slipping away in the morning mist to be lost among islands.*[15] I felt I knew to the full how Prince Genji felt when he longed to gallop back to the Capital on *a moonlit roan,*[16] as we rowed on down the coast until we reached Tomo in the land of Bingo.[17]

Offshore from the busy post town lay a little island by the name of Taiga, where a number of *asobi* had left the sad world behind to live together in a group of huts. Destined from birth to ply that deeply squalid trade, that condemned them to endless rebirth in the lower realms, they had long lived a life of scented robes, their one thought to find a man to love more fully, wondering as they combed out their hair each morning upon whose pillow it would tangle again that night, waiting at evening for customers, at daybreak left to sigh over another loss, and I was impressed and moved that they had turned their back on all that to live here now in seclusion.

'How do you follow your religious practice?' I asked. 'How did you come to awaken to the Buddhist Way?'

One of the nuns replied, 'I am the leader of the *asobi* on this island. Once I collected lovely girls and sold their various charms to passersby, happy when someone paused upon his way, lamenting as each disappeared again. I swore eternal love to unknown men, beguiling them with drink and affection *transient as the dew beneath the flowers,* until, past fifty, impelled perhaps by some karmic prompting, I awoke one day to the truth of this mutable world of ours, and once awakened there was no returning. So I came to this island, where my practice is each morning to climb the hill and gather flowers, which I offer to the buddhas of the three worlds.'

Envying them their life, I stayed here several days and then went on my way again. 'When will you return to the Capital?' they asked as I left, and I thought to myself, *It may be that I go no more.*

isa ya sono	For all the nights
ikuyo akashi no	I pause to sleep and wake with dawn
tomari to mo	port after port
kanete wa e koso	there could be no sure way
omoi-sadamenu	to set my passage

I arrived at the island of Itsukushima, where from afar the great shrine gate soars up from the flooding waves, and a vast expanse of roofed galleries stands out there in the bay, with a huge crowd of boats drawn up to them. There was to be a great religious ceremony, and all the priestesses were busy here and there, it seemed. On the twentieth day of the month a stage was set up over the water, surrounded by galleries, and the priestesses appeared from the altar for a rehearsal of the performance. There were eight of them, all wearing variously coloured short-sleeved robes beneath white cloaks. The music was the usual shrine music, but I was shaken by memories when I learned that the dance was the one that the famous Chinese beauty Yang gui-fei performed for her emperor.[18] The formal brocade clothing worn by the dancers on the stage's right and left on the day of the performance was just like that of Bodhisattvas.[19] The glittering headdresses and ornamental hairpins of the dancers made them seem very much as one imagines Yang gui-fei would have looked. As the darkness drew in the music soared still more beautifully, and I was particularly struck by the sound of the 'Autumn Wind' piece.

The ceremony ended at nightfall, and the great crowd of people all returned to their various lodgings. The shrine was left forlorn and empty, with only a few others who stayed on through the night to pray. The near-full moon that rose from the mountain behind seemed to emerge from the very shrine itself, and reflected in the rising tide all about, it appeared to dwell both in the sky above and there in the water's depths.

18

A Gift for the Capital
by Sōkyū

By the mid-fourteenth century, the rulers in Kamakura had been defeated and the centre of power had shifted back to the old Capital, although not without considerable bloodshed and political upheaval. The road that ran between the two did not cease to be the important highway it had now been for well over a century and a half, but other roads and other places were also increasingly accessible and travelled. Among these was the area of the main island that lies to the north of Kamakura, known as Michinoku or Oku, once the farthest outpost of the nascent Japanese nation and still, particularly in its remoter parts, considered the back of beyond.[1]

The travel chronicle known as A Gift for the Capital (Miyako no tsuto) is the first extant work in the kikō travel chronicle genre to describe travel in Michinoku, although in many ways it is the inheritor of a far longer tradition of poetic travel writing related to this area. Place names from the Michinoku region appear back in the eighth-century Manyōshū,[2] establishing these sites as early utamakura, and this literary heritage was reinforced in the following century by references in the enormously influential Ise Tales to the wandering hero's sojourn in the area.[3] Michinoku's literary importance was sealed in the following centuries by its significance in the lives and poetry of the two great forerunners of the wandering poet-monk tradition, Nōin and Saigyō,[4] who were revered by the literary travellers who came after them. Sōkyū, the author of A Gift for the Capital, is in every way the inheritor of this wandering poet-monk tradition, and his travel chronicle in turn became an important reference point for Bashō's famous travels in Oku over three hundred years later.

We know little about Sōkyū, although he was an important poet of his day whose poems appear in imperial anthologies, and he is mentioned

*in passing in the diaries of several literary men of the time. Although
'the Capital' was the centre of his world as it had been for all the writers who came before him,*[5] *A Gift for the Capital suggests that Sōkyū
came from northern Kyushu, a provincial origin still far from usual
among the literary classes. How or when he came to be a monk he does
not say, but he evidently belonged to the reclusive rather than the
monastic tradition, inclining him to follow Buddhist teachings through
the practice of meditation rather than scholarly study. He seems to have
had strong connections with the Zen sect, which had arrived in Japan
from China at the end of the twelfth century and was by now well
established. It is telling that he describes his impulse to travel in terms
of the urge to meditate in nature, a tradition that had gained considerable influence in religious circles from the late Heian period onwards,
idealized in the depictions of reclusive holy men found in* Senjūshō.[6]
*A Gift for the Capital describes Sōkyū's wanderings beyond Kam-
akura in terms of 'seeking out teachers of deep understanding', and the
Bearded Monk on the mountain with whom he spends a winter is
clearly in the tradition of* Senjūshō's *holy men.*

*Sōkyū was thus a serious and dedicated recluse monk, and his recur-
ring references to the Buddhist teaching of Impermanence symbolized
by a life of wandering are surely deeply felt. He was not a primarily
literary traveller in the mode of the authors of* Journey along the Sea
Road *or* Journey to the East, *whose journals record the ten days or so
spent on the populous Tōkaidō between Kyoto and Kamakura, pausing at the time-honoured sites; his journey lasted about three years and
took him far into truly remote country in search of spiritual teachers.
Yet A Gift for the Capital is essentially a literary work that uses a
light brush to touch in occasional references to religious matters, and
devotes most of its energies to depicting the experiences of Sōkyū as littérateur, seeking out famous places and composing poetry at* utamakura
in the style of his forebears.

*That long tradition of literary wandering monks, traceable back
through Saigyō and Nōin to the late tenth-century Zōki*[7] *and beyond,
sees no uncomfortable contradiction between relinquishing our deluded
attachment to the phenomenal world and being moved to tears by
the passing blossoms or some sad tale of old. Such poetic sensibility is
indeed the hallmark of the aesthete monk, and in his travels Sōkyū was
particularly intent on seeking out others of like mind, such as the man*

with whom he spends a night in deep conversation in his tastefully rustic house with its scattered plum blossoms by the eaves beneath a hazy moon, and whose death he later laments in anguished terms.

Sōkyū seems to have been a sociable traveller for all his reclusive vows, and there is a sometimes startling contrast between the darker tones of the spiritual wanderer's lonely sorrows on the road and the pleasures of encounters with other men of sensibility, epitomized in his light-hearted indulgence in poetic play with the friends he meets up with[8] *in Musashino as he is returning. While his travels in Michinoku have taken him far from the beaten poetic track, at Musashino he is suddenly back in hallowed literary territory and it seems fitting that he should throw off the sorrows of the journey for a few days and go travelling with friends to visit local* utamakura *and have some poetic fun together. The scene gives us a fascinating glimpse of the more frivolous social pleasures that poetry could provide, and a humorous portrait of the excesses associated with the literary traveller's notorious urge to collect souvenirs.*

It seems Sōkyū set off from Tsukushi (Kyushu) around 1350–52, and his travel chronicle begins, in a short section included here, by briefly alluding in poetic terms to time spent in religious reclusion en route to the Capital, where he pauses briefly before setting off along the Tōkaidō toward Kamakura. The following extract takes up his story from the spring of his third year of wandering, as he travels on from Musashino on his adventurous journey into the northern provinces, and follows A Gift for the Capital *to its close. (See Map 5)*

FROM *A GIFT FOR THE CAPITAL*

There was back in the Kan'ō era (1350–52) a certain recluse monk. Though lacking the will to penetrate the iron ramparts of the higher mysteries, he yearned to follow in the footsteps of those who dwelt *beneath tree and upon rock*,[9] and with the thought that nowhere could be his permanent abode, he set off from the land of Tsukushi. Hither and yon he wandered; a certain connection he knew of led him to make his bed among the clouds of Mount Ōe and dwell with the dews of Ikuno Moor, and thus wandering he came at last to the mountain in Tanba[10] called Iya. Here he stayed out the year, not bothering to construct a shelter worthy of the name, and in the third month of the following spring he went up to the Capital, where he remained a few days, visiting the holy places of Kiyomizu and Kitano, before making up his mind to set off to the East on his austerities.

[. . .] *Having travelled up the Tōkaidō, Sōkyū continued his wanderings west and north.*

On I wandered, hither and yon, seeking out teachers of deep understanding, and I stayed for a long time on Mount Chichibu. Here lived a hermit who never once left his retreat to so much as venture out into the village. Apparently the villagers spoke of him as the Bearded Monk, but no one knew where he had come from or what manner of person he had been.

I stayed out the winter there, and when spring arrived I set off once more. As I was crossing over to the land of Kōzuke, I chanced upon someone who gave me a night's lodgings in his home. It was very early in the third month, and the hazy moonlight through the branches of a plum tree by the eave, its blossoms now finally scattered, lent an air of refined elegance; the place itself, with its pine pillars and tasteful fence of woven bamboo, suggested that some special circumstance must lie behind this choice of rustic lifestyle.

The master of the house came out to greet me, and asked sympathetically after the sorrows of my journey, with evident sensibility. He went on to enquire in detail about what lay behind my decision to take the tonsure. 'I too am far from unaware of the impermanence of this world,' he told me, 'but I am entangled in many ties that bind me to the world and the final step has to this day remained no more than an intention. Our talk tonight has brought home to me my own indolence in failing to make that commitment. Please stay for a while,' he entreated me, 'and rest from the rigours of the journey.' But I needed to hasten on my way, and I set out with promises to call again on my way back that autumn.

In the autumn around the eighth month, wondering what

might have become of him, I went out of my way to call in there and visit, only to learn that he had recently died and the seventh-day ceremony[11] was about to be held. Inexpressible sorrow filled me at the transiency of life, and in my sadness I berated myself for not having arrived a little earlier – I had so warmly promised to return, and for all that words cannot be trusted, he must have felt betrayed. I asked how his dying had been, and in tears the family told me that he had spoken of me until his final moments. Though far from the first time I had understood the nature of this mortal life, now the suddenness and unpredictable nature of death came home to me afresh. They told me that although his artistic tastes had lain in many directions, he was particularly absorbed by the art of *waka* poetry, so I asked after his long-cherished hopes in life and then, brush tracing my thoughts, wrote this short passage on the wall before I left:

Last spring around the tenth day of the third month, on a long journey through remote lands, I came seeking out the scent of plum blossom, and by the eave of a little dwelling in the Eastern style, delighted in the moonlight. All night long I soothed the sorrows of travel in talk with the master of the house, speaking of matters past and present, reciting poems from China and Japan. This temporary lodging held my heart, but I hastened on into the clouds of the long road ahead, pledging as I set off to meet again during the three months of autumn. Now I have returned, anxious to fulfil my promise, only to find that he is gone too soon. Wracked with love for the one I saw only for one brief night and will not see again, tears of attachment soak my sleeves. Impelled by the emotions that stir within me, I can find no other way to express my grief but this. Though these 'pretty words' may be mere frivolous sin, perhaps in some distant way they can connect to the buddhas.[12]

sode nurasu	Having come back again
nageki no moto o	to find this house of grief
kite toeba	sleeves wet with tears
suginishi haru no	an empty breeze plays under
mume no shitakaze	the plum tree of that spring
	now gone

yūkaze yo	Oh evening wind
tsuki ni fuki-nase	blow across the moon
mishi hito no	and through the shadowed
	grasses
wake-mayouran	where he I knew
kusa no kage o mo	will be wandering lost

Despairing of this worthless world of ours, on I wandered aimlessly, pierced by the chill wind as I passed through Muro no Yashima and on.

Having left the Capital in spring, I was now passing the Barrier of Shirakawa at autumn's end, and the aptness of the famous poem by Nōin of Kosobe[13] – 'Though with the rising mists / of spring I rose / and left the Capital / the autumn wind blows chill / at Shirakawa Barrier' – was brought home to me. The story goes that Nōin, regretting that he had written this poem without in fact coming here, hid himself away and put it about that he had gone off East, then told the world that he had composed the poem at Shirakawa. Perhaps he did in fact come this way at some stage, for after all, he composed the travel account *Yasoshima no ki*.[14] One need not go to the lengths of Kuniyuki, who is said to have carefully smoothed his sidelocks before entering this hallowed place,[15] but it was certainly a place worthy of passing with a certain reverence, and it felt remiss of me not to do so.

miyako ni mo	The autumn wind
ima ya fukuramu	that will be blowing too
akikaze no	back in the Capital
mi ni shimi-wataru	pierces me now
shirakawa no seki	at Shirakawa's barrier gate

From here I went on into the land of Dewa and made my way on past the Marshes of Asaka, pausing to visit the famous Pine of Akoya as I went. Legend had it that when Lord Sanekata came this way he searched about for the irises traditionally used for thatch at the fifth month festival,[16] and finding only the local rushes called *katsumi*, declared that since the old texts specified only 'water plants' these amounted to the same thing, so *katsumi* were used instead.

In the seventh year of Kanji (1093) at the Empress Ikuhōmon'in's fifth month festival poetry competition, Fujiwara no Takayoshi composed the poem 'How might these irises / have grown in Asanuma's shallow marsh? – / so long of root / the hand that draws them out / tires with pulling.' This had long made me wonder if there were indeed irises in this place, so I enquired of a local. 'It's not that there are no irises hereabouts,' he told me, 'but when Lord Sanekata came this way he declared that it was pointless to put the irises of the Capital on the eaves of ignorant country folk,[17] and it was more sensible to use the local rushes.' I could see that there was indeed some sense in this explanation. I record this because the same story is also told by an old man in the local annals so it may well be true.

I proceeded to ask the way of this man, and went on towards the village of Yamada. There by the sea I found a thatched hut, not made with any eye to elegance but somehow suggestive of an interesting story, so I spent the night there with the owner. It was approaching the full moon of the ninth month; a stormy wind raged down from the mountain behind, its howl mingling with the mournful belling of a nearby stag. Before me stretched the sea, the late moon's reflection lay over the water, and as I listened to the *incessant cries of plover to plover*, I felt my heart cleansed and purified.

The next morning, setting out to cross a far stretch of plain, I asked its name and learned that it was Hashiri-i (Running Well). It seemed that the name perhaps derived from the fact that this was a long and lonely stretch of road infested with local brigands who might attack, so travellers must run desperately along it.

There were times when I slept alone, blanketed in the wind off the high peaks; times when I woke to waves pounding the rocky shore, sleeves soaked from the wandering traveller's sorrowing sleep. Times also when I chanced to hear in the grass by my pillow the small cry of insects weakening in the cold, and knew that autumn was at its end; or looking up from yet another bed in some fisherman's rough hut, knew from the sky that the moon was rising now above a flood tide.

Wandering thus, drawn on along the road, I crossed the Shirakawa Barrier and, past the twentieth day, came to the banks of

a broad river. This was none other than the Abukuma River. I had
heard tell of this remote place back in the Capital, and now standing beside it I felt the full force of how immensely far my journey
had brought me. The ferryman drew up his boat, I and the other
travellers hurried aboard, and as I gazed out over the wide water
I saw that from the layered mountain range beyond smoke was
rising. I asked the boatmen about it, and they told me that it had
begun in the same year the Kamakura government had fallen,[18]
and continued ever since. Strange indeed.

Disembarking and going on my way, I saw by the wayside a
grave mound. It was evidently the doing of passersby, with a
number of poems attached to nearby trees. Someone explained to
me that it was the grave of the long ago Chinese Prince Dong
Ping, who had died here yearning for his distant home, and it was
no doubt his longing that made the plants that grew upon his
grave mound all lean westward toward China. Moved by this
tale, I was reminded of the similar story of the green grasses that
grew on Wang Zhaojun's grave.[19] It seemed to me that any traveller who met his end beneath a foreign sky would surely long for
the night smoke of his funeral pyre / to drift toward home, and I sighed
at the folly of our worldly attachments. It moved me, too, to
wonder if the dense line of pines that grew about the grave
mound were what they call *unai-matsu,* the pines planted to mark
a grave, and the thought put me in mind of certain old tales.

furusato wa	Home – what is it
ge ni ika nareba	that still our hearts
yume to naru	even when we have died
nochi sae nao mo	and turned to dream
wasurezaruran	remember it with love?

On I went still further, sleeping a traveller's sleep sheltered beneath
the famous Pine of Takekuma,[20] where I drank in the beauty of the
moonlight that shone through its double trunk, then on over the
crossing at Natori River, sorrowing to see the water forever flowing
on without return. The *drops that fall beneath the trees of Miyagino*
were indeed, as the old poem says, too heavy for any rain hat to
withstand. The flowers with their many colours seemed a spread

brocade over the earth. One particularly caught my eye – a bush clover of unusually fine hue at a village called Motoara, a name suggesting wildness.[21] Breaking off a branch:

miyagino no	When might it be
hagi no na ni tatsu	that Motoara village
motoara no	long famed for the bush clover
sato wa itsu yori	of Miyagino
are-hajimekemu	slipped into wilderness?

So I thought to myself. People had once lived here, where now were only wild fields and shrubs, and nothing remained to be seen but one small grass-thatched hut. Moved, I wondered if *those of old had once lamented the falling flowers* of this plant too.

I heard, by the way, that the Bush Clover of Motoara was so called because the flowers bloomed on the tough old branches that remained after burning in spring the previous year, which also led to its being called 'tree clover'. It may also be because the way the branches grow is tougher and coarser than the normal bush clover. I had long thought that the Motoara Cherry of old poems was a mere name, but this new information made me wonder for the first time if it too was named so after this very village.

I now arrived at Michinoku's regional centre of Taga. From here I turned south onto the Narrow Road of Oku,[22] and went in search of Sue no Matsuyama of poetic fame. Gazing out across the piney flatland, it did indeed look almost as if *the waves poured over it*, while the little fishing boats beyond seemed to be *sailing above the tree tops*.

yūhi sasu	Evening sun pours down
sue no matsuyama	on Sue no Matsuyama
kiri harete	and as the sea mist rises
akikaze kayou	a shifting autumn breeze
nami no ue kana	plays above waves

I arrived at the Bay of Shiogama as the day darkened. The deity of this place takes the form of a salt kiln;[23] here I spent the night before the altar in prayer. A high suspension bridge is slung across the inlet on the east of the bay, which leads onto the road stretching beyond it. There is also a road that skirts the shoreline and runs on beneath the mountains. The smoke rising from the long row of fisherfolk's houses suggested that salt fires must be burning there. Perhaps it was the place I was in, but the *tow ropes of the little boats that row about the bay* seemed to be tugging at my very heart. Under the late moon an oar's soft intermittent sound filled me with melancholy. I understood then the words of the old poet:[24] 'Of the sixty provinces and more under imperial rule, none can compare to Shiogama.'

ariake no	Dawn's paling moon
tsuki to tomo ni ya	and with it fishing boats
shiogama no	rowing out across the bay
ura kogu fune mo	of Shiogama
tōzakaruramu	recede toward nothing

From here I went around the edge of the bay to see Matsushima. Just as the old poem says, *the dwellings of the fisherfolk bespoke poetic hearts* there. Here there is a temple called Enpukuji, founded by the Zen master Kakuman.[25] The monastery apparently holds about one hundred monks. The temple commands a view south over Shiogama Bay, and the term 'a thousand islands' seems to fall far short of the untold numbers visible there. One, known as Oke no Tōjima, lies far out over the sea. A vast number of islands lie between. A bridge connects to one of the distant islands east of Matsushima, where there is a temple hall by the name of Godai-dō, or Hall of the Five Greats, and indeed there are five buddhas enshrined there. To the south, by the shore under the mountain, is a narow road. Going along this path right beside the sea, one comes to a headland where pines lean out over the water, their tips soaked with the waves. The boats that ply the waters there seem to be passing right through the green of those hanging branches.

A little way off is a tiny island. This is the famous Ojima. Here a rope draws a little boat perpetually to and fro. On this island is a temple. It enshrines the three Bodhisattvas that lead the soul to the other world, and an image of the Bodhisattva Jizō. About a hundred metres to the south of Ojima lies a wonderfully moving place of deep moss beneath a thicket of pine and bamboo. This is where the people of this area have their bones laid to rest when they die. Here also is a large collection of the topknots of those who have been impelled to cut their hair and become Buddhist monks. I was deeply moved by this place and stayed several days, savouring its spiritual purity.

dare to naki	On Ojima's rocky shore
wakare no kazu o	the wild waves fling teardrops
matsushima ya	that speak of the many dead
ojima no iso no	unnamed and numberless
namida ni zo miru	as Matsushima's islands

I now decided to take to my road again, and found myself in Musashino once more. Here, to my great surprise, I met up with someone from the Capital who was eager to talk to me about the Way of poetry, and I was delighted to find several other old friends besides who joined me for a while on the road. We went about visiting the famous places thereabouts, Horikane Well among them, leaving me replete with a happy sense of fine memories of this time. This may have been how Narihira felt, I thought to myself, when he came upon the monk Sosei on Mount Utsu.[26]

It had seemed to me a great shame simply to view the very famous Sue no Matsuyama as I passed – and after all, others before me had gone so far as to collect mementos such as shavings from the Bridge of Nagara or a dried frog from Ide[27] – so I had raked up some fallen pine needles and found among them a hat-shaped pine cone which I took as a souvenir. I had also collected mementos from the Bay of Shiogama in the form of shells and so forth, and all these I now took out and showed my friend. This elicited the following poem:

sue no matsuyama	This traveller's pine hat
matsukasa wa	from Sue no Matsuyama
kitaredomo	cover me though it may

nami dani kosaba	will not keep off the flooding tears
mata ya nurenan	whose waves wash over me

In reply I composed this:

nami kosanu	Though no wave floods me
sode sae nurenu	yet my sleeves are wet
sue no matsu-	sleeping a traveller's sleep
yama matsukasa no	sheltered by this hat of pine
kage no tabine ni	at Sue no Matsuyama

Savouring our unperishing bond, I did indeed soak my traveller's sleeve with many tears, whereupon my companion:

tomonawade	What point in looking
hitori yukiken	at the salt-soaked shells you bring
shiogama no	from Shiogama Bay
ura no shiogai	since I was not there with you
miru kai mo nashi	to see it?

In reply:

shiogama no	What point indeed
ura mi mo hate wa	in the salty shells
kimi ga tame	given this bitterness
hirou shiogai	though it was all for you
kai ya nakaran	I gathered them at Shiogama?

And so I wandered on, drawn by my heart, and the days passed, and I grew haunted by thoughts of home as I hurried on my returning way – although no certain road can ever lead us back – until one night in an inn *my aged eyes woke early*, and by the *dying lamplight flickering on the wall*, I thought to keep in memory all the famous places from my journey that stayed with me so movingly, and wrote this down, adding no explanation of what came before and after, to bring it back with me as a traveller's gift to the Capital.

19

Sumida River
by Kanze Motomasa

As Sōkyū, author of A Gift for the Capital, *wandered the roads in the mid-fourteenth century he would have come across popular entertainers of many kinds, both itinerant and locally based, and no doubt paused to enjoy their performances. This thriving world of entertainment, glimpsed down the centuries from passing references in diaries and tales,*[1] *seldom impinges directly on the history of Japanese literature until the seventeenth century, but in the late fifteenth century a combination of circumstance, innovative genius and extraordinary talent lifted a provincial troupe of what were called* sarugaku[2] *performers to prominence and produced the new art form now known as Nō drama.*

In 1374, the current Shōgun Ashikaga Yoshimitsu (1358–1408) attended a performance at a shrine[3] *at the south-eastern edge of Kyoto. What he witnessed there was a form of proto-Nō, no doubt considerably different from the classic Nō performances seen today and much closer to its popular origins, but nevertheless compelling enough to impress Yoshimitsu, a connoisseur of the arts. He was particularly impressed by the troupe's leader Kan'ami (1333–84) and his young actor son Zeami (?1363–?1443), and it seems to have been his decision to become their patron that effectively propelled Nō from a form of commoners' entertainment to the refined and exquisite theatrical and literary form that it quickly became.*

Kan'ami was a gifted innovator and dramatist, who synthesized and refined the disparate elements of drama, music, song and dance to create a unified and moving theatrical experience. (A number of his plays are still performed now.) Zeami inherited, further refined and greatly enriched this new form, and his is the primary name associated with Nō today. At times his life as youthful favourite of the Shōgun must have been far from easy,[4] *but the cultural education Zeami received thanks* to that patronage flowered into plays that are still recognized today as dramatic and literary masterpieces. He is among the first examples of a lowly commoner who rose to become an esteemed and even revered practitioner within the world of Japan's high and still essentially courtly culture.

We do not know how different performance styles were in Zeami's time,[5] but the meticulous traditionalism of Nō means that we can trust that our experience of the plays is in many ways quite close to that of centuries past.[6] In a Nō theatre the audience sits before and to one side of a raised roofed stage, containing at most a single and largely symbolic prop and approached by the actors along a bridge to the left; three or four musicians (flute, and several different drums) sit at stage rear, and at stage left sits a chorus. In a typical play there are two main protagonists – the waki or 'side figure', whose role it is to introduce and frame the play's story and to interact with the main protagonist or shite, whose story it is. The shite usually wears a mask, often of a generic type ('young woman', 'warrior', and so on) and largely expressionless. Gestures are highly stylized (left hand raised to bowed face signifies weeping, and so on), the movements are slow and precisely choreographed and executed, the words are sonorously intoned and, at times of intensified emotion, sung to the accompaniment of intermittent drum beats and sometimes a high-pitched flute, which also accompany the dance performed by the shite as the emotional culmination of the play.

The combined effect of all this heightens and concentrates the performance far above any felt need for realism and towards the numinous, an effect reinforced by the plays' contents. While the waki is always a human the shite is frequently revealed in the course of the play to be supernatural, often a haunted spirit or even a deity. In a stereotypical Nō play, a travelling priest (waki) might encounter at a certain place a local person (shite) who relates a moving story associated with the place and in the process is revealed to be the suffering spirit of the person in that story, at the end released from torment by the priest's prayers. The plays build slowly towards an emotional climax and often a spiritual catharsis, in which the shite's dance plays a crucial expressive role. For all their almost excruciating slowness and extreme stylization, Nō plays can often provide an intense and somehow other-worldly experience.[7]

The theme of travel plays a prominent role in Nō drama. The typical *presence of a traveller* (waki) *who witnesses the* shite*'s story while on his journey links Nō back to collections of Buddhist tales such as* Senjūshō,[8] *with their travelling priest protagonist and his encounters in remote places. A place and its associated story is central to the structure of most Nō plays in a way that closely echoes the moving stories associated with certain places so often recorded by literary travellers in their journals. The special, compelling power of a place that is identified as a poetic* utamakura *(which can be the result of an associated story) bears a strong resemblance to the numinosity of place identified in the action of a Nō play – indeed the numinous site in a play is sometimes an* utamakura *in its own right. Nō plays present to us a world in every way outside that of normal everyday life, and travel, with its spatial, social and psychic dislocations and its potential for intense encounters with the strange and other, provides Nō with a potent realm within which its dramatic enactments can unfold.*

The play Sumida River *(*Sumida-gawa*), included here in its entirety, takes close to an hour and a half to perform. Among Nō's most famous plays,[9] it was written by Zeami's son, Motomasa (?1400–1432). Its site is the ferry crossing on the Sumida River that now flows through Tokyo but that then marked the boundary between two remote provinces, beyond which lay the far land of Michinoku. This is the site of a famous scene in* The Ise Tales, *that touchstone for literary travel writing, which gives it* utamakura *status and which lies behind the poetic exchanges between the Woman and the Ferryman. There are two travellers, one a witnessing visitor and the other the* shite, *a woman who has come from the Capital crazed with grief in search of her stolen child,[10] while the supernatural is present in the form of the child's spirit (a child who sits hidden inside the prop representing the grave mound) that finally and briefly emerges from the grave[11] in response to her anguish and prayers at the play's climax.*

As in all Nō plays, the language shifts between versions of prose (intoned) and varying degrees of a more poetic register that broadly follows a 5/7 rhythm (chanted on several tones, often with considerable ornamentation), which is indicated here with spaced phrases. In these more heightened sections, which transcend the everyday world most completely, the chorus frequently takes up the narration or speaks on behalf of a character, and at times the Ferryman and the Woman also alternate as a single voice.

SUMIDA RIVER

Waki: FERRYMAN
Wakitsure: TRAVELLER
Shite: WOMAN
Kokata:[12] CHILD'S GHOST

> [*At the centre back of the performance space, in front of the musicians, is a representation of a grave mound bearing a willow branch. Invisible inside it is the child. To soft flute music, the Ferryman enters along the bridge and goes to stand upstage, stage right.*]

FERRYMAN: I am the ferryman of the Sumida River in the land of Musashino, and today I must set out quickly and carry my passengers across. Be it known that for certain reasons there is to be an important Buddhist ceremony here, so there will be a large crowd of both monks and lay folk. [*He sits left of centre.*]

> [*Flute and drums begin, and the Traveller enters and stands by the rear left pillar, back turned to the audience.*]

TRAVELLER: Onward to the East's far reaches   clad in traveller's cloak   onward to the East's far reaches   clad in traveller's cloak   and in my heart the passing days   stretch on with the distant road. [*Turns to face forward.*]

I stand before you thus, a traveller from the Capital, going East to visit one I know there.

Cloud and mist behind me   shroud the far mountains I have crossed   cloud and mist behind me   shroud the far mountains I have crossed   along the road from land to land and barrier gate to barrier gate   to reach at last the famous Sumida   and stand now at the crossing   and stand now at the crossing.

> [*Walking forward.*]

Hastening onward, here I suddenly find myself, at the river crossing of the Sumida. And look, over there I see the ferry about to pull away. I must be quick and board! Ferryman, might I board your boat?

FERRYMAN: Most certainly. But tell me, what is that great commotion behind you?

TRAVELLER: Indeed yes, what you see there is a mad woman down from the Capital, who has lost her mind and behaves quite crazily. Everyone is gathered round to watch the fun.

FERRYMAN: If that's the case, I'll wait for her before I set off to cross.

[*Ferryman and Traveller sit stage left. Flute and drums play, and the Woman enters along the bridge, wearing a large traveller's hat and holding a sprig of bamboo grass, signifying madness. She pauses on the bridge, facing the audience.*]

WOMAN: True though it is *a parent's heart   is not by nature blind to reason's light   yet it can wander lost   through love of one's child* and now indeed wandering snowy roads   I know it to be so. How shall I tell my heart, how shall I ask   the passing travellers where my child might be? [*She proceeds to the stage.*]   Listen. Even the wind   that blows about the skies

CHORUS: comes calling on the pines and speaks there.

WOMAN: [*Drums and flute play while she moves around the stage in a short dance*] Transient the dew on Makuzu Moor

CHORUS: and must I day and night   live on, bewailing fate?

WOMAN: I am a woman who dwelt many years   at Kitashirakawa in the Capital.   Alas my only child   was taken by child traders   and when I asked for him I learned   he had crossed Ōsaka's Barrier   and gone to a far land they call the East   and my heart was crazed with sorrow   and so I wander here in search   my mind astray in longing for him. [*She weeps.*]

CHORUS: They say a parent's unforgetting heart   keeps constant though a thousand miles away   but though the bond lasts only this brief lifetime   but though the bond lasts only this brief lifetime   yet even here we cannot be together   mother and child torn apart   and I like that *grieving mother bird   whose chicks have flown and gone.   [She begins moving, indicating travel]* Here where all my heart's fierce searching   has led at last, I come   to the road's end, the border   of Musashi and Shimōsa [*she arrives near the grave*] to the Sumida River   to the Sumida River.

[*Music ceases.*]

WOMAN: [*Addressing Ferryman*] Excuse me ferryman, please take me in your boat.

FERRYMAN: And where might you be from and going to?

WOMAN: I have come from the Capital in search of someone.

FERRYMAN: Be you from the Capital or be you mad, entertain us with your crazy antics or else I will not let you board my boat.

WOMAN: How unfeeling! Surely if you are the Sumida ferryman you must cry, 'Hurry aboard, the sun goes down'![13]

To claim that someone from the Capital   whoever it may be   must not board his ferry   how could the ferryman say such an unlikely thing?

FERRYMAN: Ah, sure enough, your cultivation proves *your name is true*, and you do indeed hail from the Capital.

WOMAN: And your words likewise ring true to my ear, for Narihira once stood thus at this crossing and said: Capital bird   if your name is true   then tell me –   she whom I love   does she live or die?[14]

Look, ferryman, yonder white birds are not seen in the Capital. Tell me their name.

FERRYMAN: Why, those are seagulls.

WOMAN: Oh how unfeeling! Be they gulls or be they plovers, why do you not name these white birds on the Sumida 'Capital birds'?

FERRYMAN: [*Music begins.*] True enough, I spoke in error.   Living here as I do   at such a famous place   it was crass not to call them 'Capital birds'.

WOMAN: Those seagulls on the evening waves   go back to Narihira long ago

FERRYMAN: who asked them 'does she live or die?'   thinking of his beloved wife at home

WOMAN: as I too now come East in yearning   begging to know where my lost child might be.

FERRYMAN: In longing for his wife

WOMAN: in searching for my child

FERRYMAN: these two same loving hearts

WOMAN: travel the one road. [*She dances while the Chorus chants.*]

CHORUS: And so I too   will ask you, Capital birds   does my child live or die   along this Eastern road?   Does my child live or die   along this Eastern road?   I beg and beg   and yet unfeeling birds   you do not answer.   Rather I should call you

mere boorish country birds then   gathered here crying   just
as in that old poem   in distant Naniwa[15]   *along the shores   of
Horie River   massed with boats   the Capital birds   throng
clamouring.*   That was then on Naniwa's waters   and now I
too at the East's Sumida   *lament how very far away I am.*   Ah
well, oh ferryman   though your boat is crowded   let me
board oh ferryman   and so let me board.

FERRYMAN: So refined for a mad woman! Quick then, hurry
aboard. [*She removes her traveller's hat and holds it, then goes forward and sits, while the Ferryman stands behind her holding the
oar.*] This is a dangerous crossing. Please take care to sit still.
[*Beckons to the Traveller, who also seats himself.*]

TRAVELLER: Look, under that willow on the far bank a crowd has
gathered. What is that about?

FERRYMAN: Yes indeed, an important ceremony is taking place.
There's a moving story about it. Let me tell you while we row
across.

On the fifteenth day of the third month last year, precisely
this day in fact, slave traders arrived from the Capital on their
way further east with a young child of no more than twelve or
thirteen. The child must have been exhausted from the hard
journey for he was very ill, and he collapsed on this river bank
unable to take another step.

How hard-hearted some people are! They simply abandoned
him by the road and went their way on east. Some local people
meanwhile found this poor little boy, saw that he seemed
no common child and did all they could to care for him, but
perhaps he was fated, for he grew weaker and weaker. When it
was clear that he was dying they asked him where he came
from and his family name. [*The woman is listening increasingly
intently.*] 'I am the only child', he said, 'of one called Yoshida
from Kitashirakawa in the Capital. My father died early
and I was brought up solely by my mother, but slave traders
kidnapped me and so you find me here. I yearn for the sight
of people from the Capital, so please make a burial mound
for me beside the road here and on it plant a marking willow
tree.' He spoke like one beyond his years. Then he repeated
the invocation to Amida[16] four or five times, and all was over.

[*Overcome with emotion, the Woman weeps.*] A very touching tale it is!

Now I come to think of it, some of you would be from the Capital. Unrelated though you are, do pause to offer some Invocations for him. Look, while I've been yarning away we've arrived. Quick, quick, off the boat.

TRAVELLER: Most certainly I'll linger here today and pray for him though he is no relation. [*He rises and leaves the boat. The Woman continues to sit and weep.*]

FERRYMAN: Why doesn't that mad woman get out? Come on, out with you! Well well, how moved she is by that tale of mine. She's weeping! There now, quickly, out you get.

WOMAN: [*Seated and continuing to weep.*] Tell me, ferryman, when did this happen?

FERRYMAN: It was this very day in the third month last year.

WOMAN: And his age?

FERRYMAN: Twelve.

WOMAN: And his name?

FERRYMAN: Umewaka-maru.

WOMAN: His patronym?

FERRYMAN: One of the Yoshidas.

WOMAN: And no parent has come since?

FERRYMAN: No relative has come here.

WOMAN: And of course his mother has not come?

FERRYMAN: Naturally.

WOMAN: [*Turning to the corner and speaking with anguish.*] Oh there is good reason why   neither relative nor mother came   for that young child is the son   this mad woman has come seeking. [*She drops her traveller's hat and sprig and covers her face with both hands.*]   Is this some dream?   Oh how dreadful!

FERRYMAN: This is astonishing! Here I was assuming that no one was related to the boy   and it turns out he is your own son, you poor woman. [*He lays down his oar and helps her to stand, leads her to the grave mound, then returns to the side of the stage.*]

WOMAN: [*Kneeling before the grave.*] Believing I would somehow find him   I travelled this far way to the unknown East   to find only this marker   the sole remains of him who is no more.   Ah the cruelty of that fate   that led him here to the

East's farthest reaches   *to turn to earth upon the roadside   where now only spring grasses grow.*   Can this be my son beneath this mound? [*She lowers her head to gaze at the grave.*]

CHORUS: Oh please may they   turn this grave's earth   so that once more I might   see him before me as he was. [*Music begins. She weeps.*]

Had he lived on   he would have done much in the world yet he is gone   he would have done much in the world   yet he is gone   while I his worthless mother   am left behind alive.   His face in life   flickers before my eyes   uncertain as is this world.   Griefs blossom through our lives   tossed in the howling storms of transience   the moon that lights our night between birth and death   is shadowed by clouds of mutability.   Truly I see before me this sad world.   Truly I see before me this sad world.

FERRYMAN: Grieve as you may there's no point to it now. You must simply chant the Invocation and pray for him in the other world.

The moon has risen now   and the wind on the river   blows through the deepening night.   It is the hour for the Night Chant   and all strike their bells and sing   urging her to join. [*He strikes his bell, turning toward the Woman.*]

WOMAN: Stricken with grief the mother   cannot even pray   but throws herself upon the grave in tears. [*She weeps.*]

FERRYMAN: This is not good – though so many others are gathered here it is his mother's mourning prayers that would bring joy to him.

So giving her this bell. [*Placing the bell and hammer before her.*]

WOMAN: I know it's true, it is for my child's sake   and so I too take up the bell [*Picking up the bell and hammer and standing.*]

FERRYMAN: ceasing all grief her chant rings out

WOMAN: chanting together on this moonlit night

FERRYMAN: all hearts intent on western paradise

WOMAN AND FERRYMAN: Hail to the western paradise   to the thirty-six million realms   all with the single name of Amida

CHORUS: *Namu Amida Butsu   Namu Amida Butsu   Namu Amida Butsu*

WOMAN: [*Gazing out to front left.*] The wind and waves that sing on Sumida River join their voice to ours

CHORUS: *Namu Amida Butsu   Namu Amida Butsu   Namu Amida Butsu*

WOMAN: [*Gazing forward into the distance.*] and you Capital birds be true to your name   and add your voices too [*Strikes bell towards grave mound.*]

CHILD: [A *voice from inside the grave mound, chanting with the Chorus.*] *Namu Amida Butsu   Namu Amida Butsu   Namu Amida Butsu*

WOMAN: [*She ceases ringing the bell and approaches the grave intently.*] But listen, that chanting voice I heard was the voice of my child! It seemed to come from within this grave!

FERRYMAN: I too heard it come from there. We should cease our chanting and let the mother chant alone.

WOMAN: [*Kneeling before the grave.*] Longing to hear once more that bird   that speaks with the voice of the dead   Namu Amida Butsu [*She strikes the bell.*]

CHILD: [*Voice from inside the grave mound.*] *Namu Amida Butsu Namu Amida Butsu*, says

CHORUS: [*The child steps out from the grave and stands beside it.*] that voice from beyond   and now a seeming apparition

WOMAN: [*Gazing at the child.*] Is this you my child?

CHILD: Is this you Mother?

CHORUS: [*The Woman stands and approaches the child.*] Both reaching hands to touch and hold [*She reaches to embrace him.*] now he begins to fade once more [*the Child slips from her grasp and re-enters the grave mound*]   and she is overcome. [*She raises her hand and weeps.*]   That remembered face, that apparition [*He briefly reappears, then slips away again. She falls to one knee.*] now seen now gone again   as in the east the dawn's first light grows in the sky and he has disappeared. [*She stands and looks up.*]   What seemed her child is now no more [*She turns to the grave mound.*]   than the wild grasses left as parting sign [*She gazes about her.*]   there on the desolate mound. [*She turns to face forward, raises a hand to her eyes and weeps.*]   Alas for her   alas for her.

20

Journey to Shirakawa
by Sōgi

Like Zeami in the previous century, Sōgi (1421–1502) seems to have been from humble origins, but he too came to consort with the great and powerful and to achieve fame as a superb practitioner of his art. He was one of Japanese poetry's great wanderers, and was accorded a place alongside Nōin and Saigyō in Bashō's list of revered poets of old.

It was not only by choice that so much of Sōgi's life was spent on the road. The times he lived in were not conducive to a quiet life spent in the Capital.[1] *Although in its heyday the Ashikaga military shogunate had successfully exerted power over the nation (as well as encouraging a burgeoning of the arts), by the mid-fifteenth century it had dwindled to become largely ineffectual in the face of the growing power of the provinces. Their rulers' fractious relationships among themselves spilled over into pitched battles that engulfed Kyoto for eleven years from 1467 to 1477, leaving much of the city a smoking ruin and marking the beginning of a long and lawless era that historians term the 'Warring States period'. The Capital – that potent centre of all things cultural, refined and exemplary down the centuries – was now no longer a place to fill the traveller with longing to return.*[2]

Sōgi had the good fortune, in fact, to leave the Capital the year before these so-called Ōnin Wars broke out, heading east in the summer of 1466 for what perhaps became a longer absence than he had intended. The main purpose of this journey would have been neither poetic (to visit utamakura *sites and compose poetry there) nor religious, although he was a tonsured monk who had spent the previous years attached to the great Zen monastery of Shōkokuji in the Capital. Sōgi's reputation as a poet was by now well established, and as he moved about the country he could rely on an enthusiastic welcome and hospitality from the many aspiring practitioners of his art among the provincial warrior*

*clans, eager to learn from him. It was above all as a teacher that he trav-
elled; he was in essence a professional poet, unlike the vast majority of
the poets before him, for whom poetry was an art they practised rather
than being also a practical means of livelihood.*

Skilled composer of traditional tanka *though he was, Sōgi's primary
poetic form was* renga, *or linked verse, a complex and essentially social
art form that had evolved from the courtly* tanka *and had in his day
become something of a craze among the literate classes.* Renga *originated
in an old practice[3] of dividing the composition of a* tanka *between two
people where one composed the first three lines[4] and the other the remaining two, a kind of game in which the second person could reveal their
wit or cleverness by introducing an unusual twist or interpretation.*
Renga, *for long merely an entertaining pastime to set against the seriousness of* tanka *composition, had by Sōgi's time evolved into a serious
practice in its own right, requiring erudition, skill and the mastery of a
great many rules; and itinerant* renga *teachers were in high demand to
guide and improve their patrons' practice of the art.*

Renga's *evolution came about through the crucial development of
adding further links in chain form, so that the initial 5/7/5 + 7/7 was
extended by the addition of another 5/7/5, to which was added in turn
a further 7/7, and so on. Each of these pairs forms a coherent poem in
its own right, which must differ from the poem immediately before it
although it shares its first half with the second half of that poem. The
skill lies in adding your link in such a way that the immediately pre-
ceding link is re-interpreted to form the first half of a different poem,
while your link is in turn re-interpreted by the next poet to create a
different poem again. A* renga *is thus a series of interlocking poems
that creates an endlessly shifting and always suprising flow of differing
'scenes' that fade in and out of each other.*

A renga *(generally of a hundred links) was composed by a group at
a single sitting, led by the senior poet and transcribed by one of the
members as each link was recited.* Renga *composition was thus by
nature a social and convivial activity, and it is not surprising to find a
new sociability in* renga *poets' travel writing that belies the traditional
image of the lonely traveller in the landscape.[5] Sōgi's short travel chronicle* Journey to Shirakawa (Shirakawa kikō), *written in 1468, breaks
markedly with the dominant tradition of travel writing by clearly
depicting a group of people, rather than an ostensibly solitary traveller,*

who in 1464 travel together to visit a famous utamakura *site – the remote Shirakawa Barrier, its old barrier gate long since gone, the site of many famous poems and recorded visits.*

Journey to Shirakawa, *the first of the only two travel chronicles Sōgi wrote despite his rich experience of travel,*[6] *is in every way literary. Not only is the purpose of the journey stated to be a visit to an* utamakura, *but the descriptive content and indeed the writing itself is steeped in poetry and literary allusion. Even a straightforward and apparently realistic description such as that of the escort's bow tip visible above the long grass ahead echoes an earlier work*[7] *in a way that literary readers would have savoured in passing. The prose flows on from phrase to phrase with loose syntactical connections, carrying us irresistibly forward through sentences that can last a page or more and embrace a vast sweep of description and experience.*[8] *The description of the journey itself contains a close-textured weaving of poetic themes, primarily the time-honoured tropes of remoteness and melancholy, given added depth by the poignancy of a constant reaching after references to other sites, both real and literary, to provide the travellers with a sense of security in this intimidatingly unknown world. Much of this undoubtedly expressed their actual experience, yet though clearly based on fact* Journey to Shirakawa *should not be read as a literal record of a journey, but rather as a finely worked artefact.*

Journey to Shirakawa *ends with the hundred-verse* renga *sequence composed by the group, perhaps at their lodgings the following day. The first nine links are translated here.*[9] *Travel is an important thematic category in* renga, *although there are rules restricting and dictating its appearance. In this sequence it dominates the opening section to an unusual degree, no doubt fittingly for the circumstances of composition.*

The opening link (or hokku) *is always composed by the leader of the group, and should depict the present place and/or season, as Sōgi's does here. The second link here then shifts the implied scene to travellers settling down to sleep on the wayside in the wintry rain. The third shifts the scene to sleeping at an inn, the leaves implicitly blown over the floor where the traveller sleeps. In the fourth, the traveller at the inn cannot sleep because of the cold, the wind and the moon. The fifth radically reinterprets the previous link to refer to migrating wild geese on a cold moonlit night who cannot pause to rest. The sixth link shifts the implied scene to the sea, where rough waves prevent the wild geese from*

*landing. In the seventh, the waves instead prevent a boat from setting
out. In the eighth link the waves are whipped up by a brief downpour,
which the boatman waits out. The ninth link reinterprets the implied
boatman as a woodcutter who waits out the downpour under a mountain pine.* (See Map 5)

FROM *JOURNEY TO SHIRAKAWA*

Having fulfilled the urge to see Mount Tsukuba, and pledged to
the dew beneath Kurokami's trees,[10] I travelled on to impose myself
a while on a certain person's kindness at a place called Shioya;
then just as I was setting out again a heavy autumn rain swept in
over the sky, making me hesitate to imagine what lay ahead, yet
there was no pausing longer there, and being accustomed to the
traveller's life we set forth on our way. Our escorts two young
samurai on horseback, other guides as well, we pushed our way
ever on and in, the sound of rushing streams about us *seeming to
vie with our rain-sodden sleeves* to bring us melancholy.

Both samurai turned back, and we went on most forlornly
with just one other, and came to a place called Nasu Moor, hastening on along a path so tangled with high grasses that even our
escort's bowtip was now invisible ahead, so that I wondered miserably how we could have hoped to survive on such a road without
the aid of a warrior to guard us, for though the way through
Musashino too seems endless, yet there at least is the comfort of
knowing its famous grasses,[11] while here one feels quite lost. Then
from the withered autumn plain rose swaying dwarf bamboo
bowed deep with dewdrops, putting me in mind of the poem by
the Minister of the Right,[12] which added a touching savour to the
scene. Yet casting back I recalled the many sorrows of the past.

nagekaji yo	Enough lamenting.
kono yo wa tare mo	In this world we all
ukitabi to	journey a sad and wandering way
omoi-nasu no no	I tell myself, relinquishing
tsuyu ni makasete	my life to Nasu's dews

The others travelling with me also expressed their feelings in poems; then as the dark closed in we reached a place called Ōtawara, where we stayed the night in a rough peasant dwelling, a touching and unusual place with its fire of gathered brushwood. We spoke together of *the poor, unpalatable food*, staying up till dawn exchanging talk, between tears and laughter, but the arrival of disturbing news threatened our hopes for reaching the Barrier, until the kind old master of the house generously provided us with horses, and buoyed by this gift and in fine spirits we went on our way.

All the mountains round about were rich with autumn colours, and lovely too the leaves already scattered here and there; the plumes of pampas grasses continued unchanged from the moors of the day before, and soft cries of autumn insects so faint they seemed scarcely there at all, while the stands of oak brought to mind the wintry trees of Hirano,[13] though I found nothing here remotely reminiscent of the Capital. I felt the tears that stung my eyes in the autumn wind were mine alone, but all my companions too were melancholy as they rode along. The groves of *kashiwagi* oaks were in full colour, beautiful about the feet of the distant mountains, while the ranked stands of *kunugi* somehow gave the feel of walking beneath the shadow of Mount Sao or along Ōkawa's banks.[14] And so we went along, coming at last to a great river, whose towering banks were rich with autumn colours among dark evergreens. I thought of the Ōi River and asked its name, to be told it was Nakagawa, a name that flooded me with sudden images of the Capital.[15] Somewhat comforted by this, I crossed the river, where the torrent foamed down white about us, our floundering horses *stumbling up a spray* that drenched our sleeves, so that it seemed we might be crossing Muko River as in the *Manyōshū* poem.[16]

And now we came upon Kurokawa River, a rather more placid stream than the Nakagawa. Autumn leaves dammed the flow where other streams joined it, green mosses choked our path, and close by a nameless bird sang, at least bringing some consolation in recalling those famous lines,[17] 'better / to be here than back there / in that world of grief'. Deep in this far forest, one tree was so ablaze with colour that we fancied the Mountain Goddess herself might pause to delight in it;[18] and thus on we went, full of wonder, to arrive before long at a place called Yoko-oka.

Here we accepted the hospitality of the village head, and arranged transport for the way before us. All along the road to the Shirakawa Barrier, the sound of the little mountain streams and the wind among pines high on the peaks came to us with a somehow still deeper pathos than usual, while *on every side* whole branches had shed their leaf, exposing the homes of the poor mountain folk to plain sight; in the marshy land below the mountain the frost-withered reeds were snapped and bent, and where the stag would *come calling to his mate around the hill fields*, the watchman's hut stood leaning and deserted, the half-rotted rope that once held the watchman's clapper still dangling there, far more forlorn than any sound would be; and on we went, talking together, until in ahead we saw a particularly dark patch of green. 'Those are the trees around the old barrier gate', our guide explained, and in a daze of excitement we urged our horses forward.

When we reached the Barrier at last we were quite lost for words. The shrines to the Deities of the Two Sites[19] are a most solemn and venerable place. One of the two is dazzlingly impressive, with a hallowed air to both sacred precinct and the buildings themselves, while the other is ancient and derelict, moss for its eaves and the autumnal trees its only fence, strung not with sacred rope but with a tangle of *masaki* vine, and only worshipped now it seemed by passing stormy winds. Moved to irrepressible tears, our thoughts went to those poets of yore, Kanemori and Nōin,[20] and how touched by the melancholy of this place they must have been, and from the fullness of our feelings we too humbly offered a few poor shards of poems.

miyako ideshi	Those spring mists and breezes
kasumi mo kaze mo	when I left the Capital
kyō mireba	today gone utterly –
ato naki sora no	out of the empty sky
yume ni shigurete	a dream's chill rain is falling
yuku sue no	I do not hope to leave
na o ba tanomazu	a name behind

kokoro o ya	but here at Shirakawa's gate
yoyo ni todomen	I would leave all I feel now
shirakawa no seki	for ages yet to come
	Sōgi

Taira no Tadamori, a friend from the Capital, was evidently particularly moved to have come here with me.

omou to mo	Had you not crossed this way
kimi shi koezu wa	I would have heard distant rumour
shirakawa no	rather than truly heard
seki fuku kaze ya	the wind through the barrier gate
yoso ni kikamashi	of Shirakawa
	Tadamori

tazune koshi	Those men of old
mukashi no hito no	who came here long ago
kokoro o mo	their feelings still
ima shirakawa no	felt in the autumn wind
seki no akikaze	that blows now at Shirakawa
	Bokuō

kogarashi mo	Fierce wintry winds
miyako no hito no	have left these vivid autumn leaves
tsuto ni to ya	thinking to make them
momiji o nokosu	Shirakawa's gifts
shirakawa no seki	for travellers from the Capital
	Bokurin

These last two men are from the East, and being drawn to pursue this art of mine they came along with me from the urge to see this famous place.

And so we made our way back together to our lodgings in Yoko-oka, in company with a beautiful early moon, through an evening so lovely *it seemed made expressly for us.*

Composed at the Shirakawa Barrier on the twenty-second day of
the second year of Ōnin (1468)

sode ni mina *shigure o seki no* *yamaji kana*	Sleeves soaked against chill wintry rains along the Barrier's mountain path

Sōgi

ko no ha o toko no *tabi no yūgure*	the fallen leaves as bed dusk settles on the journey

Tadamori

sayaka naru *tsuki o arashi no* *yado ni mite*	seen from lodgings on a stormy night the clear moon

Bokurin

yosamu no sora wa *nenkata mo nashi*	under the cold night sky no way to sleep

Bokuō

ori mo izu *kumo ni ya kari no* *wataruran*	those wild geese somewhere beyond the clouds no rest for them it seems

Jun'a

shiranami araki *oki no harukesa*	rough waves far out over the bay

Sōgi

shibashi dani *kayou mo fune wa* *yasurakade*	even a brief boat journey no easy thing over such water

Tadamori

hito-murasame ni   he rests a while
hito zo yasurau   as the brief downpour passes
                                                        Bokurin

shiba hakobu   beneath a pine tree
oue no michi no   on the high ridge path
matsu ga moto   with his load of firewood
                                                        Bokuō

21

Journal of the Tsukushi Road
by Sōgi

In the late autumn of 1480, the renga *poet Sōgi set out with a small group of poet companions to travel through north-western Kyushu, then known as Tsukushi. Remote from the Capital though this area was, it had long been an important outpost and its presence in Japanese literature down the centuries made it rich in poetic associations.[1] Tsukushi was therefore fertile ground for literary travel, and Sōgi took the opportunity to compose a travel chronicle based on the trip.[2]*

Journal of the Tsukushi Road (Tsukushi michi no ki) *is a very different work from* Journey to Shirakawa, *written twelve years earlier. That compact work in some ways reads as a polished literary preamble to the hundred-link* renga *sequence that ends it, while* Journal of the Tsukushi Road *is a much more relaxed account of a sociable journey. Sōgi was almost sixty when he made this trip, still vigorous and at the height of his reputation as the greatest* renga *poet of his time, although consciousness of old age and death haunts the journal.[3] He had left the Capital some months earlier for one of his periodic lengthy absences, this time to make his way west to Yamaguchi in southern Honshu where he settled in as guest of the local warlord, Ōuchi Masahiro.*

The recent devastating Ōnin Wars had left much of the Capital in ruins, and Japan had entered a time of relative lawlessness that accompanied the growing power of local clan warlords. In such a world, Sōgi was lucky to be able to rely on the patronage and protection of cultivated and powerful men such as Ōuchi, who provided both a safe haven and a cultural space that was a happy alternative to the Capital, and protection for his travels within their domain, which in Ōuchi's case covered the Tsukushi area.[4] On this journey Sōgi would have travelled with introductions wherever he went, and been provided with armed escorts and guarantees of safe passage along roads that might be dangerous.

Journal of the Tsukushi Road *presents us with an intimate portrait of the* renga *poet's itinerant life, as well as of Sōgi himself. The extract translated here (roughly the last fifth of the journal) typically shows Sōgi and his companions finding a welcome wherever they went, lodging each night in the priests' quarters at shrines or Zen temples,[5] or with local men of culture and authority, and frequently staying a day or more to engage in a round of* renga *composition with their hosts, who went out of their way to offer every gesture of hospitality to the honoured poet. The final stays recorded in the journal are particularly interesting for the glimpses they give of the then-fashionable style of 'elegance and refinement' (fūryū), once the preserve of the Capital and its upper classes but by now aspired to by those with cultural pretensions throughout the country. The exquisite taste with which the lay monk Sugi no Mimasaka, a powerful man before his retirement from the world, has set up his mountain retreat for the visitors provides an early picture of the sensibility that would reach its highest expression in the tea ceremony not long after.[6] The beautiful garden, tasteful scroll and carefully arranged flowers of the tea ceremony are all already present here, and the judging of incense that Sōgi and his friends indulge in the following day was well on the way to becoming an equivalent ritual game in its own right.* Renga *composition, with its elaborate rules and group etiquette, can be understood in this context as a complementary elegant accomplishment.*

Elegant game though in many ways it was, however, the art of renga *poetry was a deeply serious matter. Sōgi's heartfelt prayer to the god of poetry at the shrine at Munekata speaks of the Way of poetry,[7] and this is no idle phrase. The concept of Way (michi)[8] elevated the practice of an art to something equivalent to commitment to a spiritual practice, and poetry in itself could be a form of prayer, as was Sōgi's poem offering to the god at Munekata. Sōgi, like many other professional* renga *masters, was a tonsured monk, and his constant visits to shrines and temples en route hint at a religious dedication pursued through the calling of his art.*

It is perhaps in part this solemn consciousness of spiritual purpose that lies behind Sōgi's evaluation of himself in relation to the great poets of the past. In a revealing passage, he begins by agreeing with the long-held belief that only members of the great poetic families or the aristocracy can be said to compose truly good poetry, speaking humbly of his own poems as mere 'shards',[9] but then he goes on to reach for alternative arguments to justify his final assertion that he 'need not be ashamed of my humble origins as a poet'. Commoner though he was, he dared to believe that he had a right to hold his head high as a poet in a world until then defined by the aristocratic traditions of the past.

These musings relate directly to another fascinating ambivalence that emerges in Sōgi's writing, concerning the evaluation of landscape and place. Poetic travel was by definition experienced in terms of literary tradition, and a landscape was only truly moving if it had the resonance of an utamakura. Struck by the beauty of a sweep of pine-covered dunes, Sōgi can admit that it surpasses the famous equivalent utamakura scene of Hakozaki, but remains poetically unmoved because of its lack of fame. Yet later, in a similar passage that compares another striking scene before him to its utamakura equivalent, Sōgi dares to declare that the present scene is not only deeply moving but 'indeed more so'. Just as a mere commoner can now summon the supreme confidence necessary to suggest that he need not be ashamed in the face of hallowed poetic tradition, so too the emotion provoked by the 'common' beauty of the landscape before his eyes can be acknowledged as equal if not superior to the emotion of witnessing a poetic utamakura. What is personal, immediate and part of the mere everyday world is beginning to assert itself against the elevated and elegant poetic world of precedent and tradition, in a fundamental shift in poetic sensibility that will find its full statement in the haikai poetry of later times.

In this and in other ways, Sōgi seems at times precariously balanced between two worlds. In Journal of the Tsukushi Road the tanka that form the core of traditional literary travel writing are balanced by an equal number of hokku composed for renga sessions (distant precursors of the stand-alone haiku), which here have begun to appear on their own. Sōgi's no doubt heartfelt sorrowing over the world's mournfulness and the empty nature of existence, orthodox laments for poetic travellers, are countered from time to time by his evident personal enjoyment in the journey's experiences and encounters. Sōgi brings a new lightness to travel writing that looks forward to Bashō rather than back to his poetic traveller antecedents. (See Map 4)

FROM *JOURNAL OF THE TSUKUSHI ROAD*

[. . .] As the night deepened, the rain grew fiercer and my sleep more broken, but with the daylight the skies cleared, and nothing stood in the way of our departure.

We went on past Tatara Lagoon and other such places, then paused to worship at Kashii Shrine. This was quite different from any other, with an air of melancholy about it, dense encircling trees and high grasses, the bridge spanning the mountain stream old and decayed, and only desolate moss left, it seemed, to mark the paths. The shrine itself was barely half rebuilt,[10] the temporary hall a crude construction. The shrine priests had an unenticing look, and since conversation with them would have proved depressing, my thoughts turned instead to the past. The only flourishing things there were the cedars, those sacred trees *that stand there for the gods*, a fine grove of them out beyond the shrine fence. Wishing to make some offering in their honour, I broke off a twig:

yuku sue no	Ageing toward my end
mi o futatabi to	I hold no hope
omowanedo	to come this way again
kashii no sugi ni	yet I pledge returning vows
nao ya chigiramu	to the cedars of Kashii

The deities of this shrine are Shōmo and Hachiman. The same deity here called Shōmo or Sacred Mother is known in Hakozaki as Empress Consort Jingū.[11] The sacred wood from which her image is carved is pine in Hakozaki, while here it is cedar. Thus do the gods and buddhas make themselves known in various forms according to people's differing beliefs.

We went out to the coast, and found ourselves looking onto Kashii Lagoon. It was not the season, it seemed, for there was no sign of those *children of the fisherfolk who pluck the shoreline herbs*. It was a somewhat desolate place.

From here, we made our way on among moors and mountains, to emerge once again at the sea's edge. Here we gazed out upon the sweeping scene before us, deserving of the name Thousand Mile Beach. The wind was fierce, the waves high. Somehow forlorn, I watched the tiny fish leaping from the water in apparent delight, and thought without envy that in fact they must be fleeing in fear from a shoal of larger fish beneath the surface. Shells washed about in the waves at the water's edge, and seeing them it struck me that though they were carried in and left the sea behind, they felt no sorrow; though drawn back to the sea, they felt no joy. Nothing is sadder than us creatures that have been given life. Suffering and joy in this world – both are finally sorrow. Understanding this all too well, I can only say these shells are the most enviable of all.

I asked the name of this bay, and learned that it is Mino Bay. The name has long been poetically linked to the image of empty shells.

kyō zo shiru	Emptiness – today
kono uranami no	I understand its nature
utsuse-gai	seeing these empty shells
mi no ushi tote ya	thus washed in the bay's waves
kaku mo naruran	the sad world cast off

And so with idle thoughts the time slid by, and we found ourselves arrived at Munekata. We met with the shrine's head priest, and spent that night at a Zen temple, going the next morning to worship at the shrine. It nestles on a shelf tucked into the mountainside, deep in a thick stand of trees. The gallery around the building was very dilapidated, and poorly protected from the rain, but the shrine itself was intact. To the right flowed a stream, the tide rose in the distance, while before it was a steeply arched bridge that looked to be of some importance and interest. The deity is called Tagori-hime, and she embodies two other gods as well, Tagitsu-hime and Ichikishima-hime, all sisters, the daughters of the god Susanoō-no-mikoto, god of poetry. This prompted me to compose this poem as a prayer for poetry.

hito no yo no	Oh mighty gods
sue made mamore	protect until the end

chihayaburu	of this human world of ours
kami no mi-oya no	your august father's words
koto no ha no michi	the sacred Way of poetry

Susanoo-no-mikoto's founding poem in fact surely expresses the feelings of this age of humans.[12] This god must truly be called the founding father of the Way of poetry. He is, indeed, the ultimate founder of our nation, and the spirit of the great goddess Amaterasu-no-mikoto is his own. Surely he must be worshipped as the very essence of the Way of the Gods.

The head priest's lodgings were suitably fine; the welcome he gave us was most refined, and he was meticulous in his attention to detail.

Approaching Katsura Lagoon, we saw before us Cape Kane and the island of Ōshima. I thought of the old poem[13] 'I will not forget you', and recalled the beauty of the island of Shiga. I also thought of how sad Shōni's daughters must have felt with the words 'oh whither?', and the poem 'for whom do they long?'.[14] Today as then, the wind and waves were loud, heavy drops soaked the sleeves, and plovers in ones and twos or little groups flew crying. What was in their hearts? I wondered, moved.

hama chidori	On and on
koe uchi-wabite	among the endless waves
ōshima no	of Ōshima
nami no ma mo naku	the plovers fly lamenting.
tare o kouran	For whom do they long?

This is the way of wandering beneath a traveller's sky – the world is by nature a mournful place, but we comfort our hearts with thoughts of things past. Yet hearing my travelling companions bewailing the wind and waves so fervently, I miserably blamed myself as the cause of their sorrows.

Far ahead of us into the distance stretched an extraordinary stand of beachside pines, quite the equal of and indeed surpassing the famous pines of Hakozaki, I thought, but since this place was not a famous one it did not move me greatly. It is the same with the Way of our poetry – a poem is no doubt worthless unless composed by someone from one of the lineages, or some high-ranking and famous person. Yet for all that, here and there in this work I have cobbled together around twenty poor shards of poems,[15] some in a spirit of reverence, some as prayers to the gods of poetry, others expressing my own feelings or sorrowing over traces of a vanished past, and still others prompted by the unforgettable sight of this place or that. After all, in the writings of the poet Shunzei we find the words, 'All who come to this country recite its poems; all who are born in a place such as this create its poems,' and again elsewhere we read, 'Which among the living creatures does not make poetry?'[16] Surely, then, I need not be ashamed of my humble origins as a poet.

In no time we found ourselves in Ashiya. High dunes towered like mountains, crowded everywhere with pines, with among them numerous temples. There were countless houses and fisherfolk's huts. A range of mountains rose beyond the river, the whole scene a feast for the eyes. Now a brief autumn shower drifted down, and a bright moon was rising in the evening sky, as if the scene were *made expressly for us*. It was deeply moving, in a different way from the famous Ashiya scene of 'Nada's salt fires',[17] and indeed more so.

shio yakanu	How moving this moon
ashiya no aki zo	in Ashiya's autumn sky
aware naru	undimmed by salt fires.
tsuki ya keburi o	Perhaps she came to hate
itoi-someken	that drifting smoke

Though officially winter, in the *Tale of Genji* too we find a poem calling the tenth month autumn.[18]

Here we were welcomed by Count Asō, with lavish hospitality as before. Asked to provide the *hokku* for a *renga* sequence, I composed:

oikaze no	Our boat sets forth –
matanu ko no ha no	frail leaf that will not wait
funade kana	a following wind

Someone else also requested one:

itsu kikamu	When will I hear again
ashiya no tsuki no	beneath the moon of Ashiya
yūshigure	these chill evening showers?

The next day we sent home the samurai escort whom Hiroaki had provided for us,[19] and prepared to set off by boat, following along a canal that wound on and on among the hills, but the low tide delayed us until finally the sun sank and we had only the moonlight to guide us, and we barely glimpsed the beach of Kiku no Nagahama as we passed. The lights of fishing boats coming and going among the islands, the fisherfolk's fires that burned along the shore under the mountains – all was unspeakably moving. We landed late that night, and at last reached Amidaji Temple.

The clear pure moon was just setting, wind soughed in the pines on the mountain behind, and the whole scene so touched the heart that we stayed a day there before setting off again by boat on the morning of the seventh day. As we went along the Straits of Hayato, the boatman told us that this was where the Heike would have drowned in battle.[20] How *the very oars wept salt drops* to hear it! The boat put in at Toyoura, where we paused for a while with the priest of Ninomiya Shrine, going on from there to stay with Priest Meiyū at Ryūsenji Temple.

We had much talk that night of the journey and of the situation in the Capital, and the following morning there was a *renga* gathering.[21]

okuri-kite	A wintry shower
tou yado suguru	saw me to your door
shigure kana	and then swept on

Once the session was over, the priest, another named Ryōshō whom I had known well in the Capital, and others stayed on, carousing in various ways until the dawn.

Today we all went to the mountain retreat of the lay monk Sugi no Mimasaka, a place called Ōmine. He was a man of great refinement, and his home was as elegant as the place itself was beautiful.

The garden was replete with plum and cherry trees, and he had *gathered many hues of flower and plant* surely more exquisite than anything found in the Capital. The hedge of white chrysanthemums *seeming more frost than flower* was just then in fine full bloom and rich to the gaze, while the leaves tumbling from the trees filled the garden with vibrant colour.

The following morning there was a *renga* gathering. Our host had hung a beautiful scroll, arranged exquisite flowers, lit incense to waft through unobtrusively, and prepared paper imprinted with elegant designs – all was so tasteful that he must have been rather disappointed by my clumsy *hokku* that introduced the proceedings.

kogarashi o	Stormy winds forgotten
kiku ni wasururu	at sight of the chrysanthemum
yamaji kana	on the mountain path

After we had gone a round of composing, one Chikurintei arrived, just as he had promised earlier to do. He was a dedicated follower of the Way of poetry, and his presence added greatly to the pleasures of the occasion.

The following day we played *go* and told stories, and that night we judged incense together and exchanged sake in elegant sake cups, all most impressively refined. Next morning, still rather dazed, we set off once more, and our host again revealed his fine sensibility by preparing a litter for the journey through the mountains, since the road was so bad.

It would be thirty-six days from the day of our departure until today. Travelling these remote lands, there have certainly been hard roads over mountain and river. But owing no doubt to the benevolence of the country's rulers, we were unhindered by difficult river crossings like those swift waters of Wu Canyon, nor did we meet with frightening paths like that of Taixing.[22] This whole journey has been satisfying in every way. Today, the twelfth day of the tenth month, I returned to my lodging in Yamaguchi, and completed the writing of this chronicle.

22

The Death of Sōgi
by Sōchō

Among the renga poet Sōgi's devoted followers was a man named Sōchō (1448–1532), who in his turn became one of the finest renga poets of his day. He too was a great traveller, as befitted a renga master, and like Sōgi he was a commoner who emerged from the provinces[1] and made his way to the Capital as a young man, where he took the tonsure and became associated with one of the great Zen monasteries,[2] Daitokuji. Here he encountered the famous, and famously irreverent and eccentric, old Zen monk Ikkyū (1394–1481), a friendship that no doubt encouraged Sōchō's own somewhat roguish tendencies.

In the autumn of 1501 Sōchō was living as a guest of the local warlord of Suruga in the East when for unspecified reasons he set out for the Capital. En route, he chose to make a lengthy detour across Japan to visit his old master Sōgi, who was presently a guest of the warlord of the remote Niigata area on the Japan Sea coast, where Sōchō too stayed out the year. Sōgi was by now in his eighties and nearing his end but when Sōchō, ageing and unwell himself, decided to turn back for home via some healing hot springs, Sōgi insisted on setting out with him for what would prove his last journey. Sōgi's final journey and death are movingly described by Sōchō in The Death of Sōgi (Sōgi shūenki), a work written for a friend to carry to the Capital to report the death of the master to Sōgi's many followers there.

The Death of Sōgi is thus not intended solely as a literary work, although Sōchō was a professional poet and his writing naturally draws on the literary tradition. Like Journal of the Tsukushi Road, it provides a window into the life of travelling renga poets, who stopped off on their journeys to hold renga sessions with their hosts wherever they went. The fashion was now for a series of hundred-link renga sessions that built up a poem often of a thousand links over a number of

*days, which would have been taxing for all concerned but most par-
ticularly for the aged and ailing Sōgi. The portrait of him that Sōchō
gives us here reveals not only his immense courage and stamina in
undertaking this arduous journey[3] when his end was so near, and his
stubborn love of the road, but also the depth of his dedication to poetry.
We see him balanced on the point of death en route, yet managing to
rally enough not only to continue to compose but to take part in yet
another thousand-link renga gathering that lasted for three intense days.
The poignant poems of old age[4] culminate in the moving lines he
recited as he lay dying, a link in an unfinished poem which with his
dying breath he bequeathed to his disciples to continue without him.*

*Two dreams recorded here give the strongest indication of the degree of
Sōgi's poetic attainments. The first is the hokku vouchsafed to Sōgi in a
New Year dream (considered particularly auspicious) by the god of Kitano
Shrine, the deified form of the great poet and scholar Sugawara no Michizane, in a sign of Sōgi's direct communion with the sacred and numinous
realm that lay at the heart of poetry. The other is the dream he had as he
was dying, in which he found himself in the presence of the great thirteenth-
century poet Fujiwara no Teika, implying that he had thereby been
welcomed among the ranks of Japan's most august poets.*

*For all the high seriousness of renga poetry at this time, however,
another less serious version was rapidly gaining popularity as well. It
was known as haikai no renga, light or comic renga, and harked back
to the origins of renga itself as a form of light relief from the serious
composition of waka.[5] Often salacious and tending to gently mock the
rules of renga and poetry generally, it was typically composed in
relaxed group sessions after serious renga composition, and Sōchō was
an early master of the form. Although it was not intended for public distribution and seldom recorded for posterity, we can imagine that some
of the arduous renga sessions that Sōgi and others took part in on this
journey would have ended with this kind of entertainment.[6] It was
essentially the hokku composed for haikai no renga, rather than those
of renga proper, that evolved into the later haikai poetry that Bashō
raised to a poetic seriousness equivalent to Sōgi's renga.*

The Death of Sōgi *provides an incidental picture of life on the road
at a time of widespread clan warfare. Travellers had to gain what information they could as they proceeded, to avoid becoming entangled in
either battles or casual raids, and general lawlessness was rife. Many of*

the warlords who hosted the renga *poets on their journeys were taking time off from military engagements to indulge in cultural pursuits. Among the poets' stops along the way it is interesting to note the passing mention of Edo, then no more than a castle with its surrounding small town, which one hundred years later would become the governing centre of Japan*[7] *(present-day Tokyo).*

Roughly the first half of The Death of Sōgi *is given here. The second half consists of a brief record of the group's subsequent journey, and the poems composed by others in memory of Sōgi* (tanka, *and a final long* chōka*). (See Map 5)*

THE DEATH OF SŌGI

As an old man, Sōgi seemed to grow weary of the hermitage that had been his home for years. At the beginning of spring, making arrangements to leave the Capital, he composed this *hokku*:

mi ya kotoshi	Drifter as I am
miyako o yoso no	like the spring mists this year
	I'll rise
harugasumi	and leave the Capital behind me

That year as autumn ended he set off to journey beneath traveller's skies along the Koshi Road, with no thought of the mountains that might bring him home again, and in the land of Echigo sought out an old acquaintance,[8] staying there two years.

Learning that he was there, at the end of the sixth month of 1501 I set forth on the road out of the land of Suruga, over Ashigara Mountain, Fuji's peak seen to the north, following the waves on Ojima's coast in the seas of Izu, the rocky shores of Koyurugi, a glimpse of Kamakura as I passed, seeing as if before my eyes that past age where the Minamotos and the nine generations of rulers once had flowered,[9] and it seemed to me that the beach pines of Tsurugaoka's shrine and the snow-heaped roofs were quite the equal of the famous shrine of Iwashimizu. Those mountain scenes, those valley deeps, could scarcely be plumbed by a brush's words. Here for the last eight or nine years, they say, battles have

raged between the Yamanouchi and the Ōginoyatsu,[10] dividing
the eight lands so that travellers have a far from easy time of it,
but I gathered news from here and there, and thus made my way
on through Musashino, past Ueno, and arrived at last at Kō in the
land of Echigo around the first day of the ninth month.

Here I visited Sōgi, and we spoke together of all that had passed
since we saw each other last. I was planning to go on to the Capital, but those long hard roads through far places bore down on
me now and I became ill, and so the days passed. At length, past
the twentieth day of the tenth month, I recovered, and was of a
mind to set off when a wild snowstorm blew up. The waves of far
Nagahama receded from my grasp; any hope of Mount Arachi[11]
must be still more unlikely, I was told. So I chose to stay on in a
meagre traveller's lodgings and see out the year there, waiting
for the spring, while day after day the snow swirled down and
the snowdrifts piled higher. Even the locals complained that they
had never seen such snow, and I bore it still harder. I sent this to
a friend:

omoiyare	Think of me here
toshitsuki naruru	lodged under snows
hito mo mada	lamented as unmatched
awazu to ureu	even by those who know
yuki no yadori o	the snows of many years

Then, on the tenth day of the year's last month, around ten in the
morning, there was a great earthquake, and the earth continued
to be tossed about many times a day, the tremors continuing for
five or six days. Many people died, houses collapsed, and even the
place where I stayed seemed in danger, so I had to seek fresh lodgings where I saw out the year.

On the first day of the new year there was a *renga* gathering,
with a dream poem[12] of Sōgi's as *hokku*.

toshi ya kesa	The year dawns this morning
ake no igaki no	over the sacred crimson
	fence
hitoyo matsu	round those miraculous pines

When the meeting was over, I celebrated the master with:

kono haru o	This spring
yasoji ni soete	adds to your eighty years
jūtose chū	the start of a new
	decade –
michi no tameshi ya	another setting forth
mata mo hajimen	along the Way you tread
	before us

In reply he composed:

inishie no	Far back
tameshi ni tōki	my old road stretches now
yasoji dani	and with what pain
suguru wa tsuraki	I climb yet higher
oi no urami o	over eighty years

On that same day, the ninth, we composed the first twenty-two of another *renga* sequence, for which Sōgi's opening *hokku* was:

aoyagi mo	The sacred *masaki* tree
toshi ni masaki no	this new year surpassed
kazura kana	by spring's green willow

From the end of the month my old illness returned, then a cold added to my woes, and so the days dragged on. By the end of the second month I was better, but I set aside my plans for visiting the Capital and instead announced that I would return to Suruga, taking in the hot springs of Kusatsu in the land of Ueno on my way.

'Ah, let me come with you then,' said Sōgi. 'It is a miserable thing simply to wait on here for the end that will not oblige me by coming; everyone's pity here fills me with shame, and it would only be depressing to go back to the Capital. A man I know in the land of Mino keeps sending to encourage me to come and take refuge there for my remaining years.' There was talk, too, of longing to see Mount Fuji once more, and it seemed wrong to leave him there and return home alone, so I could only agree, and thus we set off along the Shinano Road, made our way across the stones of Chikuma River, took in the wild fields of Suga no Arano, and on the twenty-sixth day arrived at Kusatsu.

In the same land there is also a famous hot spring called Ikaho. Hearing that the baths were good for the palsy, Sōgi set off to go there and we parted ways. It was there that he grew ill and was unable to take the waters. Fearing he might not survive to see the dawn of the fifth month's short night, he composed:

ika ni sen	What is to be done?
yūtsukedori no	Old, I wake early
shidari-o no	from my traveller's sleep
koe uramu yo no	longing for what the young resent
oi no tabine o	the bright cock's dawn announcement

In the land of Musashino at the Iruma River crossing there is a place called Uwado, the stronghold of the Yamanouchi, and here we rested for more than twenty days. There were many men of refinement and sensibility there, and we held a thousand-link *renga* gathering.[13] From there we moved to Kawagoe in Miyoshino where we stayed for more than ten days, then went on to the establishment by the name of Edo in the same land.

By now Sōgi seemed on the point of death, but he rallied again and continued to compose, and his strength seemed to be returning; in a place not far from Kamakura we held another thousand-link gathering that began on the twenty-fourth day and ended on the twenty-sixth, in which he composed ten links or more each session, more than he had managed earlier, many fine ones among them. To the lines:

kyō nomi to sumu	Already far behind those days I lived
yo koso tōkere	fearing each one my last

he added the following links:[14]

yasoji made	When did I ask
itsu ka tanomishi	that I should live till eighty?
kure naran	Yet now my days die to their end
toshi no watari wa	No man will ford that river
yuku hito mo nashi	from this year to the next
oi no nami	Wave upon wave these years
iku kaeriseba	bring in old age. How many crossings
hate naran	before the end arrives?

I realize now, looking back on it, that this might have been intended as a farewell poem before death.

For the two days of the twenty-seventh and twenty-eighth we rested here, and on the twenty-ninth day we were setting off for the land of Suruga when, around midday, he was stricken with 'worms'.[15] We tried what remedies we had but they had no effect, and there was nothing to be done. We found lodgings in a place called Kōtsu and saw out the night there; the next day came horses, men and a litter sent from Suruga, with Sojun[16] hastening there on horseback, and with this help we reached Yumoto at the foot of Mount Hakone the following day.

He felt somewhat better than he had on the road, and after a meal of rice cooked in spa water and some talk, managed to drift off to sleep. All were very relieved, and after making preparations for the next day's mountain crossing we went to bed, but late in the night he was in terrible pain. We rolled him about to ease it, and he told us that in his dream he had met Count Teika.[17] Then he recited 'Oh thread that holds my soul / if you must break, break now', which we who heard him recognized as in fact the famous poem by Shokushi Naishinnō.[18] He then recited lines that seemed to come from our recent thousand-link *renga* session – 'Rising to float / into the moon I gaze at'. 'I can't manage to add the next link, you must all do it for me,' he said playfully, and as he spoke his breath ceased, like a lamp flickering out.

All were beside themselves with grief, but though our hearts were distracted with sorrow, we comforted ourselves with the thought that it was surely a love of travel that had brought the passing dew of his life to meet its end upon this final wayside pillow. They say that in China too there were wanderers who spent their days and met their end upon the road, to become protective wayside gods.[19]

tabi no yo ni	Wandering through this world
mata tabine shite	itself a wandering journey
kusamakura	I sleep the wayside traveller's sleep
yume no uchi ni mo	and in this dream of life
yume o miru kana	I dream again

This poem by the priest Jien[20] would surely have been what any person of true feeling would think of on this night.

Ashigara Mountain is mournful enough, heaven knows, even to cross under normal circumstances. We set him in the litter as if he were still living, and carried him along, following before and after until we reached a forest temple in a place called Momozono, on the border of Suruga. Jōrinji, it was called. It was just on dusk when we settled in. Here we spent a day preparing, and then on the third day of the eighth month, as dawn was breaking, at a spot tucked in a little behind the temple's front gate where a pure stream flows, and set about with cedar, plum and cherry trees, we buried him, planting a marking pine as we recalled together the man we knew in life. Over the grave we placed an oval stone,[21] and around it we set up a little fence. There we remained for seven days of mourning, and then we set out for Kō . . .

23

Journal of the Kyushu Road
by Hosokawa Yūsai

Hosokawa Yūsai (1534–1610), the author of Journal of the Kyushu Road *(Kyūshū michi no ki), was an impressive man by any standards – a powerful member of the military ruling class, he was a strong man and a formidable fighter, who served and later advised three successive rulers. He was also a man of wide-ranging cultural interests that included the tea ceremony, Nō drama and flower arranging; and above all he was renowned as one of the leading scholars of his day, deeply schooled in the classics and in poetry. Yūsai is thus the epitome of those cultivated military men who for centuries had sought to combine a warrior's life with the practice of refined cultural arts.*

   It is as a literary man that we meet Yūsai in this travel journal, written in or soon after 1587, but although the journal itself makes no more than glancing mention of military matters, as befits a literary work, its circumstances are steeped in warfare. Five years earlier, Yūsai had taken the tonsure and become a lay monk in response to the death of his lord, Oda Nobunaga (1534–82), a great and ruthless warlord who had gone a long way towards defeating his many rivals and becoming default ruler of Japan before his betrayal by one of his generals,[1] who ambushed him and forced him to commit suicide. Nobunaga's achievements were taken over and extended by another of his generals, Toyotomi Hideyoshi (1536–1598), who inherited Yūsai's allegiance, although as a lay monk Yūsai no longer took an active part in military campaigns.[2]

   Having brought most of Japan's key areas under his control, in May 1587 Hideyoshi set out with a 16,000-strong army to subjugate the powerful and recalcitrant Shimazu clan[3] that effectively controlled most of Kyushu. Yūsai's two sons were members of the expedition, and Yūsai clearly itched to be part of the action. Unable to fight alongside his sons as he no doubt yearned to do, he reached for his writing brush instead, making the journey to Kyushu and back an opportunity to create a literary travel chronicle in time-honoured tradition.

The opening section of Journal of the Kyushu Road, and particularly its first poem, makes it clear that it was in the spirit of loyal retainer that he undertook this journey, and there is little doubt that the journal was intended to be presented to Hideyoshi as a gift, but it was as a littérateur that Yūsai travelled. Having retired from the world, Yūsai's form of service to his lord was to act as a kind of cultural mentor, and this is the role he played when he arrived in Kyushu to join Hideyoshi in time to celebrate the success of his campaign. In a later part of the journal (not included here), Yūsai is among those gathered around Hideyoshi to take part in cultured entertainments as he relaxes after the victory,[4] and we see Yūsai as literary master leading the renga sessions that were such an important part of the cultivated life of the day.

Journal of the Kyushu Road adheres strictly to the norms of the literary travel journal, in which the prose descriptions are essentially incidental to the poetry composed along the way. It gains added interest for us, however, not only through the circumstances of its composition, but because Yūsai's journey to Kyushu traversed a remote part of Japan seldom otherwise recorded in early literature, the western part of the main island's Japan Sea coastline. From his castle in what is now the area around Maizuru, north of Kyoto on the Japan Sea coast, it took Yūsai about three weeks to travel down to the western tip of Honshu, from which he crossed to Kyushu, and his journal reveals how difficult that journey was at times. For much of it he travelled by boat – the roads were poor, the terrain was generally mountainous and the coastline rugged, and sea travel was both faster and smoother in good weather. Bad weather caused them numerous delays, however, and at one point came close to drowning them. Local sea-going vessels seem not to have improved markedly from those of previous centuries,[5] and Yūsai's descriptions of his boat journey are strongly reminiscent of those in Tosa Diary six and a half centuries earlier, with the boat hugging the coastline and constantly putting into tiny ports, and the hapless travellers at the mercy of wind and wave and the boatmen's pronouncements about when and whether to proceed. He does not seem to have felt much urgency to travel fast, however, and makes several side trips to places *of interest. Essentially, despite his stated urge to hasten to lend his support to Hideyoshi in Kyushu, Yūsai depicts his journey as the leisurely and entertaining adventure of a cultured traveller.*

As a leading poet of his day, Yūsai is made welcome along the way much as Sōgi and other renga poets were before him, and his journal reveals the central place that renga still held in the upper echelons of society. The traditional tanka was still considered the paramount poetic form, but Yūsai's journal also records numerous hokku that he composed for the renga sessions that he was invariably invited to lead, and he does not hide the fact that he found this role onerous at times. He was a highly skilled poet but not a great one, and his poetry generally follows the taste of the day with much playful punning, often on place names (which loses much of its force in translation). His occasional serious tanka on time-honoured themes such as transiency and longing seem more poetic exercises than deeply felt, and the real energy is in his lighter poetry.[6]

In this he epitomizes a shift that had begun a century or more earlier, with renga increasingly the dominant poetic practice and a mounting interest in and acceptance of the lighter or haikai mode. The hokku that Yūsai records in Journal of the Road to Kyushu were composed to lead off formal renga sessions, but the practice of relaxing with a round of rougher and more humorous haikai-style renga was by now well-established, although these were still relatively seldom recorded for posterity. It is interesting, however, to find in Yūsai's journal several examples of tanka in the haikai mode,[7] unthinkable in this context in an earlier age.

In fact, much was on the verge of changing in Japan with the advent of Hideyoshi's successor Tokugawa Ieyasu (1542–1616), who completed the unification of Japan within Yūsai's lifetime (in 1600), ushering in two and a half centuries of peace, and along with it fundamental cultural shifts. Balanced just at the point where the medieval era tipped into the early modern, Yūsai unwittingly helped to nudge[8] the old classical literary traditions towards the new literature of the coming centuries, in which haikai became the dominant mode. (See Map 4)

FROM *JOURNAL OF THE KYUSHU ROAD*

In this year of Tenshō 15 (1587), at the beginning of the third month, our noble ruler[9] set forth to settle the private hostilities between the Ōtomo and the Shimazu clans in Kyushu. My sons Yoichirō and Genba were of the party, and although I had taken the tonsure and so could no longer take active part myself, it felt somehow unpardonable to be lingering uselessly at home while his expeditionary forces were far away, and thus on the nineteenth day of the fourth month I sent a boat around to the county of Kumano.[10]

I left Tanabe on the twenty-first day and stopped that night at Miyazu, arriving at Matsukura Castle in Matsui on the twenty-second, but when the following day had dawned and we were busy preparing for the onward journey, it began to rain and did not let up all that day. At this point my host's son, the lay Zen monk, arrived to detain me; we beguiled the time with numerous rounds of the sake cup together, and I spent that night there.

On the twenty-fourth day the weather cleared beautifully and it was declared that we had a following wind for our sail, so we set off. Ashiura Mountain being close at hand:

kanarazu no	At journey's end
tabi no yukue wa	the victory must be sure –
yoshiashi mo	I will not weigh the future
towade fumi-miru	but set my feet firm on my way
ashiura no yama	at Mount Ashiura[11]

This came to me because of the words in a classic military manual: 'He who is determined to win a battle must not attempt to divine its outcome'.

And so, at around the Hour of the Dragon,[12] the boat put out from a place called Minato, and as the day darkened that evening we made port at Igumi, on the border between Tajima and Inaba. Our lodgings were fearfully cramped, with men of every class from high to low tossed in to bed down together for the night, so I composed:

shūjū wa	Travellers that we are
tabi ni shi areba	master and servant both
sato no na no	lie huddled up together
ikumi ni shitaru	in the inn at Igumi
kari no yado kana	just as the village name
	suggests[13]

On the twenty-sixth day we put the boat out from Mikuriya in the land of Hōki, landing again at the barrier gate of Niho in the land of Izumo, where I took in the sights before proceeding along the shoreline until I learned that we had come to Nishiki (Brocade) Bay. Here we paused.

fune yosuru	My boat puts in
nishiki no ura no	at Brocade Bay
yūnami no	where waves at evening weave
tatamu ya kaeru	fold and return
nagori naruran	as if to speak my longing[14]

This is the poem I composed here. We stopped that night at the house of a fisherman in nearby Kaga.

aware ni mo	Poor little thing
imada chi o nomu	the fisherman's young child
ama no ko no	still suckles at the breast
kaga no atari ya	and cannot leave
hanarezaruran	motherly Kaga's bosom[15]

Twenty-seventh day. The boatmen announced that the wind and rain were so wild they would find it hard to put out to sea, so since the prospect of waiting idly about filled me with gloom, I ordered the boat to wait for a break in the weather and then go around to meet me down the coast, while I set off in the same direction on foot to view the shrine at Kizuki.[16]

About seven miles down the road I found it, deep in a grove of trees among remarkable hills. After looking about, I enquired of a man I took to be one of the priests there, and learned that this place was Sada Shrine, which worshipped the gods Izanami and

Izanagi.[17] We spoke about this and that until the hour grew late and the rain began to pour, so I sought for lodgings where I could dry out my clothes and there I stayed the night.

chihayaburu	Oh powerful and great
kami no yashiro ya	pillars of the land
ametsuchi to	oh shrine of gods
wakachi-sometsuru	where first heaven and earth
kuni no mihashira	were parted

Twenty-eighth day. Leaving Sada, at a place called Aika I boarded a small lake-going craft and went around to Hirata. The boatman told me that this lake was called Ou.

isomakura	Plovers pillowed
urami ya ou no	on the rocky shore
urachidori	cry in lament
mihatenu yume no	at their bitter waking
samuru nagori ni	from an unfinished dream[18]

And thus as dusk set in I reached the shrine of Kizuki. I looked at various things there, starting with the main hall and taking in the smaller shrines, and learned that the Senge and the Kitamura, the two head priest families, had originally been provincial stewards.[19] Having viewed the houses of both, I then took lodgings, and was resting after a rough-and-ready *meal on oak-leaf dishes* when Kasai of Wakasa[20] came to call, so I invited him in. He played a drum, and was with a large group of youngsters. They wished to perform a piece, so things were set up for the evening's entertainment. Both the stewards sent over snacks and sake produced in the area, then more flute players and drummers crowded in, and there was dancing[21] until all hours. It was all most unexpected.

Twenty-ninth day. In the morning calm, the men who had brought the boat around by sea arrived, and told me to *hurry aboard as the sun was rapidly climbing*. In haste, I composed:

kono kami nò	The best offering
hajimete yomeru	to this god must be a verse

koto no ha o	whose rhythm echoes
kazouru uta ya	the syllables he sang here
tamuke naruran	in that first sacred poem

This poem was merely a stringing together of thirty-one syllables by way of a shrine offering, prompted by the words in the *Kokinshū* preface, 'Thirty-one-syllable poetry began when the god Susanoō arrived in the land of Izumo'.[22] I sent this poem, written on a poem card, to the Senge house, but the master replied suggesting that since both lineages were involved it might be better to send to both, so I sent the same poem to the Kitashima house as well, being too rushed to compose another for him.

I had also been asked by the shrine's Buddhist priest[23] to provide the *hokku* for a *renga* sequence, so I sent this:

unohana ya	White deutzia flowers
kami no igaki no	bloom as offering
yū-kazura	on the sacred fence

But as we were boarding, word arrived from the Senge house saying that this *hokku* would be used for the *renga* to be composed by the Kitamura establishment, and requesting another for their own *renga* gathering.[24] I sent back several times explaining that I was too busy to compose another one, but perhaps due to local custom they would not take no for an answer, so in the end, rather than cause hurt by my refusal, I did my best to come up with something. Hearing the announcing call of a *hototogisu*:

hototogisu	Hototogisu
koe no yukue ya	its call fading
ura no nami	out among offshore waves

Twenty-ninth day. We stopped at Ōura in Iwami, and the following morning proceeded on to the port of Nima. Iwami's seas are reputed from of old to be rough, and it was indeed among whitecaps that we rowed along the rocky shoreline beneath beetling cliffs, prompting me to compose:

kore ya kono	Through wild wind and wave
ukiyo o meguru	our frail boat plies
fune no michi	across the seas of Iwami
iwami no umi no	making its way
araki namikaze	as through this floating world

From here we disembarked and climbed over to Kaneyama,[25] where we saw above the town the castle by the name of Yamabuki, or golden kerria.

shiro no na mo	This castle bears
kotowari nare ya	a golden name with reason
mabu yori mo	since the silver ore
horu shirogane o	dug from Kaneyama's veins
yamabuki ni shite	is transformed to gold

I was asked to provide a *hokku* for Jionji Temple where we stayed the night, and seeing the maples in the garden I composed:

miyamagi no	Deep among mountains
naka ni natsu o ya	young maple leaves
waka kaede	speak of coming summer

We went on to Yunotsu, where we stayed at Hōtōin Temple. Here we reminisced about the volume of *renga* from a previous year that we were shown. On the third day of the fifth month I was asked to provide a *hokku*, and that evening there was a one-hundred-link *renga* gathering.

nami no tsuyu ni	Bamboo grass
sasajima shigeru	on rocky Sasa Island
isobe kana	lush in the waves' spray

Fifth day. As our boat was putting out, word came that another *renga* gathering was planned for later and I was requested to provide the *hokku*, so on the spot I composed:

ukigusa no	Fifth month irises
ne ni hikare-yuku	drift on the water, drawn
ayame kana	by roots of floating weed

Seventh day. Setting off from Hamada, I saw from the boat a place I was told was called Takatsu, reminding me of Hitomaro's poem[26] 'I have watched my fill / of this floating world / in the moon that drifts / through the pines of Takatsu / on Iwami's shore'.

utsuri-yuku	The ages come and go
yoyo wa henuredo	all changes
kuchi mo senu	but unchanging still
na koso takatsu no	the fame of those words
matsu no koto no ha	that sang of Takatsu's pines

One way and another, we reached the land of Nagato (or Long Entrance), and as we rowed along, watching the shoreline and islands go by, I was told that one of them bore the name Karishima (Impermanent Island), putting me in mind of the temporary and transient nature of life.

minahito no	All pray that life
inochi nagato to	will be long as Nagato
tanomedomo	yet this world
yo wa karishima no	is no more than passing foam
nami no utakata	on Karishima's waves

Still in Nagato, hearing our boatmen talking together about a ship from China that had arrived in the port of Urano Obata, I decided to go to see it. We rowed quite a distance to get there, and paused a while to take it in.

ware mo mata	Like him of old
ura-zutai shite	I too have rowed my boat
kogi-tomenu	hugging the shores
morokoshi-bune no	to where a mighty ship
yorishi minato ni	from far Cathay lies
	anchored[27]

Hearing that the seas around Ago Bay were high:

kotsuzumi no	Do they strike in time
dō ni shirabe ya	with the chin drum's rhythm
awasuran	those pounding waves
utsu oto takashi	beating so high
ago no uranami	around the Bay of Ago?[28]

Tenth day. Setting out from Setozaki, the wind was wild, and a good half of the waves rose higher than our boat. My companions were so terribly seasick and ashen that I gave orders to turn back, and although it was not much more than a single mile to where we could pull in under the shelter of a mountainside, it felt like a thousand. We managed to make it back to where we had spent the previous night, but the wind grew still wilder, tearing at the vegetation, and the sea surface was *cloaked with glittering light*. It was reported that a boat that had gone out before us had sunk, though no one knew who was in it, and we went to bed that night feeling we had narrowly escaped death, awakening next morning to weather that seemed a continuation of the day before, for the wind and rain never ceased. The crashing waves vied with the roar of the sea surge, and our boatmen lamented that there was no way we could put out that day.

Discussing the matter, we decided that we should proceed on foot to the next border crossing, and on the eleventh day we set out from Setozaki with borrowed horses and other equipment. We paused to take a look at Taineiji Temple, hearing that this was where Ōuchi Yoshitaka had taken his life,[29] then pushed our way on through deep mountain country, and that night, still in the land of Nagato, we stayed at Myōeiji Temple.

The incumbent priest emerged to welcome us and we spent all night in discussions of the Buddhist Law and such matters. On the following morning as we were preparing to leave I composed:

katachi naki	Pillowed that night
yume chū mono o	on the firm bed of Buddhist Law
kokoro to mo	I knew

nori no mushiro ni   this formless dream
fushite koso shire   is all Mind[30]

This was prompted by the words that go something like 'The movements of the mind are formlessness; it penetrates the universe', but it is probably a rather unwieldy poem.

Going by Toyoura Shrine,[31] visited by the emperor long ago:

mizu moranu   At Toyoura Shrine
ike no kokoro no   the banks hold tight
fukasa o mo   the deep pond's waters
toyoura no miya no   reflecting still
tsutsumi ni zo shiru   that great depth of heart

I decided to eat our travellers' fare at a place called Tarai, and with the plan of climbing up to where we could seek shelter, my retainers first bathed their feet, complaining about the painful bean-like blisters they had. Hearing this:

sashi-irete   Popping all those blister beans
araeru ashi no   into the washing bucket
mame o ōmi   anyone would think
umadarai to ya   it was instead a trough
hito no miruran   to feed our travelling horses

Arriving at the border,[32] we paid our respects at Amidaji Temple. Beside it was another temple which the locals have long referred to as 'the palace',[33] where a priest showed us around. After seeing the image of Emperor Antoku and other Heike effigies, we were shown various poem cards[34] old and new, where I found poems by people I had known.

moshiogusa   The kelp-dark sleeves
kaku tamoto o mo   of this poet too
nurasu kana   soaked by salt tears
suzuri no umi no   to see where the brush has flowed
nami no nagori ni   that dipped in the inkstone's
                                        waves[35]

24

Bones on the Wayside
by Matsuo Bashō

Much had changed in the century between Hosokawa Yūsai's voyage to Kyushu and the autumn day in 1684 when the haikai *poet Bashō set off from his home on the outskirts of the thriving metropolis of Edo (Tokyo) on the journey that produced his first piece of sustained travel writing,* Bones on the Wayside (Nozarashi kikō), *translated here in full. The great warlord Tokugawa Ieyasu, who had brought the whole of Japan under his control in 1600, had set up his new government in Edo (although the emperor remained as figurehead in the old capital of Kyoto), enforcing a peace that lasted until the middle of the nineteenth century. Very quickly, Japan experienced a great surge of modernizing energy. Soon there was more wealth, more industry, greater urbanization, and a marked improvement in roads and infrastructure. Life was still far from easy for those in the lower levels of society and in the provinces, but now many commoners had the leisure and ability to travel, and the main roads were thronged.*

Above all, education began to spread beyond the confines of the upper echelons, and a newly wealthy urban merchant class was emerging, eager for learning and culture. Yūsai's disciple Matsunaga Teitoku (1571–1653), a classically trained poet, rode this wave. Rather than the elegant classical renga *that had dominated poetry since the fifteenth century, he chose to promote the less demanding and more enjoyable* haikai *or playful version of linked verse that depended for its effect on wit, wordplay and homely everyday realities. The* haikai *style he propounded quickly became immensely popular, only to be replaced in popularity a few decades later by what became known as the Danrin style of* haikai, *which brought new freedoms and possibilities to what was by now the established poetic form of the new era.*

Matsuo Bashō (1644–94), revered today as haiku's greatest poet,

*began life in the provinces of Iga Ueno, in the mountains east of Osaka,
and first started to write* haikai *verse there as a young man in the heyday of Teitoku's style. In 1672 he took the bold step of moving east to
the new centre of Edo to establish himself as a professional* haikai *master, where he followed the trend by composing in the newly popular
Danrin style. A mere eight years later, however, he made a surprising
move that distanced him from the* haikai *world of the city and marked
the beginnings of his poetic independence, when he left Edo and set up
his 'hut'[1] beyond the edge of the city at Fukagawa on the banks of the
Sumida River. It was a move that proclaimed his new self-identification
as a poet in the tradition of the recluse poets of old, turning his back on
the social world and devoting himself to poetry as a Way in the manner
of earlier poets such as Nōin, Saigyō and Sōgi, whom he came to identify as his true masters.*

*It was only a matter of time before Bashō followed the tradition of
his poetic models and took to the road. Four years after his move to
Fukagawa he and a disciple set off, in time-honoured fashion, to travel
the great Tōkaidō road and beyond. Unlike his poetic forebears, he
went in the opposite direction, travelling west towards the old Capital
much as his poetics were drawing him back to a time when literary
culture was the direct legacy of that city's elegant* waka *tradition. If
Bashō had chosen the old-fashioned path of writing* tanka *or classical*
renga, *he would no doubt have produced from this journey a travel
journal in the style of Sōgi or other poet-monks, and indeed the more
austere sections of* Bones on the Wayside *resonate strongly with the
medieval travel chronicle tradition. But Bashō was a* haikai *poet,[2] and
in this work he was feeling his way towards a form of travel writing
that might embody the* haikai *spirit, as he was simultaneously feeling
his way towards his own poetic style.*

The haikai *spirit that Bashō inherited from the Danrin school and
before was not simply a matter of witty poetry that drew its references
from the everyday world. Its essence was a smile-provoking inversion or
juxtaposition of incongruous elements, and it depended for much of its
effect on the classical tradition that it playfully turned on its head. To
write or appreciate* haikai *verse, one needed at least a basic acquaintance with the classics[3] and particularly with* waka, *whose refined
language, permissible topics and images, and rules of composition were
all a potential target for* haikai *parody. The presence of a single word*

deemed low or vulgar and therefore impermissible in waka*'s rarefied lexicon*[4] *was enough to mark a verse as* haikai, *bringing an otherwise elegant composition humorously down to earth.*[5]

Bashō *took the sardonic grin of* haikai*'s playful wit and transformed it into something far subtler – a smile that could be tender, wistful or deeply melancholy as well as various shades of wryly humorous and self-mocking. His* haikai *verses frequently registered a poignancy that was both gently ironic and at times a close echo of the* aware *sensibility of an earlier age, thereby, in a neat piece of reverse irony, returning the* haikai *spirit to intimate dialogue with the very sensibility it defined itself against.*

The poems of Bones on the Wayside *display the range and character of Bashō's version of* haikai *at a time when he was rapidly evolving what would become known as the Bashō style* (shōfū).[6] *The tone varies, often with a* haikai-*like abruptness, through shades of serious to light, the extremes of which can be seen in the contrast between the first and last poems. Although chronological, for the most part* Bones on the Wayside *follows the time-honoured pattern of the personal poetry collection* (shikashū) *expanded into a discontinuous narrative of the journey, and its latter half makes no pretence at narrative at all. Haiku-like, it presents a series of swift sketches of moments that barely amount to hints of a greater totality of experience.*

In fact, the journey lasted more than six months, and involved lengthy periods during which Bashō busied himself with meeting followers and composing linked verse with them. His wandering travels took him to many places in the Kinai area of western Japan, and he twice visited his old home in Iga. The dramatic opening poem with its vision of dying on the road may have expressed a real dread at what might prove a dangerous journey, although it was also a statement of commitment to the ideal of the wandering poet-monk of old embodied in the opening amalgam of quotations from the Chinese classics. In fact, despite the disturbing image of the abandoned child by the roadside (still a not uncommon sight even then), travel in Bashō's day was much less challenging than in previous centuries. The ironic distance between the projected image of the wandering poet and the realities of this often sociable journey add one more layer to the subtle ironies that resonate in Bashō's writing and that he would continue to explore. (See Map 1)

BONES ON THE WAYSIDE

'Off on a thousand-mile journey I take no food; under the dark of the moon I enter the realm of the immortals'[7] – thus said the old sages, and I lean on their staff to follow, leaving my ramshackle hut by the Sumida, in the eighth month autumn of the first year of Jōkyō (1684), the wind's voice somehow chill to the ear.

nozarashi o	Bones on the wayside
kokoro ni kaze no	haunting my heart –
shimu mi kana	how the wind pierces

aki totose	Ten autumns here –
kaette edo o	now instead it's Edo
sasu kokyō	I mean by home

The day I crossed the barrier[8] rain was falling, the mountains hidden in cloud.

kiri shigure	Mist, chill rain –
fuji o minu hi zo	Fuji hidden
omoshiroki	is all the more entrancing

A man by the name of Chiri[9] helped me on my journey, tending to all my needs, thoughtful in every way. We have a deep communion of spirit; truly a friend to be trusted, this man.

fukagawa ya	Fukagawa hut –
bashō o fuji ni	its *bashō* tree
azuke-yuku	left in Fuji's hands

Chiri

As we went along the Fuji River, we came upon an abandoned child of around three, crying pitifully. Unable to withstand the wild waves of the floating world, tumultuous as this river's currents, its parents must have left their child here on the wayside to live out its brief life. The autumn winds *about the little bush clover* will toss that flower to earth tonight or wither it by morning, I thought, and as we passed I took some food from my sleeve and threw it to the child.

saru o kiku hito	You whose heart breaks to hear
sutego ni aki no	a monkey's scream – what of
	this child
kaze ika ni	in the cry of autumn wind?[10]

Why do you weep, child? Is it because you think your father hates you, your mother rejects you? No, he does not hate you, nor she reject you. Heaven has ordained it, that is all. Weep, then, for the cruelty of your fate.

The day we crossed the Ōi River, it rained all day long.

aki no hi no ame	Day of autumn rain –
edo ni yubi oran	in Edo they'll be counting up
ōigawa	and know we're at the Ōi[11]

Chiri

Composed on horseback:

michinobe no	Hibiscus by the wayside –
mokuge wa uma ni	eaten
kuwarekeri	by my horse

A moon five days past full, faint in the sky, very dark below the mountains, *whip dangling as I rode, many miles and still no cock-crow.* Dreaming along, as in Du Mu's 'Early Departure',[12] I *suddenly awoke* at Saya no Nakayama.

uma ni nete	Asleep on my horse
zanmu tsuki tōshi	half dreaming – a far moon
cha no keburi	tea smoke

We visited Matsubaya Fūbaku[13] in Ise, and stayed about ten days. No short sword at my waist, a cleric's cloth sack around my neck, and in my hands a Buddhist rosary – *dressed like a monk yet of the world, a layman despite the shaven head*. Though I am no monk, my shaved head classed me as a man of Buddha, and I was forbidden entry before the gods.

I paid my respects before the Outer Shrine. It was dusk, the shadowy form of the great shrine gate loomed dark, here and there a sacred lantern glowed, and the pine wind from *that high and holiest peak* pierced me through, stirring my heart to deep feeling.

misoka tsuki nashi	Month's end
chitose no sugi o	moonless – the ancient cedars
daku arashi	gripped by stormy winds

There is a stream at the bottom of Saigyō Valley. Here I saw women washing yams.

imo arau onna	Women
saigyō naraba	washing yams –
uta yomamu	Saigyō would have made a
	poem

On my way back that day I called in at a tea house, where a woman named Chō, or Butterfly, begged me to use her name in a *hokku*. She produced a piece of white silk, so I wrote on it:

ran no ka ya	Scent of orchids –
chō no tsubasa ni	sweet incense
takimono su	lit on a butterfly's wing

I called at the thatched hut of a recluse.

tsuta uete	Vines in the garden
take shigohon no	storm winds
arashi kana	through scant bamboo

At the start of the ninth month I came back to my old home,[14] and found *the sedge by my mother's house* now frost-withered and gone.[15] All was changed; white had touched the temples of my brothers and sisters and their brows were furrowed, and we could only thank heaven that we had lived to meet again. My older brother opened the little funerary bag he carried and said, 'This is your mother's white hair. Pray for her soul. It's like opening Urashima Tarō's magic box[16] – your face has aged too.' We wept a while.

te ni toraba kien	Gone as it touches
namida zo atsuki	the hand – hot tears
aki no shimo	on autumn's frost

We made a pilgrimage into the land of Yamato, and at Takenouchi in Katsuge, Chiri's native home, we stayed some days resting our legs.

watayumi ya	Soothed by the cotton bow's
biwa ni nagusamu	soft lute pluck
take no oku	in these bamboo depths[17]

I paid a visit to Taema Temple at the foot of Mount Futakami, and saw the pine in the garden, which must be around a thousand years old – huge enough to hide Zhuang-zi's legendary ox.[18] Insentient and unfeeling though it is, how blessed, how holy to have been drawn to grow in this Buddhist confine and thus escape the wicked axe.

sō asagao	Dying over and over
iku shini-kaeru	monks, brief morning glories
nori no matsu	on the great tree of Buddha's Law

Alone I made my way far up into Yoshino. The mountains were deep indeed, white clouds heaped on the peaks, valleys buried beneath a haze of rain, with here and there a woodsman's humble hut; each axe stroke to the west echoed in the east, and the bells of the many temples rang far down into my heart. Of those who in the past came to these mountains to turn away from the world, many found escape and refuge in Chinese and Japanese poetry. Indeed it is justly referred to as Mount Lu.[19]

I stayed a night in the lodgings of a temple.

kinuta uchite	Priest's wife
ware ni kikaseyo ya	let me hear
bō ga tsuma	the beat of your fulling block[20]

The place where Saigyō once lived in his hermit's hut lies not far in to the right of the Oku no In shrine, along a faint path used by brushwood gatherers and across a steep valley. It moved me to reverence. The dripping spring he wrote of[21] seems unchanged today, water still falling there *drop by drop*.

tsuyu toku toku	Slow water drop by drop
kokoromi ni ukiyo	I long to try
susugaba ya	rinsing away the world

If Po-i were in our own land, he would surely rinse his mouth here. If Hsu-yu were to hear tell, he would wash his ears.[22]

The autumn light had grown long and slanted by the time I had climbed and descended the mountain, passing many a famous place as I went, until I came at last to pay my respects at the grave of Emperor Godaigo.[23]

gobyō toshi hete	Years gone now your grave
shinobu wa nani o	twined with weeping fern
shinobugusa	remembering what?

From Yamato we went through Yamashiro, along the Ōmi Road and thus to Mino, past Imasu and Yamanaka, and there beyond we came to the grave of the legendary Lady Tokiwa. Moritake of Ise wrote of 'the autumn wind like Yoshitomo' – I wonder what the point of resemblance was.[24] Borrowing this I wrote:

yoshitomo no	Autumn wind
kokoro ni nitari	chill as the heart
aki no kaze	of Yoshitomo

Fuwa Barrier:[25]

akikaze ya	Autumn winds
yabu mo hatake mo	desolate over bush and field
fuwa no seki	at Fuwa Barrier

The night we stayed in Ōgaki we were guests in the home of Bokuin.[26] When I set off from Musashino on this journey I did so with bones on the wayside haunting my thoughts, so now I wrote:

shini mo senu	Journey's far end
tabine no hate yo	and I haven't died –
aki no kure	late autumn evening

At the Kuwana Hontōji Temple:[27]

fuyu botan	Winter peonies –
chidori yo yuki no	plovers calling
hototogisu	are snowy *hototogisu*[28]

Weary of nights spent on the road with *grass for pillow*, I went out to the beach while darkness still lingered in the sky.

akebono ya	Dawn –
shirauo shiroki	the whitebait's
koto issun	inch of whiteness

I went to pay my respects at Atsuta Shrine.[29]

The shrine building is badly gone to ruin, earth walls collapsed and smothered in grass. Here a rope was strung to mark the remains of a subshrine, there a stone was placed bearing the name of the god once worshipped at that site. Overgrown with mugwort and weeping fern, in fact it moves the heart more than it would in splendour.

shinobu sae	Even the weeping fern
karete mochi kau	dry and forgotten –
yadori kana	I buy rice cake at the stall

Written as I went into Nagoya:

kyōku kogarashi no	Mad verses
mi wa chikusai ni	and buffeted by cold winds –
nitaru kana	just like old Chikusai[30]

kusamakura	Wayside sleep –
inu mo shigururu ka	a dog barks in the night
yoru no koe	chill in the same rain
	perhaps

I set off to look at the snow.

ichibito yo	Market traders
kono kasa urō	I'll sell you this hat
yuki no kasa	this snowy hat

Seeing a traveller:

uma o sae	Even the horse
nagamuru yuki no	looks good
ashita kana	this snowy morning

I spent all day by the sea.

umi kurete	Darkening sea –
kamo no koe	a wild duck's cry
honoka ni shiroshi	faintly white

Shedding straw sandals as I went, casting away my walking staff, I saw out the year in traveller's sleeps.

toshi kurenu	The year ends –
kasa kite waraji	clad in traveller's hat
hakinagara	feet in straw sandals

Yet so saying, in fact I greeted the new year back in my family's home in the mountains.

ta ga muko zo	Who's the new son-in-law? –
shida ni mochi ou	ox laden with rice cake and
	fern shoots
ushi no toshi	this new Year of the Ox[31]

On the road into Nara:

haru nare ya	Spring's here –
na mo naki yama no	the nameless hills
usugasumi	hazy

I stayed at Nigatsudō[32] in prayer and meditation.

mizu-tori ya	The Water-drawing –
kōri no sō no	icy monks'
kutsu no oto	wooden shoes clatter

Going up to the old Capital, I called on the mountain home of Mitsui Shūfū at Narutaki.[33]

Plum forest:

ume shiroshi	Plum blossoms so
	white –
kinō ya tsuru o	someone must have just
	stolen
nusumareshi	old Lin's cranes[34]

kashi no ki no	There stands the oak
hana ni kamawanu	oblivious
sugata kana	of the blossoms

At Saiganji Temple in Fushimi I met the priest Ninkō.[35]

waga kinu ni	Fushimi peach blossom
fushimi no momo no	drop your precious dew
shizuku seyo	upon my robes[36]

On the way to Ōtsu, crossing the mountain:

yamaji kite	Along the mountain path
nani yara yukashi	somehow so touching –
sumire-gusa	wild violets

Looking out over the lake:[37]

karasaki no	Karasaki's distant pine
matsu wa hana yori	hazier
oboro nite	than the blossoms

At Minakuchi I met an old friend I hadn't seen for twenty years.

inochi futatsu no	Our two lives
naka ni ikitaru	lived to now –
sakura kana	cherries in bloom

A monk from Hirugakojima in Izu, on pilgrimage since last autumn, had heard of me and followed me to Owari to ask if we could travel together.

iza tomo ni	Well then together
homugi kurawan	let's chew on wheat ears
kusamakura	grass for pillow

This monk told me that Abbot Daiten of Engakuji[38] had passed away at the beginning of the year. I could scarcely believe it was true, and hurried to send a message to Kikaku from the road.

ume koite	Mourning the plum blossom
unohana ogamu	I pray to deutzia flowers –
namida kana	these tears[39]

Sent to Tokoku:

shirageshi ni	A butterfly's torn wing
hane mogu chō no	left for the white poppy
katami kana	as keepsake[40]

I stayed again with Tōyō.[41] About to leave on my journey east:

botan shibe fukaku	Emerging from deep
wake-izuru hachi no	among the peony's stamens
nagori kana	a lingering bee

I stopped at an inn in the mountains of Kai.

iku koma no	At this inn
mugi ni nagusamu	the travelling horse
yadori kana	comforted with grain

At the end of the fourth month I returned to my hut. Recovering from the fatigue of the journey:

natsu-goromo	Summer robe –
imada shirami o	I still haven't caught
tori-tsukusazu	all the lice

25

The Narrow Road of Oku
by Matsuo Bashō

In the spring of 1689, Bashō and his disciple Sora set out on a journey of more than five months that would take them into the northern lands of Oku and down the Japan Sea coast to the Kyoto area and beyond. Bashō's last and greatest travel journal, The Narrow Road of Oku *(Oku no hosomichi),*[1] *had its genesis in this journey, although he worked on it for years after his return*[2] *and it was not finally published until after his death in 1694 at the age of fifty.*

Only four years separated Bashō's first travel journal, Bones on the Wayside, *from his last, but they were years of crucial development for him. They were also years during which he travelled increasingly. In 1687 he and a companion spent five months on the road, travelling through much the same area as the* Bones on the Wayside *journey, a trip which produced his other important travel journal* Knapsack Notes *(Oi no kobumi). Besides this there were also several smaller journeys written up in briefer travel journal form, and no sooner had he returned from the last of these than he began preparing for this arduous journey into the northern lands and beyond.*

Why did Bashō travel so intensively in the final decade of his life? One practical reason that lay behind these journeys was the professional poet's need to keep in touch with and cultivate followers, much the same need that in earlier centuries had kept the renga *poets such as Sōgi on the road for so much of their lives. Unlike the urban* haikai *poets, Bashō's followers were largely based in the provinces, and although his travel journals often do not mention them explicitly,*[3] *much of his time on these journeys was spent in their company, composing* haikai no renga *with them and tutoring them in his rapidly evolving poetics. This is not the aspect of travel that Bashō is primarily concerned with in his journals, however. Like the medieval writers of travel chronicles before him, he wrote as a poet, and his journals are concerned with the poetic experience of travel. Like them, he records the places and experiences that prompted the poems which fill the journal, and depicts his journey as a poet's journey, a straying through the landscape taking time to visit* utamakura *and other places of historical or cultural interest.*

In this and in many other ways, The Narrow Road of Oku *follows the pattern of medieval travel writing,*[4] *not only because this was a naturally inherited form but because Bashō deeply identified with the great poet-travellers of the past. Yet in this, as in his poetry, he had to find his own way within that identification.* The Narrow Road of Oku *is the result of a process that began with* Bones on the Wayside, *to create a viable new form that embodied the* haikai *sensibility just as the old travel journals had embodied the* waka *sensibility, while holding the two in a mutually enriching relationship. For him as for the 'men of old' with whom he identified – Nōin, Saigyō and Sōgi particularly, together with the great Chinese poets such as Du Fu and Li Bai – travel was both spiritually and poetically of central importance, and this was surely the essential reason for his deep and abiding urge to be on the road. It was perhaps above all through travel that Bashō found his answers to the question of who he really was and could be as a poet.*

Bashō was reaching back towards the 'men of old' across a space that was more than the space of time. He lived in an era which was already in many ways fundamentally different from theirs, and the haikai *that he practised placed him firmly outside the bounds of the great* waka *tradition within which the earlier Japanese poets wrote and experienced the world. His yearning is at times palpable, and it is really only in* The Narrow Road of Oku *that he found a way to forge a new poetry and poetic self that brought him into a viable relationship with the past that was capable of deepening rather than destabilizing his own* haikai *poetics.*

The famous opening section of The Narrow Road of Oku, *which echoes the travel chronicle tradition of poetic prefatory statement and brief self-portrait, is a finely crafted passage that not only announces the themes of much of the journal but also embodies key elements of Bashō's* haikai. *The twin themes of travel and the flux of time are woven together in the resonant opening images with their classical overtones, seamlessly followed by an essentially* haikai *shift to lowly commoners who 'spend their days in journeying, and call the journey home', a reference and implicit self-identification inconceivable within the earlier traditional* waka *aesthetics. This in turn expands back towards the classical again with a reference to Bashō's revered 'men of old' in a restatement of the solemn opening passage of* Bones by the Wayside. *The passage continues in the same vein, with poetic images of the journey and its enticements time and again brought back to earth by mundane or* haikai *images (cobwebs, tattered leggings and hat cord, and moxa treatments).*[5] *Bashō the poet is both a Traveller self-consciously walking in the footsteps of the ancients, and simultaneously a common traveller plodding the roads and affectionately engaging with the everyday world, as we will find him for much of the journal.*

In Bones on the Wayside *this play across the spectrum from the sonorous and classical to the humorous and touchingly mundane is largely confined to the poetry that forms its core. By the time Bashō came to work on* The Narrow Road of Oku, *however, he had begun to perfect a form of prose that fitted and extended the* haikai *aesthetic. He termed it* haibun, *or* haikai *prose.*[6] *It essentially follows the age-old pattern of* kotobagaki *prose passage culminating in one or several poems, although on occasion* haibun *prose could exist on its own terms without a poem. This prose is generally typified by a light vernacular elegance that avoids self-conscious reaching after classical poetic effect, elliptical sentences, concision, and frequently also inclusion of Chinese vocabulary and prosody (parallel and contrasting language and rhythms, etc.). Many of the passages in* The Narrow Road of Oku *exist in their own right as independent* haibun, *and the journal itself, with its light descriptive touch and its sinuous interweaving of* haikai *scenes (Buddha Gozaemon, little children, fleas and mosquitoes) and more serious and introspective material, can be seen as an experiment in extended* haibun *writing.*

Yet although The Narrow Road of Oku, *like the travel chronicles of earlier centuries, is essentially episodic and structured around its poems, it is subtly pervaded by the theme of time announced in its opening passage. Visits to* utamakura *in particular focus Bashō's deep preoccupation with the past, and with mutability and change, the grand themes of poetry and of travelling poets down the ages as well as of Buddhist philosophy, but of particularly vital concern to Bashō in his endeavours to bring the past into a viable new relationship with the everyday realities of the present.*

This returning theme is especially strong in the early part of the work, most of which is translated here.[7] *As Bashō and Sora proceed further on*

*their journey, the predominance of present experience in the journal
grows stronger as the* utamakura *become less frequent. The late style
that Bashō was evolving during this journey leaned increasingly towards
what he termed 'lightness'* (karumi), *a simplicity and directness that
transcends the weightier wisdom and aesthetics of the past and penetrates to the heart of everyday experience. We are left to wonder what
form his writing would have taken if he had lived on into real old age.*
(See Map 5)

FROM *THE NARROW ROAD OF OKU*

The months and days are passing wayfarers through endless ages, and
travellers too the years that come and go. Those who float their
life away on boats, or meet old age plodding before a horse – they
spend their days in journeying, and call the journey home. And
many of those men of old too died on the journey.

I myself for who knows how many years now have felt the straying wind-torn clouds entice me, my thoughts always of wandering.
I roamed the sea coast,[8] and in the autumn of last year returned to
sweep the cobwebs from my ramshackle hut by the river; the year
drew to its end, *spring mists rose* in the sky, and the gods of wayfar-
ing possessed my mind with all-consuming thoughts of crossing
the Shirakawa Barrier, the little roadside gods beckoning me until
I could settle at nothing. And so I patched my tattered leggings,
replaced the cord of my traveller's hat, burned moxa to give my legs
new strength, and with the moon of Matsushima[9] lighting my
heart, I left my house in another's keeping and moved to Sanpū's
retreat in preparation for the journey.[10]

On the pillar of my hut I hung the first sheet of a hundred-link
verse.

kusa no to mo	Time for my hermit's hut
sumi-kawaru yo zo	to change dwellings too –
hina no ie	a home for dolls now[11]

It was the last quarter of the third month, first light pale in the
sky, *the dawn moon grown dim*, Fuji's peak a hazy shape, and

forlornly I wondered when I might see again those blossoms on the boughs of Ueno and Yanaka.[12] Intimate friends had gathered the night before to farewell us by boat. When we left the boat at a place called Senju, my heart was heavy with thoughts of the thousand miles that lay ahead, and I wept salt tears at the parting of ways in this phantom world of ours.

yuku haru ya   Spring passes –
tori naki uo no   birds cry, fishes'
me wa namida   eyes brim with tears

This was the first poem written with my traveller's brush, my spirits reluctant at the way before me. Farewellers lined the road, and must have stayed to watch our departing figures until they disappeared.

This year, the second year of Genroku (1689) I believe it is, my impulsive thoughts had turned to this long journey to the northern lands, and though the hardships in far places would doubtless *weigh my head with whitening snows*, my insubstantial hopes were stirred to dream that I might one day return, having seen at last those places I had only heard of – and so at last we arrived that first day at the waystation of Sōka.

The weight I carried on my bony shoulders gave me the most pain that day. I had begun with plans to carry nothing, but there was no help for it – I found I must take a paper cloak against the chilly nights, light summer robe, rain gear, ink and brush and so on, and the parting gifts that I had not the heart to leave, and it all proved a troublesome burden on the road.

I paid my respects at Muro no Yashima shrine. My companion Sora told me that the deity of this place is called Kinohanasakuya-hime, and is an avatar of Mount Fuji. The name Muro no Yashima, Cauldron Cavern, comes about because this deity sealed herself in a doorless cavern and proved her claims of purity by giving birth in flames, and thus was born the god Hohodemi no Mikoto.[13] This is also the reason why poems of this place customarily refer to smoke. The fish called *konoshiro* is also forbidden to be cooked and eaten here because the smell is reminiscent of burned flesh. These are some of the stories and legends told of this place.

Thirtieth day. We stayed at the foot of Mount Nikkō. The master of the inn told us that his name was Buddha Gozaemon. 'People call me that because honesty is my motto in all things,' he said, 'so you can rest easy here tonight on your travels'. Wondering what manner of buddha had manifested here in this sullied world to give succour to poor pilgrims in monk's garb such as ourselves, I watched the way he acted, and found he was innocent of all knowingness and guile, honest through and through. He was like the Confucian ideal of one who is close to virtue through firmness of will and straightforward sincerity, a man worthy of deep respect for his innate purity of being.

On the first day of the fourth month, I paid my respects at the mountain. Long ago, the mountain's name of Nikkō was written a different way, but when Saint Kūkai[14] founded the temple here he gave the name its present meaning, 'Light of the Sun', no doubt foreseeing how it would shine for a thousand years to come. Today its holy light illuminates the heavens, its blessings penetrate the farthest corners of the land, and all live in peace and safety within its radiance. Further words fail me, and I lay down my brush in awe.

ara tōto	Oh hallowed light
aoba wakaba no	sun on green leaves
hi no hikari	on new spring leaves

Spring mists draped Mount Kurokami (Black Hair Mountain), still white with snow.

sori-sutete	Black hair shaved
kurokamiyama ni	now at Mount Kurokami
koromogae	time for summer robes[15]

                                                              Sora

My companion Sora has the family name of Kawai; his given name is Sōgorō. His hut stands beside mine under the leaves of the *bashō* tree,[16] and he helps me with the daily labour of water and firewood. Delighted by the chance to come with me on this journey to see the famous views of Matsushima and Kisakata, he offered to help soothe the pains of my journey; at first light on the morning we set off he shaved his head and donned monk's robes, and took the Buddhist name of Sōgo from his old name. This is what lies behind his verse at Mount Kurokami. The word *koromogae* in the last line is powerful and effective.[17]

After a climb of more than two thousand metres, you come to the waterfall. It *leaps from the summit* of a cavernous cliff to tumble forty metres into the rocky depths of a green pool. You seclude yourself in the cave behind it to look out through the veil of water, which gives it its punning name of Urami Falls.[18]

shibaraku wa	For a short space
taki ni komoru ya	first summer retreat[19]
ge no hajime	behind the waterfall

Having an acquaintance in Nasu no Kurobane, we set off on a straight course across the plain towards it. Our sights were set on a still-distant village when rain began and darkness set in. We took lodgings with a farmer, and the next day walked on over the plain.

There in a field we came upon a grazing horse, and approached the man mowing hay nearby with our sorry tale. Mere farmer though he was, he was far from lacking in feeling. 'Let me see,' he mused. 'This plain is crisscrossed with paths, you know, and unwary travellers like yourselves can easily take a wrong turn. I worry you'll get lost, so best take the horse and where it stops send it back,' and he lent us his horse as guide.

Two little children came running along behind as we rode along. One was a little girl, who told us her name was Kasane. It was an elegant and unusual name.

kasane to wa	Kasane, your name
yaenadeshiko no	must mean the layered petals
na naru beshi	of the pretty pink[20]

Sora

Before long we came to a hamlet, and here we tied some money to the saddle and sent the horse home.

We called on the local lord's steward, a man by the name of

Jōbōji. He was delighted by the unexpected visit, and we talked all day and long into the night; his younger brother Tōsui came calling morning and evening, we were taken to his home and invited in by his relatives, and so the days passed. One day we strolled out to the edge of town and looked at where they used to do the Dog Shoots[21] long ago; then we pressed on through *Nasu's bamboo grasses* to visit the grave mound of Lady Tamamo.[22] From there we paid our respects at Hachiman Shrine, and learned that this was the deity to whom Nasuno Yoichi had prayed when he shot the distant fan with his arrow[23] – a tale that filled me with awe at the power of the gods. It grew dark, so we returned to Tōsui's house.

There is a mountain ascetic[24] temple here called Kōmyōji, where we were invited and prayed at the Gyōja Hall.[25]

natsuyama ni	Praying to those magic clogs
ashida o ogamu	among summer mountains –
kadode kana	off on a journey

Behind Unganji Temple is the place where Zen master Butchō[26] has a mountain retreat. He told me once that he had written this poem on a rock by his hut with a piece of pine charcoal:

tateyoko no	Barely five foot square
goshaku ni taranu	this grass-thatched hut
kusa no io	yet I am reluctant
musubu mo kuyashi	to build even this
ame nakariseba	were it not for the rain

When I took staff in hand aiming to go to see it, others eagerly joined me, calling together still more, the young ones in loud high spirits as we went along, and in no time I found we had reached the climb to the temple. The mountain view has great depth to it, the valley path winding into the distance, forests dark with pines and cedars, moss dripping, and the air cold despite the season. Having passed the ten famous sights along the way, we crossed a bridge and entered through the temple gate.

In search of the remains of Butchō's retreat I scrambled up the mountainside behind the temple, and there it was, a little hut built on a rock up against a cave. I felt as if I were seeing before my eyes Zen master Yuan Miao's sign 'Death's Boundary' that he hung before his cave, or Fa Yun's rock cavern.

kitsutsuki mo	Even the woodpecker[27]
io wa yaburazu	doesn't harm this hut
natsu kodachi	deep among summer trees

We made our way to The Killing Stone, with a horse the steward sent on with us. The fellow who led it asked me for a poem card.[28] Impressed with the elegance of the request, I wrote for him:

no o yoko ni	Turn the horse aside
uma hiki-mukeyo	across the plain –
hototogisu	a *hototogisu*

The Killing Stone stands in the shade of a mountain where a spring bubbles up. Its poison is still potent as ever, and the sand around it is smothered deep in piles of dead wasps and moths.

Saigyō's willow *where the pure stream flows on*[29] is in the village of Ashino, still standing on a path between the rice fields. The local magistrate, a certain Kohō, had so often told me how he longed to show me this willow, and I had wondered just where it was – to find myself here today, pausing in its very shade.

ta ichimai	Paused by the willow
uete tachi-saru	a whole rice field planted
yanagi kana	before I leave

Uncertain day piled on day as we went on, and now as we came at last to the Shirakawa Barrier, my heart settled to the journey. I felt with what reason the poet wrote of his yearning to 'send word back / to the far Capital' from here.[30] This is one of the three greatest of the barrier gates, and has moved many poets. Summer's soft green treetops touched me the more deeply with Nōin's *autumn wind* in my ears and the vision of Yorimasa's *crimson leaves*[31] before my eyes. Whitethorn bloomed through the *mantling white* of deutzia blossom, lovelier to me than snow. Kiyo-suke[32] wrote of how a traveller of old tied his cap with particular care and wore his finest clothes to cross here.

unohana o	Deutzia flowers
kazashi ni seki no	tucked at my ear as formal wear
haregi kana	I cross the barrier
	Sora

In this way we came over the pass, and in due course arrived at Abukuma River. To the left rose the high peak of Mount Aizu, to the right the regions of Iwaki, Sōma and Miharu, while a long stretch of mountains marked the boundary of the lands of Hitachi and Shimotsuke. We passed the place called Mirror Pool, but the day was cloudy and we saw no reflections.

At the post town of Sukagawa we called on a man named Tōkyū, who kept us there four or five days. His first question was what we had done when we crossed the Shirakawa Barrier. 'Exhausted body and soul from the long hard road,' I told him, 'enthralled by the landscape, and harrowed with thoughts of the past, I could not muster my thoughts to compose anything worthwhile.

fūryū no	First poem
hajime ya oku no	for a poet's journey north[33] –
taue-uta	a local planting song

Well it just didn't feel right to simply cross without at least some poem . . .' I finished, whereupon he added a second link, a third then followed, and so on until we had made three sets of linked verse.

By the inn where we stayed, sheltering under a large chestnut tree, there lived a recluse monk. Saigyō gathering chestnuts deep among mountains lived perhaps just like this,[34] I thought, savouring that tranquillity, and I jotted down:

The character for 'chestnut' combines the meanings 'west' and 'tree', connecting it with Buddha's western paradise. All his life, they say, Saint Gyōgi used this wood for both his staff and the pillars of his hut.

yo no hito no   Blossoms most folk
mitsukenu hana ya   never notice –
noki no kuri   chestnut by the eave

About five miles on from Tōkyū's home was the waystation of
Hiwada, and beyond this rose Mount Asaka, close to the road.
There are many marshes in this area. It would soon be the season
for the cutting of the *katsumi* reeds, so I asked people to show me
the plants known as flowering *katsumi*, but none knew which
they were. Here and there we wandered in search, murmuring
katsumi katsumi[35] as we went, until the setting sun was low over
the mountain rim. Turning right at the double pines of Nihon-
matsu, we quickly took in Kurozuka Cave,[36] then stayed the night
at Fukushima.

The next morning we went on to Shinobu to visit the Shinobu
Rubbing Rock.[37] The rock is in a little village far in under the
mountains, and sits half buried in the earth. The village children
came up and told us that it used to be up on the mountain, but
passersby had damaged the barley fields to try rubbing barley on
the rock,[38] and this had angered the local farmers so much that
they pushed it down into the valley below, to lie there face down.
Could this be so?

sanae toru   Hands at work
temoto ya mukashi   planting Shinobu's seedlings –
shinobuzuri   hands moving long ago

Crossing the river at Tsukinowa, we arrived at the waystation of
Senoue. There we learned that the ruins of Superintendant
Satō's[39] establishment lay to the left a mile and a half away, up
against the mountains, at a place called Sabano in Iizuku village;
so we set off to see it, asking directions as we went along, until
we found our way to a hill by the name of Maruyama.

'This is where the Superintendant's residence once stood,' we
were told, 'and at the foot of the hill is the site of the old castle
gate . . .' We listened in tears as our guide talked on. An ancient
temple off to one side also held the gravestones of the Satō family,
with among them moving memorials for the two wives of the

brothers who died in battle. Women though they were, they were renowned for their courage, and the thought of them provoked fresh tears. That famous Grave of Weeping[40] might have been here before me.

We went into the temple to ask for tea, and found carefully preserved there Yoshitsune's sword and Benkei's travelling satchel.[41]

oi mo tachi mo	Sword and satchel
satsuki ni kazare	out for display on Boys' Day –
kaminobori	carp streamers

This was on the first day of the fifth month.[42]

That night we stayed in Iizuka. There was a hot spring where we bathed, before taking lodgings in a miserable hovel with only a thin mat to lay over the earth floor. Lacking a lamp, we spread our bedding to sleep by the light of the hearth. The night was loud with thunder and pouring rain, the roof over me leaked, a plague of fleas and mosquitoes kept me awake, and my old illness came back to torment me almost to death.

When the brief night at last gave way to dawn, we set off on our journey again. The hardships of the night still lingered with me, and I was reluctant to face the road that day. We borrowed a horse and went on to Kōri. With such a distance still before us, this illness made me anxious, but I rallied myself with thoughts of arduous pilgrimage in far lands, life's transience and the Buddhist readiness to relinquish all, and death on the journey as the will of heaven, so that a little courage returned to me, and I swung manfully along the road, through the great border gate and into Date.

Passing Abumizuri and Shiroishi Castle, we entered the province of Kasajima, where I asked where we might find the grave marker of Captain Sanekata. I learned that the villages we saw beneath the mountain far to the right were Mikawa and Kasajima, and there we would find the roadside shrine where he fell, and the autumn grasses of Saigyō's poem.[43] The road was dreadful after the recent fifth month rains, and I was exhausted, so we simply took these in from a distance as we passed. The names of Minowa and Kasajima are both redolent of the rainy season:[44]

kasajima wa	Where's sheltering Kasajima? –
izuko satsuki no	fifth month's
nukari-michi	boggy road

We stayed in Iwanuma.

The Pine of Takekuma[45] does indeed make one feel *fresh to the world*. Two trunks rise from the single base, showing that it is still as it always was. It brings to mind above all the monk Nōin, who wrote 'Now the old pine / has vanished',[46] no doubt because the man who came here as governor of Mutsu had had the pine cut down to make the pilings for the Natori Bridge. I had heard that down the passing years it had been cut and replanted several times, but lo and behold here it stood in all its splendour, looking just as it had for those *thousand years*.

When I left Edo, Kyohaku had written in farewell:

musashino no	Show him
matsu mise-mōse	late-blooming cherry
osozakura	the Pine of Musashino

And so in answer:

sakura yori	Three months the two trunks
matsu wa futaki o	waited for me
mitsuki koshi	longer than the cherry

We crossed the Natori River and came into Sendai, on the day of the Iris Thatching.[47] We found lodgings, and stayed four or five days.

Here lives an artist by the name of Kaemon, who I had heard was a man of some sensibility, and now I came to know him. He told us he had spent years searching out famous places of old whose locations had grown obscure, and he showed us around these for a day.[48]

The thick growth of bush clover at Miyagino conjured up for us that famous autumn flowering; the pieris were in flower at Tamada, Yokono and Tsutsujigaoka. We entered a pine grove so dense that no light filtered through, and were told that this was the famous Undertree. It was because the dew here long ago also lay thick that the poet wrote: 'Tell your lord / to wear his broadhat'.[49] We worshipped at the Yakushi Hall, Tenjin Shrine and other places, and thus the day drew to a close.

Our host drew a beautiful map of the famous places of Matsushima and Shiogama as a gift for us. He also gave us for the journey two pairs of straw sandals with special blue-dyed thongs – the crowning proof of his fine sensibility.

ayamegusa	For thongs
ashi ni musuban	to bind around my feet
waraji no o	the blue iris

Guided by his map, we followed the Narrow Road of Oku,[50] and at the edge of the mountains we found fields of the matting rush which, the old poems say, was used for many years to weave the matting sent to the local lord.

The famous Tsubo no Ishibumi is in Tagajō in Ichikawa Village.

The stone is over six feet high and around three feet wide. The carved lettering is faintly visible beneath the moss. It records the distance to the borders of the land in the four directions, and this is followed by the words: 'This castle was built in the first year of Jinki (724) by Lord Ōno of the East, Chief Overseer and Commander of the Subduing Forces.[51] It was restored in the sixth year of Tenpyō-hōji (762) by the Emi Lord Asakari, Commander and Governor of the Eastern Sea and Mountain Provinces. Dated this first day of the twelfth month.' This would mean it was built in the reign of Emperor Shōmu.[52]

Many famous *utamakura* sung of since ancient times in poetry have come down to us, but mountains crumble, rivers change their flow and roads are altered, stones become buried in the earth, trees age and are replaced by young ones, and thus time passes and the world changes, and all the traces of the past grow obscure – yet here beyond question was before my eyes a monument that has stood a thousand years, where I could read the minds and hearts of the ancients. At this reward for my journey, at the sheer joy of living to this moment, I forgot all the pains of travel, and simply wept.

Bashō and Sora

Chronology

mid–late 7th century Princess Nukata
? – *c.* 708 Kakimoto no Hitomaro
710–94 Nara Period
mid-8th century *Manyōshū*

794–1185 Heian Period

825–80 Ariwara no Narihira
late 9th–mid 10th century *The Ise Tales (Ise monogatari)*
?872–?945 Ki no Tsurayuki
***c.* 920** *Kokinshū* (full title *Kokin wakashū*)
***c.* 935** *Tosa Diary (Tosa nikki)*
mid 10th–early 11th century Zōki
***c.* 998** *Ionushi's Pilgrimage to Kumano (Ionushi)*
?966–*c.* 1025 Sei Shōnagon
***c.* 1001** *The Pillow Book (Makura no sōshi)*
***c.* 1008** *The Tale of Genji (Genji monogatari)*
966–1041 Fujiwara no Kintō
***c.* 1013** *Wakan rōeishū*
988–?1058 Nōin
***c.* 1050** *Nōinshū*
1008–? Sugawara no Takasue's Daughter
***c.* 1060** *Sarashina Diary (Sarashina nikki)*
1127–92 Retired Emperor Goshirakawa
***c.* 1170** *Dust Dancing on the Rafters (Ryōjin hishō)*

1185–1333 Kamakura Period

1118–90 Saigyō
early 13th century *The Tale of the Heike* (*Heike monogatari*)
1205 *Shinkokinshū* (full title *Shinkokin wakashū*)
early–mid 13th century *The Tale of Saigyō* (*Saigyō monogatari*)
early–mid 13th century *Senjūshō*
c. 1224 *Journey along the Sea Road* (*Kaidōki*)
1242 *Journey to the East* (*Tōkan kikō*)
?–1283 Abutsu
c. 1279–80 *Diary of the Waning Moon* (*Izayoi nikki*)
early 14th century *Pilgrimage to Kumano* (*Kumano sankei*)
1258–? Lady Nijō
c. 1310 *A Tale Unasked* (*Towazugatari*)
1333 Kamakura shogunate defeated

1336–1573 Ashikaga shogunate, Muromachi Period

14th century (dates unknown) Sōkyū
between 1353 and 1367 *A Gift for the Capital* (*Miyako no tsuto*)
?1363–?1443 Zeami
?1400–1432 Motomasa
1421–1502 Sōgi
c. 1430 *Sumida River* (*Sumida-gawa*)
1467–77 Ōnin Wars
1467–1568 Warring States era
1468 *Journey to Shirakawa* (*Shirakawa kikō*)
1480 *Journal of the Tsukushi Road* (*Tsukushi michi no ki*)
1448–1532 Sōchō
1502 *The Death of Sōgi* (*Sōgi shūenki*)

1573–1603 Azuchi Momoyama Period

1534–82 Oda Nobunaga
1536–98 Toyotomi Hideyoshi
1542–1616 Tokugawa Ieyasu
1534–1610 Hosokawa Yūsai

1587 *Journal of the Kyushu Road (Kyūshū michi no ki)*
1600 Battle of Sekigahara

1603–1868 Edo Period

1571–1653 Matsunaga Teitoku
1644–94 Matsuo Bashō
1684 *Bones on the Wayside (Nozarashi kikō)*
1687 *Knapsack Notes (Oi no kobumi)*
1689 *The Narrow Road of Oku (Oku no hosomichi)*

The Japanese Calendar

The calendar used throughout the classical period was a lunar–solar calendar based on that used in China. The year was divided into twelve months of either 29 or 30 days, the beginning of each month coinciding with the new moon. Days and months were conventionally referred to by number ('the fifth day of the eleventh month', for example), although months also had individual names. The fifteenth day of each month was the day of the full moon.

The year began on the first day of spring (the first day of the first month), which follows the pattern still used in China today. Thus, new year generally fell on the new moon of the Julian calendar's February, spring being months one through three; summer, months four through six; autumn, months seven through nine; and winter, months ten through twelve.

Years were commonly referred to by imperial reign name or *nengō*, so for instance the eighth year of Engi (Engi 8) refers to 908 in the Julian calendar.

The day was divided into twelve 'hours' of approximately 120 minutes each, named with the twelve zodiac signs, as seen in the diagram below. Thus the Hour of the Horse fell between 11 a.m. and 1 p.m., and so on. The same zodiac cycle was also applied to directions.

Zodiac Hour Names and Associated Directions

Outer Circle: Zodiac Names, Quarters, Semi-quarters
Second Circle: Modern Hours

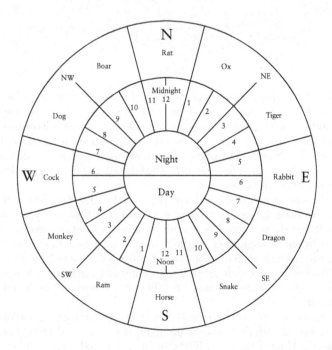

Glossary

asobi Also at different times termed *yūjo*, *asobime*, etc. Female entertainers of various kinds, either itinerant or based at waystations along the roads, who usually combined selling sexual favours with song, dance and musical performance.

aware Poignancy. The experience of being deeply touched or moved by something, or the thing that provokes this feeling. From an earlier more neutral or positive meaning it evolved to express feelings of pathos or sorrow, particularly at the transience of the phenomenal world. See also *mono no aware*.

Azuma See **The East**.

banka Elegy, lament. An early poetic category.

barrier gate See *seki*.

biwa A form of the Chinese *pipa*, distantly related to the wider family of stringed instruments that includes the lute. It was played by courtiers as well as by lower-class professional story-tellers (*biwa-hōshi*), but ceased to be fashionable in the Edo period.

Capital *Miyako*. The term commonly used to designate the imperial seat of power. From 794 until 1869 this was the city now known as Kyoto. Its heyday was the Heian period (794–1185).

chōka 'Long poem'. A poem of varying length but longer than a *tanka*, in loosely alternating five- and seven-syllable rhythm. *Chōka* are frequently found in the earlier poetry of the *Manyōshū*, but largely dropped from favour thereafter.

dai Poetic topic. An assigned topic on which a poem would be composed, usually in a group gathering. A poem composed in this way was termed a *daiei-ka*.

fūryū Elegance and refinement. An aesthetic sensibility cultivated in the arts particularly from the late medieval period onwards.

The East *Higashi no kuni* (earlier termed *Azuma*). A general term distinguishing the area to the east of the **Capital**, which came to be identified with the region centring on Kamakura and later Edo.

haikai 'Playful, humorous, light, vulgar'. Originally a term distinguishing frivolous or light poetry from the serious and elegant *waka*, it came to be particularly associated with *haikai no renga* and was often used as an abbreviated form of this term.

haikai no renga Light or comic *renga*, as distinguished from *renga* proper. Sometimes referred to simply as *haikai*. Originally a form of linked verse composed for comic entertainment, often after a more serious *renga* session, in the early Edo period *haikai no renga* evolved to become a poetic practice in its own right. Matsuo Bashō is its best-known practitioner. See also *renku*.

haiku Literally, a *ku* in a longer *haikai no renga* sequence. The term was occasionally used to denote the *hokku* that began the sequence, which was sometimes recorded and appreciated as an independent poem.

haiku Here distinguished from *haiku*. The current term both in Japan and internationally to denote a short, usually imagistic verse form traditionally composed in seventeen syllables. The present meaning of this word appeared in the late nineteenth century, although the term was in occasional use before that time. Now also retrospectively applied to earlier *hokku* read as stand-alone verses.

hanka Envoy. A poem in the *tanka* form frequently appended to a *chōka* in the *Manyōshū*, that repeats and rephrases the central emotional statement or image of the poem.

headnote See *kotobagaki*

hiragana See *kana*

hokku The opening seventeen-syllable *ku* in a *renga* sequence. It was composed by the leading poet in the group, and its material was derived from the present situation. The status of its composer, the importance of this verse in the linked verse sequence, and the fact that (unlike the subsequent verses) it reflected the immediate circumstances of its composition, all inclined the *hokku* to receive particular attention in its own right, and it was sometimes preserved in the form of a free-standing verse, leading eventually to the evolution of the haiku.

hototogisu A kind of cuckoo, whose song is poetically associated with early summer.

imayō 'Songs of the moment'. Songs performed by entertainers, which became popular at court in the twelfth century.

jo Prefatory section of a poem, usually containing an image or description that leads into the poem's statement, often by means of word play or association.

kagura Sacred dances associated with ceremonies for the gods performed in shrines or in the imperial palace.

kana Phonetic script derived from the earlier *manyōgana* in the late Nara / early Heian period, at first closely associated with the private and personal world of women's writing and letters, and with the composition of poetry in the Japanese language (*waka*) and its associated prose. Its modern simplified form is called *hiragana*. An equivalent and more angular *manyōgana*-derived phonetic script, now called *katakana*, evolved separately as an aid to reading Chinese texts in a form of Japanese translation (see *kanbun*).

kanbun 'Chinese writing'. The Japanese term for writing in the Chinese language, which in Japan was read either as Chinese, or as a convoluted form of Japanese whose method of reading was coded by means of diacritical marks added to the text (*kanbun kundoku*). *Kanbun* was the preserve of males, both courtiers and monks, during the Heian period, and was associated with official and public life and religious texts. From the late Heian period, it increasingly infiltrated Japanese *kana* writing and the associated native Japanese language.

kikō Travel chronicle. A combination of the personal poetry collection (*shikashū*) and diary (*nikki*) forms that emerged in the Kamakura period. *Kikō* are generally self-consciously literary works structured to varying degrees around poems composed on a journey and their associated places, frequently *utamakura* sites.

kiryo no uta Poem on the subject of travel. A poetic category.

Kokinshū Full title *Kokin wakashū* ('Collection of Ancient and Modern Waka'), *c.* 920. The first and most important of the imperial poetry collections, containing over one thousand poems.

koto Thirteen-stringed musical instrument derived from the Chinese *zheng*.

kotobagaki Headnote. A usually brief prose introduction to a poem, supplying information on the circumstances of composition and/or the poem's topic (*dai*). In *kikō*, the *kotobagaki* form was often expanded to merge with the more general diary entry form, creating a semi-continuous, poem-centred narrative of a journey.

ku A division of the *tanka* form, either the first or upper *ku* of 5/7/5 syllables or the second or lower *ku* of 7/7 syllables. From this, the term evolved to designate also a link in *renga* and *renku*, and finally a stand-alone verse of 5/7/5 syllables (cf. **haiku**).

manyōgana The earliest method of writing the Japanese language. A complex script that used Chinese characters sometimes for their meaning and sometimes to phonetically spell out the syllables of Japanese words.

makurakotoba 'Pillow word'. A poetic epithet, most usually in the form of a word or phrase conventionally attached to a place name.

Makurakotoba were much used in *Manyōshū* poetry and less frequently later.

michi 'Way' or 'path'. The word took on richly symbolic connotations through its Buddhist use (derived primarily from the expression 'the Way of Buddhism'), and from the late Heian period onwards came to express a pursuit to which one is wholeheartedly dedicated, and which by implication becomes a means to enlightenment. See also *suki no tonseisha*.

Michinoku *Michi no oku*, 'the far reaches of the road'. The northern region of the main island of Honshu, for centuries one of the farthest outposts of the Japanese nation. See also **Oku**.

michiyuki 'Going-along-the-road'. A set-piece depiction of the route of an emotionally intense and usually unhappy or tragic journey through enumeration of places along the route, poetically evoked. Its heightened form of lyrical prose in loosely 5/7 syllable rhythm is termed *michiyuki-bun*.

michiyuki-bun See *michiyuki*.

miyabi A refined aesthetic associated with the culture of the Heian court. The word derives from *miya*, here meaning the imperial court.

monogatari Narrative prose tale, usually fictitious, that came to prominence in the Heian period. Written in the Japanese language for and sometimes by women, *monogatari* were typically anonymous courtly romances, but the term was later extended to cover military and other forms of narrative tale.

mono no aware 'The poignant nature of things'. A more abstract term for *aware* and a key concept in Japanese aesthetics.

nikki Diary or journal (literally 'daily record'). The origins of *nikki* were the day-to-day records of official events written in Chinese by courtiers, but the word was appropriated to apply to the Japanese language (*kana*) free-form diary-like accounts of private life, thoughts and poetry written by women, most famously in the Heian period.

Nō **drama** (Also Noh.) A highly stylized form of drama that combines music, dance, masks and chanted or sung words to present a play that frequently includes supernatural elements. *Nō* drama emerged in the late fifteenth century and quickly evolved into a courtly art with a large repertoire of plays whose language ranges from the colloquial to the elegant and poetic. See also *sarugaku*.

nusa Strips of cloth or paper traditionally offered at shrines by way of prayer to a deity.

Oku Abbreviation of **Michinoku**. The literal meaning is 'innermost place'.

renga Linked verse. Originally a *tanka* whose composition was divided between two people, usually in the form of statement and clever response, the term came to designate a form of extended group composition in which an initial *ku* of 5/7/5 syllables (or **hokku**) was completed by the addition of a 7/7-syllable *ku*, which in turn formed the beginning of a new poem by the addition of a further 5/7/5-syllable *ku*, and so on. *Renga* were generally composed in group sessions of varying numbers of poets, according to a complex set of rules. Hundred-link *renga* were the most common, but these could be extended to marathon thousand-link *renga* composed over several days.

renku A name now commonly applied to **haikai no renga**, to distinguish it from **haiku**.

sarugaku A form of popular entertainment that included elements of comic skit, song and dance, performed by troupes of players. *Sarugaku* was an important precursor of **Nō drama**.

seki Barrier gate. These were set up on the borders between provinces, to check the credentials of travellers and sometimes to impose a toll. They largely ceased to function with the passage of time but remained landmarks along the way, and their ruins became evocative of the past.

setsuwa Anonymous, usually short narratives derived from oral stories, often containing Buddhist themes.

shikashū Personal poetry collection, generally made to be circulated among friends and acquaintances.

shite The main role in a *nō* play. See also **waki**.

shugendō A syncretic amalgamation of Buddhist and native religious beliefs and practices, whose practitioners (commonly termed **yamabushi**) devoted themselves to rigorous ascetic acts, often in remote mountains. They were commonly credited with having special powers.

shugyō Ascetic and devotional practice with the aim of attaining enlightenment.

sōga Also *sōka, enkyoku*. An elaborate style of lengthy song that became popular in the late thirteenth century. Its ornate and rhythmic language, replete with word play and allusion, borrowed heavily from the **waka** poetic tradition.

suki no tonseisha One who has taken Buddhist vows and retired from active engagement with the world to devote himself to the Way of Buddhism in a form that combines religious devotions with the dedicated practice of one or more of the arts, often poetry.

tanka 'Short poem'. A poem of thirty-one syllables in the rhythm 5/7/5/7/7, although this count could occasionally be varied for effect. The term is often used interchangeably with **waka**, since it was for centuries the exclusive form for poetry composed in the native Japanese language (as distinct from poetry in Chinese).

Tōkaidō The Eastern Sea Road. The main road that connected the **Capital** with the eastern provinces and beyond, which in the Edo period became the great highway linking the old Capital with Edo (now Tokyo). It followed various routes and went by various names in earlier centuries, such as Eastern Road (*Azumaji*) or Sea Road (*Kaidō*). Its association with literary travel began early, and a vast corpus of poetry grew up around its many famous *utamakura* sites. Although this name only became established in the Edo period, it is used for convenience here in discussing earlier centuries.

uguisu A kind of bush warbler, whose song is poetically associated with spring.

uta Song, poem. A term denoting poetry generally in the classical period, and often used synonymously with *waka* (*tanka*).

utamakura From an earlier more general meaning, the word later came to denote the name of a place with specific poetic associations owing to its presence in past poetry, its historical importance, etc., and by extension also such a place itself.

waka 'Japanese poetry'. A term that distinguishes poetry written in the native Japanese language from that written in Chinese (*kanshi*). It came to be identified specifically with the *tanka* form that dominated Japanese poetry for centuries, and is often used interchangeably with that term.

waki 'Side figure'. The secondary role in a *Nō* play, often a travelling priest. See also *shite*.

yamabushi Mountain monk. See *shugendō*.

Notes

Introduction

1. *what we would today call genres*: The concept of genre is largely irrelevant to the way literature was conceived in Japan, a lack of strict boundaries that encouraged the kind of rich cross-fertilizations that fed the tradition of travel writing.
2. *haikai*: A distinction is made throughout this book between the *haikai* poetry that Bashō and others of his time wrote, and the 'haiku' that we know today. For more on this, see Glossary.
3. *scarcely distinguished in that early time*: The word *uta*, which was the common term for poetry and today is the word for song, originally denoted simply a rhythmical set of words for singing. (See Glossary for this and other Japanese terms.) The singing (chanting) of poems was for long the primary method of composing and communicating them, while writing was used largely for purposes of recording them (except in the case of letters).
4. *the trajectory of Japanese literature . . . the works of Bashō*: See the Chronology for a timeline of dates for the historical periods together with those of the translated works and their authors.
5. *largely turns its back . . . charted here*: Travel journals more or less modelled on their medieval predecessors continued to be written by some Edo period travellers with literary pretensions, but these were on the whole essentially old-fashioned gestures towards a tradition that had long since run its course.
6. *they passed through difficult mountain terrain . . . crossings between tides*: Such places of notorious danger on the road were known as *nansho* (difficult places), and were the sites of many accidents. They are vividly described in a number of the texts translated here.
7. *boats largely cease . . . distantly seen across the water*: The main exception included here, the late sixteenth-century *Journal of the Kyushu Road*, describes a hazardous journey made partly by boat that

closely resembles that described in *Tosa Diary* more than seven centuries earlier, suggesting how little had changed.

8.   *women diarists*: Men also wrote diaries during this period, but they were generally dry official records in Chinese and hence outside the scope of this book.

9.   *Buddhist monks*: This term is loosely used to include men and occasionally women who took Buddhist vows and 'turned from the world', but were by no means always or usually confined to monasteries.

10. *fed into the new forms of literature that emerged in the middle ages and later*: This influence is particularly strong in *The Tale of the Heike* and in the evolution of Nō drama, both forms of performative literature.

11. *here termed asobi*: Asobi is somewhat arbitrarily chosen from among the various terms for them in different periods.

12. *One of the few comforts . . . for the road*: Except for local forays to famous places for the primary purpose of group poetry composition, however, the literature produced by travellers was a by-product of the journey rather than its immediate purpose. Even Bashō, who presents his journeys as being purely literary in intent, combined his travels with important time spent promoting his school.

13. *China's writing system . . . the Japanese language*: This earliest phonetic writing system for the Japanese language, known as *manyōgana* (literally, '*Manyōshū* makeshift'), is the distant origin of the modern *hiragana* script. See the introduction to *The Ise Tales* for a further discussion of this process.

14. *so with Bashō's travel journals*: His earlier travel journals such as *Bones on the Wayside*, translated here, make this particularly clear.

15. *a series of . . . that culminate in a poem*: This tendency is particularly evident in the medieval travel chronicles, which form the core of classical Japanese travel writing. Those included here are chosen in part for the relative weight that they give to the prose; the majority of travel chronicles were often little more than collections of poems composed on the journey, interspersed with brief prose prefaces.

16. *the traveller himself*: Women travellers did exist, and a few are represented in these pages, but travel in this period was overwhelmingly the preserve of men.

17. *the remarkable continuity of poetic form and rhythm*: The early emergence of the *tanka* form of 5/7/5/7/7 syllables, and its later abbreviation to the 'haiku' form of 5/7/5 via the evolution of linked verse, can be traced through a consecutive reading of the works in this book.

18. *Celebration and delight ... a relatively minor role*: After the early *Manyōshū* poetry that celebrates the land (a conventional way of celebrating its ruler), celebratory poetry is largely limited to poetry composed in praise of the native gods and their shrines. Most travel journals include at least one and often a number of such poems, together with conventional reverent description of shrines visited. The excerpts in this book exclude many of these passages, which are usually too conventional to be interesting for the general reader.

19. *the landscape itself ... his longing for home and absent loved ones*: Many of the travel poems in the *Manyōshū* seamlessly combine the themes of travel and love in this way.

20. *There were times ... rising above a flood tide*: Lack of defining subject and verb tense allows this passage to also be understood as general statement ('There are times when one sleeps alone ...' etc.), reinforcing the slippage between personal and suprapersonal experience.

21. *it was essentially in poetic terms that literary travellers generally portrayed it*: The extreme example of this is the heightened writing style known as *michiyuki-bun*, exemplified here in Chapter 10.6 of *The Tale of the Heike* and in *Pilgrimage to Kumano*, in which prose takes on rhythmic and lyrical intensities that lift it towards poetry.

22. *assumes but seldom makes explicit*: A lack of explicit subject is inherent in the Japanese language, allowing for ambiguities that the shifting interpretations found in linked verse in particular exploited (see note 20 above). In other cases, context provided by the *kotobagaki* could determine a poem's interpretation.

23. *he was in a sense imagining himself as a figure in a scene*: A nicely ironic instance of this is found in *The Ise Tales* 9, where the (supposedly) real-life travellers decide to compose acrostic *daiei-ka* poems 'on the theme of Travel', then weep at the moving image of the Traveller evoked in the man's poem.

24. *continued to search out the place identified with this scene*: It is still visited by hikers today, along a path known as 'The Narrow Path of Vines' (*tsuta no hosomichi*), a reference to its description in *The Ise Tales*.

25. *almost as a pilgrim will offer up a prayer*: The almost religious nature of this gesture is not unrelated to the custom of offering poetry at shrines, both shrines and *utamakura* sites being equally important places on the itinerary of literary travellers.

26. *Those who ventured ... the wilds of the literary unknown*: The fifteenth-century linked verse poet Sōgi's *Journey to Shirakawa* is a

particularly compelling expression of the role that *utamakura* played for the adventurous literary traveller (see Chapter 20).

27. *particularly from the late twelfth-century figure of Saigyō onwards*: The wandering poet-monk Saigyō's own life and poetry contributed greatly to the evolution of the Traveller figure, but it was above all the anonymous and undatable *Tale of Saigyō* (see Chapter 11) in its many versions that distilled it for future ages.

28. *very different travel works*: One of the last remaining links with the old travel writing tradition was the continuing inclusion of poetry in many of these works, although the poems were for the most part humorous *haikai*-style poems.

A Note on the Translations

1. *the prose can intensify . . . the qualities of poetry*: The distinction between prose and poetry is generally less absolute than in modern English. Heightened 'poetic' prose bears a familial relationship with the long poems (*chōka*) of the early *Manyōshū*, which are reproduced here in the same way, with a continuous line of spaced phrasing.

2. *passing allusive echoes embedded in the prose*: One telling example is the famous opening words of Bashō's *The Narrow Road of Oku*, which are a loose restatement of words and sentiments recognizable from a number of classical Chinese texts (see p. 264).

3. *depends on syllable count rather than line division*: *Waka* is usually written in two lines that divide the first three units, or *ku* (5/7/5) from the second (7/7). *Hokku* (which later became haiku), evolving as it did from the *waka's* first three units, is written in a single line.

1. Manyōshū

1. *first extant work of literature*: The two main works that antedate it, *Kojiki* (712) and *Nihon Shoki* (720), are semi-historical chronicles.

2. *eastward . . . the present-day Tokyo area*: a region then designated by the general name 'The East' (*Azuma*). During this period and for some time after, the outer boundaries of this area as well as some of its remoter regions continued to be the scene of armed confrontations with the earlier inhabitants (known collectively as *Ezo* or *Emishi*), who were only with difficulty 'pacified'.

3. *its stock images*: The most important and pervasive is the epithet *kusamakura* (grass for pillow), a poetic term which came to evoke

the hardship of travel, and continued to resonate in literature down the centuries.

4. *sea travel . . . in these poems*: A far quicker form of travel than overland, and used whenever possible, particularly for the busy route between Yamato and Tsukushi.

5. *composed and transmitted orally . . . only later*: Most of the composers would have been illiterate. Writing had been introduced from the continent only relatively recently, and the writing system used in the *Manyōshū* was extraordinarily cumbersome and beyond the reach of the general populace.

6. *a communal poetic tradition*: From social group composition and performance to the pervasiveness of allusive borrowing, Japanese poetry long continued to be a far more communal and shared phenomenon than lyric poetry in the West.

7. *the forms of poetry*: For more on poetic forms and terms, see Glossary.

8. *my translations*: *Chōka* make frequent use of poetic epithets (*makurakotoba*), which I only occasionally translate, as their meaning is often unclear and they are frequently used primarily for their sound.

9. *The history . . . remains unclear*: The *tanka* seems to have evolved early and possibly independently of the *chōka*.

10. *the assigned topic*: Poems composed at social gatherings were generally responses to set topics (*dai*), a custom inherited from China. See Introduction, p. xix for the influence of this on the evolving tradition of travel writing.

11. *388/89*: Throughout, numbers refer to the ordering found in *Manyōshū*.

12. *Sasanami in Ōmi*: An area along the shore of Lake Biwa which was briefly the seat of the capital from 667 to 672.

13. *the island of Samine*: Samine is one of the many small islands of the Inland Sea, off the coast of Shikoku (Sanuki).

14. *a specifically Buddhist sensibility*: Although Buddhism had already been introduced from the continent, its influence was still insignificant in this period.

15. *themes found in the early poetry of sea travel*: Compare poem 3333 above.

16. *composed in spring in the third month*: Months were numbered according to the lunar calendar equivalent to the present-day Chinese calendar; see 'The Japanese Calendar' for more information.

2. *The Ise Tales*

1. *a permanent capital*: It remained Japan's capital almost without break for more than a thousand years.

2. *even fewer knew how to read it*: For this reason the *Manyōshū* became largely unreadable to later generations, and only a few of its poems were preserved in anthologies. Its influence was carried through indirectly in the continuing evolution of *waka* poetry, although its poems seem to have been known to at least one of *The Ise Tales'* creators.

3. *whose poems . . . the work's earliest form*: Their main source is generally believed to be a now lost collection of Narihira's poetry, although a number of poems and similar headnotes are found in the *Kokinshū* (possibly derived from the same source).

4. *a courtier*: Though the grandson of an emperor, Narihira never attained a commensurately high rank, largely because his father had been disgraced through his association with a failed coup and reduced to commoner status.

5. *the monogatari . . . at the time*: See Glossary. Few of these tales have survived. The crowning achievement of the genre was Murasaki Shikibu's *Tale of Genji* (*Genji monogatari*, c. 1004–1012), whose hero seems to have been partly modelled on the hero of *The Ise Tales*.

6. *elegant excursion*: Such aristocratic excursions, derived from Chinese example, always involved at least one occasion for the composition of poems on a place or scene.

7. *the land of Suruga . . . Mount Utsu*: One of the Tōkaidō's routes crossed Mount Utsu by a notoriously steep and difficult road.

8. *our Mount Hiei . . . a salt cone*: Mount Hiei, to the immediate northeast of Kyoto, is the tallest mountain in the vicinity. The writer assumes an audience familiar with the Capital. A salt cone (*shiojiri*) was a cone of sand over which sea water was poured to extract salt.

9. *Sumida River*: The Sumida River now flows through Tokyo.

10. *Michinoku*: This was still the outermost area of the Japanese nation, considered a wild and uncouth region.

11. *bonded . . . this brief life*: It was believed that the male and female silkworm make a single cocoon together.

12. *Even her poetry was rustic*: The image of the silkworm in particular betrays her as a mere country girl. The poem is in fact a variation on a *Manyōshū* poem (3086).

13. *she composed this*: This humorously boorish poem includes Michi-noku dialect words.

14. *She was delighted by this*: The apparently complimentary poem in fact insults her by implying that, like the famous local pine, she is rooted to the locality and not quite human.

15. *home they went again*: It would have been usual for all those pres-ent to compose a poem. It is implied that this poem was so impressive that they returned without composing any themselves.

3. *Tosa Diary* by Ki no Tsurayuki

1. *a direct . . . Tsurayuki's original manuscript*: The original manuscript, long forgotten, was discovered and copied in 1235 by the great poet Fujiwara no Teika (1162–1241), and again not long after by his son Tameie (1198–1275), whose more faithful copy was in turn re-discovered in 1975 and gives us the work as we know it today.

2. *makes its slow way*: Records of the time indicate that in calm wea-ther the journey would have taken only thirteen days. The extracts given here abridge much of the description of delays at ports along the way, as well as omitting the early section largely devoted to a lengthy leave-taking.

3. *precisely whose experience is being described*: Not only subject but sometimes object are left unstated, as well as the distinction between plural and singular (see also Introduction, p. xix). The lack of a clear 'I' in *Tosa Diary*'s first-person account, and the vagueness and ambivalence of subject and grammatical person, often suggest 'we' as the closest translation.

4. *elegant confusion*: The poem in the twenty-first day entry is a typ-ical example. Fanciful surmising, such as in the poem in the fifteenth day entry, is a related common characteristic of this poetry.

5. *the Kokinshū . . . by imperial decree*: This immensely influential work was ordered by Emperor Daigo (r. 897–930) though con-ceived by his father Uda (r. 887–97), and later inspired an important series of imperial poetry collections that continued to appear until the mid-fifteenth century.

6. *a legitimate poetic form among the men at court*: The enthusiasm for *waka* of Emperor Uda and his son (see previous note) spurred on this acceptance. Formal *waka* matches (*utaawase*) were held at court, and there was fresh interest in the composition of *waka* on set themes and scenes depicted on screens (see Introduction, p. xix), at which Tsurayuki excelled. Many of the poems in *Tosa Diary*

seem to have begun their life as screen poems, and the lightly
sketched natural descriptions in the diary are often reminiscent of
the screen painting style.

7.   *a prose work in kana . . . Chinese literary mode*: Like *The Ise Tales* and
     other writing in Japanese of the time, Chinese ideograms were
     incorporated only occasionally in *kana* writing. A poetry collec-
     tion titled *Shinsen manyōshū*, which had appeared a generation
     earlier, had broken with tradition by mischievously matching
     native *waka* with similarly themed well-known Chinese poems in
     mock imitation of court poetry matches. There is also speculation
     that Tsurayuki may have had an important hand in the creation
     of *The Ise Tales*, another semi-playful experiment in *waka*-style
     Japanese-language narrative writing.

8.   *had little influence on the history of Japanese travel literature*: This
     puzzling fact can perhaps best be explained by the vagaries of
     manuscript history. A work could only gain circulation through
     laborious copying, and lack of subsequent reference to *Tosa Diary*
     suggests that it was never widely circulated, so that it soon disap-
     peared from sight (see note 1 above).

9.   *the Hour of the Dog*: Around 8 p.m.

10. *Twenty-seventh day. Our boat set off from Ōtsu, bound for Urado*: The
     previous recorded days were taken up with elaborate leave-taking.
     They are proceeding downriver from Ōtsu (the site of modern-day
     Kōchi) to the nearby port of Urado.

11. *there was one among us . . . as he watched*: Typically, this sentence
     has no subject, although the description implies that the subject is
     not the writer. It could equally be interpreted as the child's mother.

12. *With a voice like that . . . apparently exclaimed*: A joking reference to
     two Chinese proverbs describing the power of a beautiful voice
     (see *Dust Dancing on the Rafters*, p. 100). 'Apparently' indicates that,
     being a woman, the writer would not in fact have understood the
     Chinese quotations.

13. *Fujiwara no Tokizane, Tachibana no Suehira*: Both are unidentified.

14. *New Year sake and medicinal spices for it*: The spices are Chinese
     medicinal herbs traditionally used to spice the celebratory sake
     drunk at New Year to ward off illness in the coming year.

15. *tooth-hardening foods*: Foods traditionally eaten at New Year, such
     as venison, pheasant and white radish, believed to harden the teeth
     and thereby ensure a healthy old age.

16. *suck on salted sweetfish . . . clamped to theirs*: Sweetfish (*ayu*) was one
     of the tooth-hardening foods. The innards were sucked out through
     its mouth.

17. *Masatsura*: Unidentified.
18. *the White Horses ceremony*: The traditional parading of twenty-one white horses before the emperor, held on the seventh day of the new year.
19. *the Festival of Young Herbs*: Seven types of herb were gathered and eaten on the seventh day in a ritual meal to ward off evil and illness.
20. *boxed food*: *hiwariko*, a compartmentalized box much like today's *bentō* box, containing a portable meal.
21. *no one composed one in return*: Courtesy required that an offered poem receive one in response.
22. *would that ... flee before it*: By Ariwara no Narihira.
23. *until we crossed the province's border*: They are about to leave Tosa province, whose governor Tsurayuki has been. It was the custom to accompany travellers as far as a boundary, which often involved a journey of several days. (See also *Manyōshū* poem 135, and *Sarashina Diary*.)
24. *This was a day ... particularly intense*: It may have been a significant anniversary. This sentence has been variously interpreted.
25. *one among them ... homeward journey*: *Kokinshū* 412, anonymous.
26. *Funtoki and Koremichi*: Unidentified.
27. *past its tenth night*: And therefore heading towards full. In the lunar calendar, the fifteenth day fell on the full moon, so it is now two days short of full.
28. *for fear of arousing ... go so deliciously with sea squirts*: There was a superstitious belief that the sea god would be attracted to a beautiful woman and seize her. Shellfish and *bêche-de-mer* (sea cucumbers) were commonly eaten together, giving rise to this risqué joke.
29. *a day of abstinence*: Certain days were prescribed days of abstinence, requiring purification observances and vegetarian food.
30. *festival red bean stew*: It was the tradition at court to cook red beans on this day, to avert evil influences.
31. *the hour of the hare*: Around 6 a.m. The intervening days had all been spent in the port waiting for good weather.
32. *though it was spring*: The first day of the new year had marked the beginning of spring.
33. *black birds*: Possibly cormorants.
34. *it did sound clever somehow*: The concise balancing of contrasting images echoes the construction of a typical line of Chinese verse, although a boat's captain could not be expected to be familiar with such things.
35. *pirates*: The Inland Sea swarmed with pirates, who were sometimes referred to by the name *shiranami* (white waves).

36. *And so we went on*: It is now the fifth day of the second month, and after many delays they have come unscathed as far as Izumi, south of present-day Osaka.

37. *the god of Sumiyoshi was a fierce sea god*: They were passing Sumiyoshi, whose unruly deity was renowned for his tendency to stir up angry waves until suitable offerings were made.

38. *Two precious eyes, but only one of these*: An expression commonly used to emphasize that something was particularly precious in being unique. The saying is appropriate here in likening a mirror to an eye.

39. *the navigation markers*: Markers indicating a sea lane. They are arriving at what is now the port of Osaka Bay, the mouth of the Yodo River that will take them upstream to the Capital.

40. *fishing with fine rice to catch fingerlings*: This seems to have been a saying of the time. Rice was considered more precious than fish.

41. *the Nagisa Villa*: An imperial villa, famous in its day as the gathering place of Prince Koretaka's poetic salon, which included such luminaries as Ariwara no Narihira.

42. *Planning to arrive . . . we took our time*: After further slow progress upstream, they are arriving at the Capital on the sixteenth day.

43. *Unlike the Asuka River . . . have never changed*: A reference to a well-known anonymous poem.

44. *High on the moon . . . katsura tree*: A reference to a well-known Chinese legend that a *katsura* (*Cercidiphyllum japonicum*) stands on the moon.

45. *I plan to destroy this forthwith*: Tsurayuki is following custom by humbly suggesting that what he has written is strictly private and not worthy of wider circulation.

4. *Ionushi's Pilgrimage to Kumano* by Zōki

1. *pilgrimages to shrines and temples*: The accepted distinction between temple (*tera*, Buddhist) and shrine (*jinja*, native or 'Shinto' religion) is maintained in this book. In practice, owing to religious syncretism there was often little distinction between the two, as was the case with Kumano's main holy sites.

2. *in the first section of his shikashū*: The second section reverts to typical *shikashū* form, with poems presented in random order. The third section presents a kind of hybrid form. It follows Zōki's journey to and from distant Tōtōmi but traces it strictly through sequential placing of the poems composed along the way, without expanding their *kotobagaki* into broader descriptive or narrative passages as does the first section.

3. *the third person protagonist in his own story*: An interesting variation on the playful disguising impulses seen in both *The Ise Tales* and *Tosa Diary*, the first suggesting Ariwara no Narihira through veiled use of anonymous third person style, the second taking a fictional first person style to depict the real author with humorous objectivity.

4. *a real journey*: Despite the lightly fictional effect of the third person narrative form, the work makes no attempt to disguise the fact that it describes Zōki's actual experience.

5. *wittily allusive conversational exchange ... poetic core*: Wit and wordplay continued to be prized elements in poetry and poetic exchanges, and the teasing conversational exchanges Zōki depicts rely on a similar style of wit and allusive reference. Unfortunately the passage of time and the limitations of translation detract somewhat from the effect of this clever banter.

6. *earliest recorded myth ... numbers of people*: Kumano is first mentioned in the section of the *Nihon shoki* (720, one of Japan's two earliest attempts at historical record) that details the events of the 'Age of the Gods' (*shindai*). By Zōki's day its rapidly increasing popularity as a pilgrimage site was further boosted by numerous imperial pilgrimages.

7. *a powerfully attractive centre of devotion*: Not only Hongū but the entire sacred mountainous area surrounding it was believed to embody the Pure Land paradise to which Amida worshippers aspired. The deity at Nachi, which Zōki later visits, was in turn considered an avatar of the Bodhisattva Kannon, inspiring a cult in which seekers after Kannon's promised land (Fudaraku) set out to sea from Nachi in tiny unprovisioned boats in what amounted to a suicidal journey to attain paradise.

8. *he set off to visit ... to purge his sins*: This is an early example of the combination of aesthetic pleasures and ascetic rigour that was the hallmark of many later Buddhist poets and their writing.

9. *went to Yahata to pray*: Iwashimizu Hachiman Shrine at Yahata (Yawata) is to this day an important place of worship.

10. *the shrine of Sumiyoshi*: An ancient and important shrine in present-day Osaka; see p. 298 note 37.

11. *he thought quietly to himself*: A reference to the fact that poetry was usually composed aloud, this also echoes the poem's theme of hidden worship.

12. *Here I have hung ... from sight and mind*: This obscure poem seems to refer to the ritual of copying part of the Lotus Sutra and tying it to a branch in the shrine as offering. The image of the hidden jewel

derives from the Lotus Sutra parable of a priceless jewel secretly hidden in the robes of an ignorant man.

13. *more transient . . . dew upon the grass*: Here and below, italics indicate material embedded in the text that contains allusive echoes of previous literary works but is not overtly quotation.

14. *a heavenly maiden frequently appears on the beach*: This widespread legend, also the subject of the famous Nō play *Hagoromo*, tells of an angelic maiden who descends to the beach to bathe wearing a robe of feathers.

15. *unfeeling though he was*: A monk should have transcended human feeling. (See also *The Tale of Saigyō*, p. 126, where Saigyō repeats this phrase in a famous poem.) The tension between Buddhism's renunciation of all attachment and the poet's sensitive responsiveness to the phenomenal world lies at the heart of much Buddhist poetry.

16. *the name will conjure her*: The word 'back' (*se*) in the mountain's name is homophonous with the word for 'husband'.

17. *sunk from sight upon the flooded rocks*: An allusion to *Manyōshū* 1394: 'Perhaps because this grass / has sunk from sight upon the flooded rocks / when the tide washes over / seeing it so much less / I long for it the more.' The poem laments how rarely the lover can catch a glimpse of his beloved, here implying that his friend has been elusive.

18. *a day spent longing*: 'A day spent longing / is a long long day / but now rare chance is ours / yet even on this night / would you deny me?' The friend quotes another *Manyōshū* poem (2079) as a joking complaint that in fact Ionushi has been the elusive one, and should spend more time with him now that they have met here.

19. *the beach lilies of Kumano's bays*: 'As many times / as the many-folded leaves / of the beach lilies of Kumano's bays / so many times more / does your heart think of him than me' (*Kokin rokujō* 1935–6). The friend is teasing him that someone else holds more attraction than his own company.

20. *Not a single night spent folded*: 'My heart thinks / of no other more than you / and this beach lily of Kumano's bays / has spent not a single night / folded in another's arms.' The *hanka* to the previous poem.

21. *Why then you have no cause*: 'If you have not met / even for a single night / why then you have no cause / to lament either her / or you yourself' (*Shūishū* 678). The implied meaning here is, 'Well then, don't grumble'.

22. *Sleeve pressed to eyes . . . Mount Later*: This final exchange parries quotations of conventional expressions found in various poems of parting.

23. *Sacred Boat Island*: The gods were believed to have arrived at Kumano by boat, which became the boat-shaped rock named Mifune-shima that lies offshore from Hayatama Shrine in the Kumano River.

24. *Tada Mountain*: An early name for Nachi Mountain, where there is an important shrine and sacred waterfall.

5. *The Pillow Book* by Sei Shōnagon

1. *a powerful means ... educated women*: The most famous of the Heian women's diaries from this period to survive is *The Gossamer Diary* (*Kagerō nikki*, 954–74), by a woman known only as 'the mother of Fujiwara no Michitsuna'.

2. *associated primarily with women*: The *monogatari* writers were anonymous but it is generally believed that they were written largely by men, although women were overwhelmingly their primary audience.

3. *if she knew more about the world beyond the Capital*: As the daughter of a provincial governor, she may well have experienced travel at least to one of the provinces in the company of her father.

4. *Conventional poetic pathos was not her mode*: Sei was a skilled poet, as custom required, but her talent lay in the realm of wit and repartee, and *The Pillow Book* is notable for how few poems it includes.

5. *nothing quite like The Pillow Book was ever written again*: Three centuries later Yoshida Kenkō harked back to *The Pillow Book* in his *Essays in Idleness* (*Tsurezuregusa*), but that is in many ways a very different work.

6. *sleeves tumbling out in profusion*: An ox carriage was roofed and had fine reed blinds at the sides, through which the ladies inside could see out while remaining invisible. It was the custom at this time to arrange one's long sleeves to hang outside the blinds for display.

7. *the temple at Hase*: Hasedera, at the edge of the Yamato plain, has long been an important and immensely popular site of Kannon worship. The journey from the Capital would have taken several days.

8. *the famous Yodo Crossing*: A river crossing just south of the Capital, in present-day Fushimi.

9. *the temple at Kiyomizu*: Kiyomizudera, today one of Kyoto's top tourist destinations, was a popular pilgrimage site to rival Hase. It stood not far beyond the southern edge of the Capital.

10. *the four-word verses of the Kusha Sutra*: This sutra is divided into 600 'verses' (*ge* or *zu*) of four words each, to aid in recitation.

11. *a mountain monk*: Commonly called *yamabushi*. A follower of the *shugendō* sect and a version of the ascetics that Ionushi lived among at Hongū (see Glossary).

12. *The young lady is in akome gown and skirted trousers*: Sei is depicting a scene such as might be found in a *monogatari* romance. An *akome* gown was a young girl's over-robe. Skirted trousers (*hakama*) were wide-legged trousers worn under the gown.

13. *what I believe is called the 'oar'*: Sei chooses to distance herself elegantly from the world of such workaday words. It is likely that the young man is poling the boat from the stern rather than rowing.

14. *The 'white retreating waves' of the poem*: See *Manyōshū* p. 16, poem 351. Sei quotes from the version known to later generations (*Shūishū* 1327), whose final three lines are 'white retreating waves / behind a boat that vanishes / rowing into the light of dawn'.

6. *Wakan rōeishū* compiled by Fujiwara no Kintō

1. *for performance purposes*: The more literal meaning of *rōei* (a Chinese word) is 'intoned vocal performance of poetry'.

2. *a fall of snow . . . a Chinese poem on the subject*: See *Tosa Diary* p. 37 for an example of the way a quotation from a Chinese poem was recited or sung in response to an occasion.

3. *one of which is Travel*: All nine poems in the Travel section are translated here.

4. *a version of the Chinese pronunciation . . . more or less comprehensible as Japanese*: This laborious method of reading Chinese in the Japanese fashion was known as *kanbun kundoku*. Its notation method gave rise to the *katakana* phonetic syllabery still used to provide an approximate pronunciation of foreign words.

5. *How might I find . . . the Barrier at Shirakawa*: This poem established a lineage of traveller's poems at the barrier gate of Shirakawa which echoed down through the poems of Nōin, Saigyō, Sōgi and finally Bashō, among many others.

7. Eight Poems by Nōin

1. *largely limited to provincial governors and their entourages*: Absence from the Capital could be perilous for one's career, although aristocratic families generally gained their wealth from large country estates that required visits from time to time.

2. *To what extent . . . is less clear*: With his aristocratic connections, it is probable that he would have taken the occasional opportunities

offered to stay at wealthy homes en route, as well as spending time at local temples, and more than likely that he did not travel alone. There is also a theory that one of his purposes for travelling was horse dealing.

3. *the 'way' of the aesthete recluse (suki no tonseisha)*: Men who combined religious practice with the dedicated pursuit of an art, frequently that of poetry, and attempted as far as possible to philosophically integrate the two.

4. *cultivated and literary men*: Cultivated women could and did take the tonsure and become 'lay nuns', but custom dictated that they remain closeted at home and they played little part in the emergence of recluse literature.

5. *a way of life . . . religious awakening*: The early thirteenth-century work *Hōjōki* by Kamo no Chōmei is the quintessential expression of this way of life and its guilty pleasures.

6. *utamakura*: See Glossary, and Introduction p. xx. All the poems translated here invoke an *utamakura* name either in the headnote or in the poem itself. It seems only fitting that the pre-eminent compendium of *utamakura* is assumed to have been compiled by Nōin.

7. *balancing . . . an imagined elsewhere*: Poem 88 doubles this effect by imagining from the Capital (with an implied yearning to share the experience) the friend who is in a position to embody the image of the lone traveller haunted by longing thoughts of the Capital.

8. *it was nevertheless Nōin's autumn wind . . . his ears*: See *The Narrow Road of Oku*, p. 269.

8. *Sarashina Diary* by Sugawara no Takasue's Daughter

1. *Kazusa*: Roughly present-day Chiba prefecture, near present-day Tokyo.

2. *Like other women of her class . . . a male relative*: Women's personal names were seldom used outside the family circle.

3. *evocative places . . . woven into poetry*: The route's poetic importance for travellers was first established by the famous 'Going Down to the East' (*Azuma-kudari*) sections of the *Ise Tales* (see Chapter 2). Later travellers, including *Sarashina Diary*'s author, used these poems and stories as touchstones for their own poetic responses at the appropriate places.

4. *a well-established characteristic of travel for the educated classes*: See, for example, *Tosa Diary* (Chapter 3), in which the composition of occasional poetry provides constant entertainment and solace for the travellers on their dangerous journey.

5. *Place names . . . in so much Japanese poetry*: Many of these structur-
    ing place names are *utamakura*, as was the norm for literary travel
    writing. The relative weight given to prose description and the
    focus on personal experience, however, show that this work draws
    its essential inspiration from the diary form rather than from the
    poetry collection style.

6. *written many decades later in old age*: The *Sarashina Diary* seems to
    have been written when the author was in her early fifties (con-
    sidered old at the time), when she was recently widowed and
    probably only a few years before her death (the date of her death is
    unknown).

7. *others by previous women diarists*: Prominent among them was the
    lengthy description of a pilgrimage to Hase in *Kagerō nikki* (954–
    74), written by a relative of this author known by the name of
    'The Mother of Fujiwara no Michitsuna'. Although men also under-
    took pilgrimages and retreats, it is the women diarists who have
    left us detailed accounts of this important form of travel. See also
    p. 301, note 1.

8. *the Eastern Road*: An earlier name for the Tōkaidō that linked the
    Capital with the eastern provinces.

9. *Hikaru Genji*: The romantic hero of *The Tale of Genji*. Hikaru
    means 'to shine brightly'.

10. *the Healing Buddha*: Yakushi Nyorai; believed to save sentient
    beings from suffering and illness.

11. *the year I turned thirteen*: A child was considered to be one year old
    at birth.

12. *the preliminary move*: It was customary to choose an auspicious
    day to leave the house and settle briefly nearby while final prepar-
    ations for a journey were made. See also *The Narrow Road of
    Oku*, p. 264.

13. *Ikada . . . our hut was virtually set afloat that night*: The name Ikada
    means 'raft', which prompts this playful image.

14. *had to travel on separately*: Childbirth involved ritual defilement,
    which necessitated her travelling separately from the general party.

15. *a somehow quite incongruous scene, given the circumstances*: The image
    of moonlight filtering into a ramshackle dwelling is an elegant lit-
    erary trope, hence incongruous for the unromantic situation of a
    nursemaid in childbirth.

16. *the others . . . turned for home*: See p. 297, note 23.

17. *murasaki*: A plant from which precious purple dye was made.
    Musashi, an *utamakura*, was poetically associated with fields of
    murasaki.

18. *an estate*: The text is unclear, possibly due to mistranscription. I follow one among several interpretations.

19. *the fire huts*: Manned huts that stood at the palace gates, where sentry fires were kept lit at night.

20. *something very fragrant*: The scent of her incense-infused clothing would have hung in the air as they passed, although her face was hidden.

21. *Narihira's poem ... the Sumida*: See section 9 of *The Ise Tales*. She is here referring to the poem as found in Narihira's personal poetry collection. In fact, the Sumida was on the border between Shimōsa and Musashi.

22. *asobi*: See Introduction, p. xvi for a discussion of these travelling entertainers.

23. *aoi*: Sometimes translated as 'heart-vine'. A delicate plant whose heart-shaped leaf is the motif for the great Kamo Shrine in the Capital. Being strongly associated with the Capital, the incongruous sight of it here was particularly touching.

24. *Smoke ... flames leaping from it*: After a few centuries of dormancy the volcano was beginning to be active again at this period.

25. *The Barrier Gate of Kiyomi*: This and the following several places are *utamakura* sites, which are here the focus of the journey's description.

26. *The Fuji River flows out from Mount Fuji*: This river is geographically out of sequence in the story.

27. *The famous Yatsuhashi*: See *The Ise Tales*, p. 28.

28. *Miyaji Mountain ... late in the tenth month*: Miyaji means literally 'Palace Road', and the following poem plays with the conceit of the mountain's beauty remaining untouched thanks to its imperial status. The tenth month was well into December by the Western calendar.

29. *as in the old poems*: The poems play on the name Shikasuga, which can be read as the hesitant expression 'and yet'.

30. *The lake*: They were travelling along the eastern shore of Lake Biwa.

31. *it being the custom ... the Hour of the Monkey*: Weary travellers customarily waited until nightfall to arrive home, to avoid attracting undue attention, so they delayed their departure until around 3 p.m.

32. *A half-made Buddha figure ... staring down at us*: This statue of Miroku Bosatsu was being made for nearby Sekidera Temple. It was completed and placed in the worship hall in 1022.

33. *Ishiyama Temple*: A popular pilgrimage site near Lake Biwa.

34. *the purification ceremony ... that followed the enthronement*: The ceremony involved a spectacular imperial procession to the Kamo River. The new emperor was Goreizei (1025–68), whose enthronement occurred in 1045.

35. *Hase*: See p. 301, note 7.

36. *the Uji maidens in Murasaki's tale*: Ukifune and her two sisters, whose life at Uji is depicted in the final chapters of *The Tale of Genji*.

37. *the Uji mansion of the Chancellor*: Fujiwara no Yorimichi's mansion at Uji, to which the author's connections at court would have given her access. It was later to become the famous Byōdōin Temple.

38. *Mount Kurikoma*: An area near Uji notorious at the time for its bandits.

39. *Tōdaiji Temple. Isonokami Shrine*: Tōdaiji, among Japan's most famous temples, is in Nara. The great Isonokami Shrine is beyond it, near present-day Tenri. Its name is poetically associated with immense age.

40. *The Inari god*: The deity of Inari Shrine in southern Kyoto was associated with cedars whose saplings were believed to have supernatural powers and were carried home and planted by pilgrims.

41. *Narasaka*: A hill to the north of Nara, notorious for its thieves.

42. *the famous fishing weirs*: The Uji River is associated in poetry with the weirs of woven stakes placed across the river to trap fish.

43. *Kurama Temple*: A sacred mountain temple to the north of Kyoto.

44. *the promise of that cedar*: A reference to the dream of the sacred cedar during her previous visit to Hase.

45. *Circumstances took me down to Izumi*: Her brother was governor of Izumi at the time.

9. *Dust Dancing on the Rafters* compiled by Retired Emperor Goshirakawa

1. *haunting presences ... down the centuries*: Perhaps their best-known appearance is towards the end of Bashō's *The Narrow Road of Oku*, where he spends the night in the room next to two travelling *asobi* and overhears them lamenting their fate.

2. *they left no personal record of their lives*: A few *Manyōshū* poems such as poem 3140 (see p. 19), though anonymous, seem to be spoken in the voice of an *asobi*, and may have been composed by one, although recorded and perhaps tastefully adjusted by a literate hand.

3. *a Chinese legend ... as they sang*: See also *Tosa Diary*, note 12.

4. *clearly found the songs of commoners intriguing*: See, for instance, the sailors' songs recorded in *Tosa Diary* (p. 42).

5. *passing aristocratic vogue*: After a brief flare of popularity *imayō* quickly lost its importance in court circles, and within a hundred years it had almost disappeared.

6. *detailed performance notes that have unfortunately been lost*: The original work is recorded elsewhere as consisting of ten volumes, plus ten volumes of the companion *Kudenshō*, but both were long believed to have disappeared. In 1911 several volumes plus some fragments were discovered, but unfortunately the performance notes are among the missing material.

7. *asobi and other itinerant entertainers*: The flexible term *asobi* covers both wandering and locally based women entertainers, as well as those based in the ports who plied their trade on boats. *Kugutsu*, both men and women, were also itinerant entertainers who added juggling and other performance skills to their singing. This floating underworld also included itinerant priestesses and gamblers such as we find in songs 364 and 365, as well as wandering ascetics (song 300) and other pilgrims, beggars, pedlars and a host of other nondescript drifters.

8. *the arduous and immensely popular Kumano pilgrimage*: Goshirakawa himself undertook the Kumano pilgrimage thirty-four times.

9. *Easy Pine of Yasumatsu . . . the Beach of Chisato*: The song pivots on the word 'easy' (*yasu*), and proceeds to list other famous landmarks along the Kumano route.

10. *Nyaku-ōji*: Near present-day Waka no Ura. One of the ninety-nine *ōji* shrines along the various main Kumano routes, and a place where it was traditional to pause before facing the hard seven-day mountain walk to the main shrine at Hongū. (See Map 2).

11. *Yawata*: The location of Iwashimizu Hachiman Shrine, an important pilgrimage site often reached by boat from the Capital, down the Kamo and Katsura rivers to the port of Yodo below the shrine.

12. *So set your boat out . . . oh Bodhisattva!*: Hachiman, the god of the shrine, was commonly believed to lift the suffering from the sea of earthly passions into his boat and take them to the far shore of salvation. The town on the river below the shrine was renowned for its prostitutes and *asobi*, who approached potential customers on boats.

13. *Suzu Cape . . . Koshi Road*: He or she is travelling along the Japan Sea coast road from Suzu Cape on the Noto Peninsula. The poem puns on the word *ashiura*, a kind of fortune-telling done by pacing,

homophonous with 'sole of the foot' and also the name of a mountain in this area. Other transcriptions of this song give a different reading.

14. *a-priestessing*: The young girl is an itinerant *miko* or priestess, who often acted as a medium for the spirits of the dead as well as telling fortunes.

15. *Tago Bay*: Present-day Suruga Bay, on the Izu Peninsula.

16. *Sumiyoshi . . . Nishinomiya*: Two important shrines, the first in present-day Osaka and the other near present-day Kobe.

17. *Kai . . . Shinano*: Kai is present-day Yamanashi prefecture, Shinano Pass is in the mountainous Shinshū area.

10. *The Tale of the Heike*

1.   *The Tale of the Heike*: This and the following sections are not presented in strict chronological order, since it is impossible to pin them to precise dates. The order here is determined by their historical relevance, *The Tale of the Heike* being placed first in order to introduce the historical developments that shaped the subsequent works.

2.   *remained the preserve of that little world*: Monks such as Zōki (Chapter 4) and Nōin (Chapter 7) could and did write literary works (largely poetry), but they were composed within the terms of courtly literature. Only near the end of the Heian period did religious literature begin to evolve as a separate tradition.

3.   *anecdotally traced . . . the blind reciter Shōbutsu*: This is found in *Essays in Idleness* (*Tsurezuregusa*, c. 1330), section 226.

4.   *an ancient tradition of blind musicians . . . of pre-literate societies*: The *rhapsodes* who transmitted and performed the Homeric epics of ancient Greece, and the bards who recited England's early epic *Beowulf*, are two among many examples.

5.   *a stringed instrument called a biwa*: The tradition of performance of the *Tale* with lute-like *biwa* accompaniment, inherited down the centuries, still precariously exists today, and can be seen in online videos.

6.   *within a few decades of the defeat of the Heike in 1185*: Both its anonymity and its many variant versions make it impossible to date *The Tale of the Heike*. The version from which the following extracts are translated includes material from *Journey Along the Sea Road* (Chapter 13) as well as other texts, that suggests a date later than 1223.

7. *the title*: The work's title was quite possibly a later addition.
8. *michiyuki-bun ... down the intervening centuries*: See Glossary.
    Michiyuki-like passages occur in the popular songs of *Dust Dancing on the Rafters* (Chapter 9), and increasingly in literature from the Kamakura period onwards.
9. *Yoshitsune*: Minamoto no Yoshitsune (1159–89), the head of the Genji forces.
10. *that ancient poem that speaks of 'fireflies by a stream'*: 'Are they stars / filling a cloudless sky? / Or perhaps fireflies by a stream? / Or are these the fires the fishermen burn / off the beaches where I live?' *The Ise Tales* 87.
11. *after the Heike were defeated ... Yoshitsune was killed in the far north*: After the defeat of the Heike, Yoshitsune's older brother Minamoto no Yoritomo (1147–99) established rule in Kamakura. He turned against Yoshitsune and had him pursued and killed in Michinoku in 1189.
12. *Hakuga no Sanmi*: A grandson of Emperor Daigo and a renowned *biwa* player.
13. *the uncertain tides ... tidal beach*: The *naru* of the name Narumi forms a pun with *ika ni naru*, 'how will things turn out?'
14. *Yatsuhashi ... those eight tangled spider's legs*: See the *The Ise Tales* 9 (p. 28).
15. *a place like this*: It is implied that Jijū is an *asobi*. Other versions of the text here specify that it was the *asobi* Yuya with whom he exchanged poems.
16. *'What miserable karmic fate has led me to this?'*: According to the Buddhist law of karma, one's present fate is the result of actions in a previous life.
17. *'cross this way again'*: He quotes Saigyō (1118–90), whose famous poem at Saya no Nakayama (see The Tale of Saigyō, p. 122) was already well known. The following sentences briefly slip into the rhythm and style of lyrical *michiyuki* lament.
18. *Utsu's vine-tangled path*: See the *The Ise Tales* 9 (page 28).
19. *Though I do not lament ... Shirane Mountain*: This poem is a variant of a poem found in *Journey along the Sea Road*, written some time after 1223, an indication of the complex textual history of the *Tale*. The following description of the view from below Mount Fuji also owes much to the description of this place in *Journey along the Sea Road*.
20. *'If you loved me ... you never really did'*: This seems to be a quotation from an *imayō* (see Chapter 9), now lost.

11. The Tale of Saigyō

1. *Nōin*: See Chapter 7.

2. *depicted at sometimes unusual length in the introductory headnotes to the poems*: These *kotobagaki* sections plus their poems were here and there loosely strung together in his personal poetry collection *Sankashū* to form larger travel narratives, much as we find in *Ionushi* (see Chapter 4), encouraging posterity's tendency to personalize his poems into story.

3. *closely concerned with the fate . . . were ruined by them*: Most particularly Emperor Sutoku (1119–64), whom he had served in his youth. Sutoku's faction was defeated in the Hōgen Rebellion and in 1156 he was exiled to Shikoku, where he later died.

4. *in spring . . . the second month's full moon*: 'I pray / that I may die / in spring beneath the blossoms / under the second month's / full moon.' The spring full moon was the fifteenth day of the second month, also the traditional death date of the Buddha. In fact, Saigyō died a day later.

5. *The Ise Tales*: See Chapter 2.

6. *built around a series of his contextualized poems*: The creators of the *Tale* freely re-contextualized, re-interpreted and even occasionally rephrased the poems they used, much as did the creators of *The Ise Tales*.

7. *it bears a familial relationship with . . . Tale of the Heike*: The poetic diction of much of the prose in *The Tale of Saigyō* also occasionally rises to the 5/7 rhythms of the *michiyuki* (indicated in this translation with spaced phrasing).

8. *The complicated textual history of The Tale of Saigyō*: This protean work presently exists in at least twelve often very different textual forms, and probably once had many more.

9. *the depiction is in purely poetic terms*: More realistic touches are afforded by the story of the abusive warriors on the Tenchū ferry, and the later casual reference to the monk whose bones had been scattered by dogs.

10. *the famous Shirakawa Barrier*: For previous poems on this *utamakura*, see also the *Wakan rōeishū* poem by Fujiwara no Kanemori (p. 73) and poem 101 by Nōin (p. 78).

11. *in the sutras . . . countless kalpas of good deeds*: The source of the quotation is unknown. A *kalpa* is a vast stretch of time.

12. *Rather than despise and hate you . . . Bodhisattvas*: From the 'Jōfukyō' chapter of the Lotus Sutra.

13. *Saya no Nakayama*: In present-day Shizuoka prefecture. This mountain pass, whose name evokes the darkness of night, was renowned as a particularly challenging place to cross.

14. *Whatever ... apprehended with the senses*: From the Kongō Sutra (*Vajracchedika-prajnaparamita* in Sanskrit).

15. *On he went*: In this brief passage, the language shifts to the sonorous *michiyuki* style of lyrical travel depiction.

16. *like dew on leaf-tip or the drop beneath*: A frequently quoted phrase from a poem expressing the idea that it matters little who dies first, as the other must soon follow.

17. *for him ... the message they might carry*: A reference to the common poetic conceit that migrating wild geese carry a message from a distant loved one. Being a monk, Saigyō could expect no lover's message.

18. *Narihira ... nor yet in dreams*: See the *The Ise Tales* 9.

19. *Narihira's poem ... the season*: See the *The Ise Tales* 9.

20. *Sanekata ... a bird's single call*: Fujiwara no Sanekata (?–998), a skilled poet, was sent as a form of exile to govern Mutsu Province in Michinoku, where he died. The second quotation is from a Chinese poem by Tachibana no Naomoto, which appears in *Wakan rōeishū* (see p. 72).

21. *In autumn dusk ... touch it*: Most commentaries agree that the heart 'that should no longer feel' refers to Saigyō's status as a monk, who should be free of worldly passions. Compare Nōin's poem 109 (p. 78).

22. *the poets of old ... tomorrow's path*: Numerous poems had been composed on the theme of Musashi's purple *murasaki* grasses. The poem he quotes is by Fujiwara no Tamekane (1254–1332).

23. *Bodhisattva Fugen ... the eight scrolls of the Lotus Sutra*: Fugen (Samantabhadra in Sanskrit) is one of the Buddha's attendants, often depicted seated on a white elephant. The Lotus Sutra is one of the most important of the Buddhist texts.

24. *Reside in a quiet place, and pursue your Practice*: An admonition to pursue a devout and reclusive life, found in the introductory chapter of the Lotus Sutra.

25. *Empress Yūhōmon'in*: 1076–96.

26. *well acquainted with the circumstances of the empress*: She was the sister of Retired Emperor Toba, whom he had served in his youth.

27. *Though with the rising mists ... at Shirakawa Barrier Gate*: See p. 78.

12. Senjūshō

1. *to implicitly . . . identify him as Saigyō*: His name only appears once in the collection, in 3:1 translated here, but a number of other tales use devices such as quotations from famous Saigyō poems to suggest his identity. Saigyō's historically unattested meeting with the hermit of Musashi in *The Tale of Saigyō* (see p. 127) presents a more poetic version of the hermit encounter, and may well have suggested his role in *Senjūshō*.

2. *The wandering narrator monk . . . the realm of the common people*: This is an early version of the wandering monk acting as framing and narrating device that we find later in the *waki* role of Nō plays (see Chapter 19). It may well be that the Saigyō figure of *Senjūshō* influenced and partly inspired the development of the *waki*.

3. *ideally suited for the role . . . Saigyō's legendary figure*: The Saigyō narrator may have been a later addition to an earlier version of the collection.

4. *a word that functions . . . religious sensibility*: See Glossary and Introduction, p. xvii.

5. *his association with the utamakura Matsushima*: This story was on Bashō's mind when he visited Matsushima in the late seventeenth century.

6. *his choice of the utamakura Utsu for his retreat*: Utsu carried complicated Buddhist overtones both from its early association with the tangled depths of the mountains in the *The Ise Tales*, where the name is punningly related to the concept of reality versus dream or illusion, and the punning association of the name with melancholy and world-weariness. Perhaps for this reason, it became known as a popular place of retreat for hermits (see *Journey to the East*, pp. 161–2, for an example of a *Senjūshō*-style hermit at Utsu).

7. *the Koshi Road . . . Noto*: The Koshi Road was the road along the Japan Sea coast. Noto is Noto Peninsula, near Kanazawa.

8. *famous Naniwa*: The poem puns on the name Sumiyoshi (literally 'good to live in') in Naniwa Bay, whose associated poetic image is its pine trees. See also *Sarashina Diary*, p. 98.

9. *'even this heart, that should no longer feel'*: See *The Tale of Saigyō*, p. 126.

10. *Yamashina Temple*: An alternative name for Kōfukuji Temple in Nara.

11. *Mount Miwa . . . Kasuga deity*: Mount Miwa is a sacred mountain in Yamato, south of Nara. The Kasuga deity is the deity worshipped at the great Kasuga Shrine in Nara.

13. Journey along the Sea Road

1. *The road that linked the old Capital . . . thronged with travellers*: It is interesting to compare this account of the road with that of *Sarashina Diary* 200 years earlier (see Chapter 8). The journey now took a mere two weeks, and travellers were well supplied with inns and readily available supplies of food.

2. *Journey along the Sea Road (Kaidōki)*: *Kaidō* (Sea Road) was the contemporary name of the highway later known as Tōkaidō (Eastern Sea Road). Its western section followed the coast more closely than did the later Tōkaidō. See Map 2.

3. *its prose bears the strong imprint of Chinese literary prose*: A brief sample of this style can also be found in the description of the journey to Hiyodori Pass in *The Tale of the Heike* 9.9. This work was clearly influenced by *Journey along the Sea Road* at some point in its evolution, and it is possible that its Chinese-inflected passages owe their style at least in part to that of *Journey along the Sea Road*.

4. *'what has moved me' (mono no aware)*: An early use of this term for the movingly poignant nature of things, which came to bear a heavy literary and philosophical freight as exemplifying the Japanese sensibility.

5. *Saigyō, Nōin and Zōki*: See in this volume *The Tale of Saigyō* (Chapter 11), the poems of Nōin (Chapter 7) and *Ionushi's Pilrimage to Kumano* (Chapter 4) respectively.

6. *Buddhist themes*: Though overwhelmingly Buddhist in tenor, *Journey along the Sea Road* is unusual in its embrace of Confucian morality, seen for instance in the author's guilt at deserting his ageing mother and in his reaction to the sight of children working in the field.

7. *its various forebears*: These include the two important earlier lay travel diaries, *Tosa Diary* (Chapter 3) and *Sarashina Diary* (Chapter 8).

8. *Ionushi*: See Chapter 4.

9. *schooled in the Chinese and Japanese classics*: Many of the passing allusions are to poems found in *Wakan rōeishū* (see Chapter 6), and thus would have been instantly recognizable to an educated reader.

10. *the nine-tiered pagoda*: A large pagoda in the grounds of Hosshōji Temple, in Kyoto's present-day Okazaki area. Like so much else in Kyoto, it was later burned in the Ōnin Wars of the fifteenth century.

11. *those fierce sculptures guarding either side*: Wooden sculptures of fierce guardian deities can still be found on either side of the gates

of larger temples today. Compare the description of passing this temple in *Sarashina Diary*, p. 92.

12. *On, on I travelled, farther still*: See *Wakan rōeishū*, p. 71.

13. *among the four*: The four great roads that led from the Capital were the Eastern Sea Road, the Northern Land Road, the Western Sea Road and the Tamba Road.

14. *Yui Beach*: Close to Kamakura, his destination.

15. *plucking egu herbs ... wet with tears*: "'The sleeves I soaked / as I plucked for you the *egu* herbs / in the running stream / among those mountain fields / are still undried."' (Anon.). His tears both recall the poem and come in response to recalling it from the scene before him.

16. *hearts have gone awry / as in the mountain's name*: 'Yoko' in the name Yokota ('Sideways Field') carries connotations of being false or awry.

17. *the rain that night ... in Bai Juyi's famous poem*: Bai Juyi's poem appears as poem 555 in *Wakan rōeishū*: 'They lie beneath brocaded curtains under the blossoms / while in my thatched hut at Mount Lu I hear night's rain beat down.'

18. *the figure of old Ji Kang*: A Chinese sage, poetically associated with pine trees.

19. *an arrow to pierce a tiger rock like that swift arrow of old*: This refers to an ancient Chinese tale about a hunter who mistook a rock for a tiger and pierced it with his arrow.

20. *a scene to hold captive Shun'e's untethered horse*: This refers to a poem by the late Heian poet Shun'e, in which an untethered horse is held captive by the sheer beauty of a reedy landscape.

21. *the god within, a Buddhist avatar*: It was commonly believed that the gods of Japan's native religion were avatars of Buddhist deities.

22. *the sacred syllable*: Meditating on the syllable 'A', the first syllable of the Sanskrit script, was a key Buddhist meditation practice.

23. *the morning tide ... before it turned*: Travellers had to wait for the ebb tide in order to cross tidal beaches at several places along the route. (See also *Sarashina Diary*, p. 91, on Narumi Bay).

24. *Why did those young boys of legend ... in that boat?*: This refers to a Chinese legend of a boatload of young boys who set off to find the fabled land of Penglai which held the secret of immortality, but failed and grew old as they sailed.

25. *has no heart to feel*: See p. 311, note 21. It is generally believed that the expression 'has no heart to feel' refers to his status as a monk, who has chosen to transcend the phenomenal world.

26. *Yatsuhashi*: Made famous in *The Ise Tales*, see p. 28.

14. *Journey to the East*

1. *the personal and immediate finds its meaning . . . through the centuries*: See Introduction, p. 21 for a further discussion of this.

2. *write a poem in turn*: It is interesting to note that in at least one famous *utamakura*, Mount Utsu, there was by now a version of a billboard where one could read the poems that other passersby had written here and post one's own.

3. *irises and little bridges, as poetic tradition required*: This scene from *The Ise Tales* had become a motif in art as well, and these stylized depictions of little curved bridges and irises in turn influenced the reconstruction of the scene for later visitors.

4. *which would probably still have been there*: Forty-seven years later, their disappearance is lamented by Lady Nijō: see p. 182.

5. *saintly recluse hermits . . . as seen in Senjūshō*: See Chapter 12. The hermit of story 5:9 also escapes the adoring crowds by retreating to Mount Utsu, which was clearly considered a particularly suitable place for retreat.

6. *Jin and Zhang*: Powerful dynastic warrior families in early Han China.

7. *Tao Qian*: A poet recluse who turned his back on the city and retreated to live in poverty.

8. *that time when the tribute horses are brought in*: A ceremony held at this time in which horses sent from the provinces as tributes were ceremonially met at the entrance to the Capital.

9. *that traveller who travels still beneath the late moon's light*: This refers to a Chinese legend of a lord who, pursued by his enemy, saved himself by imitating a cock crow and thus causing the barrier gate to open for him although dawn had not yet come.

10. *Ariwara no Narihira and that poem he wrote on the irises*: See *The Ise Tales*, p. 28.

11. *Minamoto no Yoshitane*: A member of the Heian court, dates unknown.

12. *Ōe no Sadamoto*: Governor of Mikawa; died 1034. He took the tonsure on the death of the woman he loved.

13. *the former Musashi governor*: Hōjō Yasutoki, who was governor of Musashi 1219–38.

14. *the Duke of Shao*: Said to have died *c.* 1000 BC.

15. *like long-ago Fushimi village*: A reference to a poem that speaks of the now-crumbling village near the early capital at Nara.

16. *All night long beneath my bed / I see the clear heavens*: A poem found in *Wakan rōeishū*, atributed to Miyoshi no Yoshimune (dates unknown).

17. *the sutra*: The words are from the Lotus Sutra.

18. *those swift waters of Wu Canyon*: Described in similar terms in a poem by Bai Juyi. The following sentence refers to another poem by him.

19. *Kotonomama*: The name means literally 'just as it is'.

20. *'lying stretched to bar my view'*: *Kokinshū* 1097, Anon. 'I long for a clear sight / of Kai's mountains / but heartlessly / the dark pass of Saya / lies stretched to bar my view.

21. *Counsellor Muneyuki*: Fujiwara no Muneyuki (1174–1221), a high-ranking noble in the court of Emperor Gotoba. The following is a poetic description of the uprising known as *Jōkyu no Ran*, in which Gotoba sent forces to defeat the ruling Kamakura government, which then seized the Capital, executing many of the nobles and sending Gotoba into exile in the Oki Islands. Muneyuki was among those taken to Kamakura in captivity. He was executed en route. (Compare p. 114ff.)

22. *sunagashi*: Decorative *washi* paper in which flowing water is suggested by a sinuous scattering of gold or silver flakes across the sheet.

23. *Tatsuta's tangled swirls of autumn leaves*: From an anonymous *Kokinshū* poem. The autumn leaves of Tatsuta River were a famous motif in poetry and art.

24. *overgrown with vines and maples, just as of old*: See *The Ise Tales*, p. 28.

25. *Shu Qi . . . Xu You*: Two Chinese recluse monks renowned for living simply with nature.

15. *Diary of the Waning Moon* by Abutsu

1. *With her went one of her older sons, a high-ranking priest*: Because this is clearly stated in the introductory passage, I often use 'we' rather than 'I' in the translation, although there is no grammatical distinction in the text.

2. *demonstrating her mastery of the poetic tradition in her poems*: This involved not only allusion to previous poems but elaborate poetic techniques that are largely untranslatable.

3. *culminating, surprisingly, in a long chōka*: These long poems, popular in early poetry (see Chapter 1), had virtually disappeared by the ninth century. Abutsu's virtuoso *chōka* was one more example of her mastery of the poetic tradition.

4. *her case still unresolved*: It was finally settled in her son's favour in 1313, thirty-four years after her journey to Kamakura.

5. *almost as though . . . nor yet in dreams' encounter*: See *The Ise Tales*, p. 28.

6. *a particularly exalted person*: Abutsu's daughter, whose own daughter was the consort of the retired emperor Gofukakusa.

7. *Oh moon, seek after me*: 'Oh moon, seek after me / follow my footsteps/ as I go crying, crying / like plovers loath to leave / the Beach of Okitsu' (Fujiwara no Teika).

8. *An inkstone*: A smooth stone used for grinding ink to write with.

9. *how many layers . . . have been flung at you*: The image plays with the expression 'to cast wet robes on someone', meaning to cast aspersions about someone having a lover. The poem echoes the situation playfully suggested in the previous poem.

10. *the stench of the inn at night*: A line from a poem by Bai Juyi.

11. *What will become of me / oh Bay of Narumi*: Recorded in *Utatane*, also by Abutsu (date unknown). 'What will become of me/ oh Bay of Narumi before me here /when my fond thoughts/long to be elsewhere/ in that distant place?'

12. *Who drew that smoke . . . its unknown end?*: Compare Saigyō's Mount Fuji poem in *The Tale of Saigyō*, p. 125.

13. *the words of the Preface to the Kokinshū*: The first of the following poems refers to the description in the Preface to 'a high mountain, which grows from earth and mud at its feet to reach to the skies at last'. The second refers to the description of the comfort of poetic composition on hearing that one of the old poetic reference points has changed: 'The poet may learn that Fuji's smoke has now disappeared, or that the Bridge of Nagara has been rebuilt.'

14. *worthy of the description 'upon the waves'*: The translation follows one possible interpretation of an obscure section of the sentence.

15. *Surely the gods . . . from ancient times*: Abutsu is alluding to her claims to the right to pass on to her son the poetic lineage of her husband.

16. *Ashigara Pass*: An important *utamakura* which she would have been sorry to miss. It was a difficult mountain crossing, and the main highway now followed a different route.

16. *Pilgrimage to Kumano* by Myōkū

1. *Nō drama . . . similarities in singing and possibly dancing style*: For Nō drama, see Chapter 19. Their presence is seen particularly in the *kuse* section that is associated with the culminating part of Nō plays.

2. *their remarkable length*: The ancient *chōka* was the only other continuous Japanese poetic form of any length.

3. *attributed to one of two creators*: Several are also attributed to 'a certain court lady', and some speculate that this may have been Abutsu (author of *Diary of the Waning Moon*, Chapter 15), who was in Kamakura at roughly this time.

4. *the mountainous Kumano region in present-day Wakayama prefecture*: See *Ionushi's Pilgrimage to Kumano* (Chapter 4) for an earlier literary depiction of this journey.

5. *a continuous litany . . . the* ōji *shrines*: Besides the names of many of these shrines (some rather different from today), the song also weaves in other place names, some perhaps real and others simply *utamakura* added in for poetic effect.

6. *the gods*: This term should be understood loosely. Kumano had long been a place of elaborately syncretic religious beliefs in which gods and buddhas were conceived as avatars of each other.

7. *the surrogate experience of the pilgrimage itself*: Miniature versions of the Kumano and other pilgrimages can still be found today, which the proxy pilgrim traverses worshipping at each tiny shrine along the path and thereby gaining equivalent blessings.

8. *through mountainous country . . . Hongū Shrine on the Kumano River*: The route described here follows more or less exactly the route still traversed today, and most of the *ōji* can be identified with those that still exist. The Kumano pilgrimage route is now a popular World Heritage site.

9. *sweet-scented orange . . . some past owner*: This apparently irrelevant description is in fact an acrostic for Tachibanamoto Ōji, whose name is divided between *tachibana* (sweet-scented orange) and *moto* (past or original).

10. *a bird's single call*: See *Wakan rōeishū*, p. 72.

17. *A Tale Unasked* by Lady Nijō

1. *Emperor Kameyama, Gofukakusa's arch-rival*: The enmity between the two was complicated and long-standing, but focussed finally on a succession dispute that led to two alternating lines of succession in subsequent generations.

2. *some time after 1306, when its story ends*: The date of her death is unknown.

3. *she carried her heartbreak with her through life*: She had several further encounters with Gofukakusa over the years, in which he continued to proclaim his love for her. One of the last scenes in

A *Tale Unasked* describes her running barefoot and in tears down the street as she follows his funeral procession.

4. *The Tale of Saigyō*: See Chapter 11 for a version of this tale.

5. *Semimaru*: A semi-legendary early Heian period poet and musician of noble birth who was said to be blind. He was believed to have lived in a hut in the hills near the Ōsaka Barrier Gate. The quotation is from poem 1851 of the *Shinkokinshū*.

6. *that lingering face / that still haunts my heart*: The face is that of a past lover, perhaps Gofukakusa.

7. *brought back old times for me*: She had been a fine performer on the *biwa* at court.

8. *linking it with love*: The poem cleverly hinges on the *suru* of *koi suru* (to love) and the place name *Suruga*.

9. *I found no flowing streams there*: A reference to *The Ise Tales* (see p. 28).

10. *he would always send a sacred horse*: Horses were a common though extravagant form of offering to a shrine's god.

11. *Now . . , a cedar grove of green*: The poem relies on two puns, one on *naru* (come, become) and Narumigata (an *utamakura* in the area where she was), the other on *sugi* (to pass, and cedar).

12. *trail lingering in the wind*: See *The Tale of Saigyō*, p. 125.

13. *Where were those vines . . . Mount Utsu*: The thronging words are all the past poems written about the famous vines by travellers. The dreams image alludes to Narihira's Utsu poem (see p. 28).

14. *the late Shogun Yoritomo*: Minamoto no Yoritomo, who established the shogunate in Kamakura. Shogun was the title of the head of the military government.

15. *slipping away in the morning mist to be lost among islands*: See *Wakan rōeishū*, p. 73.

16. *how Prince Genji felt . . . on a moonlit roan*: *The Tale of Genji*, Chapter 13 'Akashi'.

17. *the land of Bingo*: Present-day eastern Hiroshima prefecture.

18. *the one that the famous Chinese beauty Yang gui-fei performed for her emperor*: Yang gui-fei (719–56), a famous beauty, was the adored consort of emperor Xuan-zong (r. 712–56). The dance was said to be one that he had created from a dream of an angel dancing. It reminds Nijō of her own life as the emperor's favourite.

19. *The formal brocade clothing . . . just like that of Bodhisattvas*: Performers representing Bodhisattvas in temple performances wore heavily brocaded clothes.

18. *A Gift for the Capital* by Sōkyū

1. *considered the back of beyond*: The name Michinoku signified the road's farthest reaches, while Oku, its abbreviated form, means literally 'innermost place'.
2. *Manyōshū*: See Chapter 1.
3. *The Ise Tales . . . sojourn in the area*: See Chapter 2, particularly episode 14.
4. *Nōin and Saigyō*: See Chapters 7 and 11 respectively. Nōin's poems 101, 109 and 149, included here, are examples of his Michinoku *waka*. Saigyō's travels in Michinoku are depicted in *The Tale of Saigyō* in the sections following the extract included here, which take him as far north as the Shirakawa Barrier, where Michinoku was felt to truly begin.
5. *'the Capital' . . . all the writers who came before him*: The central importance of Kyoto was only finally replaced in the seventeenth century when Edo (present-day Tokyo) became the centre of government, although the emperor continued to live in Kyoto and it remained the official capital until the mid-nineteenth century.
6. *Senjūshō*: See Chapter 12.
7. *Zōki*: See Chapter 4.
8. *light-hearted indulgence . . . friends he meets up with*: It is interesting to compare this with Zōki's playful encounter with a friend on his way to Kumano (see p. 58f).
9. *beneath tree and upon rock*: An allusion to the practice of living and meditating in nature.
10. *Mount Ōe . . . Ikuno Moor . . . Tanba*: All three are in the vicinity of Kyoto.
11. *the seventh-day ceremony*: An important ceremony held seven days after someone has died.
12. *these 'pretty words' . . . connect to the buddhas*: There was a debate among Buddhists about whether poetry was mere 'wild and pretty words' which falsely distracted the heart from perceiving reality's true nature, or whether it could be a means to enlightenment.
13. *Nōin of Kosobe*: See Chapter 7. Nōin owned land in Kosobe, in present-day Osaka prefecture.
14. *Yasoshima no ki*: This seems to have been a poetic journal written by Nōin, probably focussing on his journey to Shirakawa and beyond. It is no longer extant.
15. *carefully smoothed his sidelocks . . . hallowed place*: The courtier Kuniyuki is said to have been so awed by Nōin's poem on the

Shirakawa Barrier gate that he took care to groom himself before visiting it. See p. 270 (*The Narrow Road of Oku*) for a further echo of this.

16. *Lord Sanekata . . . the fifth month festival*: Fujiwara no Sanekata was a courtier and poet who was exiled here. On the fifth day of the fifth month, iris leaves were traditionally laid on roofs.

17. *it was pointless . . . on the eaves of ignorant country folk*: The man uses the expression *nan no ayame mo shiranu* which puns with the two meanings of the word *ayame* (iris / understanding) to mean both 'wouldn't know what an iris was' and 'wouldn't have a clue about things'.

18. *the same year that the Kamakura government had fallen*: The Kamakura shogunate had been defeated in 1333, less than twenty years earlier.

19. *the long ago Chinese prince Dong Ping . . . Wang Zhaojun's grave*: Dong Ping (d. 78) was believed to have lived and died in Japan. Wang Zhaojun (first century BC) was said to have longed so much for her homeland that her grave in the desert grew green. Both references are derived from Chinese poetry.

20. *Pine of Takekuma*: A double pine that had come to symbolize two lovers in poetry.

21. *Motoara, a name suggesting wildness*: The name, which literally means something like 'fundamentally wild', appears in a famous early poem about Miyagino's bush clover (where the name implies 'rough-rooted'), which prompts the poem here.

22. *the Narrow Road of Oku*: The name of a section of road between Taga and Sendai. The name was later used as the title of Bashō's famous travel journal.

23. *a salt kiln*: A kiln on the seashore for boiling sea water to make salt. The sacred salt kiln here is the embodiment of a deity.

24. *the old poet*: Ariwara no Narihira. The words come from section 81 of *The Ise Tales*.

25. *Enpukuji, founded by the Zen master Kakuman*: Kakuman was not in fact the founder, but was head of the temple from 1306 to 1308.

26. *This may have been . . . on Mount Utsu*: See p. 28. The mountain monk whom the protagonist meets later became identified with the late ninth-century poet Sosei. Sōkyū's unexpected meeting in Utsu with like-minded poets seemed to him as delightful and unlikely as this imagined meeting of the two famous poets in the same area.

27. *others before me . . . a dried frog from Ide*: A reference to a story of Nōin and another poet proudly showing each other these souvenirs taken from famous *utamakura* places visited on their travels.

19. *Sumida River* by Motomasa

1. *glimpsed down the centuries . . . in diaries and tales*: See, for instance, *Sarashina Diary*, p. 88 and *Journal of the Kyushu Road*, p. 241.

2. *sarugaku*: Although it is unclear exactly what *sarugaku* consisted of at this time, it was essentially a form of comic skit that often included dance and song. In the process of evolving to become Nō, *sarugaku* combined with other popular entertainment forms such as *dengaku* (a form of song and dance accompanied by music) in a complex amalgam.

3. *a performance at a shrine*: Sarugaku's close relationship with shrine performance is still evident both in the structure of the Nō stage and in important elements both of performance and of content.

4. *far from easy*: Eventually, under Yoshimitsu's successor, Zeami was exiled to the remote island of Sado and is thought to have died there.

5. *We do not know how different . . . in Zeami's time*: Nō later became popular with the warrior class, whose tastes influenced it in various ways including emphasizing its more stately and ceremonial qualities, resulting in the drawn-out and slow-moving performances seen in theatres today.

6. *our experience of the plays . . . centuries past*: The four schools of Nō performing today were founded around the beginning of the sixteenth century. Their textual and performance traditions differ, but only in relatively minor ways.

7. *somehow other-worldly experience*: Many elements both of performance (particularly the music and dance) and of content have their roots in spirit possession, mediums and trance, and Nō has frequently been described in terms of shamanic rite and exorcism.

8. *Senjūshō*: See Chapter 12. Saigyō, the implied narrator of the *Senjūshō* stories, is himself the subject of several Nō plays.

9. *Among Nō's most famous plays*: It provided Benjamin Britten with the inspiration for his opera *Curlew River*, composed after seeing *Sumida River* performed in Tokyo.

10. *her stolen child*: Kidnapping and trafficking of children for labour in the remote provinces was not uncommon.

11. *finally and briefly emerges from the grave*: Zeami argued that the child should not emerge but only speak from within the grave, and some performances honour his opinion.

12. *Wakitsure . . . Kokata*: Meaning 'Companion of the Waki' and 'Child Role'.

13. *if you are . . . 'Hurry aboard, the sun goes down'!*: The references in this scene are to *The Ise Tales* 9 (see p. 30).

14. *Capital bird . . . live or die?*: See *The Ise Tales*, p. 30. The following exchange continues to refer to *The Ise Tales* 9.

15. *in that old poem . . . distant Naniwa*: A poem by Ōtomo no Yakamochi.

16. *the invocation to Amida*: The invocation to the Bodhisattva Amida, '*Namu Amida Butsu*', is repeated by believers as a prayer for the soul's salvation.

20. *Journey to Shirakawa* by Sōgi

1. *a quiet life spent in the Capital*: Despite his many extended journeys, Sōgi did have a home in the Capital to which he continued to return until his last years.

2. *The Capital . . . longing to return*: Although the emperor and his court remained in Kyoto until 1868, when they moved to the new capital of Tokyo, the imperial court had long since ceased to play a dominant political role.

3. *an old practice*: Examples are recorded in the *Manyūshū*, and *renga* practitioners traced their art to even earlier records. For definitions of these two poetic forms, see Glossary.

4. *the first three lines*: Explained in this way for convenience, although *tanka* are not written using line divisions, the only sructural division being between the 17-syllable 5/7/5 section and the following 7/7 section.

5. *belies the traditional image . . . in the landscape*: Sōkyū's pleasure in the company of other poets in Musashino (see *A Gift for the Capital*, pp. 198–9) provides a foretaste of this conviviality, which was an aspect of poetic composition from earliest times. The solitary traveller implied in traditional travel writing is in fact often a literary fiction, as occasional mentions of a companion make clear.

6. *his rich experience of travel*: From his mid-forties onwards Sōgi spent much of his life on the road, although this included lengthy periods as the guest of provincial rulers and other followers.

7. *echoes an earlier work*: See *Sarashina Diary*, p. 86. Scholars today work hard to identify such allusions and subtle echoes, which include many traceable to *The Tale of Genji*, which Sōgi was deeply versed in.

8. *sentences that can last . . . description and experience*: Although the translation attempts to give a taste of this, it would be impossible to translate sentence for sentence into readable English. An example

is the third and fourth paragraphs of the translation, which in Japanese constitute a single sentence.

9. *The first nine links are translated here:* The prose section of the journal is translated in its entirety.

10. *Mount Tsukuba . . . Kurokami's trees:* Mount Tsukuba was an *utamakura* of particular importance to *renga* poets as the place where the first linked verses were said to have been composed. Kurokami Mountain, an *utamakura* associated with dew beneath the trees, is the old name for Mount Nantai, the main peak in the volcanic range at Nikkō.

11. *there at least is the comfort of knowing its famous grasses:* The *murasaki* grass of Musashino had been a constant poetic reference for poets down the centuries. His thoughts have turned to Musashino owing to his allusion here to the Musashino description in *Sarashina Diary* (see note 7 above).

12. *the Minister of the Right:* Minamoto no Sanetomo (1192–1219). 'Hail leaps / from the warrior's gauntlet / as his hand reaches to arrange / the arrows in his quiver / on Nasu's grassy moor'. Minister of the Right was a high-ranking court title.

13. *Hirano:* A shrine near the Capital poetically associated with its reddish cedar trees.

14. *Mount Sao or along Ōkawa's banks:* Mount Sao and Ōkawa River are both places near the Capital famous for their *kunugi* oaks.

15. *Ōikawa . . . sudden images of the Capital:* Ōikawa and Nakagawa were both names of rivers in and around the Capital.

16. *crossing Muko River as in the Manyōshū poem:* 'Swift flows the water / in the deeps of Muko River / and as I cross my roan / stumbles up a spray / that soaks me through.' Anon.

17. *those famous lines:* An anonymous poem in the *Kokinshū*. 'Melancholy / though this mountain village is / yet it is better / to be here than back there / in that world of grief.'

18. *the Mountain Goddess:* A deity of the mountains, poetically associated with autumn leaves.

19. *the Deities of the Two Sites:* Nisho Gongen is the collective name of two deities from two prominent shrines in the distant Kansai area, worshipped by the shogunate. The two shrines at the Shirakawa Barrier were dedicated to these gods.

20. *Kanemori and Nōin:* Two famous poets who had visited the Shirakawa Barrier. See p. 73 for Kanemori's Shirakawa poem, and p. 78 for Nōin's. The poems here contain allusions to these poems.

21. *Journal of the Tsukushi Road* by Sōgi

1. *rich in poetic associations*: See, for instance, a number of the *Manyōshū* poems included in Chapter 1 of this anthology.

2. *took the opportunity . . . based on the trip*: It was probably composed as a gift for his host, and possibly commissioned by him.

3. *consciousness of old age and death haunts the journal*: In fact he lived another twenty-one years (see Chapter 22, *The Death of Sōgi*).

4. *which in Ōuchi's case covered the Tsukushi area*: He had invaded and seized it from a rival warlord two years earlier, in an act typical of the time.

5. *Zen temples*: The Zen sect of Buddhism had risen to a position of great importance largely through its association with the ruling class, and the arts of this period and later were strongly associated with Zen philosophy.

6. *that would reach its highest expression in the tea ceremony not long after*: Although already in the process of evolving at this time, the tea ceremony as we know it today is considered the creation of Sen no Rikyū (1522–91).

7. *speaks of the Way of poetry*: The translation makes explicit what is implied in the poem.

8. *The concept of Way (michi)*: See also p. 76 for an earlier discussion of this term.

9. *mere 'shards'*: The same term is used in *Journey to Shirakawa* (p. 215) to describe the poems of this group of poets in relation to those of the great poets of old.

10. *barely half rebuilt* : It had burned down eleven years previously.

11. *Empress Consort Jingū*: Dates unknown, perhaps third century.

12. *Susanoō-no-mikoto's founding poem . . . this age of humans*: This deity is credited with composing the first *tanka*, making him the founder of Japanese poetry, associated with the beginning of the age of humans in the famous preface to the *Kokinshū*.

13. *the old poem*: 'Though I have passed / fearsome Cape Kane / of the mighty gods / I will not forget you / gods of Shiga' (*Manyōshū* 1230, Anon.).

14. *the words 'oh whither?', and the poem 'for whom do they long?'*: References to the Tamakazura chapter of *The Tale of Genji*, which describes the young girls' journey along this coast and the poems composed en route.

15. *around twenty poor shards of poems*: He is referring only to *tanka*. The *hokku* that he records did not count as true poetry in the traditional sense.

16. *'All who come to this country . . . does not make poetry?'*: The first quotation is from Fujiwara no Shunzei's (1114–1204) treatise on poetry *Korai Fūtaishō*. The second is from the preface to the *Kokinshū*.

17. *the famous Ashiya scene of 'Nada's salt fires'*: From *The Ise Tales* 87.

18. *calling the tenth month autumn*: In the lunar calendar of the time, the tenth month falls roughly in December.

19. *whom Hiroaki had provided for us*: Hiroaki, a personal friend and governor of an area they had passed through, had provided two samurai to escort and guard them on their travels.

20. *the Straits of Hayato . . . would have drowned in battle*: The Strait of Shimonoseki (here Hayato) separates Kyushu and Honshu. Here in 1185 occurred the famous battle of Dannoura, in which the Heike clan met their final defeat against the Genji. (See Chapter 10 for historical background to this conflict).

21. *a renga gathering*: The following poem is Sōgi's *hokku* for that gathering.

22. *Wu Canyon . . . paths like that of Taixing*: See *Journey to the East*, note 18. In the same poem, the path of Taixing is described as rough enough to break carriage wheels.

22. *The Death of Sōgi* by Sōchō

1. *who emerged from the provinces*: His father was a swordsmith in what is now Shizuoka prefecture.

2. *became associated with one of the great Zen monasteries*: Like many others of the time, including Sōgi, his association did not extend to entering the monastery itself; indeed he proceeded to have a wife and children in defiance of monastic vows.

3. *this arduous journey*: Their journey would have passed through snowy and difficult country.

4. *poems of old age*: Although I refer to them as poems for convenience, links in *renga* were not considered to be independent poems.

5. *a form of light relief from the serious composition of waka*: See the discussion of this evolution on p. 229.

6. *we can imagine . . . this kind of entertainment*: The late-night carousing that Sōgi records in *Journal of the Tsukushi Road* (Chapter 21), for instance, would almost certainly have involved *haikai no renga* composition, although Sōgi was privately somewhat disapproving of this frivolous poetry.

7. *the governing centre of Japan*: Kyoto remained the imperial capital until the Meiji Restoration of 1868 that began Japan's modern era.

8. *an old acquaintance*: The local warlord of Echigo, present-day Niigata prefecture.

9. *where the Minamotos ... once had flowered*: The three Minamoto rulers and the nine Hōjō rulers who governed from Kamakura in the thirteenth to fourteenth centuries.

10. *the Yamanouchi and the Ōginoyatsu*: Two rival branches of the local Uesugi clan. Their battles began in 1488 and lasted sixteen years.

11. *The waves of far Nagahama ... Mount Arachi*: Both *utamakura*, which he would have passed by on his route to the Capital. Nagahama is on Lake Biwa and Arachi is in Fukui prefecture.

12. *a dream poem*: A poem received from a sacred source via a dream. This *hokku* refers to the thousand pines said to have grown overnight where the shrine to the deity of Kyoto's Kitano Shrine (the spirit of the scholar Sugawara no Michizane) was founded.

13. *a thousand-link renga gathering*: Ten consecutive sittings during each of which a hundred links were composed.

14. *the following links*: Two separate links of 7/7 followed by 5/7/5 are given, in which Sōgi provides the 5/7/5 (i.e. the second pair is not connected to the previous one but would have appeared in a different place in the *renga*).

15. *stricken with 'worms'*: Exactly what kind of parasitic worm is unclear from the name. His illness may in fact have been an intestinal disease of some kind that was put down to an infestation of worms.

16. *Sojun*: A local high-ranking warrior and follower of Sōgi.

17. *Count Teika*: The great poet Fujiwara no Teika (1162–1241).

18. *Shokushi Naishinnō*: A princess and accomplished poet (d. 1201) with whom Teika was said to have had a love affair.

19. *They say that in China too ... protective wayside gods*: Echoed in the opening section of Bashō's *Narrow Road of Oku* (p. 264).

20. *Jien*: A famous poet-monk (1155–1225).

21. *an oval stone*: Commonly used to mark the grave of a Zen priest. Sōgi's grave at Jōrinji is now marked by a small stone pagoda.

23. *Journal of the Kyushu Road* by Hosokawa Yūsai

1. *one of his generals*: Akechi Mitsuhide (1528–82). Yūsai found himself uncomfortably close to the wrong side in this incident, his son having married Akechi's daughter Tama three years earlier. Tama is normally known by the name Gracia, which she took when she

later defiantly converted to Christianity in reaction to Hideyoshi's proscription of that religion when he returned from Kyushu.

2. *no longer took an active part in military campaigns*: This did not prevent him from later taking up arms to protect his castle, which he ably defended against a two-month siege in 1600.

3. *to subjugate the powerful and recalcitrant Shimazu clan*: Yūsai echoes Hideyoshi's official justification for this campaign, which was the need to 'settle the dispute' between the Shimazu and a rival clan that was resisting them.

4. *those gathered around Hideyoshi . . . after the victory*: These include Yūsai's contemporary Sen no Rikyū, Hideyoshi's revered tea master and the man who established the tea ceremony in the form still practised today.

5. *Local sea-going vessels . . . those of previous centuries*: This is evident too in the curiosity Yūsai shows towards the large Chinese trading vessel that had reportedly docked not far away. Japan did have ships capable of travelling between Japan and China, but they were seldom seen along the Japanese coastline.

6. *the real energy is in his lighter poetry*: Yūsai himself would have been horrified at this judgement. For all his indulgence in the more frivolous poetic fashions of the day, he saw himself as a staunch upholder of the classic *waka* tradition, and was revered as such by all those he taught.

7. *several examples of tanka in the haikai mode*: In the following extract, the poem 'Popping all those blister beans . . .' is one example of this mode.

8. *Yūsai unwittingly helped to nudge*: One of Yūsai's students was Matsunaga Teitoku (1571–1653), who went on to play a crucial role in popularizing *haikai no renga* composition among the less educated classes through his playful Teimon style, thereby setting in motion a new literary trend that two generations later produced the masterful poems of Matsuo Bashō.

9. *our noble ruler*: Toyotomi Hideyoshi, the *de facto* ruler of Japan at the time. Yūsai refers to him here by his title only.

10. *the county of Kumano*: The boat docked at the port of Kumihama on the west side of Tango Peninsula, where he planned to board it for the journey.

11. *Mount Ashiura*: The poem plays on the name Ashiura, which is a kind of fortune-telling and can also mean 'sole of the foot'. See also poem 300 in *Dust Dancing on the Rafters* (Chapter 9) and accompanying note (p. 307).

12. *the Hour of the Dragon*: Roughly 8 to 10 a.m.

13. *just as the village name suggests*: Ikumi, a variation on the name Igumi, can mean 'to hug or huddle together'.

14. *My boat puts in . . . as if to speak my longing*: A poem expressing his hopes of return that plays with words and images associated with the name Nishiki.

15. *Poor little thing . . . motherly Kaga's bosom*: A humorous play on the place name Kaga, a variation of 'kaka' (mummy). Although this poem is within the norms of punning *waka* poetry, in its lowly subject matter and humour it belongs to the *haikai* mode.

16. *the shrine at Kizuki*: From the context this seems to refer to the great Izumo Shrine, although the name given here is that of a different place.

17. *Izanami and Izanagi*: The two progenitors of the nation's gods. They caused the parting of heaven and earth and the creation of the islands of Japan.

18. *Plovers pillowed . . . an unfinished dream*: The poem plays on the name Ou, which can also mean 'to bear (a grudge)'.

19. *provincial stewards*: The early system of local stewardship. When the system changed in the fourteenth century, these families were usually granted headship of the local shrine.

20. *Kasai of Wakasa*: Unidentified, but probably a popular entertainer.

21. *dancing*: The type of dancing named here suggests that it was an energetic form of Nō dance (see p. 201).

22. *'Thirty-one syllable poetry . . . the land of Izumo'*: The poem said to be composed by the god Susanoō, who is worshipped at this shrine, was by tradition the first poem composed in the thirty-one syllable *tanka* form that came to embody Japanese poetry down the centuries.

23. *the shrine's Buddhist priest*: There had long been a close relationship between Buddhism and the native religion of the gods, so a shrine such as this could incorporate a Buddhist component.

24. *this hokku . . . another for their own renga gathering*: The opening *hokku*, traditionally composed by the leading poet at a *renga* gathering, could now be composed in advance by a prestigious poet who did not take part in the gathering, another step on the route to the eventual independence of the *hokku* and the evolution of today's haiku.

25. *Kaneyama*: Site of a famous silver mine.

26. *reminding me of Hitomaro's poem*: Hitomaro was a famous seventh-century poet; see Chapter 1 for a sample of his poems.

27. *Like him of old . . . lies anchored*: This poem recalls the poem in *Tales of Ise* 26: 'Astonishing / the tumult of my tears / these sleeves

a heaving harbour / all because a mighty ship / from far Cathay has come'.

28. *Do they strike in time . . . the Bay of Ago*: The name Ago is homophonous with 'chin'. The chin drum (*kotsuzumi*) is propped on the shoulder near the chin with the left hand and beaten with the right.

29. *where Ōuchi Yoshitaka had taken his life*: Ōuchi (1507–51) was the military governor of a number of provinces in the area. He committed suicide following an insurrection among his retainers.

30. *this formless dream / is all Mind*: A reference to the Buddhist doctrine that the phenomenal world is ultimately a product of the mind. The following quotation has not been identified.

31. *Toyoura Shrine*: The remains of an ancient shrine which legend states was visited by Emperor Chūai (dates unknown) during a military expedition. The following poem weaves in the words of a poem by Fujiwara no Tadahira.

32. *the border*: Shimonoseki, at the western tip of Honshu. From here the traveller crosses the strait to northern Kyushu. See p. 226 for Sōgi's description of this place.

33. *the palace*: Presently called Akama Jingū. It houses the spirit of the child emperor Antoku, who had drowned nearby when the Heike clan were defeated in the sea battle of Dannoura (see Chapter 10 for historical background to this conflict).

34. *poem cards*: It was the custom for visitors to compose a poem and leave it as an offering.

35. *The kelp-dark sleeves . . . the inkstone's waves*: The poem plays with sea images that proceed from the pun on *kaku* ('to write', and 'to gather seaweed').

24. *Bones on the Wayside* by Matsuo Bashō

1. *his 'hut'*: Although his home was referred to in this way in accordance with the convention of the hermit's 'grass hut', it was probably a somewhat more substantial, though modest house.

2. *Bashō was a haikai poet*: Although he is now considered a haiku poet, Bashō was a poet of linked *haikai* verse, and most of his poetic activity was devoted to its group composition. The poems that we find in his travel writing and poetry collections, now anachronistically identified as 'haiku', are *hokku* by origin, verses intended to lead off a linked verse poem. For further clarification of these terms, see Glossary.

3. *one needed at least a basic acquaintance with the classics*: Teitoku's
    stated motive for promoting the *haikai* style was to thereby intro-
    duce people to the classics.

4. *deemed low or vulgar ... in waka's rarefied lexicon*: These words
    included any Chinese-derived word, since *waka* was by definition
    poetry in the native Japanese language, as against Chinese poetry.
    This distinction did not extend to *waka* prose, although Chinese-
    derived language was used there only for particular effect.

5. *The presence of ... humorously down to earth*: These subtleties, often
    crucial to the effect of a verse, can seldom be conveyed in transla-
    tion since non-Japanese readers have difficulty registering the
    slippage between standard and non-standard classical poetic lan-
    guage, imagery and allusion. An example in the following text is
    the third poem, whose language and imagery (mist, autumn rain,
    Mount Fuji) set up expectations of a classical *waka* sentiment,
    which is humorously inverted when Fuji turns out to be both
    invisible and all the better savoured for it.

6. *he was rapidly evolving ... the Bashō style (shōfū)*: It was during
    this journey that the five *haikai* linked-verse sequences published
    as *Fuyu no hi* (*A Winter Day*), the Bashō school's first import-
    ant collection, were composed by Bashō and his followers in
    Nagoya. It is particularly interesting to note that more than a quar-
    ter of the verses in *Bones on the Wayside* have a non-standard
    syllable count, half of these being in 7/7/5 form (the standard form
    is 5/7/5).

7. *'Off on a thousand-mile journey ... the realm of the immortals'*: An
    amalgam of quotations from *Zhuang-zi* and *Jiangxi Fengyue* (a clas-
    sic collection of Zen verse teachings).

8. *the barrier*: The mountain pass of Hakone.

9. *Chiri*: Naemura Chiri (1648–1716). The *bashō* tree of his poem is a
    banana tree that grew beside Bashō's house in Fukagawa, from
    which Bashō took his name. The house looked onto a view of dis-
    tant Mount Fuji.

10. *You whose heart breaks ... in autumn wind?*: In Chinese poetry, the
    scream of the monkey was traditionally portrayed as tearing the
    hearer's heart with anguish.

11. *Day of autumn rain ... at the Ōi*: This river was renowned for
    becoming uncrossable when the rains swelled it.

12. *as in Du Mu's 'Early Departure'*: Du Mu (803–53) was a Chinese
    poet. The previous words loosely quote from his poem 'Early
    Departure'.

13. *Matsubaya Fūbaku*: An Edo disciple who had returned to his family home in Ise, site of the great Ise Shrine.

14. *my old home*: In Iga Ueno (present-day Mie prefecture).

15. *the sedge by my mother's old house frost-withered and gone*: His mother had died the previous year.

16. *Urashima Tarō's magic box*: A reference to the legend of a fisherman who spends enchanted time in the underwater palace of the Sea Dragon King and returns with a magic box to his village to find that many years have passed and all has changed except himself. He goes against the Sea Dragon's command and opens the box, and suddenly he too is old and grey. Bashō had been away for nine years.

17. *Soothed . . . in these bamboo depths*: Someone is beating cotton into wadding by plucking a bow-shaped beater against it. The last line nods towards the place name Takenouchi, literally 'in the bamboo'.

18. *Zhuang-zi's legendary ox*: This refers to a mention in *Zhuang-zi* of a tree left to grow so old and huge that an ox can hide behind it.

19. *Mount Lu*: Mount Lu in China was renowned as a place where recluse poets chose to live. Saigyō was the most famous of the many poets associated with Yoshino.

20. *Priest's wife . . . fulling block*: Bashō has in mind a poem by Fujiwara Masatsune (1170–1221): 'Autumn's mountain wind / on Yoshino – / as the night grows long / the cold sound of the fuller's beat / in the old Capital.'

21. *The dripping spring he wrote of*: 'Drop by drop it falls / from a rock cleft / pure spring water / barely enough to catch and yet / enough for this home of mine.' (Attributed to Saigyō.) The little spring still drips there near a replica of his hut.

22. *Po-i . . . Hsu-yu*: Legendary figures renowned for their purity and rejection of the world. Po-i retired to the mountains rather than compromise his principles, and subsisted on fern shoots until he starved to death. Hsu-yu was offered the kingdom, but washed his ears at this defilement of them and likewise retired to the mountains.

23. *Emperor Godaigo*: 1288–1339. Emperor at a time of the ascendancy of the shogunate in Kamakura, Godaigo attempted and failed to wrest back power, then fled with his loyal followers to Yoshino where he established an alternative court.

24. *Lady Tokiwa . . . what the point of resemblance was*: Tokiwa was the mistress of the warrior Minamoto no Yoshitomo (1123–60), and fled after his death. She was believed to have been killed by robbers here. Arakida Moritake (1473–1549) was a *renga* poet and important early practitioner of the *haikai* style. The reference is to a link in

a *renga* intended to suggest that the autumn wind was Yoshitomo's mourning spirit visiting his beloved's grave. Bashō was probably feigning ignorance of this to make his own poem effective by contrast.

25. *Fuwa Barrier*: At Sekigahara (Saga prefecture), site of a long-ago barrier gate. An *utamakura*. In 1600 a decisive battle had been fought here.

26. *Bokuin*: 1646–1725, an important disciple of Bashō.

27. *Kuwana Hontōji Temple*: The priest of this temple was a *haikai* practitioner.

28. *Winter peonies – hototogisu*: Peonies should bloom in late spring, when the *hototogisu* sings, so these winter plovers are filling the *hototogisu*'s role for the unseasonal peonies.

29. *Atsuta Shrine*: An important shrine in Nagoya.

30. *Chikusai*: The eccentric protagonist of a popular story of that name who travelled about composing mad verses (*kyōku*), and at one point set up a quack doctor's practice in Nagoya.

31. *Who's the new son-in-law? . . . this new Year of the Ox*: A man is following the old custom of taking special new year food on ox-back to present to his parents-in-law, in the Year of the Ox.

32. *Nigatsudō*: An ancient and important hall in the grounds of the great Tōdaiji Temple in Nara. The Water-drawing ceremonies are held here for fourteen days from the first day of the second month.

33. *Mitsui Shūfū at Narutaki*: Shūfū was the nom de plume of Mitsui Tokiharu (1646–1717), whose hermitage at Narutaki on the northwestern outskirts of Kyoto was a meeting-place for poets.

34. *old Lin's crane*: The poem is based on a conceit. In the note he appended to this poem when offering it to Shūfū, Basho added that he looked exactly like the famous recluse poet Lin Bu (967–1028), who was said to love plum blossoms like a wife, and his pet cranes like children.

35. *Ninkō*: The nom de plume of Hōyo, the incumbent priest at Saiganji Temple in Fushimi, just south of the Capital.

36. *Fushimi peach blossom . . . upon my robes*: Ninkō, who was eighty when Bashō visited him, is offered this poem in deep respect. The village of Fushimi was poetically associated with peach blossom.

37. *the lake*: He has arrived at Lake Biwa and gazes across it to Karasaki, an *utamakura* poetically associated with the ancient pine tree that grew in its shrine precincts.

38. *Abbot Daiten of Engakuji*: The incumbent priest at the Zen temple of Engakuji in Kamakura. He was a *haikai* poet. Bashō's disciple Kikaku had studied Zen with him.

39. *Mourning the plum blossom ... these tears*: Mourning Daiten through the plum blossom blooming when he died, Bashō offers prayers for him to the humble roadside flowers as substitute.

40. *Tokoku ... as keepsake*: Tsuboi Tokoku (?1657–90). A favourite disciple who lived in Nagoya. He accompanied Bashō on a subsequent journey. The poem refers to their recent parting.

41. *I stayed again with Tōyō*: He has arrived back in Atsuta, where he stayed with Tōyō early in the journey.

25. *The Narrow Road of Oku* by Matsuo Bashō

1. *The Narrow Road of Oku (Oku no hosomichi)*: The Japanese title, which has been translated variously, refers to a stretch of road that carries the travellers into the northern lands of Oku (Michinoku). In this title 'oku', literally 'innermost place' or 'hinterland', is generally taken to include connotations of an inward or spiritual journey. The title also carries *haikai* echoes of Narihira's famous 'narrow path of vines' (*tsuta no hosomichi*, see p. 28).

2. *he worked on it for years after his return*: A number of the poems in this journal were revised and in some cases composed later, and the prose material was extensively reworked, reordered or newly composed and inserted.

3. *often do not mention them explicitly*: In the section translated here, Jōbōji, Tōkyū and the artist Kaemon are mentioned by name.

4. *In this and in many other ways ... medieval travel writing*: See Introduction for a more detailed discussion of this and other aspects of Bashō's writing.

5. *'poetic' images of the journey ... moxa treatments*: This shifting theme is also announced in the opening *hokku*, where the traditional poetic 'hermit's hut' humorously transforms itself into a 'doll's house' in a typical *haikai* twist.

6. *He termed it haibun, or haikai prose*: Some of *haibun*'s characteristics are already present in the prose of *Bones on the Wayside*, which like *The Narrow Road of Oku* includes versions of a number of short prose-plus-poem pieces composed independently and later brought together there. It was only later, however, that he began to term such writing *haibun* and to consciously refine it as a style.

7. *most of which is translated here*: The following extract comprises a little over a third of the complete work.

8. *roamed the sea coast*: This refers to the journey of 1686–7 recorded in *Knapsack Notes*.

9. *the moon of Matsushima*: Matsushima, one of the great *utamakura* of northern Japan, is poetically associated with the dawn moon.

10. *moved to Sanpū's retreat in preparation for the journey*: Sugiyama Sanpū was one of Bashō's followers, whose retreat was nearby. Bashō was following the old custom of beginning the journey by moving to a nearby place where one paused for farewells and final preparations.

11. *the first sheet . . . a home for dolls now*: The first sheet of a *renga* contains eight links. The verse he gives here is the *hokku* or opening verse, and alludes to the fact that the new residents of his house included a little girl who would soon be celebrating the Dolls' Festival there (celebrated on the third day of the third month).

12. *Ueno and Yanaka*: Ueno and Yanaka in the nearby city (now central Tokyo), both famous for their cherry blossoms, are implicitly visible in the near distance.

13. *this deity sealed herself . . . Hohodemi no Mikoto*: Konohanasakuya-hime undertook to prove her faithfulness to her husband and therefore the divine origin of her child by giving birth to him in a sealed cavern which she set on fire.

14. *Kūkai*: 774–835. A renowned Buddhist saint who established the Shingon sect. He was credited with travelling the land and founding numerous temples, but he was not in fact the founder of the religious complex at Nikkō.

15. *time for summer robes*: On the first day of the fourth month, winter robes were replaced with lighter ones for the new season. The words also suggest Sora's recent taking of Buddhist robes.

16. *under the leaves of the bashō tree*: see p. 331, note 9.

17. *koromogae in the last line is powerful and effective*: This word, a poetic season word for summer, is written here with the characters used to mean taking monks' robes (taking Buddhist vows), adding religious overtones to the everyday meaning 'to change robes'.

18. *Urami Falls*: Urami, here meaning 'seen from behind', is also a word meaning 'bitter resentments'.

19. *first summer retreat*: The first day of summer is the beginning of the summer retreat for Zen monks. Recluse monks commonly meditated in caves.

20. *Kasane . . . the pretty pink*: *Kasane*, which means 'layers', suggests the elegant layered gowns of that name worn by ladies in the Heian period. The poem uses the image of the double pink, a small carnation-like flower that grows wild and blooms in early summer, and is associated with girls.

21. *the Dog Shoots*: An enclosure where dogs had been shot at for arch-
    ery practice centuries earlier.

22. *Lady Tamamo*: Legendary consort of a twelfth-century emperor,
    she was in fact a fox, which fled to Nasu when it was exorcized, its
    spirit becoming the poisonous Killing Stone (see below, p. 269).

23. *Nasuno Yoichi . . . with his arrow*: This refers to the tale of how this
    warrior of the Genpei Wars prayed for success to the Hachiman
    deity of his home land of Nasuno, before plunging into the sea on
    horseback and shooting a perfect bull's-eye through the fan tied to
    the mast of an approaching enemy ship.

24. *a mountain ascetic*: A practitioner of rigorous ascetic practices in
    mountainous country.

25. *the Gyōja Hall*: Dedicated to the early, semi-mythical mountain
    ascetic saint En no Gyōja. He is traditionally depicted wearing very
    high *geta* clogs, on which he reputedly strode magically over
    mountains. It was the custom to pray to his *geta* to give one's legs
    power before a journey.

26. *Zen master Butchō*: Bashō's Zen master for several years from
    around 1680. He died at Unganji in 1715.

27. *Zen master Yuan Miao . . . even the woodpecker*: Yuan Miao retreated
    to a cave for fifteen years, erecting this sign outside. Fa Yun, his
    disciple, named his own cave retreat 'Phantom Dwelling', the
    name Bashō gave to his hut on the shores of Lake Biwa. Woodpeck-
    ers were reputed to knock down temples with their pecking.

28. *a poem card*: A long, narrow card on which a poem is written, suit-
    able for hanging as a scroll.

29. *willow where the pure water flows*: Passing here, Saigyō composed:
    'Here in this willow's shade / where the pure stream / flows on by
    the wayside / briefly I pause / and stand.'

30. *the poet wrote of . . . from here*: A reference to Taira no Kanemori's
    (?–991) poem at the Shirakawa Barrier. See *Wakan rōeishū*, p. 73,
    where the poem is attributed to Fujiwara no Kanemori.

31. *Nōin's autumn wind . . . Yorimasa's crimson leaves*: For Nōin's poem,
    see p. 78. Minamoto no Yorimasa's poem is: 'Still the green leaves
    of summer/ I saw them in the Capital / but crimson now / they fall
    and lie / at Shirakawa's Barrier.'

32. *Kiyosuke*: Fujiwara no Kiyosuke (1104–77) recorded this story
    in the tale collection *Fukurozōshi*. See also *Gift for the Capital*,
    p. 193.

33. *First poem / for a poet's journey north*: The Shirakawa Barrier was
    considered the real beginning of the journey into the northern
    Oku region.

34. *Saigyō gathering chestnuts . . . just like this*: A reference to a poem by Saigyō, 'Deep among mountains / I gather up / dripping water from the rock / and garner from the ground / the fallen chestnuts.'

35. *katsumi, katsumi*: His words echo a line from a poem in *Kokinshū*. For *katsumi*, see *Gift for the Capital*, p. 193.

36. *Kurozuka Cave*: Said to be the home of a witch.

37. *the Shinobu Rubbing Rock*: Long famous for the mottled *shinobu* (fern-leaf) dye pattern supposedly produced by rubbing it.

38. *to try rubbing barley on the rock*: Probably a reference to a local belief that rubbing barley leaves on the rock would allow one to see the person in one's thoughts. *Shinobu* is also a verb meaning to achingly recall something.

39. *Superintendant Satō*: A twelfth-century superintendant of this area who was killed in the Genpei Wars.

40. *Grave of Weeping*: The grave of a beloved local governor in China that provoked tears in all who visited.

41. *Yoshitsune's sword and Benkei's travelling satchel*: see p. 309, notes 9 and 11. He and his loyal attendant Benkei (d. 1189) travelled through this area in their flight north from Yoshitsune's brother Yoritomo.

42. *the first day of the fifth month*: Close to the day of the Boys' Festival (the fifth day of the fifth month, roughly mid-June in the western calendar), when paper carp streamers were flown in front of houses.

43. *Captain Sanekata . . . Saigyō's poem*: Fujiwara no Sanekata (d. 998), a court poet who was exiled to the northern realms. According to legend, he was struck from his horse and killed by the roadside gods of Kasajima shrine when he rode past them without dismounting. Saigyō's poem at Sanekata's grave was: 'His name alone remains / unfaded / but here on the autumn plain / in memory of him I find / this scene of autumn grasses'.

44. *The names of Minowa and Kasajima . . . the rainy season*: *Mino* means straw raincoat, and *kasa* means rain hat.

45. *The Pine of Takekuma*: An *utamakura*, poetically referred to as 'the double pine'.

46. *Now the old pine / has vanished*: Written on his second visit, when the pine he had seen last time had disappeared. 'Now the old pine / has vanished – / I might have come / the thousand years of its life / too late to find it.' For Nōin, see Chapter 7.

47. *the Iris Thatching*: On the fourth day of the fifth month, the day befoe the Boys' Festival, iris leaves were traditionally laid on roofs to ward off misfortune.

48. *he showed us around these for a day*: The following section names a number of local *utamakura* and the poetic images associated with them.

49. *Tell your lord / to wear his broad-hat*: A reference to the anonymous poem: 'Servants, tell your lord / to wear his broad-hat / for the dews of Miyagino / beneath the trees are heavier / than any rain.'

50. *the Narrow Road of Oku*: See *A Gift for the Capital*, see p. 321, note 15. This was one of the places named as an *utamakura* in *haikai* poetics.

51. *Commander of the Subduing Forces*: The titles are approximate. This castle was built as a stronghold in the ongoing struggle to defeat the earlier inhabitants of the region.

52. *the reign of Emperor Shōmu*: 724–49.

Index

Entries in bold are defined in the Glossary.

THE SONGS OF THE SOUTH

An Ancient Chinese Anthology of Poems by Qu Yuan and Other Poets

'From of old things have always been the same:
Why should I complain of the men of today?'

Chu chi (*The Songs of the South*) and its northern counterpart, *Shi jing*, are the two great ancestors of Chinese poetry and contain all we know of its ancient beginnings. *The Songs of the South* is an anthology first complied in the second century AD. Its poems, originating from the state of Chu and rooted in Shamanism, are grouped under seventeen titles. The earliest poems were composed in the fourth century BC and almost half of them are traditionally ascribed to Qu Yuan. Covering subjects ranging from heaven to love, work to growing old, regret to longing, they give a penetrating insight into the world of ancient China, and into the origins of poetry itself.

Translated with an Introduction and Notes by David Hawkes

ISBN: 978 0 14 119 870 5

THE ANALECTS

Confucius

'The Master said, "If a man sets his heart on benevolence, he will be free from evil"'

The *Analects* are a collection of Confucius's sayings brought together by his pupils shortly after his death in 497 BCE. Together they express a philosophy, or a moral code, by which Confucius, one of the most humane thinkers of all time, believed everyone should live. Upholding the ideals of wisdom, self-knowledge, courage and love of one's fellow man, he argued that the pursuit of virtue should be every individual's supreme goal. And, while following the Way, or the truth, might not result in immediate or material gain, Confucius showed that it could nevertheless bring its own powerful and lasting spiritual rewards.

Translated with an introduction and notes by D. C. Lau

ISBN: 978 0 14 044 348 6

THE PILLOW BOOK

Sei Shonagon

'I wonder if it's wrong to feel a fascination with the way those in
high places live'

Written by the Court gentlewoman Sei Shonagon (c. 966–1017)
ostensibly for her own amusement, *The Pillow Book* is one of the
greatest works of Japanese literature. A fascinating exploration
of life amongst the nobility at the height of the idyllic Heian period,
it describes the exquisite pleasures of a confined world in which
poetry, love, fashion and whim dominated, and harsh reality was
kept firmly at a distance. In sections ranging in size from brief
reflections to longer, lyrical tales, Shonagon moves elegantly across
a wide range of themes including nature, society and her own
flirtations and frustrations, to provide a witty, unique and deeply
personal insight into a woman's life at Court in classical Japan.

Translated with an Introduction and Notes
by Meredith McKinney

ISBN: 978 0 14 044 806 1

THE TALE OF GENJI

Murasaki Shikibu

Written in the eleventh century, this exquisite portrait of courtly life in medieval Japan is widely celebrated as the world's first novel – and is certainly one of its finest. Genji, the Shining Prince, is the son of an emperor. He is a passionate characteer whose tempestuous nature, family circumstances, love affairs, alliances, and shifting political fortunes form the core of this magnificent epic.

Edited and translated by Royall Tyler

ISBN: 978 0 14 303 949 5

MONKEY

Wu Ch'êng-ên

'Dear Monkey! He set out on his cloud trapeze, and in twinkling
he had crossed those two hundred leagues of water'

Monkey depicts the adventures of Prince Tripitaka, a young
Buddhist priest on a dangerous pilgrimage to India to retrieve
sacred scriptures accompanied by his three unruly disciples: the
greedy pig creature Pigsy, the river monster Sandy – and Monkey.
Hatched from a stone egg and given the secrets of heaven and
earth, the irrepressible trickster Monkey can ride on the clouds,
become invisible and transform himself into other shapes – skills
that prove very useful when the four travellers come up against
the dragons, bandits, demons and evil wizards that threaten to
foil them in their quest. Wu Ch'êng-ên wrote *Monkey* in the mid-
sixteenth century, adding his own distinctive style to an ancient
Chinese legend, and in so doing created a dazzling combination
of nonsense and profundity, slapstick comedy and spiritual
wisdom.

Translated by Arthur Waley

ISBN: 978 0 14 044 111 6

AS I CROSSED A BRIDGE OF DREAMS

Lady Sarashina

'I lie awake,
Listening to the rustle of the bamboo leaves,
And a strange sadness fills my heart'

As I Crossed a Bridge of Dreams is a unique autobiography in which the anonymous writer known as Lady Sarashina intersperses personal reflections, anecdotes and lyrical poems with accounts of her travels and evocative descriptions of the Japanese country-side. Born in 1008, Lady Sarashina felt an acute sense of melancholy that led her to withdraw into the more congenial realm of the imagination – this deeply introspective work presents her vision of the world. While barely alluding to certain aspects of her life such as marriage, she illuminates her pilgrimages to temples and mystical dreams in exquisite prose, describing a profound emotional journey that can be read as a metaphor for life itself.

Translated with an Introduction by Ivan Morris

ISBN: 978 0 14 044 282 3

SANSHIRO

Natsume Soseki

'Even bigger than Japan is the inside of your head. Don't ever surrender yourself – not to Japan, not to anything'

Soseki's work of gentle humour and doomed innocence depicts twenty-three-year-old Sanshiro, a recent graduate from a provincial college, as he begins university life in the big city of Tokyo. Baffled and excited by the traffic, the academics and – most of all – the women, Sanshiro must find his way amongst the sophisticates that fill his new life. An incisive social and cultural commentary, Sanshirō is also a subtle study of first love, tradition and modernization, and the idealism of youth against the cynicism of middle age.

With an Introduction by Haruki Murakami
Translated by Jay Rubin

ISBN: 978 0 14 045 562 5

TAO TE CHING

Lao Tzu

'Have little thought of self and as few desires as possible'

Whether or not Lao Tzu was a historical figure is uncertain, but the wisdom gathered under his name in the fourth century BC is central to the understanding and practice of Taoism. One of the three great religions of China, Taoism is based upon a concept of the Tao, or Way, as the universal power through which all life flows. The *Tao Te Ching* offers a practical model by which both the individual and society can embody this belief, encouraging modesty and self-restraint as the true path to a harmonious and balanced existence.

Translated with an Introduction by D. C. Lau

ISBN: 978 0 14 044 131 4